P9-DCI-021

"I can't imagine too many people dumb enough to take you on."

Joe gave a wolfish grin. "Yet you never hesitate."

Affronted by the suggestion that she might be dumb, Luna said, "I believe I've avoided you."

Joe subtly kicked the sheet lower. Apparently, not subtly enough because her eyes shifted, then stayed glued to his abdomen. "Avoided me?" he asked, to keep her from noticing that he'd noticed her looking. "So that wasn't you with me in the dark hallway at Zane's wedding, kissing me and clawing my back and arching up against me and—"

She was off the bed in a flash. "A touch of modesty wouldn't hurt, you know."

"Modesty is for wimps." He kicked the sheet farther away.

Being stubborn, Luna refused to look. "All right. So, I kissed you. It was a momentary lack of sanity."

Joe nodded in mock sympathy. "I have that effect on a lot of women."

Her eyes got glassy with her determination to stay on northerly ground. "Which is why I came to my senses and walked away."

It gave Joe a lot of satisfaction to point out one irrefutable fact. "But you're back."

"Only out of necessity." As if she couldn't help herself, her gaze flicked over him. Her breath caught; her cheeks warmed. Softly, she said, "There's no denying it, Joe. You'd be a treat."

More from Lori Foster

Too Much Temptation
Never Too Much
Unexpected
The Secret Life of Bryan
When Bruce Met Cyn
Just a Hint—Clint
Jamie
Murphy's Law
Jude's Law
The Watson Brothers
Yule Be Mine

Anthologies

All Through the Night
I Brake for Bad Boys
Bad Boys on Board
I Love Bad Boys
Jingle Bell Rock
Bad Boys to Go
I'm Your Santa
A Very Merry Christmas
When Good Things Happen to Bad Boys
The Night Before Christmas
Star Quality
Perfect for the Beach
Bad Boys in Black Tie
Truth or Dare
Bad Boys of Summer
Delicious

SAY NO
TO JOE?

LORI
FOSTER

ZEBRA BOOKS
KENSINGTON PUBLISHING CORP.
http://www.kensingtonbooks.com

ZEBRA BOOKS are published by

Kensington Publishing Corp.
119 West 40th Street
New York, NY 10018

Copyright © 2003 by Lori Foster

All rights reserved. No part of this book may be reproduced in any
form or by any means without the prior written consent of the
Publisher, excepting brief quotes used in reviews.

To the extent that the image or images on the cover of this book
depict a person or persons, such person or persons are merely
models, and are not intended to portray any character or characters
featured in the book.

If you purchased this book without a cover you should be aware that
this book is stolen property. It was reported as "unsold and destroyed" to the Publisher and neither the Author nor the Publisher
has received any payment for this "stripped book."

All Kensington titles, imprints, and distributed lines are available at
special quantity discounts for bulk purchases for sales promotion,
premiums, fund-raising, educational, or institutional use.

Special book excerpts or customized printings can also be created
to fit specific needs. For details, write or phone the office of the
Kensington Sales Manager: Attn.: Sales Department. Kensington
Publishing Corp., 119 West 40th Street, New York, NY 10018.
Phone: 1-800-221-2647.

Zebra and the Z logo Reg. U.S. Pat. & TM Off.

First Printing: August 2003
ISBN-13: 978-1-4201-4247-1
ISBN-10: 1-4201-4247-X

20 19 18 17 16

Printed in the United States of America

Chapter One

Sprawled out flat on his stomach, his big body stretched end to end on the full-sized bed. Two women loomed over him, touching him, quietly oohing and ahhing. They were so absorbed in their scrutiny, they didn't even notice Luna's entrance, hadn't heard her knocks. She shook her head, but she understood, indeed, she did.

After all, Joe was buck naked.

And he had a . . . tattoo on his ass?

Huh. Luna squinted to read the ornate script wrapped around a three-dimensional heart. It looked like it said *I Love Lou*. She frowned. Now what was that about? She knew without a single doubt Joe Winston was into women, not men—as witnessed by the two Barbie dolls presently pampering him.

One of those women whispered with longing, "I do wish he'd wake up."

The other sighed. "I've been trying for half an hour. No luck."

Luna cleared her throat, and when the women

looked up, startled and somewhat guilty, she explained, "The front door wasn't locked."

Rather than question her sudden presence or order her out, as Luna expected, the women shared a glance and flushed. The breasty blonde even dropped her hands from Joe's back where she'd been petting him.

The redhead bit her lip in nervousness. "Ummm . . . Who are you?"

Seeing that Joe hadn't moved, was apparently, in fact, sound asleep just as they'd said, Luna seized her opportunity. She stared with contrived contempt at both women, raised her chin in disdain, and uttered with complete absurdity and unrivaled fiction, "I'm his wife. Get out."

That they didn't question her told Luna all she needed to know. These women weren't important to Joe or they'd have already learned all about his aversion to marriage. She almost smiled as the women tripped past her—until she saw the bottle of pills on Joe's nightstand.

Striding forward, Luna read the label and saw that they were rather powerful pain pills. She frowned and set them aside. No wonder he was out cold. But what had happened to him? Why was he medicated?

"Joe?"

He didn't move, but he did give a slight, snuffling snore and shifted the tiniest bit. His shoulders, as wide as a tank and just as sturdy, drew her hand. Luna touched him, felt the hot silk of his taut flesh—and realized she was trembling. Not that she was nervous about her mission. Nope. But hey, Joe was naked, and if that wasn't enough to make any red-blooded female shake, then what could?

She hadn't seen him in three long months. The last time he'd asked her out, he'd told her if she refused him, he wouldn't ask again.

She'd refused.

His thick blue-black hair lay in disarray, a sharp contrast to the rumpled, snowy white pillowcase. His heavily whiskered jaw appeared clenched, and as Luna looked closer, she saw a purplish shadowing around his eye. A bruise?

Sitting on the side of the bed, Luna shook his shoulder. "Joe, wake up."

At her nearness, his nose twitched; then with a slight frown, he drew a slow, deep inhalation of breath. With exaggerated effort, he got one thickly lashed eye to open. The seconds ticked by while they stared at each other.

Abruptly his other eye snapped open and Luna got snared in his flinty, dark blue gaze. In a voice deep and rough from sleep, he said, "I thought I recognized that scent."

Bemused, Luna pulled back. "Sorry, champ, but I'm not wearing perfume—"

Her statement strangled in her throat when Joe rolled to his back with a rumbling groan of agony. His new position gave her a shocking display of his battered ribs along with a variety of bruises and scrapes on his chest, face and abdomen.

Someone had hurt him.

Outrage blossomed, but the outrage was tempered by awareness because he also provided her with a full frontal view of his gloriously naked body—and wow, what a view it was.

Joe Winston might be a bonified jerk, a sexist pig in fact, but Luna had no complaints with his physique. He was all bulky strength, long bones, dark hair and sinew. And sex appeal, the man had it in spades.

She was trying to convince herself to look away when Joe snagged her upper arms and dragged her over him.

"You don't need perfume," he purred in what could only be a tone of seduction.

Alarm shot up her spine. "Oh, no, big boy. Hang on there . . ."

Even weak and apparently drugged, Joe had no problem overpowering her, big overgrown lug that he was. She ended up with her breasts crushed to his massive hairy chest, her legs caught between his. He grunted in pain, then growled in appreciation.

"Joe," she started to object—and his mouth covered hers.

Luna recognized the danger of the moment even as she thrilled at the strength of his thick arms circling her, the press of his groin into her belly, the damp heat and gentle hunger of his mouth. The summer temperatures outside had nothing on Joe. The man was too hot. It had always been like this with him. He touched her, and common sense fled.

Without her conscious permission, Luna's eyes drifted shut and for only a moment, a single moment, she gave in, kissing him back, taking his taste and giving him her own.

He made a sound of hunger as his big, hard hand opened on her back, mostly bared by her halter top. His fingertips were rough, warm, and before she could assimilate that, they slid low to her bottom to enclose an entire cheek. He gently squeezed.

Like a shot, Luna sprang from the bed to glare down at him. She was breathless and annoyed and damn it, he still looked good enough to eat.

Deep blue eyes narrowed on her face, expressive and intent. "Come back here."

He said that as if he really expected her to obey. She almost did. "You," she accused, valiantly resisting temptation, "are drugged."

Amazingly, his hand slid to his lap and he laid his fingers lightly against himself. Wearing a crooked smile, Joe murmured, "I'm still fully functional."

Her jaw loosened; her mouth fell open. Oh, Lord. It took a lot to knock her off kilter, and this qualified. Luna wanted to swoon, to fan her face. She wanted to touch him, too, to feel the strength of him, the hot silk of his flesh, the crisp black hair.

Absurd. Men, even big, muscular, overconfident hulks, did not affect her this way, to the point she had trouble breathing or forming a coherent thought. She swallowed hard and managed to keep her eyes on his face. "I didn't come here for that, Joe."

"No?"

"I came to talk."

"Let's talk in bed."

His purring tone sank into her bones, weakening her resolve. Trying for a little attitude, she summoned a teasing smile. "You're the only man I know who gets aroused by pain medicine."

His gaze slid over her breasts beneath the brightly colored halter edged in shiny beads. "I've been on pain meds for three days now, honey. Trust me, they don't turn me on."

Suspicion dawned. "You're not as out of it as I thought, are you?"

He groaned, winced, and forced himself a little straighter in the bed. "Out of it, no. Not anymore. In pain, yes. Give a hand, will you?"

Mouth flat, eyes watchful, Luna wrapped both

hands around his thick upper arm. Muscles bunched and flexed against her palms, raising her awareness level even more. He braced against her, then shoved himself upward in the bed until his back rested on the pine headboard. He looked pale from the effort and so battered she almost softened toward him.

"Jesus," he muttered, "my ribs are killing me and my knee hurts like a son of a bitch."

She could see that. He was tense with the pain, his forehead damp. But Joe wasn't a man you coddled, especially not while he was in a bed and naked.

Once he was propped up, he let out a slow, cautious sigh.

Choosing discretion over titillation, Luna tossed the top sheet over his lap.

Joe blinked at her. "Getting to you, huh?"

Yes. "Not at all." His long, hairy legs still showed, so she spread the sheet over his lower body and tucked it in around him, doing her best to ignore his knowing smile and the way the sheet tented with his semi-arousal.

"Thanks," he murmured with a lot of irony; then he cautiously stretched, settling in a bit more. "I'm glad you're here."

"Of course you are." Luna put herself a safe distance from the bed and the reach of those long muscular arms. "You looked to be suffering greatly with two women fawning all over you."

"Suffering? Yeah, that about sums it up. Why do you think I was playing possum?" He kicked the sheet loose until his right leg was again visible, clear up to the paler skin of his hip. "The insatiable tyrants don't understand that I'm only human, and subject to injury."

Refusing to give herself away, Luna kept her gaze glued to his face. "You're telling me they were here for sex?"

"Did either of them look like Florence Nightingale to you? And I don't have any money, so they couldn't be after that. What else is there but sex?"

Luna rolled her eyes. "I can't believe I came here."

"Yeah, me either. Why are you here, by the way? Oh, wait, you're my wife, right?"

His expression was alight with devilish delight, enhanced by his slightly crooked nose and the small gold hoop in his ear. Joe would enjoy embarrassing her, making her ill at ease. But she had no time to be embarrassed, no time for second thoughts.

Drawing a fortifying breath and praying he wouldn't give her a hard time about it, Luna said, "The truth is Joe . . . I need you."

Joe did his best to hide his reaction to the thumping, grinding pain in every muscle, bone and joint. He glanced at the clock and saw that it was nearing eight o'clock. He'd been in bed forever it seemed, and God, he felt like something the cat had mauled, killed, and then dragged in. But he couldn't afford to be distracted with the annoying pain right now.

Luna had sought him out, and by God, he'd take advantage of the moment if it killed him.

"As I recall," he said around a wave of discomfort, "you told me to get lost. Sounded pretty sincere to me, too."

Seeing Luna Clark flush was a unique experience. Usually she was all brass balls and feminist pique. Not once had he ever witnessed any insecurity in her.

Her chin rose. "You know why, Joe."

"Because you're cold-hearted?" The second he said it, he held up a hand. "No, don't abuse my already abused body. One more blow and I'm done for."

She did look ready to clout him, not that he didn't deserve it. Whenever he got near her, it seemed he had no control over his wayward tongue, his better sense, or his lust. But damn it, her continued rejection nettled him so much that more often than not he behaved like a complete ass.

Uncomfortable with that fact, Joe shifted, and a groan slipped out without his permission.

She inched closer. "What happened to you anyway? Did you accost another woman and she took a ball bat to you?"

Joe hid his grin. "A little grab-ass is not accosting." At the worst of times, Luna could amuse him. And now he finally had her where he wanted her.

His cousin Zane had called yesterday to explain that Luna would be visiting, that she had a situation—which was as much explanation as Zane would give—and that she could use his special skills. Naturally, Joe had agreed to help out. Hell, Luna was the best friend to his cousin's wife, which made her practically family. And Joe would do anything for family.

Yeah. That sounded plausible enough to suit him.

She'd gotten here sooner than he'd expected, though. He'd thought to have a few more days to recoup before he had to pit wits with her.

Her mesmerizing eyes shone with annoyance and disbelief. "I barely knew you, Joe. I brought you a sandwich, and half a minute later you had your hands all over me."

Despite his aches and pains, the memory warmed Joe. Locking onto her gaze, he said in his defense, "You have that kind of bottom, honey. All round and soft."

Her color deepened. "Of all the stupid, sexist—"

"It's irresistible," Joe insisted, and meant it. "It begs for a man's hands. It—" There looked to be an explosion imminent, so Joe wisely let that go for now and instead distracted her. "And for your information, no, I didn't get beat up by a woman." He snorted. "How absurd is that?"

"I dunno." Her body vibrated with tension. "I'm ready to beat you up."

Oh, he'd love for her to get close enough to try. For that brief moment when he'd pulled her over him, touching body to body in all the right places, he'd felt alive. Aware. Hungry in a way that had eluded him since . . . well, the last time he'd touched her. Damn.

But she kept her distance. Smart girl. "If you want the gory details, some slimy bastard snuck up and blindsided me. I think it was a two-by-four, though, not a ball bat."

"Ohmigod."

Finally, a dose of the sympathy he deserved. Joe grunted. "That's right. The first blow was to my head, and I still have the lump to prove it. Knocked me on my ass." He gingerly touched the tender spot behind his left ear. "That's all I remember until I came to." And for good measure, he added, "I barely managed to make it home."

Little enough exaggeration there. Getting up the steps to his second-floor apartment had seemed a monumental feat, especially with his twice-cursed bum knee. Even with the help he'd had, it had proved damn difficult.

With a very satisfying, very womanly look of concern in her beautiful light brown eyes, Luna moved closer to the bed. "You've seen a doctor?"

"Yeah, and had a whole series of X rays and pokes and prods. Nothing's broken, though it feels like half my body is crushed. Final verdict was that I'd live, and with some well-placed ice packs, bed rest, and pain meds I should be good as new in a week or so."

Her concerned gaze skimmed over him. "Are you able to move much?"

Now we're talking. "The hips work just fine, honey. Course, it'd probably be easier if you did all the— hey, c'mon now, Luna, I was just teasing." He barely managed to hold in his laugh. "Don't storm away."

She pivoted on her heel and stomped back toward him. Joe braced himself, waiting for the blast of her ire. She surprised him by drawing a deep breath, then another. And one more.

He sighed. She was such a volatile, passionate woman, which made tweaking her temper fun. He raised a brow. "Got control of yourself?"

She gave one sharp nod.

The little liar. She wanted to bludgeon him. "Good." He patted the side of the bed next to his hip. "So tell me about this 'needing me' stuff. I'm all ears."

"God, Joe, you're exasperating." She dragged a hand through her hair. Today it was soft brown, shoulder length, silky straight. But Luna was such a chameleon, constantly changing on him, Joe wouldn't be surprised if it was red tomorrow and blond the day after. To date, he'd seen her with just about every shade and style to her hair, to the point he had no clue what her natural coloring might be. First time he got her naked, he'd find out, though. He could hardly wait.

In the meantime, he liked it that she kept him guessing. The novelty drew him. Yeah, that was it. The novelty.

From the very beginning, Luna had intrigued him. And he hadn't lied—the woman had a killer ass. He'd picked up on that the moment she'd come sashaying into his cousin's computer store where he'd been helping out during a difficult time. Because Joe had been doing Zane a huge favor by minding the register, Zane had asked Luna to bring him lunch.

At first, Luna had been more than pleasant, flirting in a way that Joe now realized was a natural part of her nature, not a come-on for him personally. She'd looked at him with those slanted, golden eyes, and he'd seen what he wanted to see: an invitation.

Under normal circumstances, Joe kept a clear head at all times. But with Luna, nothing felt normal. In so many ways, she shot his perspective all to hell. On that particular day, she'd turned to set the meal on the checkout counter, presenting Joe with a perfect view of that delectable rear end, and without even thinking about it or the possible consequences, he'd . . . touched her.

That is, if you could call a pat, followed by a full-palm squeeze, a mere touch. Soft, warm, resilient . . . He'd gotten one handful and immediately wanted more. A whole lot more.

But Luna had gone rigid, and from one second to the next Joe found himself wearing his lunch instead of getting to eat it. She'd stormed out without giving him a chance to apologize or explain or coax her into a better mood.

It hadn't been easy, but Luna had eventually for-given him. After all, the chemistry was there, as un-deniable to her as it was to him. At Zane's wedding, Joe had finally managed to ease her into one long, wet, blistering kiss that had haunted his nights for three months now.

After that, he'd tried repeatedly to get her alone. Hell, he'd even tried being on his best behavior. Not that his best was all that good. At thirty-six, he'd had a lot of time doing just as he damn well pleased. And the jobs he'd had—bodyguard, bounty hunter, private dick—had only made him meaner, a little nastier. It came with the territory and in some cases was outright necessary.

But for Luna, he *had* tried and had been damn uncomfortable in the process.

And still she'd turned him down.

Joe mentally rubbed his hands together. Now, however, fate had thrown her for a loop, and ac-cording to Zane, she needed someone exactly like him. Someone unscrupulous, someone hard, fearless. Someone who could kick ass when nec-essary.

He needed to recuperate before he undertook the ass-kicking part. But for Luna, for a chance to appease his overwhelming lust, he'd manage.

Luna looked very undecided, so Joe held himself still, even held his breath, and after half a minute, just when he thought he might suffocate waiting for her to make up her mind, she came to him.

She sat on the side of the bed, hip to hip. "You'll behave, Joe."

"Absolutely." Joe waited, but she didn't say any-thing more. "Yeah?"

She looked at him, scowled, looked away.

Oh, now this was good. "Shyness?" he taunted in

a low tone. "From Luna the loony? Luna the goddess of the moon? Luna the—"

"All right!" Brows drawn, expression stern, she said, "I have two kids."

Joe choked. And damn it, given his injuries, choking hurt. He held his ribs and wheezed and tried to catch his breath. Surely, he'd misunderstood. Zane had claimed she had a problem that only he could handle, and Luna herself said she needed him. But Joe assumed they meant to deal with a threat of some kind, a pushy boyfriend, an impatient landlord, even something financial. He could handle any and all of those. But kids? What the hell did he know of kids, other than that he didn't want any?

Finally, eyes watering, Joe sputtered, "The hell you say? Must've been one quick birth."

"Are you going to be serious or not?"

Joe clutched his aching ribs. "Believe me, sweetheart, I'm as serious as a nun on Sunday."

She drew a big breath. "I have a cousin who passed away two years ago. She left two kids. No one knows who their father is, so now they need a guardian." She stared at her hands in her lap, and for a moment, it appeared she might actually cry.

Typically male, Joe felt himself melting. There was just something about a tearful woman that made a man feel more like a man, protective and strong, the conquering hero ready to comfort the vulnerable little lady. And when that little lady happened to be Luna . . . Well, she was usually so brazen and self-assured it really threw him to see her like this. If he weren't so beat up and sore, he'd pull her close and hold her, snuggle her into his chest, rub her back . . . That'd be real nice, for sure. But odds were if he got her that close, especially while she was being all soft and female, he'd do something to get himself slugged.

Better not try it.

But while he waited for her to compose herself, he could at least hold her hand. Her nails were painted fuchsia, and she wore several silver rings. Small-boned, her hand felt delicate in his.

Shit. He hadn't wanted to think of Luna as delicate. He wanted to think of her only as sexy. Hot. Provoking.

His.

He'd had a lot of fantasies about her needing him, but not like this. Not all the emotional stuff. This time the groan was silent, caused by a cramp in his brain, not his body.

"How did she die?" He kept his tone gentle, low.

"A stupid car wreck. She left one night for groceries and never came home again." Luna sniffed. "They've been through the wringer, Joe."

He tilted his head, trying to see her averted face. Teasing her seemed his best recourse. "I swear, if you cry, I'll fall apart, too, and then where will we be?"

She snorted at that. In the next instant, she shed the vulnerability, once again as cool as the other side of the pillow. "They've been through several guardians, but no one permanent. I spoke with Willow, Chloe's daughter, for about half an hour. She sounded almost . . . desperate. I don't like that."

"Chloe was your cousin?" Joe stroked her knuckles with his thumb, marveling at how soft she felt, distracting himself from the emotional issues trying to crowd his brain.

She nodded. "We met once or twice when we were younger, but I barely remember her at all. I didn't even realize she'd passed away. No one notified me of the funeral."

"So why are they contacting you now?"

"I'm all that's left. Willow isn't quite fifteen yet, but she sounds much older. She's been trying to take care of her younger brother and deal with the constant changes. It's too much. I have to go there."

"Course you do." Joe gave her hand a squeeze. He couldn't imagine what Luna thought he might add to the equation. Hell, he wasn't a family man, but he also wasn't a complete bastard. "So where do I fit into this?"

"Then, you're willing to help?"

He gave her a level look for that ridiculous question. "You mean you don't know? And here I thought you were Luna, goddess of the moon, all powerful, all seeing . . ."

Again, she looked ready to hit him.

Joe laughed. "Come off it, honey. You assumed before you came here that I'd help, otherwise you wouldn't have asked."

She acknowledged that with a shrug. "All things considered, I thought I could probably count on you."

Ah ha. A cocky grin tilted his mouth. "You mean because of the sexual chemistry between us."

Far too serious, Luna gazed at him. "No. I meant because deep down, you're one of the best men I know." Her gentle voice took him by surprise. "Zane certainly trusts you."

Now damn it, that threw him completely off guard. He'd had all kinds of sexual banter ready to go and she had to hit him a low blow by complimenting his oft-maligned character.

While Joe mentally fumbled, Luna went on unfazed. "But before you agree, you should know that the kids are a handful. Willow hinted that they'd riled some of their neighbors with harmless pranks, and now some people are . . . well, blaming them for all kinds of things and generally giving them a hard time."

"A hard time, huh?" Joe smirked. It had to be more than that or Luna wouldn't be trying to coerce him along. She wasn't exactly helpless herself, and in the normal course of things, he had no doubt she could handle a few annoying neighbors. She'd sure handled him, and in the process, she'd made it more than plain that she wanted nothing to do with him. It said something about her present situation that she'd come to him now.

It also emphasized her faith in his abilities. *You're one of the best men I know.* Now, didn't that beat all? She wasn't here because she wanted him, but out of some misconstrued notions on his nobility. Joe clenched his teeth. She was sure to be pissed when she found out that he didn't have a noble bone in his body, and it wouldn't really be fair—to her or to the children—for him to get involved.

But how bad could a couple of kids be? They were little people, right? Limited in their destructive abilities. Neither he nor his sister had married yet, so they were a long way off from supplying any babies to the family, much to their mother's annoyance. But between his four cousins, there was a gaggle of kids ranging in age from eighteen months to nearing fifteen. Joe enjoyed them whenever he visited. Kids could be charmers, as long as they weren't *his* kids.

Having made up his mind, he pushed away his ever-present physical discomfort and faced Luna. "All right. Let's hear it."

"It?"

"The scoop. What have the rugrats done? How much trouble are they in?"

"I don't know that I'd really call it trouble," she hedged. "There are just a few people hoping to run them off."

"What kind of people?"

Luna looked him over, then said, "Big people."

"Big, huh?"

"And scary."

He grinned. "That right?"

"And mean."

"I am not mean."

"I didn't say you are. I said the people bothering the kids are mean."

"Right. And you figure you'll fight fire with fire by shoving me under their noses?"

It was her turn to grin. "However imposing and unscrupulous they are, you have to be more so, Joe. I've seen you in action when you were helping Zane, and I've heard all the stories your cousins have told. You can handle anything and anyone."

"Probably." Then with a frown: "But I am not mean." Why it mattered so much that she understood that, Joe couldn't say.

"You'll be perfect. Those bullies won't know what hit them."

"You still haven't told me what's being done. Why are bullies bothering them?"

Luna frowned at a particularly ugly bruise below Joe's left pectoral muscle. She looked as if she wanted to touch him, and Joe waited, hoping she would, even though he knew he wasn't up to a romp at the moment. But Luna simply lifted her gaze back to his face. "Willow said it's because their mother was never married, and now they're orphans."

"And no one has any idea who the dad is?"

"No. He's never paid child support, never been around. I didn't want to dig, but Willow volunteered that there wasn't a dad, and never would be."

"Damn."

"Sad, huh? How can a town blame children for being illegitimate or orphaned? Yet, none of the guardians have ever made a move to adopt them. They just keep drifting away, abandoning the kids for one reason after another."

It sickened Joe, but he knew that small towns could be really funny about that sort of thing. In so many ways, they were worse than big cities. At least in a big city you could be anonymous and no one gave a damn who you were or what you did. "Who's the guardian now?"

"An aunt. She's sticking around just until I arrive, but she made it clear that she's impatient. There was another cousin before her. I'm told his wife got a job transfer and they didn't want to lug the kids along. Before that was a semiretired great uncle, who claimed the kids were too troublesome. The aunt is the third one. Now she wants to get married, and her fiancé doesn't want to be saddled with two children."

Imagining how young kids must feel without any stability, Joe scowled. But to have Luna take over . . .

As a bona fide free spirit, Luna was too exotic, too bold and far too sexy to be a mother. Not only that, but she worked as a psychic, or rather a psychic's assistant. There were plenty of times when Joe thought she had legitimate *woo-woo* ability. On several occasions, she'd seemed to know more than she should, especially about him.

As if she'd read his mind, Luna flipped her hair and forged on. "I've already passed the back-ground check, but I'll have to do the home study once I'm settled there. I'm not overly concerned because while I might not be the ideal mother—"

"You said it, not me."

With no interruption to her explanations, Luna pinched him on the arm, making him lurch. "—CPS is way overworked, and anytime kids can be placed with a relative, they tend to bend over backward to see it happen, or so the social worker told me. Even though I'm a distant, unknown relative, I'm still preferable."

"Yeah? Preferable to *what?*"

A golden fire lit her eyes, alerting Joe to the pos-sibility of another pinch. He caught her hand to deter her. "Does the social worker know about your propensity for causing pain?"

"Don't be a baby, Joe. I didn't hurt you."

True enough. Added to his other various aches and pains, a mere pinch was negligible, but God knew he didn't need any more.

"I'm going to move there."

Thrown off guard once more, Joe asked, "There where?"

"North Carolina."

Joe gave a start of surprise. Well, hell. Luna already lived over an hour south of him, in Thomasville, Kentucky. Any more than that was just too damn far for his convenience. He'd have to find a way to talk her out of relocating.

He wanted her in his bed. For how long he hadn't decided yet. But until he did decide, he wanted her within reaching distance. Kids he could handle. Bullies he could handle.

Never knowing how it felt to have Luna under him . . . Now, that was too much to consider.

Chapter Two

"Maybe we should talk about this."

"My mind's made up. They're alone, Joe. Two whole years they've lived with uncertainty, going from one adult's set of rules to another. At first, I thought to bring them here, but the house was given to them free and clear in the will, with the proviso that the guardian live there."

Joe frowned over that. Why would their mother insist the kids stay in the same area? Surely, she knew how difficult it would be for most adults to relocate. Added to the automatic responsibilities of raising someone else's children, it was a lot to ask.

Picking up on his thoughts yet again, Luna said, "I bet Chloe meant the house as an incentive. You know, like free rent, since the mortgage is paid off. She probably didn't want it sold because it'd be too easy for a guardian to sell it, spend the money, then leave the kids again. Besides, the kids have had enough change. It's their home and they shouldn't have to move. For the past two years, it's been the only constant in their life."

Luna sounded so set on leaving, something close to desperation crept in on Joe. He shrugged it off and scowled. "What about your life here? Your job with Tamara, your friends, your family?" *What about me?* He didn't say it out loud, and even thinking it made his guts cramp. But damn it, he wanted to matter to her a little.

Her shrug was negligent, unconcerned. "My family is already scattered around the country, and we've never been close. Believe me, it won't matter to them what I do."

"No?" The idea of relatives not caring seemed alien to Joe, but then he came from a big, close family. That thought brought another, and he realized he really didn't know much about Luna's background.

Luna shook her head but didn't elaborate. "I can find work anywhere, and I can always visit Tamara and Zane and the others."

Disgruntled, Joe rolled his eyes. Obviously, the thought of being out of *his* reach didn't distress her one iota. But he'd find a way to change her mind about that. "So what's my role in this? You want me to beat the shit out of anyone giving the kids a hard time? Will I need to hurt anyone?"

Luna looked amused by his offer. "Give it up, Joe, because I'm not buying it."

"What?" His innocent act was a bit rusty, but he thought he'd pulled it off.

"Zane already warned me that you'd say something stupid like that. He said you take every opportunity to exaggerate your own reputation."

Zane ruined all his fun. But Joe still remembered a time when Zane had accused him of being

a hit man, so apparently he'd bought into the reputation at least a little. Joe grinned. "So what is my
role?"

"I just want you there for backup and to intimidate the more aggressive people." Luna looked him
over, her gaze lingering on his chest, his shoulders.
Her eyes warmed and her brows lifted in feminine
approval. "Even battered and bruised and moaning
with every other breath, I can't imagine too many
people dumb enough to take you on."

Joe gave a wolfish grin. "Yet you never hesitate."

Affronted by the suggestion that she might be
dumb, Luna said, "I believe I've avoided you."

Joe subtly kicked the sheet lower. Apparently,
not subtly enough because her eyes shifted, then
stayed glued to his abdomen. "Avoided me?" he
asked, to keep her from noticing that he'd noticed
her looking. "So that wasn't you with me in the
dark hallway at Zane's wedding, kissing me and
clawing my back and arching up against me and—"

She was off the bed in a flash. "A touch of modesty wouldn't hurt, you know."

"Modesty is for wimps." He kicked the sheet farther away. It couldn't go any lower without baring
him completely.

Being a stubborn witch, Luna refused to look.
"All right. So, I kissed you. It was a momentary lack
of sanity."

Joe nodded in mock sympathy. "I have that effect on a lot of women."

Her eyes got glassy with her determination to
stay on northerly ground. "Which is why I came to
my senses and walked away."

It gave Joe a lot of satisfaction to point out one
irrefutable fact. "But you're back."

"Only out of necessity." As if she couldn't help herself, her gaze flicked over him. Her breath caught; her cheeks warmed. Softly, she said, "There's no denying it, Joe. You'd be a treat. But I don't intend to be one more notch on your bedpost."

So, he was a treat, was he? A few of his aches diminished beneath the rush of pain-numbing lust. "I understand completely," he soothed. "There's no reason to get defensive."

"I am not defensive." She turned her back on him and crossed her arms beneath her breasts, looking very defensive.

"How about I be a notch on your bedpost? I wouldn't mind. Course, you might have to notch it twice, not that I'm bragging or anything . . ."

Another loss of temper seemed imminent. Through her teeth, Luna growled, "Will you go along with me or not?"

Her black jeans were low slung, snug, hugging that exquisite rear end to perfection. She turned back to him, and when she moved just right, Joe could catch a small glimpse of her belly between her jeans and her colorful halter. For a woman with generous hips and breasts, Luna's waist was surprisingly narrow, her belly only slightly rounded. More than anything, she reminded him of a pinup girl from days gone by. Lush, curvy. Sexy.

"I'm still considering it," he muttered, thoroughly distracted with thoughts of getting her naked so he could do a better inspection of her assets.

"I'll pay you."

Well, that shot his pleasant imagery all to hell. "Forget that. I don't want or need your money."

She propped her hands on her hips. "But you just told me that you were broke."

Joe waved that away, then had to hold his ribs

when pain skittered through him. "I always say that so women won't get ideas. It's better than claiming I'm a lousy lover, which I doubt anyone would believe anyway."

Her eyes narrowed dangerously. "So you lied?"

"Course not." He tried to look offended. "I just exaggerated, that's all. I mean, I'm not wealthy or anything. But I've always lived a moderate lifestyle alone, I've always been employed, and I'm always good at what I do. I have enough put away to be comfortable."

"You are such a pig."

"I'm a realist," he corrected. "Women have been trying to drag me to the damn altar for years. They're more inclined toward temporary liaisons rather than long-term relationships when they think I'm poor."

"Fine, whatever. I really don't care what you tell other women. But I insist on paying you for your time."

"No." He'd rather she be indebted to him. Not that he'd use the debt to blackmail her into bed or anything, but if she softened toward him, if she saw him as her hero, maybe she'd quit fighting him so hard.

"Be reasonable, Joe. I have no idea what we're walking into, so I might need you there for a week or a month. Can you afford that long off work?"

Knowing his own abilities, Joe figured it'd take a week, ten days tops, to get the lay of the land, uncover any problems, and get it all straightened out. Then he could concentrate fully on Luna—and her gratitude.

He grinned shamelessly as he said, "Yeah, I can." When she started to argue again, he held up a hand.

"Here's the thing. I was ready to dump this place anyway. Too many people feel free to drop in unannounced and—"

"You mean too many women."

He answered her pointed glare with a grin.

"Maybe if you quit handing out keys . . ."

"Now, that's one accusation you can't lay on me. I do not hand out keys." Just the opposite. He valued his privacy, his bachelor status, above everything except family.

"So how did Barbie and her friend get in?"

"Barbie?" All this grinning was making his jaw ache as much as his ribs. "You mean Beth? She got in with Amelia, the other one who was copping feels off my drugged body when you arrived. And before you ask, no, I didn't give Amelia a key either. We had a date the night I got jumped, and so she's the one who took me to the hospital and brought me home. I'm assuming she kept a key, and God knows I haven't been fit enough to see about changing locks."

An arrested, thoughtful expression replaced Luna's look of annoyance. "She was with you, but she wasn't hurt during the attack?"

"I was away from her when it happened." And that had been the only blessing of the night. Joe couldn't bear the thought of a woman being hurt while under his protection.

With her head down in thought, Luna took a slow turn around his bedroom. Except for the clothes that he'd dropped on the floor the night he was hurt, the path was clear. Since the attack, he hadn't gotten dressed, had barely eaten, and rarely even ventured from the bed except that morning to clean his teeth and get a drink. He'd

been prepared to scrounge up some food when
Beth and Amelia had dropped in.

Of course, they hadn't thought to feed him. He
figured he'd lost a good eight pounds in the last
few days.

"So you were on a date with Amelia, but away
from her side when some goon jumped you?" Luna
tapped a foot. "That's rather convenient, isn't it?"

"For who?"

"Her?"

The blatant insinuation threw him. "I had no
idea you had such a suspicious nature."

Luna shrugged and waited for him to explain.

Her insinuations rubbed him raw. "It was not a
conspiracy. In case you failed to notice, Amelia is
still fond of me. And that's even after I turned her
down for anything more serious."

"More serious?"

He shrugged. "They all seem to get marriage
minded. But she was okay with just keeping it . . ."

"Sexual?"

Joe grinned.

In her driest Luna-the-goddess tone, she said,
"Dumb question." Then, with remaining suspicion: "So tell me, Joe, how exactly did it happen?"

Joe gave up. "I'd run out to the parking garage
to get my truck because it was raining. I *am* a gentle-
man, you know."

"Right."

Did she have to sound so facetious? "I'd just gotten the truck unlocked when I got hit from behind. I went down, got beat on some more, but I'd
already blacked out, so I have no idea how much
time passed. When I didn't return to the restau-
rant, Amelia came after me and found me on the

ground. She might have been the person who scared the guy off, you know. He might have killed me otherwise. It sure as hell feels like he was trying."

Other than burning concern in her gaze, Luna let all that go by. "Did she call the police?"

"I was just coming around when she got there. She took me to the hospital, and when they finished with me, I spoke with the cops there. Not that I expect them to be much help. I didn't see who it was, so there wasn't much to go on."

Luna didn't look at all convinced. "Amelia didn't see anyone either?"

"No. She heard some noises in the garage, but I was alone when she got there."

"Hmmm. You must have been out for a quite a while." Joe glared at her, and she said, "Okay, so Amelia adores you even though you turned her down for marriage. Do you have any idea who might not feel the same?"

"Oh, I've got my suspicions." Even as Joe said it, his muscles clenched in anger, causing him additional discomfort. When he caught the son of a bitch again, he'd even the score and then some.

"Meaning?"

Joe shook himself. Now wasn't the time for savage thoughts of revenge, not when Luna was within reach. "Meaning it was probably Bruno Caldwell, the same bastard who shot out my knee."

Her eyes widened. "That's why you sometimes limp? You were *shot?*"

Joe grunted. "What, you thought I hurt it playing softball?"

"I don't know." She looked dumbfounded. "I didn't . . . I never really thought about it. I mean, I know you've had some edgy jobs, but . . ."

Joe almost laughed. Obviously, she had no idea

how dangerous his life had been at times. "I should have taken Bruno apart when I had my chance, but by the time I'd recaptured him almost a year later, I felt law abiding again and stupidly turned him over to the authorities."

"Law abiding *again?*"

He shrugged. "The injury forced me off police work, which put me in a . . . bad mood." *What an understatement.* He'd been in a killing rage for months. "I admit to being a little unruly for a while there."

"They fired you?"

"Worse. They offered me a desk job." And he hadn't been able to stand it. He liked to get in the thick of things, not fill out the endless paperwork after the dust had settled. "I was plenty pissed about it for a while there. Then I got over it and became a bounty hunter instead."

"A bounty hunter with a limp?"

"No, smart ass. Well, only when I overdo it." Damn it, what had she expected him to do? Sit around and twiddle his thumbs? Not likely. He'd have gone nuts in less than a month.

"Right. So you caught this Bruno character and turned him over to the police."

That was simplifying it a bit, but Joe didn't say so. Luna couldn't understand about the hassles of tracking someone who didn't want to be caught, and who had the resources to stay hidden. Especially a petty, ruthless bastard like Bruno. "That's about it."

"You two have quite a history, it seems."

"You could say that. I arrested him and got shot in the bargain. He jumped bail and went missing for a while, until I caught up to him again. He was locked up until he hijacked a truck during a work detail, and now he's hiding again. Or rather, he was hiding until he decided I was a problem he had to get rid of."

"My God. You think he wants to actually *kill* you?"

Joe shrugged as if it didn't really matter. Truth was, he didn't intend to get caught off guard again. From now on, he'd be ready for Bruno. And when he caught him again, the son of a bitch would pay. "He doesn't have much choice if he wants to stay free. He knows I'll get him. Eventually."

Luna slumped up against the dresser and her voice went weak. "If he doesn't get you first."

Joe used her obvious concern to his advantage. "Exactly. If I'm staying with you for a while, in North Carolina no less, I'll be out of reach." *At least until I'm fit enough to retaliate in kind.* "Bruno would never think to look for me there. It'll also throw the more persistent ladies off the track. They won't be able to find me, and they'll give up, too."

Luna began pacing again. "Just until you come back." As she paced, she picked up his jeans, his T-shirt, his socks.

Acrimony filled her tone, and that pleased Joe. Could she be jealous? He hoped so. "Yeah, well, I was thinking of relocating to Kentucky anyway, to be closer to the cousins." *And to you.* "You know, I do believe Zane misses me between visits."

That gigantic falsehood had her pinching her mouth together to keep from snorting, or spilling the truth as she knew it. Zane liked Joe more now than he had a year ago, but he would forever be leery of him. In their younger days they'd competed for women, and too often, Joe had won.

Now that Zane was in love, he refused to see beyond that. He knew Joe didn't poach, and he trusted his sweet little wife, Tamara, but it still made him uncomfortable to let Joe too near her.

Twitting Zane was about as close to honest fun as Joe had these days.

"Joe." Luna dumped the clothes into a pile on the foot of the bed. "You're trying to make this sound like I'd be doing you the favor, instead of the other way around."

"You will be doing me a favor." *You'll be giving me the opportunity to wear you down.*

She crossed her arms beneath her breasts. "That's absurd and you know it. No, don't argue with me. I have to be honest with myself here, too. I'm in over my head and I need your help. That means I have to pay you, just like anyone else would."

Joe scowled. "You want honesty, honey? Then I'll give you honesty."

Because he wanted to be more upright for this confrontation, Joe shifted a little higher in the bed. It hurt to move—hell, it hurt to breathe—but it would hurt more to lose this opportunity. He wasn't used to being celibate, and it sucked. He hated it. But damn it, he wanted Luna, not some other woman. She'd crawled under his skin three months ago, and having her there was like an interminable itch. It was driving him nuts.

Once he was settled and could quit gritting his teeth, he gave Luna a dead-on look. "There's something you should know."

Luna moved toward him with concern. "Joe, are you all right?" She had a hand stretched out to him.

"I still want you."

She halted in midstep.

"I'm not going to stop wanting you until I have you."

She took a step back.

Just saying it turned Joe on. Her exotic eyes were wide, darkened with surprise; her lips parted. Joe's voice dropped to a low rumble. "About a dozen times in a dozen different ways, Luna. And even that might not be enough."

Her mouth closed.

Joe shrugged, though he felt far from cavalier. "I figured you should know."

The seconds ticked by; then in a chilling whisper, she said, "You're making it a stipulation? I have to sleep with you if I want your help?"

Now that pissed him off. "No. Hell no. I don't need to force women into my bed."

"Oh." His tone had her blinking before she settled into another frown. "Then what exactly did you mean?"

"I meant that I'm not going to stop trying. We'll be playing house, babe, under the same roof, in close proximity. Believe me, I'm going to use that to my advantage."

Slowly, her smile appeared. "And you think I won't be able to resist you? Oh, that's too funny, Joe. You've got so much ego it's falling out your ears."

Joe smiled, too. He did love a challenge. "So long as you don't object to me giving it my best shot."

"Thank you for the warning. I'll be on my toes." Still amused, she shook her head, picked up his dirty clothes, and sashayed out of the room. In the doorway, she stopped and looked at him over his shoulder. "I'm going to rustle you up something to eat. You look thinner to me. Then we'll make plans on when to leave."

"Thanks. I'm starved."

"No, Joe, thank you." Her smile now was genuine, softened with her relief. "I really do appreciate your willingness to help."

She appreciated him. Perfect, Joe thought. Things were working out just as he hoped.

Luna held her serene smile until she got out of sight. Then she groaned and swallowed hard. Beneath her breast, her heart thumped in heavy, exaggerated beats.

Since meeting Joe Winston, her life had gone through some drastic upheavals. She didn't like it. She didn't like him.

Liar.

Part of the problem was that her basic nature rebelled against needing anyone. She lived her life to her exact specifications; she was independent, capable, mature and self-sufficient.

Yet, she now needed Joe.

As a feminist, she couldn't abide men like Joe Winston. They saw women as weaker beings meant to be protected, sometimes cherished. But never as equals.

Her body didn't care.

In her present situation, he was perfect for her, and so dangerous that she trembled whenever she thought of him. For three months now she'd wavered, wanting to call him, wanting to be with him. She went to sleep with him on her mind and woke with the need to touch him.

She'd always enjoyed her sexual freedom, but now other men held no interest, seeming small, pale, even insubstantial in comparison to Joe's cocky confidence and larger-than-life capability. Nothing threw him.

Well, the mention of kids had strangled him for

a moment there. It had almost been funny, watching Joe's reaction. But the painful truth was that Joe knew more about kids than she ever would. His four cousins had them in various ages, and Joe seemed at ease with them all. He held babies, conversed with toddlers, related to a teen. He was comfortable in all situations, but then, he'd come from a good family, and so he understood the dynamics and workings of a family unit.

She didn't.

Joe appealed to her in ways she'd never experienced before. If it had just been sexual, there wouldn't be a problem. She'd have indulged an affair and walked away.

But Joe was also loyal, funny, ruthless in defense of his family, and . . . He made her feel more feminine, like the stereotypical little woman, weaker against his obvious strength, pampered in the face of his masculine appreciation.

Damn the man for his diabolical tactics.

Resisting him had proved a personal struggle, but she'd held firm, reminding herself again and again that Joe wasn't a man to play with. He wasn't just a lick of fire, where she could get singed. He was an inferno, ready to consume her if she gave him the chance. Nothing with Joe would ever be half measure. Not the physical pleasure he'd give, and not the way he made her feel.

Now, as he'd just informed her, he had his chance. Luna groaned again. She'd just have to keep her mind busy on other things—and two kids ought to take care of that.

More laundry awaited her in his small kitchen where a stacked washer/dryer combo was neatly stashed in a pantry. Joe was tidy for a man, his clothes in a basket, his kitchen clean except for some dirty dishes in the sink and some papers on the table. Luna drew a shaky breath and got to work.

He was willing to help her, but she had to help him first. She had a load of laundry going and the makings for grilled cheese sandwiches out on the counter when his phone rang.

No doubt, a woman wanted his attention. Luna meandered into his bedroom, nosiness and a tad of jealousy making her dislike herself. But Joe hadn't answered the bedside phone. His eyes were closed, his expression weary, pained.

He'd been so badly hurt . . .

With false sweetness, she asked, "You want me to get that?"

Before he could reply, the answering machine picked up. Sure enough, a feminine voice purred, "Joe? Where are you? You haven't answered the phone in days. Call me, okay?"

Joe never opened his eyes.

Teeth gritted, Luna said, "Another admirer, huh?"

Rather than answer that, he sniffed the air. "I thought you were going to fix something to eat?"

"How about grilled cheese? You don't have much in the way of groceries."

"I usually eat out." Then, with appreciation and a touch of weariness: "That sounds great. I didn't know you cooked."

Was that sheet even lower? The material barely maintained his privacy, and what the soft cotton did cover, it didn't really conceal. There were some clear bulges and ridges. Luna eyed his body and felt her insides turn liquid. Even with the dark ugly bruises, he was so damn gorgeous. His shoulders were sleek and taut and thick, his chest covered in that fine, crisp hair so that his small brown nipples were almost hidden. Muscles layered his rib cage, and even at ease in the bed, his abdomen was sharply defined. That teasing trail of dark hair bisecting his body and dipping beneath the sheet was finer, silkier, than that on his chest.

Luna cleared her throat. "Grilled cheese is hardly brain surgery. But for the record, I cook. Nothing fancy, but I can read recipes." She patted her fanny with both hands. "As you can see, I'm not starving."

One eye opened, bright with interest. "You're a woman, not a little girl. You've got dangerous curves, babe, and they make me nuts."

He sounded so sincere, her pique evaporated. But how could she reply to *that*? She chose to change the subject instead. "You want to eat in bed or can you make it to the table?"

Finally opening both eyes, Joe grimaced and took a critical accounting of his body. "I have to get out of bed. I'm as stiff as a spinster's upper lip." He struggled into a sitting position with his legs over the side of the bed. Luna gazed down the long line of his back to his tight behind—until he groaned.

Her concern doubled. She'd always thought of Joe as invincible, probably because that's how he thought of himself. He gleefully dove into danger without a single thought to personal risk, secure in his belief that he could handle anything and anyone. He played at careers that scared other men to death.

Even the bruises hadn't detracted from his air of impenetrable strength. But he was just a man, and right now, he was hurt. "Maybe you should stay in bed. I'll bring the food here—"

"I want to take a shower," he rumbled in a low tone, while holding his side. "The hot water is bound to ease my sore muscles." He stood . . . and left the sheet on the bed.

Luna gawked. She couldn't help it.

Glancing at her as if he wasn't buck naked, as if his body wasn't a rock-hard sculpture of masculine perfection, Joe asked, "Can I have ten minutes, do you think?"

Luna swallowed. And stared. And stared some more.

"Luna?"

He wasn't quite standing straight, was more bent to favor one side of his ribs, off kilter thanks to his injured knee. He had a three-day beard shadow, unkempt hair, and eyes so blue they torched her even from across the room.

He smirked and awkwardly lifted the sheet, holding it in front of his lap. "Better?"

Luna pulled herself together. She wasn't a wilting virgin. She'd seen naked men before. None of them had looked like Joe, but still . . . She went to him and took his arm. "Sit here and wait for me. I'll get the shower ready first, then I'll help you."

Joe braced one hand against the footboard, one around his middle, and eased back down to the mattress. He had his injured leg stuck straight out and he was breathing hard. After several seconds ticked by, he asked, "Help me, how exactly?"

"I'll get things ready for you so all you have to do is step under the hot water."

"Wanna scrub my back for me, too?"

She almost smiled at the hopeful way he asked

that. The man couldn't move without gritting his teeth, and still he flirted. "Your back will have to go unscrubbed until you're capable of doing it yourself. But I'll start the shower and help you in. How's that?"

"I'd prefer you shower with me—no? All right, I'll take what I can get. So far, all I've managed is to clean my teeth and hit the john. Anything more than that was impossible."

Luna stalled. "You haven't eaten in three days?"

He shook his head, drawing her attention to his hair. It was thick and black and silky. Without thinking, Luna smoothed it away from his forehead. Joe looked up at her, his eyes warm and aware. Their gazes clashed and held.

She jerked her hand away.

He was nice enough not to say anything about it. "The first day I stayed drugged and slept. The second day I was hungry enough to hobble into the kitchen but I didn't have anything ready to eat and cooking wasn't worth the effort."

Outrage filled her all over again. "What about the women trooping in and out? None of them offered to cook for you?"

He raised a brow, surprised by her vehemence. "Not a Martha Stewart clone in the bunch."

"Your taste in women is deplorable."

He looked her over, and even in his present condition, he managed to put a load of sensual regard into his expression. "Oh, I dunno. I think I have great taste in women."

Unsure how to reply to that, Luna asked instead, "Where do you keep your underwear?"

Joe drew back. "Forget it. I'd have a hell of a time wrestling them on over my leg."

"I'll help you." She'd never survive if he remained in the buff. In her entire adult life, she'd never known anyone so cavalier about nudity. Joe was as comfortable out of clothes as in them.

"Spoilsport," he accused, but added, "third drawer on the left-hand side."

Luna pulled out a pair of black cotton boxers, then went back to Joe. "Do you need help walking?"

"God, I hope not." He sounded disgruntled, then in pain as he pushed to his feet and slowly moved forward. "I'm too old for this shit," he mumbled under his breath.

Luna rushed ahead of him to the hall bath. She opened the door wide, then started the shower so it'd get nice and hot. She was just straightening when Joe limped in behind her, dropped the sheet to the floor and stepped cautiously into the tub without a word.

Luna whipped around, giving him her back, but not before she saw him crowd his big body in under the steamy spray. She heard his carnal sigh of pleasure.

Sympathy welling, Luna stepped out of the bathroom and went about finding a couple of towels and a washcloth. He spent several minutes just standing beneath the hot spray before finally soaping up a bar and scrubbing clean.

Waiting in the hall, Luna fretted. "You okay?"

"Much better, thanks."

"When are you due for another pill?"

"An hour ago."

Of all the idiotic . . . She yanked the curtain part way open. Joe had suds in his hair, trailing over his massive shoulders and down his chest to his abdomen. Luna sputtered a moment—until Joe opened one eye and gazed at her quizzically. "You want something, honey?"

"Why didn't you take your pain medication?"

"I was playing possum, remember?"

She rolled her eyes. "Finish up and you can take the medication with your food."

"Yes, dear."

She snapped the curtain closed again and started to move away.

"Do all wives nag this much?"

"Probably."

He laughed, then said, "I'm done."

He did sound refreshed, at least she thought so. Keeping her face averted, Luna opened the curtain again to turn both spigots off. "There. Now I'll just—"

"Help me dry off?" He reached for her and soaked her shoulder as he braced against her to step out, grousing and groaning with every move. A puddle formed around his big feet while he looked down at her and waited.

Luna hesitated, but she just wasn't sure. She'd never imagined Joe asking for help. He'd always seemed too proud for that, too intent on being the big man. Was he truly incapable of doing it himself? With Joe her thoughts were always mired with conflicting emotions and needs.

"That's okay," he finally relented, his voice shaded by disappointment. "I understand. Forget I asked." He clenched his jaw as he bent to pick up the towel, then wrapped it around his waist.

Luna felt selfish and wretched and mean. She'd barged into his home, run off his girlfriends, asked him for an enormous favor, and he'd not once complained. He'd agreed to help her. For free. His only stipulation was that she had to understand up front that he wanted her.

She did understand, because she wanted him, too. But contrary to his sexual suggestions, he was in no shape right now to do anything about it. He needed her, as much as she needed him.

She reached for the other towel.

Chapter Three

Less than a minute later, Joe knew he'd made a serious tactical error, but it was too late now to re-trench. Luna bent close to him as she gently blotted the towel over his shoulders and across his upper chest, along the length of his arms. He stared down at the top of her head while inhaling the flowery fragrance of her hair and the earthier scent of her body. He could feel her warmth and the soft touch of her breath.

Unbelievably, his knees felt weak, so Joe widened his stance and braced one outstretched arm against the tile wall. If he let her get to him like this, the towel would soon prove inadequate covering. And she'd already made her feelings on his nudity plain. She didn't like it.

Or maybe she liked it too much. Either way, he didn't want to push her too far too fast. She might just balk and walk out on him.

Hesitating, Luna asked, "You okay?"

No. "Yeah."

Lightly, she rubbed the towel lower, over his abdomen.

He'd misjudged his own control by a long shot, he realized, as the old John Henry reared up to say hello.

Of course, Luna noticed. Even covered by white terrycloth, a bobbing erection was a tad hard to miss. She made a face. "You really should control that, you know."

"Can't." Then Joe thought to add, "Especially if you're going to talk about it."

"My lips are sealed."

"Don't talk about your lips either."

She wasn't offended. In fact, she laughed.

Joe could barely keep himself upright, and Luna was amused. "My back," he said, and lust put such an edge into the two words that he sounded horribly pained rather than turned on. He was used to being playful with women, teasing while keeping ultimate control. With Luna, he felt like a berserk marauder. He couldn't even spell control, much less utilize it.

She moved behind him . . . and hesitated yet again. Joe held his breath until he heard her say, "I'm wondering . . . Who is Lou?"

Annoyance over the damned tattoo made him antsy. "No one." He wasn't up to relating a long, ridiculous tale at the moment.

The towel brushed over his back, down the length of his spine. She'd dried his front with a brisk, detached purpose, but with his back, she wasn't really giving it her all, was sort of lingering over the task. "I saw the tattoo when I first got here. It says you love him."

Joe choked on a furious wave of indignation.

"Not a *him*. Good God, woman, don't start rumors like that."

"I'm not the one wearing that sentiment permanently emblazoned on my rear."

Damn it, he'd have to explain after all. Usually, he didn't care enough to bother. But no way did he want Luna to get the wrong impression. "Don't you dare laugh."

She made no promises. She bent to dry his legs, and Joe thought he might strangle for a whole different reason. Strike this one from the fantasy books; it was too difficult to enjoy. "Louise was another marriage-minded woman I used to date."

"Was?"

Talking helped a little. It gave him something else to focus on other than her touch and scent and warmth. "I think I may have cured her of those ridiculous notions. Now, do you want to hear this or not?"

"I'm listening."

Joe closed his eyes and concentrated hard on the story rather than the position of Luna behind him and all the places she touched. Was she dragging this out on purpose just to torment him? It wouldn't surprise him. Her three-month rejection of him, despite their shared interest, proved she had a real mean streak. He could actually feel her breath on the back of his injured knee.

"Joe?"

Seeing no way around it, Joe rushed through his story. "I quit seeing Louise because she got too clingy, even though I'd told her up front that I wasn't into any type of permanence. Unlike Amelia, she didn't accept that I wanted to remain a bachelor. She kept pushing and pushing. So I bailed."

"Meaning you stopped seeing her at all?"

"Yeah. A month or so later we ended up at the same party. She was being nice, which should have been my first clue that she was up to something, because whenever things didn't go her way, Louise was a real bitch. Halfway through the night she slipped something into my beer and I woke up in a damned tattoo parlor. I was stretched out on a table, my jeans around my ankles, and some wiry little weasel was writing *I Love Louise* on my ass. I came to before he could finish."

A faint snicker was heard from behind him, then Luna stood. She wore a wicked grin, but she didn't laugh. This attitude she had of treating him like an asexual being grated big time, especially since he couldn't return the favor. She was a sexy woman, and he knew it in every pore of his being. His awareness of her defied all reason.

"All done, except for a few places that I refuse to touch."

Joe gave her a heated look. "Chicken."

"Just cautious."

Joe held out his hand, and Luna tossed the towel to him, then turned her back. Hastily, feeling a little self-conscious, Joe finished drying. He let one towel drop to the floor and shielded himself with the other. On top of acute sexual frustration, his every muscle pulled and ached. The hot shower had eased him, but not enough.

He winced a little as he moved, and Luna said, "Let me help you get your boxers on."

"Forget it. Just keep your back turned." He'd tortured himself enough for one day. If she bent down in front of him—a position sure to put lecherous thoughts in any male mind—he wasn't sure he'd be able to take it.

With a modicum of swearing and a few stifled groans, Joe donned his underwear. Luna hovered at his side, not watching but still *there*, burning him, making him edgier. He hated to admit to his own weakness, but it was a good thing she didn't want him fully dressed. Wearing jeans and a shirt would have been more than a little uncomfortable.

As they headed for the kitchen and sustenance, Luna held his arm. He noticed that she walked slowly to make it easier on him. Though it was necessary, that nettled him too. Damn weakness. When he'd started this, Joe had planned to let her assist just to have her close. He hadn't planned on actually needing her help.

When the opportunity arose, he'd kick two asses just to prove to her that he could.

"So what did you do when you came to and realized what was going on?"

They'd reached the hall and were almost to the kitchen. "I was out of it enough that I tore the place up first."

"First?"

He slanted her a look. "Want all the gory details, huh?"

"That depends on how gory they get. I can't imagine you hitting a woman or beating down an innocent man."

"Your idea of innocent probably varies from mine, but no, I didn't hurt the tattoo artist." *Much.* "Let's just say he now understands that he should never touch someone who isn't coherent enough to agree to a tattoo."

"And the woman?"

Joe grunted. Far as he was concerned, Louise had gotten off easy. "She's from a rich family, with an influential daddy and society mamma. Big into appearances. They think their little girl is so sweet and innocent. I think they have big plans of her hooking up with a senator's son or something." He shook his head, grinned. "It's for sure they never pictured her slumming with me."

"What's wrong with you?"

She actually sounded affronted on his behalf. Joe laughed. "I'm not a mamma's dream son-in-law, that's for sure. I explained to Louise that if she came near me again, for any reason, I'd advertise our association to all and sundry, and let a certain little secret of hers out of the bag. That stopped her cold and turned her real apologetic, real quick."

Luna's eyes lit up. "What kind of secret?"

Shaking his head, Joe said, "You want me to kiss and tell? Shame on you." He maneuvered his body into a straight-backed kitchen chair. It wasn't what anyone would call cozy, but it beat staying in bed, especially since he'd been in bed alone. Luna pulled another chair toward him so he could prop up his leg, and that helped a little. "Thanks."

She didn't sit. She just stood there, arms crossed under her breasts, her foot tapping.

Watching her, Joe grinned. She looked as cool as ever, but also determined. Why not tell her, he thought. It'd be fun to see her reaction. "Louise likes it pretty rough. She's big into game playing."

"Sex games?"

Tilting his head to see her lush behind, Joe murmured, "Give me a few days and I'll show you."

A wave of warm color filled her face, and Luna took a step back. "I'm not that curious."

"Liar."

She ignored that to say with disapproval, "So she

shared her sexual fantasies with you, and you're using them against her now?"

"She had my ass tattooed!"

Lips twitching, Luna said, "Okay, so I guess you were justified."

"Damn right." But he felt compelled to add, "Normally, I figure what goes on between the sheets stays there. And besides, I doubt I'd have really told. It was just a threat."

"Why don't you have the tattoo removed?"

The very idea made him shudder. "Forget that. It hurt bad enough waking up with the damn thing. And it itched for days. No way am I having it lasered off."

"A sensitive tush, huh?" Before Joe could tell her to quit discussing his ass, she added, "Aren't you worried about what women will think when they see it?"

He gave her a look. "Any woman who gets my pants off already knows what to think."

"Sorry." Silently laughing, Luna held up both hands. "Forget I asked."

"You're forgiven. Now, about that food . . . ?"

Playing domestic goddess, Luna cooked two cheese sandwiches in a skillet until the bread was golden brown and the cheese was nice and gooey. She poured a tall glass of milk and scrounged around until she found some chips.

Joe sat back and enjoyed the sight of her. She still moved like a seductress, all fluid with the expected sway of hips and the delightful jiggle of breasts. But seeing her at his stove with a spatula in hand added a whole new perspective. It almost looked homey, and that should have sent him into a panic. Instead, it made him smile. Luna cooking for him. He never would have thought to see the day.

When she'd finished with the food, he expected her to join him at the table, but she went after one of his pain pills instead. He thankfully tossed it down, but grumbled, "Damn things make me sleepy."

"Then you better eat up now, before you start nodding off." She cut her sandwich, keeping one half and giving him the other. Silence reigned while they ate, but Joe was aware of Luna stealing looks at him. He wondered what she was thinking, and finally she said, "Did you play rough with her?"

He paused in the middle of taking a large bite. Lowering the sandwich back to the plate, he asked, "Got that in your head still, huh?"

She shrugged, but he could tell her nonchalance was feigned. Knowing she thought about it made him think about it. With Luna.

A wild little romp, once he'd recovered enough to really enjoy it, might be just what he needed to get her out of his system. But he wouldn't want to hurt her, or be as rough with her as Louise enjoyed.

He cleared his throat. "I always aim to please, honey, you can be sure of that. But I have to admit it wasn't something I really got into." Joe eyed her averted face and raised one brow. "Of course, if you wanted to . . . ?"

Fighting off a blush, Luna said, "That's real generous of you, Joe, but no thanks. It's not my thing."

Joe took the last bite of his sandwich. "Good."

After his hot shower, food and medication, Joe felt much better. Not good, not entirely up to par, but better. Sated on several levels but still tense on at least one, he watched Luna move around his kitchen, tidying up, preparing coffee. Damn but it felt good to be here with her. He wanted her, but it was more than that. He liked watching her move, enjoyed talking with her, hearing her tease. "Thanks for feeding me."

"You're welcome."

It was strange, but Joe didn't feel as ill at ease as he might have with any other woman. Of course, Luna wasn't trying to get on his good side. Different women had offered to cook for him, to clean, too. But it was always in an effort to become part of his life. Luna didn't want him in her life, at least not permanently. She'd only come to him because she had to. "This isn't as painful as I thought it'd be."

"What's that?" She set a cup of steaming coffee in front of him, then propped her hip against the table beside him.

"Letting you coddle me."

Her laugh was throaty and warm and . . . arousing. "Is that what I was doing? And here I thought I was just trying to get you back into fighting form."

Joe narrowed his eyes. Could her concern really be so mercenary? He didn't think so.

After he'd taken several appreciative sips of the coffee, she asked, "When do you think you'll be able to go?"

Now he felt challenged. "We can leave whenever you want." *Just please don't let it be right now.*

Very gently, Luna leaned closer and stroked the bruises over his ribs. Joe froze. Just as casually, she brushed his still-damp hair back. "I don't think you're in any shape to travel yet, do you?"

Nope, not mercenary at all.

Joe studied her, then caught her hand when she started to move away. "Honestly? I'll be better able to help you in a couple of days."

Her disappointment showed, but so did her understanding. "I want you to take as much time as you need."

Maintaining his hold on her hand, Joe admitted, "The thing is, I don't want you to go without me if you think there might be trouble."

He waited for an explosion. From the first, he'd known that Luna had an independent streak a mile wide. She did and said exactly as she pleased and bristled at any insinuation that she might not be able to handle things on her own.

Joe almost slid out of his chair when she nodded. "I could stay here with you, help you out until you're feeling better. Then we could leave together, in say, two days?"

Shock kept his tongue glued to the roof of his mouth for several seconds. "You'd do that?"

"You're going to help me," Luna pointed out. "The least I can do is help you."

From his toes to his ears, Joe detected over a hundred different aches and pains. Just breathing hurt. Sitting in the chair hurt. It didn't matter. One thought leapt to the forefront of his brain and crowded out all other considerations: he had only one bed. He looked at Luna and smiled. "Hell of an idea."

She couldn't hide her relief. "That's great. I can use the time to help you get packed up."

So she wanted to pack for him, too? Joe sipped at his coffee while reevaluating his thoughts. Perhaps Luna was more domestic than he'd given her credit for.

"We needed that long for you to pass the background check, anyway."

He spewed his coffee. "The what?"

"Background check." Frowning, she grabbed up

a paper napkin and handed it to him. "Anyone staying with the kids has to have one. Don't worry about it. I already gave CPS your name, address and phone number last week, when I first decided to go. The check should be done before we take off."

"I don't want anyone poking around in my background!"

Luna cocked a brow. "Got something to hide?"

"Yeah, *my life.*" Fuming, Joe shoved himself to his feet. It was an awkward show of anger given his level of discomfort and the fact he wore only boxers. Stomping was out of the question; the best he could do was limp.

"Just calm down, Joe."

He opened his mouth to refuse, and his phone rang. "Damn it."

Luna raised a brow. "Want me to get that?"

"No. Ignore it."

"It could be important."

"It's not."

Exasperated, she said, "It could be the woman from Children's Protective Services. Maybe you've already been given the stamp of approval." Luna reached for the phone, and the answering machine picked up.

A feminine voice said, "Hey, Joe. It's Alyx. I want to come visit, but I don't want to walk into anything like I did last time. I swear, that little show stunted my growth." A husky, amused laugh followed the statement. "Is the coast clear?"

Joe grinned, but before he could explain why this caller didn't irk him, Luna snatched up the phone.

"No, the coast is not clear." She glared at Joe, her scowl ferocious. She listened, then said, "I'm

Joe's wife, that's who I am. No, I'm not joking. Joe's a married man now, so you don't need to bother calling him back. Understand?"

Joe stood there in horrified fascination. Watching Luna at work was like seeing a train wreck—devastating but unstoppable. "Uh, Luna . . ."

Her mouth curled in a wicked smile. "No, he can't come to the phone. Why? Because I said so. Now be a good girl and get lost, okay?"

She hung up the phone. Then, as if that awful little debacle hadn't just occurred, she said, "The background check is rudimentary. If you don't have any arrests or outstanding warrants or records of drug abuse, you should pass with flying colors."

A little poleaxed, Joe blinked. It took him a second, then he started to laugh. He wrapped his arms around his middle and chuckled so hard that he had to slump into the wall. It hurt like hell, but he couldn't stop himself.

"What," Luna demanded, "is so funny?"

"That was Alyx," he managed to gasp around his hilarity.

One brow shot high. "Are you telling me she's special to you?"

"You could say that, yeah." He looked at Luna and started chuckling all over again.

Luna went rigid. "*How* special?"

He got the laughter under control, but continued to grin. Luna looked so put out, so disapproving and . . . *jealous*, Joe couldn't help but touch her cheek. "Real special."

She looked ready to spit. "Well, excuse me for tampering with your love life," she all but sneered. "I was under the impression you weren't serious about any woman."

Joe wouldn't admit it, but he knew he'd already

gotten very serious about Luna. This was going to be fun. "Alyx," he informed her, "is my sister."

She pulled back. "Your . . . ?"

"Sister."

"Well good God. Why didn't you say so?"

Joe dragged her close and hugged her. "You didn't give me much of a chance." She was so embarrassed, she didn't fight him. She tucked her face into his chest and groaned. Joe liked holding her, so even though he felt like a steamroller had gone over him, he didn't move to the chair. "Don't sweat it, honey. She'll call back. Trust me. Sometime within the next minute, she'll—" The phone rang. "There you go."

To keep her at his side, Joe looped one arm around Luna's shoulders, then lifted the receiver. He glanced at the caller ID, smiled, and said into the phone, "Alyx doesn't waste much time, does she? No, Mom, everything's fine, I promise."

Luna stared up at him in horror, then mouthed, *Mom?*

Joe nodded, but spoke into the phone. "No, I'm not being held hostage." He laughed. "That was just Luna. Yeah, she's sane, she just goes off on these tangents sometimes."

Luna started to hit him in the ribs, saw his bruises, and gave him a dirty look instead. Joe squeezed her.

"That's a dumb question." His brows drew down. "I know what she said, but no, I'm not married. That's just her way of keeping other females away from me. Yeah, possessive. No, I don't mind." Joe laughed again. "I'm *fine*."

Obviously peeved, Luna pushed herself away from him, so Joe gave up and gimped his way into the chair. He sat back, stretched out his legs, and scratched his belly.

Wide-eyed, Luna watched him. Or rather she watched his hand on his stomach. Nice.

"Tell Alyx I owe her one, but no, she can't visit. Because I'm going to be going out of town, and before you ask, yes, I'd have told you first." He glanced at Luna and rolled his eyes. He was thirty-six years old and still his mother fretted. "I'm not sure, but I'll get in touch when I get there and let you know, okay? Yeah, love you, too. Smack Alyx for me." He grinned. "Bye."

He laid the phone on the table and turned to Luna. She looked devastated. "Hey, what's wrong?" Had his teasing really bothered her so much? "You okay?"

She turned her back on him and began rinsing cups in the sink. Quietly, her voice strained, she said, "Of course I'm okay. Why wouldn't I be?"

He didn't know, but he could hear it in her tone. She was bothered about something. Joe silently left his chair and stepped up close behind her. Her light, feminine fragrance filled his head. He inhaled deeply.

Little by little, he was starting to feel human again. The pain pill had kicked in, dulling his sharper aches and making him mellow. But he didn't feel that awful urge to drop into bed and fade into oblivion the way he had earlier. Luna was here, and he didn't want to waste a single second of his time with her.

He crowded into her, but stayed cautious. With Luna, he never knew when she might let a pointy elbow get the better of him. "You really threw Alyx into a spin. You know what she thought?"

"That I'm a nut?"

He put his hands on her waist and nudged closer still until he was pressed up against her behind. Damn. If only all of him felt as responsive as his dick. "Maybe. But she also thought someone had killed me or taken me prisoner."

Luna relaxed back against him. "The idea that you might marry is too ludicrous to be considered, huh?"

"For right now, yeah." Joe nuzzled her hair, quickly falling in lust again. "You have to understand Alyx. We're close. She knows there's no way I'd get married without telling her first, so therefore, she assumed foul play."

"Does she know about you getting beat up?"

"No way. If she did, Alyx would be on a manhunt herself, and I'd have to worry about her as well as everything else." Joe slid both hands around her to her belly.

Luna made a small sound of yearning. "Joe . . ."

He pressed his mouth to her neck, the sensitive spot where her neck met her shoulder. He spread his fingers wide.

"You shouldn't keep things from your family, Joe."

He inched one hand higher, one lower. "You don't know my family," he rumbled. "They'd go nuts worrying. They know what I do and they know it's sometimes dangerous. The fewer details they're aware of, the better."

Luna sighed. "That's nice."

Pausing in his seduction, Joe bent around to see her face. "Nice?"

"To have family like that, I mean. To worry about you. To . . . care."

Temporarily sidetracked, Joe propped his chin on top of her head. He'd never before realized how short Luna was in comparison to his six feet, three inches. He guessed her to be around five-six, but she had such a presence about her, he'd always thought her taller. "You don't?"

"No, not really." As if catching herself, she turned in his arms and gave him a chiding shake of her head. "Look at you, trying to work your moves when you can barely stand up."

"Hey, I'm up." He looked at her mouth. "In more ways than one."

She fought a smile. "I thought we weren't going to talk about that."

"Not then." Pressing into her so that she couldn't miss his rising erection, he murmured, "But now . . ."

"No." She flattened her hands on his chest and stared up at him. She had the most beautiful caramel-colored eyes, lightened with glowing gold flecks. "We have to finish talking about your background check."

A frown replaced his grin. "Oh, yeah. I'm pissed about that."

"Do you have a criminal record?"

He considered swatting her for that impudent question. "Of course not. I used to be a cop, remember? I got picked up a few times, but that was just—"

"You've been arrested?" She went wide-eyed in shock again, then shook her head as if she expected no better.

Joe locked his jaw. "Sometimes in the thick of things, it's tough to see who's the good guy and who's the bad."

She gave him a cynical look. "And you like to blur the edges?"

"Sometimes." He rolled one shoulder. "Police have to be cautious. So I've been hauled in a time or two, but I've always been released."

She slid away from him and moved to the other

side of the table. "So there's nothing to worry about, right? You've never been arrested, so you have nothing to hide."

"I didn't say that."

She clutched the chair in front of her. "So you do have something to hide?" Annoyance clouded her eyes. "If they reject you, then that means I'll have to go alone. I might as well leave now instead of wasting time waiting for you."

His molars would be dust by the time they finished this tooth-grinding conversation. "You're not going without me."

"Wanna bet?" She started to pace again.

Joe caught her arm when she neared him. "I'll pass, all right? They might frown over my job, but it's legit. That still doesn't give you the right to go snooping—"

"What exactly is your job? I know you used to be a cop, then a bounty hunter."

"I've done a lot of things," he said evasively, knowing he'd walked the gray areas more than once. "Private detective work, bouncer. Right now I hire out as a bodyguard."

"A bodyguard? For who?"

"Anyone who needs protection." All this gabbing got to him, so he turned to leave the room. "Mind if we finish this conversation in bed? I'm about shot."

"Oh, of course not." She hustled along with him, reaching the bed first to turn down the sheets so he could crawl right in. "Is that better?"

"It'd be better if you joined me."

"It'd kill you if I joined you."

Joe laughed. "Bragging about your skill in the sack? Damn, no need to build the anticipation, babe. I'm already anxious."

"No! I just meant . . ." She eyed him, then shook her head. "Stop being outrageous."

"I could die happy, honey."

She sighed. "You're not up to it, Joe, and you know it. So quit trying."

"Just hoping to ease you into the idea, that's all. When I'm back to my old self, which I will be very soon, I want you to be ready. We've wasted enough time."

"I'm not going to—"

Joe caught her hand. "Shh." He pulled her to the edge of the mattress until she sat beside him. "Don't make declarations you might not be able to keep, okay? I want you, you want me. The rest will work itself out."

Flushed, Luna pulled free and stood. "I'm going to get some of my stuff out of the car." She glanced along the length of his body, now stretched out from headboard to footboard atop the mattress. Her voice sounded thick. "It's getting late and I'm tired."

Joe gave her a smug, knowing look. "I thought you wanted to hear about my job as a bodyguard."

"Tomorrow. Over breakfast."

"Away from the bed and temptation?"

She surprised him by nodding. "Exactly. Why don't you go to sleep? I'm going to shower, make a few phone calls, then turn in on the couch."

Now, that idea sucked. "Hey, why sleep out there?" He patted the mattress beside him. "You'll be more comfortable here."

She gazed at his naked chest, his stomach, his thighs, and let out a long breath. "No. I get the feeling that lying down with you right now would be frustrating and very uncomfortable. You need your rest, and I'm . . . Well, I think I'll sleep better alone, too." She started out of the room. "If you need anything, just call me."

In a near whisper, he asked, "And if I need you?"

Her back to him, one hand on the knob, she paused at the door. "I suppose we'll just have to see—when you're up to par again."

The door closed with a quiet click behind her. Very slowly, Joe's smile spread until he laughed out loud. He had her. She'd as much as agreed, thanks to his seduction tactics, and he wasn't even up to full speed yet. Just wait until he felt a hundred percent and could really turn on the heat.

He forgot his aches for the moment and, out of habit, reached for the balisong knife he always kept on the nightstand. Closed, it looked like a slim, harmless tool. Opened, it exposed a lethal blade. He'd carried such a knife for years.

With one flick of his wrist, it opened like a butterfly spreading her wings. The handles folded back and the razor-sharp blade extended. Just as easily, Joe flipped it closed again. He only locked the handles into place when he wanted to actually use the knife. The rest of the time, he played with it, perfecting his timing, his dexterity. Open, closed, open, closed. The quiet snick, click was familiar to him, soothing.

He heard the shower start, and an image of Luna naked and wet crowded into his brain. Lush breasts, full hips, honey-tinted skin . . . Snick, click. Snick, click. His heartbeat thumped, heavy and slow. He'd have her alone in his apartment for the next couple of days. Just showering and eating had left him much improved, a fact enforced by the ease with which he manipulated the knife. Even two days ago, he couldn't have practiced the smooth movements so familiar to him.

In a few days, he figured he could give her a taste of what she'd been denying for three long months. Anticipation rode him hard, and long past the time he heard Luna settle in on the couch, Joe lay awake thinking about it. Finally, sometime past midnight, he dozed off into broken sleep, tormented by the craving that wouldn't abate.

When the soft creak awoke him, he at first thought it was Luna coming to him. His whole body tensed—then he heard a quiet grunt, the sounds of stealth, and his instincts kicked in. In one fluid, silent motion, Joe left the bed, all pains pushed to the back of his mind so they couldn't interfere with how he functioned.

Someone had broken into his apartment. And Luna was out on the couch alone. If the intruder scared her, touched her—Joe would kill him. It was as simple as that.

Chapter Four

When a hard hand pressed over her mouth, Luna lurched awake. Panic surfaced, raw and real, and she tried to scream, but the big body pressing on her made that impossible.

A voice breathed into her ear, "Shhh. It's me," and she went still, her heart racing in relief even as she struggled to orient herself. Joe slowly released her mouth and in a nearly soundless command, said, "Don't move."

On her back, her gaze able to make out only the moon shadows on the ceiling, Luna held immobile for a single heartbeat. What in the world had happened? Why was he whispering? Joe started to move away, and clarity struck. In that moment, Luna realized there was a threat of some kind. She heard a faint noise in the kitchen, and Joe intended to investigate.

Determined to keep him close and away from danger, she grabbed for him. She didn't think about what she did, she just did it. Her hands barely touched warm, hard flesh before he reacted.

Fingers spread wide, he flattened one palm on her upper chest and forced her down to the couch again. "Do not move."

Uh oh. Joe sounded deadly, not like the Joe she knew best, full of teasing come-ons and melting sensuality. But like the man she knew he could be when necessary, the man she needed with her in North Carolina.

Hard, unstoppable, cutthroat—the man who could handle any situation, the man who grinned with excitement while jumping into danger.

Luna had witnessed this side of Joe once before when he'd assisted his cousin Zane in removing a threat. He'd been so lethal then, so dangerous, that she'd felt herself reacting to the power of him.

She was no less awed now. She was, however, determined to assist him, given that he wasn't in his best shape at the moment.

Quickly, without shadow or sound, Joe left her. Luna pushed up on one elbow, but she couldn't see or hear anything more than the thundering of her own heartbeat in her ears. Her palms began to sweat. She slid off the side of the couch, crouching onto the balls of her feet and her hands. *If you dare get hurt, Joe Winston,* she silently cursed, *I'll . . .* Well, she didn't know what she'd do. Visions of his already bruised, battered body invaded her brain. He wasn't up to this. He wasn't his normal invincible self. . . .

She'd managed only two cautious steps when a crash sounded and bodies came tumbling past her. "Joe!" Luna jerked to her feet and fumbled for the lamp on the end table. It came on, but immediately went off again when Joe lunged against a big masked man, knocking him into the table and upsetting the lamp. Luna let out a very undignified screech of surprise. The lamp crashed against the floor and the light bulb blew with a pop.

"Damn it," she hissed, and she ran toward the kitchen, fumbling on the way, almost tripping in the unfamiliar darkness of his apartment before feeling for the light switch on the wall. The fluorescent light flickered on, blinding her and sending slanted light and misshapen shadows onto the two men.

Joe was on the bottom. The husky man straddling him wore black leather gloves and a dark ski mask. He drew back one enormous fist, aiming for Joe's face.

The strangest feeling went through Luna. Fear melted under a volcanic tide of red-hot fury; her heart settled into a slow, fierce beat. Without her mind's permission, she found herself going forward, swinging up the fallen lamp and preparing to bludgeon the intruder's head.

She didn't get the chance. Joe's feet wedged under the other man and he suddenly went flying toward the front door. He hit the wall with a dull thud that left him dazed. In slow motion, his corpulent body sunk down to the floor.

"Joe!" Luna reached for him, but Joe was upright again and stomping forward as if he hadn't suffered a single hurt. There was no limp, no favoring his ribs. His chest expanded; his shoulders bunched. Menace pulsed off him in waves. He wore that awful little smile that didn't bode well.

He appeared so massive and strong and capable, Luna caught her breath in astonishment.

Apparently the intruder felt the same because he'd already charged to his feet and was at the door, frantically turning the lock and jerking it wide open. Joe caught him before he could go out. Using a hand on his shoulder, Joe spun him around and landed a fist against his nose with sickening impact. The intruder howled and fell backward through the doorway, fetching up against the hallway wall and quickly scrambling for balance.

Joe started through the doorway, too, intent on following.

"Joe!"

He didn't slow.

The idiotic man didn't know when to leave well enough alone. Luna dashed after him. Panic, fear and annoyance filled her voice as she gave a frantic yell. "Damn you, Joe Winston."

Joe paused for a single heartbeat, casting her a quick, dismissive red-eyed look. His gaze immediately shot back to her. Eyes narrowing even more, he looked her over, head to toes and back again. Only then did Luna recall her state of undress. She'd been in bed, wearing no more than a black T-shirt with the word *Intuitive* in silver script and black satin panties. But thank God for that, because during Joe's moment of distraction, the intruder's pounding footsteps sounded on the stairs.

Joe jerked back to attention. "Stay inside."

"Oh, no." Luna reached for him, but since he was mostly naked, there weren't many places to grab. She caught a handful of material at the seat of his shorts, almost stripping him the rest of the way when he didn't slow. She released his boxers rather than leave him bare-assed. "Joe . . ." She detested begging, but heard herself say, *"Please."*

She darted around him, putting herself in front to block his way. Dumb. In an instant, she felt her

shoulders pushed to the wall. Eyes flaring with desperation, she wrapped both hands around one
bulging, rock-hard biceps. "If you go after him,
I'm following," she threatened. "Do you hear me,
Joe Winston? I'll be right on your heels, I swear it."

Fury rippled through Joe. He pressed his chest
into hers, surrounding her with his heat, his anger.
"You'll do as you're damn well told," he roared,
and Luna would almost swear his fury parted her
hair.

"No." Breathless, defiant, she waited to see what
he'd do over her denial. His jaw locked, his nostrils flared with his rage.

They both heard the front door of the apartment building slam shut. The man had gotten
away. In the darkness of the night, he'd probably
already disappeared. There were more than a few
alleys to dart down, buildings to hide behind.
Luna's knees went weak in relief.

But only for a moment.

Joe wrapped his hand around the back of her
neck and stared hard into her face. His breath was
hot, his bare body hotter. She thought she could
feel the thumping of his heartbeat against her
breast. Frustration rolled off him in suffocating
waves.

"He's long gone, Joe," she told him. "Give it
up." He still seemed poised for pursuit, so she
added, "We should call the cops."

"I could have had him."

Oh, boy. She hadn't been prepared to see him
like this. Knowing how he could be and finding
herself the recipient of that mood were two different things. Luna tried to reason with him. "Have
you forgotten that you're hurt? What if he'd had

friends waiting outside? Or if he'd pulled a gun?" She couldn't help frowning in annoyance. "You're also in your damn underwear."

"So?"

It figured that Joe wouldn't care about something like that. "Well, your neighbors are peeking out at you now."

His head swiveled about, and he took in the curious faces of the nearby residents to the left and right of his apartment. His hand tightened on the back of her neck until she went on tiptoe. To an elderly man, Joe said, "Call the cops, will you, Rob? Someone broke into my place."

"Sure thing, Joe." Rob looked thrilled for the chance to take part in the action.

"Marilyn," he said to a forty-something woman with two kids peeking around from behind her. "I'm sorry we woke you."

"That's all right, Joe." She glanced between the two of them. "Are you okay?"

"Fine."

"You don't look fine."

"He's not," Luna told her, and became the beneficiary of another glare. She shrugged, a little apologetic, but not much. She'd done what she thought best. She'd do it again if necessary.

"I'm *fine*," Joe said again, then told Marilyn, "I'm sorry we disturbed you. Go on back to your bed."

The woman gave Luna a curious and somewhat pitying look, then ducked inside.

"Why'd she look at me like that?" Luna asked, trying to ignore the fact that Joe still had her pinned to the wall. His hand on her neck was in no way hurtful, but she wouldn't exactly call it a loving embrace either.

"Probably because she's smarter than you." So saying, Joe turned and marched her back into the apartment. Once through the door, he kicked it shut, but didn't release her. Luna found herself pressed to the wall again, and this time Joe didn't hold back.

"Don't you ever, *ever,* get in my way again. Do you understand me?"

It would be most unwise to provoke him while he was in this mood. She should soothe him, calm him down . . . "You're not my boss."

Joe's eyes flared, the blue positively glowing with molten rage. *"You could have gotten hurt."*

His roar damn near stopped her heart, but still she shrugged. "I wasn't."

Teeth grinding, he said, "Luna—"

She reached up and touched his jaw in a butterfly caress. He was warm, alive. Safe. Her voice shook when she whispered, "God, Joe, you about scared me to death."

A muscle ticked in his temple. His gaze, burning into hers, dipped to her mouth—and stayed there. He drew a fast, short breath, then another, and suddenly he was kissing her.

Or rather, devouring her.

Luna hung in his arms, her senses devastated by the heat and taste and rock-hard feel of him. His tongue thrust in, his mouth grinding against hers almost brutally. One hot palm opened over her breast and massaged, squeezed, shaped. He gave a groan of pain or pleasure, she wasn't sure which.

She tried to gather her wits, but the bombardment of her senses was too much. She wanted this, she wanted him. His pelvis pressed into hers, insistent, moving in a parody of the sex act, further demolishing her control.

She turned her face away to gasp for air and managed to inhale his hot, male scent. *"Joe."*

He reclaimed her mouth, refusing to let her move, to withdraw. Overwhelmed by the onslaught, she gave up, wrapped both arms around his strong neck, and held on. Oh, God, she should have remembered how his kiss affected her, but she hadn't, and now it was just too delicious to resist.

Everything changed with her surrender. His hold tightened, those massive arms of his keeping her plastered to his body, but it now felt cherishing rather than restrictive. His kiss gentled, went deeper, slower, longer. She could hear his rapid breaths and her own shallow panting.

With no forewarning, Joe stroked one hot palm down her back and straight into her panties. Stunned by the impact of his long fingers there, Luna arched forward in surprise, a small cry escaping her, but it didn't deter Joe. He swallowed the sound, spurred on by her response.

His fingers squeezed, then slid into the cleft of her behind, low, deep, finding her vulva in a bold, tantalizing exploration. She shuddered in response.

Joe gave a rumbling growl of triumph and lifted his head. Their gazes met, hers melting, his burning. He pushed one finger slowly into her—and a knock sounded on the door.

"Police. Open up."

Without moving, Joe squeezed his eyes shut. "Fuck."

Luna trembled from head to toe. His finger was still inside her, hot, deep, teasing. "I . . . I gathered that's what you had in mind."

"No way." He drew two deep breaths before looking at her again. His hand shifted the tiniest bit, rasping against sensitive, intimate flesh. "What I want to do to you, with you, is way beyond fucking, honey. Way beyond." Keeping their gazes locked, he withdrew his hand in a slow, sensual caress. "You remember that, okay?"

Luna had no idea what he meant by that, but the very idea both alarmed and excited her. Joe stepped back, moved her aside, and opened the door.

The door.

She couldn't breathe, was more turned on than she'd ever been in her entire life, and she now had two young uniformed officers staring at her.

Good Lord. Color flooded her face. If she survived this night, she'd strangle Joe for sure. "Excuse me," she muttered with as much dignity as she could muster under the circumstances. Her wits were scattered, and her body tingled to the point she knew she couldn't deal with anything more than modesty. On wobbly legs, she headed for the couch to retrieve her sheet, then wrapped it around herself. Joe, damn him, stood there with an erection that a blind man couldn't miss.

The cops quickly surveyed him. "Do we have the right place?"

"Yeah, come on in." Joe stepped back and held the door wide for them. He seemed as comfortable in his boxers now as he had been naked earlier. And somehow, despite his state of undress, his bruises and sleep-rumpled hair, he looked more imposing, more in charge, than the two policemen.

"I'm Officer Clark, and this is Officer Denter. There was a break-in?"

"That's right." Joe sent Luna a searing look. "I

almost had the bastard, too, but someone doesn't know when to stay the hell out of my way."

Luna lifted her chin, insulted and further embarrassed with the way the cops examined her. "You're in no shape to play macho-man."

One of the officers agreed. "She's right. You look like an elephant stomped on you."

"But not just now," the other officer said. "Those are older bruises?"

"Yeah, and I'm betting they're from the same asshole who visited tonight." Very briefly, Joe filled them in.

Officer Denter crossed his arms over his chest. "So despite being bludgeoned nearly to death—"

"It looks worse than it is."

"—you still managed to fight this guy off tonight and send him running?"

Shrugging, Joe admitted, "I've been in the business. I know what I'm doing." With little embellishment, he told the officers the variety of jobs he'd held.

To Luna's disgust, they each looked impressed and very respectful.

"So someone doesn't like you?"

"Lots of people dislike him." Luna made a face. "At the moment, me included."

Denter nodded at the bedding on the couch. "So I see." Joe groaned, drawing Denter's notice back to him. "You okay?"

Limping to the couch, Joe carefully lowered himself to the soft cushions—right where Luna had been sleeping. "With any luck, I'll live."

The other cop approached him. "Do either of you need an ambulance?" He spoke to them both, but he was looking at Joe's colorful ribs.

"I'm fine," Joe insisted. "He must have come in through the kitchen window. He didn't get a chance to take anything, and he left without saying a word."

"So you think it was an attempted burglary?"

Joe shook his head. "No, I think he was here for an entirely different reason."

"To finish you off?"

"Most likely."

Luna shivered at the cavalier way Joe said that.

"He wore a ski mask and black leather gloves, so you won't be turning up any prints. But I figured you'd want to know about it anyway."

The cops shared a look. "You were right to call us, but . . ."

"Yeah, I know. Unless someone saw something, you've got nothing much to go on."

"We'll check on witnesses," Denter told him, then went in the direction of the kitchen. Officer Clark followed.

Luna used the moment to move to Joe's side. She dropped down next to him, which caused the couch to dip and Joe to groan. Shaking her head, she put her bed pillow over his lap to afford him a little modesty, whether he wanted it or not. "Look at you. A few minutes ago you were wrestling on the floor like a world champ, and now you can barely draw a breath."

"A minute ago I was on an adrenaline high." He tipped his head to the back of the couch and closed his eyes tiredly. "And I was worried he might hurt you. Pain became a secondary concern."

He'd been worried about her? And why the heck did that matter? He'd still been an impossible, pushy—"Really?"

With a grunt of humor, Joe said, "Don't sound so surprised, babe. Of course I don't want you hurt. And in the thick of things, the body just takes over." Without changing positions, he looked at her through slanted eyes. His voice lowered to a rumble. "Anger, lust. They work about the same. You get a rush of endorphins, and it acts as a natural painkiller."

"But now you're paying for it."

He winced and touched his ribs. "Yeah."

The cops reentered. "Looks like he did come in the window. With the way that dumpster is situated, it wouldn't have been too difficult to scale the wall and use the windowsill to hoist himself up."

"That's what I figured," Joe told them.

"So if you knew you had trouble, why was the kitchen window unlocked?"

"Are you sure it was?" Luna asked.

"Doesn't look like it was forced. I think he cut the screen and came right on in."

Joe shrugged. "I keep them locked. Hell, it's ninety-five outside and I have air-conditioning, so I never open the windows. But one of the ladies might have opened it earlier."

"Ladies?" The officers looked at Luna.

Infusing her voice with disgust, she waved her hand at Joe. "He has hoards of women."

Officer Clark pulled out a notepad. His mouth went crooked as he pinched off a smile and tried to appear serious. "Ah . . . Would that include you, miss?"

"No." Luna shook her head hard for emphasis, but Joe said at almost the same time, "Yeah."

Crossing her arms beneath her breasts, Luna glared at him. *"No."*

Joe winked. "Give me a few more days."

The men shared a conspiratorial glance and laughed. Officer Clark cleared his throat. "Was it a woman who clobbered you? Because I can tell you, I wouldn't be surprised."

"That's exactly what I said." Luna nodded in satisfaction.

Joe rolled his eyes. "Absurd. The women I know don't want me dead. You can trust me on this. Besides, he sat on me, so I know he was male, not female." He slanted both officers a look. "Believe me, I can tell the difference."

Officer Denter laughed. "Never underestimate a woman. They're clever in setting things up and using men to follow through." Before Luna could find a suitable way to show her affront on behalf of all womankind, Denter started out of the room. "I'm going to check out the rest of your apartment."

"Fine. Not that much to check, though. There's just the bedroom and bathroom."

"He never made it out of the kitchen?"

"Nope. I was dozing, heard a noise and came to investigate. He'd just gotten to the kitchen door when I found him."

"I think I'll look all the same. It's routine." While Officer Denter walked off, Joe filed his report with Officer Clark. He told him about Bruno Caldwell, the man he suspected was behind his present ills. He shared his history with Caldwell and gave a generalized description, including height and portly weight, which matched the dimensions of their nighttime visitor. Luna realized that Joe couldn't be more specific because he hadn't seen the guy in a while. He said he didn't know of any distinguishing marks, other than a nasty temper and a very homely mug. He also relayed details of the attack days before, which was still quite visible on his body.

Getting more worried by the second, Luna stood by and listened. Bruno Caldwell sounded like a very bad character, and the fact that he'd hurt Joe once and probably wanted to do so again made her chest tight with anxiety. Maybe Joe was right; taking him with her would be as beneficial to him as it was to her.

Officer Clark closed his notebook. "Stocky, dark and mean describes half the guys we're after, but we'll keep an eye out for him."

"And ugly. Seriously ugly."

"Got it." Clark chewed his upper lip in thought, then said, "I don't think we should rule out other possibilities, though."

"Like women?" Luna wanted to know.

Being a diplomat, Clark shrugged. "Let's just say I'd be very careful if I was you, and no more open windows."

"You don't have to worry about that," Luna assured him. "I'm not letting any more women in until Joe is back up to speed."

"Screw that," Joe said, and pushed himself to his feet with a grunt of discomfort. "We won't be here, so it's a moot point."

"Leaving town?" Denter raised a brow as he walked back in. "Other than an illegal knife on the nightstand, the rest of the place is clear."

"The knife is mine," Joe told him.

"You carry it on you?"

"Always."

"You any good with it?"

"Very."

"It *is* illegal, you know."

"Yeah, I know."

Denter looked at Clark, and they both shrugged. Luna assumed that meant they wouldn't call him on the knife. Then Denter said, "If you get caught with it, it'll be taken away from you."

Joe nodded. "We were going to take off in a few days, but I'd rather get Luna someplace safe right away, so we'll be heading out before dawn."

Luna's mouth fell open. "But, Joe, you can barely walk . . ."

He gave her a stony don't-argue-with-me look. "I can make it to my truck just fine. You can drive. And I can get Zane's ass up here to help us pack up." He offered his hand to each officer. "We appreciate your help. If anything turns up, you can reach me on my cell phone." Joe recited the number while Clark wrote it down.

"Sounds smart to me," Denter said with a cagey glance at Luna, "if you really think the two incidents are related."

Clark nodded. "I don't encourage overreacting, but if you'd planned a trip anyway . . ." And he, too, nodded at Luna. "It might as well be now, just to make sure everyone stays safe."

"This is ridiculous." Luna chased after the men as they all headed for the door in what she viewed as a condescending male fashion. Her sheet trailed behind her, wrapping around her feet and nearly tripping her up. "I can certainly take care of myself. Besides, no one is after *me*. It's Joe they want to hurt, and he's not up to traveling. He's not up to anything."

Clark rubbed his upper lip to cover a grin. "Oh, I don't know that I'd say that."

"He's up." Denter didn't bother hiding his humor. "From what I saw, he'll survive." He thwacked Joe on the shoulder. "But do take it easy and we'll let you know if we turn up anything."

Once they were alone again, Luna fumed. "Damn you, Joe, this is not a game."

He caught her by the back of the neck and stole another kiss. That, too, infuriated her. She'd just drawn breath to curse him when he said, "I'm not taking chances with you, Luna." His big thumb rubbed her nape, warm and gentle. "I wouldn't be able to handle it if you ever got hurt."

She went speechless as he limped past her to the kitchen phone. He sounded so inflexible, she threw up her hands in defeat.

He had the phone to his ear, waiting for an answer, when Luna pointed out the time. "You realize that it's two A.M., right?"

Joe just shrugged, started to say something to her, then grinned. "Hey, Zane. What's up, cousin? It is? No shit, I didn't realize." He winked at Luna as he gave that audacious lie. "So . . . You were in bed? Yeah? Well, get your sorry ass up because I need a favor."

Luna could tell Joe thoroughly enjoyed himself. She turned on her heel and walked out of the kitchen. Her thoughts churned with a mingling of worry and anticipation and anxiety. She wanted to be with the kids. They needed her now not later. And she wanted Joe safely away from whoever intended him harm. But she couldn't bear the thought of causing him more pain, and at the same time, she found herself wanting to take care of him.

Stupid, stupid, stupid. Just because Joe wasn't the invincible macho jerk she'd always considered him to be didn't mean he'd suddenly become tame, ready for commitment and fidelity.

Just because he was worried about her didn't mean he wanted her to return the favor. From what she'd always known of Joe, the minute a woman got the notion to coddle him, he dumped her.

She'd have to keep that in mind—before she started to fall in love with the big guy. She would not be like Louise, bitter when she realized he wanted only sex. And she wouldn't be like Amelia, willing to accept half measure. The very idea was disturbing enough that she had to busy herself to block it from her mind.

By the time Joe found her some fifteen minutes later, Luna was dressed in black jeans and a silky purple tank top. Her earrings were fashioned from peacock feathers and silver hoops. She was at the bathroom sink brushing her teeth.

With a familiarity that had somehow formed in the last two hours, Joe slid his hand under her hair and curled his fingers warmly around her nape. "Zane will be here in a couple of hours. He's heading out now."

Around her toothbrush and a mouthful of paste, Luna gave him the nastiest look she could manage. Joe still wasn't standing up straight, and dark circles made his blue eyes more mesmerizing than ever. He was physically beat, exhausted, and he needed time to recoup, not a long difficult drive. But he was a bulldozer once he'd made up his mind, and she just didn't know what might be best. She felt cornered and hated it.

When she didn't reply, Joe said, "Tamara sends her love."

Luna concentrated on spitting and rinsing. She

couldn't remember any other man standing around, idly rubbing her neck while she brushed her teeth, but then, she'd never met a man like Joe.

When she'd finished, she walked around him. His hand fell to his side. "I'm packed already. I hadn't gotten that much out of my car. Tell me what you want me to do."

Joe nodded. His expression was searching, determined, but also teasing. "All right. Take off your clothes and get into my bed."

She jerked around to face him.

One side of his mouth curled, as if he'd only wanted a reaction from her, something other than her obvious disgruntlement. "Oh, you mean to get ready to leave?" He flicked the end of her nose. "Sure thing."

Together they retrieved his suitcases. While Luna packed away several pairs of jeans and T-shirts and shorts, Joe dressed. She noticed that he seemed a lot more limber now, so maybe he was feeling better. His normal masculine grace was missing, but he finished clothing himself without too much groaning and cursing.

Watching him, Luna asked, "Should you take another pain pill?"

"Hell no. I want to stay alert." He deftly buckled on a thick, black leather belt. "I'm not convinced our buddy won't return."

"You don't have to say that with so much relish, you know."

He glanced up at her, then picked up the balisong knife on his nightstand and slid it into his front pocket. "Believe me, nothing—other than you naked and willing—would give me more satisfaction at the moment than getting hold of Bruno."

She almost hit him. "Damn it, Joe, stop with the sexual barbs, okay?"

He turned away, opened the nightstand drawer, and pulled out a box of condoms. He tossed them atop his piled clothes in the suitcase. "I want you to know I want you. That was our deal, remember? I go along, you put up with my attempts at seduction."

"Seduction? I half expect you to club me over the head and drag me off by the hair any minute."

"Would that work?"

Her teeth clicked together. "No. And why me, anyway? According to you, you had two willing, adoring women here when I arrived. Why not make it easy on yourself?"

He slanted a cautious look her way and closed the suitcase. "Is this one of those tricky female questions where I hang myself no matter what I say?"

"Probably." She crossed her arms and stood in front of him, waiting. When he remained silent, she said, "It's just because I've said no, isn't it? You're not used to rejection. I'm a challenge."

His teeth flashed at her. "Your faith in my ability is awesome."

"Just repeating what you've told me, again and again."

"Well, I wouldn't lie, now, would I? But maybe I've exaggerated." He looked at her mouth, then didn't look away. "There have been other women turn me down, you know."

"Someone said no to Joe Winston, stud extraordinaire?" Luna laughed, but the way Joe watched her so intently felt like a caress. "Really? How incredible."

"It's usually not a big deal." He reached up and touched her cheek, mixing the impact of his hot look with the tenderness of a lover's touch. "When one woman says no, another says yes. Sex is just sex. But I haven't wanted any other woman since meeting you."

That threw her completely off balance. Why, it had been three months, and for a man like Joe that had to be a lifetime. "I'm expected to believe . . ."

"Believe what you want, babe." He bent and kissed her forehead, lingering for a heartbeat until her eyes closed and her lips parted. "But it won't make any difference. One way or another I'm going to get your panties off you, and then we'll both have a helluva time. I promise."

He walked away, leaving Luna befuddled and too warm and suddenly . . . curious. What would it be like to—*No.*

She couldn't start thinking that way. This trip was meant to gain her two children, not a man. Definitely not Joe. If she dallied with him, she'd end up with a world of hurt; she had no doubts about that.

For whatever unfortunate reasons might exist, Joe had already impacted her more than any other man she knew. Despite her outward appearance of flightiness, Luna prided herself on remaining grounded in reality, and her current reality was the responsibility of two emotionally needy children. Even if she wanted to risk her own heart, she couldn't let the kids become attached to him because she knew Joe wasn't ready to settle down. The most she could hope for was that he'd get along with the kids, befriend them, help her get things settled, then move on without too many hurt feelings.

And that meant she had to keep things platonic, despite what Joe wanted, and despite what, deep down, she wanted.

"Luna knows all and sees all," she whispered, mocking herself, "and Luna sees a lot of heartache headed her way." Shaking her head and shoring up her determination, Luna lugged the over-stuffed suitcase off the bed and began dragging it into the living room.

By six A.M. they were ready to go.

Chapter Five

Joe stood beside Luna while Zane slammed the tailgate shut on the truck and again checked the hitch where they'd chained Luna's small Contour. They would have already been on their way if Luna hadn't insisted on taking her car, too. She claimed she wanted her own transportation, not to be dependent on Joe. Since Joe felt the same, Zane had stopped and rented an appropriate hitch, and they were now towing Luna's car behind his Dodge Ram.

Their plans hadn't made Zane happy, but then, Zane had arrived grumbling and hadn't stopped yet. His brown hair was disheveled, his eyes tired, proof that Joe had gotten him out of a cozy bed and taken him away from his even cozier wife. Zane had always been an insatiable hound dog, but since marrying Tamara, he'd only gotten worse, much to Joe's amusement.

To further annoy his cousin, Joe said, "Damn, Zane. You're more fretful than an old woman, I swear. Tamara has you whipped, doesn't she?"

Both Zane and Luna scowled at Joe, almost making him laugh out loud. At the moment, he seemed to be the only one in a good mood. But then, he was heading off for an adventure with Luna. From his perspective, things were looking up.

"Well, shoot me for caring," Zane grouched. "I still don't understand why the hell you didn't tell anyone you'd been beat to a pulp."

"What would you have done, cousin? Come up and played nursemaid? Served me soup in bed? Held a cold compress to my head? Checked me for fever?"

Zane pokered up in indignation. "I could have put you out of your misery."

That made Joe chuckle. "Thanks but no thanks. I'm fine, getting finer by the minute actually." He blew a kiss to Luna, who appeared to search for a rock, presumably to hit him with. Damn, but she was adorable in a snit, and she'd been in a snit since he'd told her they were leaving.

Before that, though, when he'd lost his senses and nearly taken her against the wall, she'd been so hot he could have made love to her for hours without a single notice given to his aches and pains. The feel of her satiny bottom was burned into his brain. And the way her inner muscles had clamped onto his finger when he'd pressed into her . . . Damn. He couldn't wait to feel that hot, hungry hold on his cock.

"Earth to Joe."

With a start, Joe returned his attention to Zane. His voice was rougher, warmer, when he said, "If I bugged you every time some son of a bitch got in a lucky punch, you'd never see the end of me."

Zane shook his head in disgust. "You're what—almost forty now?"

"Bite your tongue! I'm thirty-six." And he was feeling every cursed year. Why, in his twenties he would have already bounced back from a similar beating. Now, however, it took all his concentration to stand up straight.

"You're old enough to stop playing the tough guy and settle down before someone gets lucky enough to kill you."

"If I settled down, I'd be bored to tears in a week. No thanks, Zane. I like what I do." But he wouldn't mind taking an extended break with Luna.

The late June sun dawned bright, breaking the lingering shadows of the hot night, forcing Zane to shield his eyes. "Think about it while you're on this trip." He glanced over at Luna, who busied herself by slipping on her dark sunglasses. "You might find marital bliss agrees with you."

Joe grinned and put an arm around Zane while they headed to the passenger's side of the truck. The hold looked friendly, when in truth Joe needed his cousin's support. He leaned heavily on Zane, making him scowl. "Why is it," Joe asked, "that every guy who ties the knot wants to see that same noose wrapped around other male throats?"

"Wisdom?"

"This is funny coming from a man who shared my sentiments not that long ago."

Zane shrugged. "Till I met the right woman. Just wait. When you meet the right one, you'll feel the same."

Joe considered them all right in one way or another. Not that he'd say so now with Luna surreptitiously listening in. She didn't respond to Zane's comments, but Joe saw the color rise in her face. Anger or embarrassment? Didn't matter to him. Either way, he found her adorable.

Over the roof of his truck, he said, "You sure you're okay driving the whole way?"

Joe couldn't see her eyes through her sunglasses, but he could hear the bite in her tone. "Would you ask me that if I were a guy?"

"Uh . . . no. But, Luna, you're not a guy."

"Just shut up, Joe." She opened her door and climbed up into the truck, sliding in behind the wheel. Joe laughed. Definitely anger.

To Zane, he said, "She's pretty damn entertaining, isn't she?"

"In rare moments." The engine kicked over with a rumble, giving Zane an opportunity to speak confidentially. "Bluster aside, you sure you're up to this?"

"Baby-sitting a couple of kids? Yeah, sure."

"It's not that easy, you know. From what I understand, you're walking into a passel of trouble with half the town in an uproar."

"No shit?" Had Luna misled him? Did it matter? Hearing that the situation might be worse than he'd been told only made Joe more determined to be there for her, to protect her and help her. To maybe see a little action.

"If I'd known you were at war with this Bruno Caldwell guy," Zane admitted, "I wouldn't have recommended you to Luna."

"Then I'm glad you didn't know . . ." Joe stiffened, and his words trailed off with the familiar prickling of his senses. Muscles drawing tight in preparation of a threat, he scanned the area and immediately focused on a car parked across the street. Behind the wheel sat a large man. His blond hair was nearly hidden beneath a low cap, and sunglasses masked his face. He wasn't looking at them now, but a hard stare was a tangible thing, and Joe had already felt it.

They were being watched.

Keeping the car and driver in sight and shushing Zane at the same time, Joe tried to decide how to proceed, but already the man began readjusting something in the seat beside him. He glanced up at Joe and put the car in gear.

"Goddammit . . ." Joe started toward the street in a trot, but he'd barely stepped off the curb before the car sped away, kicking up gravel and dust. Well-trained, Joe made note of the car model and memorized the license plate as the car went down the street.

Zane trotted up behind him. "What the hell's going on?"

"I need a pen and paper." Joe turned away and almost ran into Luna. He caught her upper arms to steady her, then said, "AM768U."

"What?"

"Remember that." He pushed past her and went to the truck to retrieve his cell phone. "Get a pen and paper for me, honey." He dialed, and got an answer on the second ring. "Hey, it's Joe. Yeah, run some plates for me, okay?"

Joe was aware of Zane and Luna standing by him, silent and watchful. He knew they were oblivious to the connections he'd made throughout his career of various jobs, but they were about to witness the advantages of knowing people.

"Ready?" Joe accepted the pen and slip of paper that Luna handed to him. As he spoke, he wrote the number down. "Gold Sebring convertible. Ohio plates. Amy-Mary-768-Unicorn. Yeah, you can call me back on my cell phone." He recited his number, then hung up.

Luna clutched at his arm. "Joe? What is it?"

Joe tucked the paper into his pocket. "We were being watched."

"You're sure?" She looked around with new awareness and irritation.

Joe wanted to curse himself. Alarming her had never been his intent, but at the same time, he knew he'd do whatever was necessary to keep her safe, and it wouldn't hurt for her to be on guard. "No, but I don't believe in coincidence."

"Was it that damn Bruno Caldwell again?"

She looked ready to do bodily harm on his behalf. Joe shook his head. "I couldn't see the guy well, but he appeared younger, with longish dark blond hair almost touching his shoulders. Bruno is mostly bald and very dark."

She twisted her mouth in thought. Joe wondered if she even knew she still held on to him. "Should we call the police?"

Slipping his arm around her shoulders and pulling her protectively close to his body, Joe asked, "And tell them what? That some bastard was watching us from across the street? There's no law against that." He urged Luna back to the truck and behind the wheel. The sooner they got out of town, the better. "No, I'd rather do this my way."

Zane tightened his mouth. "What the hell does that mean?"

"It means I trust myself and my own capabilities more than anyone else."

"I don't like this." Zane crossed his arms over his chest. At six-two, he stood an inch shorter than Joe and was a good forty pounds lighter, but at the moment he managed to look big enough. He nodded to Joe's hand. "You intend to use that on him if you catch him?"

Startled, Joe saw that he had retrieved his balisong knife without even realizing it. He was twitchy enough with the situation to flip it open and shut, open and shut. The blade was long and lethally sharp, and when he held it, it became an extension of his arm. Balisong knives weren't meant for throwing, but when Joe locked it open, he could propel it with deadly accuracy. He was so used to the knife he could open it faster than a switchblade.

When the intruder had come into his apartment earlier, he'd deliberately left the knife behind. His night vision was better than good, but with Luna on the couch, or maybe lurking around, he hadn't wanted to take any chances that she'd get sliced by accident.

Joe flipped the knife shut and tucked it away. "Yeah, I'll use it if I need to." At that moment, he met Luna's gaze and saw her apprehension. He turned away from her and muttered low to Zane, "Damn it, you're scaring Luna. Quit worrying and just close the place up tight for me, okay?"

"Promise me you'll be careful."

Curling his lip, Joe said, "Yes, Mother." Being coddled by his cousin was a most discomfitting happenstance. "By the way, I contacted Alyx. She should be here soon to lend you a hand. She knows what things are mine, and what came with the apartment. Make damn sure she's never left alone, though, okay? You know how she is. If she sees anyone spying on the place, she's liable to go right up to them and demand they turn themselves over to the law."

Zane grinned despite his bad mood. "She's still fearless, huh?"

"Fearless and flippant and brassy as hell." Joe didn't like to consider all the ways his sister's personality mirrored his own. He'd been a very bad influence on her. "I swear she'll never marry because she scares all the guys half to death."

"She's a little like Luna in that respect."

Lowering his voice even more, Joe said, "Yeah, well, Luna doesn't scare me. I can handle her."

"Spoken like a man blinded with lust. You know you're going to eventually eat those words, right?" Zane shook his head and laughed. "God, I just hope I'm around to see it."

"Don't hold your breath, okay?" He gave Zane a light shove to get him back on track. "After you pack up the rest of my stuff, turn the keys over to the landlord and split. I'm paid up a month in advance, but if there's a problem with the lease, just let me know. Alyx can store my things. Got it?"

Luna stuck her head out the window. "Are we leaving sometime today, or do you two biddies plan to gossip all damn day?"

Just that easily, she lightened his mood. "Nag, nag, nag." Joe startled his cousin by pulling him into a bear hug. His sore ribs protested, but it was worth it for Zane's reaction. He walked away while Zane sputtered behind him. After sliding into the seat next to Luna, Joe buckled his seat belt and gave a weary groan. "Mind if I doze while you drive? I'm a little tuckered out from all the excitement."

Just as Joe had intended, her anger evaporated. Funny how Luna had always hidden that wide nurturing streak of hers. He liked it. He liked her, and he had no qualms with her rush of concern. With most women, it had felt smothering, but with Luna, it just felt . . . nice.

She began fussing over him. "Do you need a pain pill? I have them in my purse. And here, I thought you might want a pillow, so I brought one with us." She pushed it behind his head while Joe reclined his seat a little and stretched out his long legs. "Get comfortable and relax. I'll wake you when I stop for gas, okay?"

Zane leaned into the car. "Quit spoiling him, Luna. He's insufferable enough as it is."

"I know," she said with gentle sweetness, "but I'd hate to see even a snake suffer."

Zane laughed while Joe pretended to be insulted, but in truth, he didn't mind her quips. He knew Luna was struggling with things. Smarting off was her way of dealing with the strength of her attraction to him. He wasn't blind. He knew she felt the chemistry almost as much as he did.

The little lady wanted him, but it scared her. *He* scared her. And for a woman like Luna, fear was unacceptable.

He'd ease her into things, Joe decided. That is, if he could keep himself in check. It wouldn't be easy if she kept being so grumpy and teasing and sexy. He leaned back and closed his eyes. "Say goodbye, Zane."

"Goodbye. And don't forget to check in once you're in North Carolina."

"We'll call," Luna promised. "Thanks for everything, Zane."

"No problem." He stepped back. "Let us know if you need any help with the kids, okay?"

"I will." She put the truck in gear.

"And, Joe? Watch your back."

Joe saluted him, and Luna pulled away. To Joe's surprise, he was sleepy. Maybe he would just rest his eyes for a little while. Luna was certainly capable of following the directions and getting them there safe and sound without his assistance.

Minutes later, Luna smiled over at Joe as he began to softly snore. His hands were over his hard abdomen, his fingers laced together. His head had slid off the pillow to slump against the door window, and the early morning sunshine glinted off the small gold hoop in his ear. His long, dark lashes softened his features, a sharp contrast to the beard shadow on his chiseled jaw and the slight kink to his once-broken nose.

Even mountains had moments of weakness, it seemed. She sighed.

Why, oh, why did that have to make him more appealing?

Given the simple clothes and shoddy residence, he'd assumed Joe Winston was broke. That assumption had to be reassessed when the expensive black muscle truck drove past the alley where he'd set up. Joe Winston was either truck poor or selective in where he spent his money. And with Joe's reputation, he'd bet it was the latter. The man didn't strike him as a fool.

With a covert attention to detail, he watched the flashy truck pass. He'd already turned off the "big ear" and removed the headphones. Good thing, too, or the rumbling of that powerful engine would have deafened him. The eavesdropping device was set to click off at any loud noise, but sometimes it wasn't quick enough to keep him from having his brain rattled.

When he'd first bought the "big ear," it had taken him a while to figure out how to use it effectively. From a distance, it picked up the slightest whisper. But it also picked up everything else, making it difficult to use in congested areas. Luck was with him this morning, because Winston had decided to slip away with the dawn. There'd been some disruption with the waking birds, but he'd heard what he needed to hear.

So, Winston was aware of Bruno. He supposed that wasn't really a big surprise. Winston couldn't have lived so long by being an idiot. The fact that Joe knew might complicate his job, but he wouldn't let it get in his way.

Not this time.

Now that the area was clear, he stepped out of the car and went to the front to remove the phony plates and replace them with the originals. He did the same at the back of the car, then tucked both fake plates into his satchel, along with the "big ear" and an assortment of other tools. For this mission, he'd packed a stun baton that delivered five hundred thousand volts of discouragement to assailants, night-vision goggles, a supply of nonlethal ammunition and the general assortment of hand and foot restraints, both steel and nylon.

He paused for only a moment. There'd been some mention of kids. That made his stomach feel a little icy and caused him a few cramps. His conscience was so old and rusty, he sometimes doubted its existence, but he wasn't so hardened that he could discount the possible threat to kids. Hell, he didn't want any innocents caught in the crossfire, but definitely not kids.

He pressed a fist to his guts and told himself he'd just have to trust Winston to keep them out of it. He had more important issues to concentrate on, like the fact that Winston had claimed his destination. North Carolina. He glanced at his watch. Yep, he'd have to haul ass to catch up.

He left the Sebring in the alley, assuming the

cops would locate it soon enough and return it to its rightful owner. If he found a minute or two, why, he'd even give them an anonymous tip. But not yet.

Before setting up this morning, he'd parked his well-used and nondescript brown sedan only a few yards away. The car was part of his necessary equipment. With a thick metal mesh screen securely fastened between the front and back seat, it served as an adequate cage for transporting captives. There were no door handles on the inside, no way to escape. Once he locked someone in back, they'd stay there until he released them. He'd be willing to bet Winston had once owned a similar vehicle.

Satisfied that all was in order, he stowed everything in the trunk, including the stupid cap he'd worn, then headed out of town. He got on 75 South, the same route he knew Winston and the woman would take. He left the window down so the humid air could keep him alert. His blond hair blew in his face, reminding him that he needed a haircut. He'd take care of that—after he took care of business.

Within twenty minutes, he caught up to the truck. They were in the slow lane thanks to towing a red Contour, and for the same reason, they were highly visible. Nice of them to make his job easier.

By all accounts, Winston was a sharp son of a bitch. But so far, he'd made one mistake after another—starting with being caught off guard several nights ago.

Unfortunately, that bitch Amelia had shown up, squawking and carrying on in a conspicuous show of concern for Winston's wellbeing, before he could make his move. Because of her, he hadn't had a chance to do his job then. But he wouldn't let another opportunity pass him by.

It didn't matter how good Joe Winston might be.

He figured he was better.

"Where the hell is this place? We've been driving for hours."

Luna took a fortifying breath. Joe was obviously tired, uncomfortable and cranky. She felt for him, she really did, but he should try it from her position. She was fed up with his attitude, her back and neck were sore from eight hours of driving, and she wanted food. Not fast food with its greasy smell and heavy taste, but real food. Even peanut butter and jelly would do, but no way in hell could she choke down another drive-through hamburger. *Ugh.*

"Not much farther," she said through her teeth, when she really had no idea. She'd called Patricia hours ago, once she was sure it was late enough for everyone to be up. Patricia would be watching for her, but with all the stops Joe had insisted on making, she'd have to wait longer than expected. "The directions say we keep going southeast until we hit Welcome County."

Joe pulled his gaze away from the passenger door side mirror. "Welcome County?"

"I know. Neat name, huh?" For most of the day Joe had either slept or eaten, which gave Luna little enough time to tell him about their destination. The man had an unbelievable appetite. He claimed to be making up for the days he hadn't eaten, so Luna had tried not to complain about stopping—again and again—at a variety of restaurants. She'd eaten a little herself, but she wasn't big on fast food.

"I've been there," Joe told her. "Back when I was still a bounty hunter. I happened into a situation where I busted a couple of guys rather than just the one I'd been tracking. The other guy had an outstanding warrant, so I contacted the officials in that area. They were more than a little relieved that I'd found him. The cop in charge told me that he'd made them all look like fools by evading arrest. When they came to get him, they thanked me and invited me down to visit. I needed a break, so I took them up on their offer."

"And spent all your time drinking and accosting the local females?"

Joe laughed. "No, smart ass. Several women tried to accost me, but I mostly spent my time fishing and boating and just lazing around. It had taken me over six weeks to catch the guy I was after, so I'd earned a break."

"You fish?"

Joe laughed. "I tell you a great story about how I nabbed the bad guys, and that's all you notice? Yes, I fish. When I get a chance. Not that I'm an expert or anything, but I found it pretty relaxing."

Pleased by his comments, Luna said, "Then you'll love where we're staying. The house is located on Quiet Lake. It's a little over fourteen acres, and they own it."

It was Joe's turn to be surprised. "They own a lake?"

"Yep. I think their mom used it to support them, but their aunt told me she closed it off after she moved in."

"But that's—" Joe glanced into the side-view mirror, fell silent, then finally said, "Look, there's a Creamy Whip. Let's get an ice cream."

Luna rubbed her forehead. "Joe, you can't be hungry still."

"Ice cream has nothing to do with hunger. Hell, it's ninety-two outside." He slid a hand over her thigh, suggestively squeezing. "Aren't you hot? I know I am. A malt would really hit the spot."

Actually, now that he'd said it, she could use some cooling down. Just being next to Joe affected her, keeping him in the forefront of her mind. "At this rate we'll never make it there, and I really want to get out of this damn truck of yours."

"You don't think my truck is comfortable?"

She took the exit and pulled into a crowded parking lot. "I think my little Contour is much, much better. Even with your seat pulled all the way up, I barely reach the pedals."

She expected some response, but Joe wasn't really listening to her complaints. He continued to idly stroke her leg while again looking in the side-view mirror. It finally dawned on Luna that he was watching something. Or someone.

With a gasp, she snapped, "Damn you, Joe, what are you doing?"

"Hmm? Oh, nothing. We're being followed, that's all."

Luna gaped at him. "That's *all*?"

"I didn't want to alarm you, but yeah." He twisted in the seat, and they both watched the road behind them as traffic went by. "He's cagey, whoever he is. He knows I'm onto him, so he kept going."

Her temper simmered. "How does he know you're onto him?"

"Because we stopped so often." Joe gave her a "duh" look. "I kept checking him. He was careful not to pull in behind us, but no matter how many times I made you stop, or how long I took, he always managed to be a discreet distance behind us."

His logic awed her. "That could be a coincidence."

Shaking his head, Joe said, "I don't believe in coincidence."

He'd said that more than once. Luna was just tired enough, just fractious enough, to slug him in the shoulder. "You bastard."

"Ow, hey." He caught her wrist and pressed her hand down to his hard thigh. "Why are you attacking me?"

Luna's fingers twitched. Joe held her palm far too close to his most dominantly male parts, and he expected her to answer questions? She could feel the heat of him and the flex of rock-hard muscle. Joe could be so diabolical. But she wouldn't let him get the better of her so easily. She firmed her resolve and said, "Why the hell didn't you tell me?"

Joe looked around, making her aware of several people gazing at them. In contrast to her voice, he sounded calm and totally unaffected. "What would you have done?" He inched her hand slightly higher. "Besides getting nervous, glancing out the rearview mirror constantly and maybe causing a wreck?"

"I would not have wrecked." But she would have been nervous. Damn him for being right. "From now on, I expect you to tell me everything. *Everything*, Joe. Do you understand?"

"Yeah, sure. Whatever you say, honey." He sounded about as sincere as a brick. Luna started to tell him so when he leaned forward and took her mouth in a warm, firm kiss. Her fingers contracted on his thigh; her mouth opened without her even thinking about it.

Joe teased her bottom lip with his tongue, then lifted away the tiniest bit. Luna felt his smile against her mouth. "What's your pleasure? Besides me, I mean? Looks like they've got quite a menu here."

He mixed sexual innuendoes in with casual conversation to the point she could barely keep up with him. Then she realized he'd released her hand, yet her fingers were still clutching his thigh, high up near his crotch. She shoved him away and did her best to ignore his triumphant laugh. "What about the guy following us?"

Joe opened his door and got out, but leaned back in to say, "I'll drive the rest of the way. He won't be able to follow."

"But . . ."

"No buts. Now, I'm getting a large chocolate malt. Do you want one? Or should we share?" He straightened away from the door. "Let's share. I like that idea. And then you can hold the thing for me."

He closed the door without waiting for her agreement and went to the back of the line leading to the ice cream window. His gait was stiff, but not hobbling, as it had been that morning. Perhaps the quiet, peaceful time during the drive and his off-and-on dozing had helped. He appeared to be improving by the hour.

Her lips still tingling, Luna gazed at him. Among the children and parents waiting for their treats, Joe stood out like a dark pirate. Surrounded by carefree kids, his big body looked even more powerful. His coal black hair blew across his forehead, teased by a gentle breeze, and his heavy brows and whisker-rough face made his blue gaze appear even sharper as he continually surveyed the lot and everyone in it. He stood loose limbed, ready—for anything. But with his aura of danger, Joe's casual stance in an ice cream line seemed ludicrous.

Someone had followed them.

Recalling that fact, Luna looked around. It occurred to her that she didn't even know what their tail looked like. How could she possibly be on the lookout if she wouldn't recognize the guy?

She was still pondering that when Joe tapped on her window, making her lurch with a short, startled shriek. He grinned. "Jumpy, aren't you? Well, scoot. I'm driving."

"Joe, I can handle it."

"No."

Her temper rose. Joe had a lot to learn about giving her orders with any expectation of having them obeyed.

"What?" he asked in all innocence when she continued to glare at him. He reached through the window and gently stroked her chin, her throat, her upper chest with an absorption totally out of place to the time and location. "I wasn't polite enough?"

Knowing she'd already lost, Luna gave up with a shake of her head and some grumbling. "You are not a polite man and you know it."

"Untrue, but either way, I'm usually right. At least in situations like this." He tucked her hair behind her ear, showing her that gentle side again and making her heart flip-flop. "Have a little trust, okay? I can outrun any tail without even trying. And we can't have that much farther to go, right?"

Luna hesitated, but the ending was inevitable. She'd be more effective in keeping a lookout, once she learned what she had to look out for. She pulled out the directions she'd been given and looked them over. "Not much farther at all."

"Great." He opened the driver's door and began crowding his big body into the seat behind the wheel, leaving her no option but to scramble awkwardly over the fold-down center armrest console. "Get your seat belt."

She glared at him over her shoulder, caught him staring at her behind, and said through her teeth, "I always do." She dropped heavily into the seat and reached for the seat belt. He acted so autocratic, she wished she could refuse him, but she wasn't willing to risk her own safety just to annoy Joe. "Give me the damn malt."

Joe laughed at her. "Yes, ma'am." As soon as she'd taken it from him, he slid the seat all the way back so his long legs would fit.

Luna took a fortifying drink of the malt. Delicious. "So who are we looking for?"

"You can't miss it. It's a plain brown sedan, usually about ten to twelve car lengths behind us. No way in hell do I want him following us into town, though. It wouldn't be safe for the kids, and I'm not going to risk them. I'd leave first."

Luna hated to even think it, but if it came down to that, she'd let Joe leave. Now that the kids were her responsibility, they had to come first. They needed her to take care of them, whereas Joe could take care of himself. Luckily, with Joe taking a few detours, they went the rest of the way with no sign of a brown car.

They took one turn after another, and little by little the scenery changed. Wide, busy highways led to narrow, mostly deserted streets, which gave way to rough asphalt roadways. If anyone had followed, they would be easy to spot. But the road behind them remained clear.

They entered Welcome County, but saw no sign of their destination, a town comically named Visitation. Tall trees surrounded them, and there was only the occasional house or trailer to show habitation. It appeared they had driven into nowhere, and Joe apparently didn't like that.

Frowning, he pulled over and slipped on a pair of black-framed reading glasses. He took the directions and map from Luna, opening the papers over the console between them. "Damn, according to the map, we should be there."

Their heads almost touched as Luna leaned in to read the map, too. She touched her finger to the paper, indicating their present location. "It looks like we should just keep going straight, or as straight as the road lets us."

"I don't like it. I haven't seen a single sign noting Visitation. What kind of town doesn't have a sign?" He cast a quick look around the deserted area. "The damn soundtrack to *Deliverance* is starting to play in my head."

Luna almost laughed, but she strangled on her humor when Joe suddenly stiffened. His gaze met hers, so icy cold and hard it filled her with unease. She could practically see his hair lifting, like a snarling dog that has scented danger.

She was about to ask him what in the world was wrong when he jerked around and somehow, without any discernible motions, the balisong knife appeared in his hand. In mingled apprehension and amazement, Luna pressed back into her seat.

Then she saw the man. He stood right next to

Joe's window, and he wasn't smiling. Good God, with his dark beard, obsidian eyes and otherworldly air, he looked like a malevolent vision. Luna's heart slammed into her ribs, then almost stopped, freezing right along with her body.

Joe suffered no such problems.

Chapter Six

Joe couldn't remember the last time he was so pissed. How the hell had someone crept up on him without him knowing? Jesus, he was getting old and slow, and maybe it was time to settle down when people started taking him by surprise over and over again.

He had the car door open and the man a good distance away from Luna before two seconds had passed. Backing him up to a thick tree trunk, Joe held him immobile with one arm across his throat and the other pressing the knife to his ribs. "Who the fuck are you?"

With no expression at all, the man stared back at Joe. And if Joe wasn't mistaken, the man was amused. There was no smile, no softening to those harsh features, but something in his dark eyes gave him away. He definitely wasn't afraid.

"If you don't know who I am," he asked calmly, "why are you attacking me?"

Damn. Joe didn't exactly have an answer to that one. He'd gone by his instincts, overwrought no

doubt under the stress of celibacy and his efforts
to keep Luna safe. Feeling defensive, Joe pressed
his arm a little tighter into the man. "You came
sneaking up on us."

"No." Other than the movement of his throat as
he spoke, the man remained immobile. "I just approached your truck to speak to you."

"Without making a goddamned sound?" Joe demanded.

The man's black eyes glittered. Though Joe had
no intention of moving, he felt compelled to take
a step back. "Perhaps," the man said in a voice deep
and somehow eerie, "you just weren't listening."

True enough, but unacceptable. "Let's get back
to my original question. Who are you?"

"Jamie Creed. I live up on the mountain."

Joe glanced past him to an impenetrable wall of
trees climbing high into a tall mountain. He saw
no road. Hell, he didn't even see a dirt path. Jamie
seemed to have just . . . appeared. Out of nowhere.
Without so much as snapping a twig to announce
his arrival. "So what are you doing down here?"

"I'm after supplies."

"What kind of supplies?"

"An inquisition?" His mouth stayed flat, his eyes
direct. "Okay. I needed more food, ammunition,
and some electrical supplies. And before you ask, I
hunt for my food, which is why I need more ammunition."

"You came here on foot?" Joe looked the man
over. He wore faded jeans, sturdy lace-up boots,
and a muscle shirt beneath an unbuttoned cam-
bric shirt with the sleeves cut off. He was lean but
hard, clean but unshaven. His beard would rival
that of a hermit's. Perhaps he was a hermit.

Joe no sooner thought it than Jamie actually

laughed. The sound was far too rough and raw to have any regular use. "My life is no real concern of yours. You're looking for Visitation." It was a statement, not a question. "Almost there. Two more miles and the road'll dip into such a deep incline, it'll appear you're driving off the side of the earth until you see the sharp left turn." Then, out of nowhere, he paused, studied Joe's face, and his eyes narrowed. "You're here for the kids."

How the hell had he come to that conclusion? Joe stiffened. "What kids?"

Raven eyes tracked his face, his shoulders, making Joe uncomfortable with the close scrutiny. Distracted, he murmured, "Willow and Austin Calder. Their ma died some time back, and they need a mother." He looked beyond Joe to the truck, and though his severe expression didn't actually change, his eyes warmed with male appreciation. He rubbed a fingertip along the bridge of his nose, his stare so intent on Luna that Joe growled. In a low whisper, Jamie said, "Yes, you're here for the kids."

As if Jamie had drawn her with but a look, Joe heard a door open and knew Luna was approaching. Damn her, couldn't she ever just stay out of harm's way? Joe started to order her back into the truck when Jamie turned back to him and pinned him with that intent stare.

"He's no threat, you know."

Luna sidled up to Joe's side, but Joe tucked her behind his back. The knife was still in his hand, and by God it'd stay there until he felt secure that all was safe. Luna, bless her for being wise just this once, stayed behind him. "Who isn't a threat?"

"The man following you." Jamie continued to look just over Joe's shoulder where Luna had gone on tiptoe to peek. "He's not the one."

Goddammit, about two more seconds of this mumbo jumbo and Joe was going to throw a punch. Jaw clenched so hard his teeth protested, Joe ground out, *"What exactly does that mean?"*

Unconcerned, Jamie shrugged, then stuck out his hand to Luna. "I'm Jamie Creed."

Luna actually giggled, infuriating Joe and making him want to toss her sexy little ass back into the truck. What the hell did she have to giggle about?

She reached beyond Joe to take the large, darkly tanned hand extended to her. "Hi. I'm Luna Clark."

And Jamie said again, "You're here for the kids."

Luna the loony didn't seem nearly as offset by that remark as Joe had been. "Why, yes, I am. Do you know them?"

"I do. It's good that you're here." He lifted her hand to his chest, flattening it there over his heart for several seconds while gazing at her with somber, profound import, almost as if he could see into her soul.

Joe heard Luna inhale and knew she was holding her breath. After several seconds, Jamie nodded with grim satisfaction. "You'll be perfect for them."

Luna gave another nerve-wracking, twittering laugh. Because Joe's rage had just doubled with something that felt sickeningly like jealousy, he snatched Luna's hand away from the other man and enfolded it in his own for safekeeping. What the hell did the stranger think, flirting with Luna right in front of him? Did he look like a man to toy with? And Luna had let him, even encouraged him.

Joe damn near snarled in frustration. "You seem to know a hell of a lot about our business."

Jamie gave another slow nod. "I often know a lot of things." He glanced up at the bright blue sky with a frown. "I should be on my way now. I need to be home before dark, and it's a long walk."

"We appreciate your help," Luna rushed to tell him.

Incredulous, Joe jerked around to stare down at her. "His *help?* How the hell did he help? By throwing out those obscure, ominous comments on things he shouldn't have known a damn thing about?"

Luna blinked at him, surprised by his venomous mood. "Well, he told us . . . I dunno. He said the kids need me and that I'm right for them and that the guy following us wasn't a threat."

Joe scoffed. "And just like that, you believe him?"

She shrugged. "Why not?"

Disgusted by her naivete, Joe turned back to Jamie—but he was gone.

"Mother fucker." Joe released Luna so he could quickly walk the area, but the man had literally disappeared from sight. There was no sign of him anywhere. The road ahead was empty, and the land to the side of the road was undisturbed and just as wooded as that from where Jamie Creed had come. Joe concentrated hard, but he couldn't see or hear so much as a rustling leaf or the snap of a twig. Either the man was a wraith or very, very dangerous.

Luna touched Joe's back. Her whisper was low, filled with reverence. "He's amazing, isn't he?"

Raw jealousy took Joe's breath. He had to fight to control himself in the face of the unfamiliar emotion. "Let's go." He flattened a hand on Luna's back and hustled her to the truck. She remained either oblivious to his dangerous mood or uncaring, because she started to whistle.

Her whistling hit a shrill note when he pulled her around and into his chest.

"What—"

Just to remind her that she'd brought him along for a reason, Joe kissed her hard. Her lashes dropped, half covering her eyes, making her look soft. For him? Or was she still thinking about that creep?

Unsure, Joe gave her a swat on the ass and said, "Into the truck, woman." She had the audacity to laugh while rubbing her behind with both hands.

Ghost or man, it didn't matter to Joe. If he ran across Jamie Creed again, he'd get some answers. Until then, Luna would be smart not to push him.

They drove the next two miles in strained silence, and suddenly, the road did indeed dip. The slope was so severe, both Luna and Joe held their breath. But just as Creed had claimed, a sharp turn brought them back onto a road. Once at the bottom of that steep incline, they could see the hill that ran down and flattened out again. The dip looked more dangerous than it really was. There were houses here, along with a large hand-painted sign that read, *Visitation. We Like It Here.*

"The directions say that the house is at the outside edge of town. We just have to stay on the main road."

They traveled another ten minutes before locating the long gravel drive to the house. It was over two hundred and fifty feet long and took them through a wooded area to a small clearing.

About an eighth of a mile to the left, the road continued, barely seen through brambles and scrubby shrubs and a few evergreens. To the right, an abundance of enormous trees formed a thick woods. They couldn't see the lake, but still the area was picturesque and very private.

In the middle of it all stood the large house, in much need of repair, but still impressive. It sported a wraparound porch that circled three sides on the first level, then another on the second story that went completely around. Doors opened on the upper level, probably to bedrooms, and two shutters were missing from the windows that flanked the doors.

The shingles were so curled and weathered that Joe wondered if the roof leaked in a rain. The porches were incredible, or at least they would be with some fresh paint. The limbs of two large trees spread out to offer shade on the front and side. No real landscaping existed, only weeds and more weeds.

Luna leaned forward for a better look. She didn't seem the least put off by the state of disrepair. "With a little cosmetic work, it'll be beautiful."

Joe put the truck in park and turned it off. "Lucky for you, I'm good with my hands."

"Brag, brag, brag. You men are all the same."

Joe laughed. "I didn't mean in the sack, witch."

"Too bad, because I didn't bring you here to work."

"Hey, I didn't say I wasn't willing. But I can be good at both, ya know." He waited until she slanted her golden brown eyes his way, then winked. "I can make you scream, and do a little fix-up."

Luna snorted. "You already make me scream— with frustration." She opened her door and got out.

Joe followed. "Only because you keep saying

no." He again surveyed the house. Yep, he could make it look a whole hell of a lot better. He'd always taken pleasure in the scent of sawdust and the satisfaction of working with his hands. Besides, it wouldn't hurt his cause to be of assistance to Luna. When she saw how much help he could be, maybe she'd quit sighing over that damn Creed.

Joe had taken only one step when he heard the ruckus.

Luna frowned at the loud voices carrying through the open front door to the yard. "Sounds like a cat fight going on."

He took her arm and started her forward. "Let's find out."

When they reached the screen door, Luna knocked, but no one answered. They could hear women arguing, one voice whiny, one determined, one disgusted and mean. Luna pulled the unlatched door open and called out, "Hello?"

They both had their heads stuck inside when the voices grew silent, replaced by the sound of approaching footsteps. The first to reach them was very tall, in her early forties, with an apron around her voluptuous figure. She was an attractive woman, but in a hard, cynical way. She stared at Joe, her expression openly assessing and appreciative. "Well now, who are you?"

Using her shoulder to lever her way in, Luna reached around Joe and stuck out her hand. "Luna Clark. I'm here for the children." The woman ignored her. She smoothed her dark blond hair, licked her lips and smiled at Joe.

Another woman, fashionably slim and dressed in a chic silk pantsuit with her dark hair loose to her shoulders, rushed into the room. "Thank God, you're here. Now you can just deal with . . ." She saw Joe, drew to a halt and started primping. "Hello."

Joe heard Luna's loud and rude snort, but he decided payback was in order. After all, she'd flirted with Jamie Creed. He offered his hand. "I'm Joe Winston. I'm here with Luna for a visit."

The woman in the apron got his hand first. "Welcome. I'm Dinah Belle, the housekeeper." She didn't let go, but her eyes slanted toward him in unmistakable invitation. "If you need anything while you're here, Joe, you just come to me."

Joe gave her his best false grin and watched her lips part in response. "Thank you, Dinah. I appreciate that." He tried to pry his hand loose, but didn't have much success until the other woman nudged her way closer.

"I'm Patricia Abbot, the children's aunt." She eyed Joe, letting her gaze linger on his chest. "My, my. I didn't realize Luna was bringing along a man."

"Is that a problem?"

Patricia twittered, and she, too, clasped his hand. "No, of course not. You're just in time for lunch. I thought we'd have a bite to eat before I leave."

"You're leaving already?" Luna asked.

Dinah frowned. "Lunch? Since when? You didn't tell me anything about lunch."

Flustered, Patricia sent a meaningful look toward Dinah. Her smile more of a snarl, she said, "I'm telling you now."

For a housekeeper, Dinah seemed pretty put out about something as simple as a meal, and not in the least respectful of her employer. She sniffed and curled her lip at Patricia.

Another woman gave a loud "harrumph." She

stood in the doorway, thin arms folded across her chest, her expression mulish. She appeared to be in her late twenties, early thirties, and unlike the first two, she had eyes only for Luna. "So you're Ms. Clark?"

Luna stepped forward. "That's me."

"I'm Julie Rose, a teacher subbing in the area for the summer. I came here to discuss the children, and I'm not leaving until I've had my say."

Patricia groaned theatrically.

Dinah shook her head.

Luna beamed. "Perfect. I'm very glad to meet you, Ms. Rose, because I'd like to talk about the kids, too. Where are they, by the way? I want to meet them."

Julie scowled at Patricia, her accusation plain. "Funny, but no one here seems to know."

Joe again had to pry his hand loose, but unfortunately, Luna wasn't paying him any attention, so she didn't notice how the women were fawning on him. It wasn't any fun—was in fact an aggravation— if Luna wasn't going to notice or care. Finally freeing himself, he stepped away from them and moved to Luna's side, well out of reach.

Luna raised her brows at Patricia. "The children?"

It was the housekeeper who replied, waving a hand negligently. "They're out somewhere. Who knows where they've gotten to? They're impossible to keep track of, always running off—"

Luna's jaw grew tight, and her tone lowered ominously. "Running off?"

"Playing," Patricia rushed to explain with a harassed look at Dinah. She gave a false laugh. "They like to play near the lake and in the woods beyond. They'll show up sooner or later."

Joe scowled. By nature he was cautious, but after

many years working in dangerous jobs he'd grown even more so. Children should be well protected and supervised. He knew from his own youth that any time you didn't know where a kid was or what he was doing, he was probably doing something that he shouldn't. "That's a little dangerous, isn't it? I thought they were only fourteen and nine."

Julie nodded. "Exactly. They need more boundaries and structure."

"Nonsense. Austin has his little pack of friends he runs with, and Willow is always surrounded by young men." Patricia lowered her voice and said in a conspiratorial, somewhat snide tone, "She's like her mother in that regard."

Julie Rose drew herself up in stiff affront. "She's a very nice, intelligent and sensitive young lady."

In an attempt to be diplomatic, Luna said, "Ms. Rose, why don't you stay for lunch also? We can discuss your concerns and you can fill me in on the children. I'm dying to hear everything about them."

After a mutinous glare at Patricia, the teacher agreed. "I'd like that, thank you. And please, call me Julie."

Patricia rolled her eyes. "This is totally unnecessary, Luna. Julie wants to tutor the children for an ungodly amount of money, and I've already told her the budget doesn't allow for it, not to mention that it's a waste of time. The little delinquents aren't interested in learning."

Dinah joined in, saying, "The only thing they put any effort into is getting into constant trouble."

That set Julie off, and the three women began to argue again. Fuming, Luna turned to Joe. "Do you believe this?"

She looked as annoyed as he felt. With the way the women carried on, you'd think the children were monsters not worth their concern. Having come from a very loving family, that attitude sickened Joe.

He touched Luna's shoulder and felt her trembling with anger. She looked ready to take off a few heads. The only other time he'd seen her this angry was when she'd first met him, and that time she'd hurled a sandwich at him.

He leaned down to her ear, kissed her temple and said, "Don't kill anyone yet, okay? Patricia is leaving soon, and then you can decide what *you* want to do about the kids."

She didn't reply, but she did suddenly say, *"Lunch?"* in a rather carrying voice that broke into their argument.

Joe grinned, liking this take-charge side of her. Luna could be a dominating force when she chose. He wondered if she'd be that dominating in bed.

It seemed possible.

Dinah sniffed again, turned on her heel, and strode away with a noticeable sway to her hips. Patricia smoothed her dark hair and pointedly ignored Julie Rose. "Yes, of course. Why don't you bring your things in and get settled. Lunch can be ready in half an hour."

"Are there rooms prepared for us?" Luna asked.

Patricia nodded. "Luna, you can take the room upstairs, first door that you come to. It's the master bedroom, and it's nice enough. You'll have your own bath, of course, but unfortunately you'll be close to the children."

Luna set her teeth. "Unfortunately?"

"Yes. They have a tendency toward nocturnal

antics." Patricia shook her head. "I finally bought earplugs so I could get some rest."

"You bought ear plugs?"

Uh oh. Luna looked ready to bite again. Joe rubbed her back in an effort to soothe her.

"As I said, that's the nicest room, so of course I kept it. It's spacious and has a lovely balcony that overlooks the lake. I've already packed my things, and I had Willow change the bedding today." She smiled up at Joe in open consideration. "Are you two, perhaps, sharing a room?"

Joe hadn't thought about this particular situation, but his and Luna's relationship was private as far as he was concerned. Luna started to answer, no doubt to blast the woman, but he beat her to the punch. "No. I'll need my own room if there's one available."

Patricia's gratified smile came slowly. "Wonderful. You can take the back room, then. It's small, but provides more privacy. Why don't you get your things and I'll show you where it is."

Feeling like a turkey on Thanksgiving morning, Joe put his arm around Luna. She stood stiff and hostile at his side. "That's okay. I'm sure I'll find it." He ushered Luna back out to the truck before she did bodily harm. Not that he didn't appreciate her possessive nature. Strangely enough, he did. Watching Luna bristle on his behalf filled him with a deep satisfaction. She may deny him, but she didn't want him with any other women either. That had to mean something.

Once they'd reached the yard, he said, "Temper, temper," just to tease her.

She shoved away from him. "Both of those women were coming on to you."

"Yeah." He grinned at her. "I sort of noticed that."

"They pretended I wasn't even there. I could have been invisible for all the notice they paid me."

"You are never invisible, sweetheart. Trust me."

"Trust you? You just stood there and let them ogle you."

"Hey, I can't help it that women—other than you, of course—find me irresistible." Joe managed to say that with a straight face while he opened the truck and pulled out their belongings.

"You don't have to sound so cocky and pleased about it, Joe." She narrowed her eyes. "And how come you're not limping at all? Trying to put on a good show for your admirers?"

"Now, Luna." Joe shook his head at her. "I'm here as the resident ass-kicker, remember? I have to give the right impression. Women are notorious gossips. Do you want them running around town telling everyone you brought a lame duck with you? How much protection would that give you?"

The seconds ticked by while Luna mulled over his words. Finally she softened, then rubbed her forehead. "You're right."

" 'Course I am."

Her jaw tensed again. "Don't push me, Joe."

"Only in bed, honey." He pinned her in his gaze. "Then I'll push you till you just can't take it anymore."

Her breath caught, she cursed low, then groaned. "You're impossible. How are you really feeling? Holding up okay?"

He allowed her the change of subject. "Stiff, a

little sore, but on my way to a full recovery thanks to your gentle care." Then, just to tweak her again, he added, "Don't fret. I'm up to handling two women on the make. You don't have to worry about them overpowering me."

"That's not funny, Joe."

"You wouldn't think so." He almost laughed at her venomous frown. She snatched up her luggage and marched away, but when she reached the porch, she found Patricia standing there and apparently changed her mind about leaving him alone. She looked over her shoulder and snapped, "Hurry up, Joe."

"Yes, honey." His damn case weighed a ton, but he hauled it up the steps without so much as a grimace. He'd meant what he said about hiding his weakened condition from Patricia. The woman was supposedly engaged, but she kept looking him over with lustful intent. To Joe, that made her very untrustworthy.

Julie Rose appeared at Luna's side. She was taller than Luna, but much slimmer, with shoulder-length mousy brown hair and mostly nondescript features. Other than her soft brown eyes, now filled with iron determination, she was as plain as a woman could be. Not overly curvy, not overly pretty, not overly anything—except plain.

"Let me help you." She took Luna's largest case and started up the steps. "We can talk while you unpack."

Maybe plain *and* pushy, Joe thought, seeing that Luna wasn't left with much choice. Appearing helpless, she glanced at Joe and hesitated, but already Patricia had him by the arm, hauling him down the hall to his assigned room.

He shrugged at Luna, blew her a kiss to let her know it'd be okay, and allowed Patricia to lead him away.

They went past the formal dining room, dusty from lack of use, and entered the kitchen where Dinah stood at a rectangular table preparing small sandwiches. She gave Joe a sly smile when she saw him. "I hope you like chicken salad?"

"I do."

"I've made plenty. A man of your size surely has a hearty . . . appetite." She looked him up and down as she said that, leaving Joe with no doubt to which appetite she referred.

Actually, Dinah wouldn't be able to appease any appetite. At present, he wanted only Luna, not any other woman, no matter how accommodating she might be. And with as many times as he'd had Luna stop along their drive, he wasn't all that hungry, either. But he needed his strength to completely recover, so he wasn't about to turn down food. He ignored the housekeeper's reference and simply said, "Thanks."

Patricia's grip was tight enough and determined enough that his ribs ached. She pulled him to the left of the large kitchen and into a smaller room off to the side. Joe stepped inside with interest. Patio doors opened to the porch at the back of the house. In the distance, he could see the impressive lake and woods.

The room was dusty, sparse and stale. One dresser and a bare cot barely big enough for a kid took up most of the space. He winced, thinking of how uncomfortable the flat, thin mattress would be to his bruised body.

Patricia laughed and cuddled up to his side, pressing a breast into his ribs. "Don't worry, Joe.

We'll have the kids move Austin's bed down here, and he can use the cot."

Joe frowned at her and moved a pace away. "That's not necessary." With any luck he'd get to spend most of his nights in Luna's room with her soft body cushioning him, but either way, he wasn't about to take Austin's bed. To Joe's mind, the boy had lost enough already.

"Oh, he won't mind. He likes camping out on the ground, down by the lake. He even sleeps on the floor sometimes. As I said, he likes to be up and around at night. Besides, he's just a kid, and a man certainly has more need of a proper bed, right?" She looked up at him with sensual regard.

Disgusted, Joe narrowed his eyes and kept his mouth flat. "No."

The finality in his tone, along with his lack of politeness, left her in no doubt as to how he felt about her suggestion. "Oh, well . . ." She faltered long enough for Joe to take her arm and lead her back to the door.

"I'll unpack now and join you for lunch in a few minutes." He moved Patricia outside the room.

She turned back to him, opened one hand on his chest, and smiled up at him. Through his shirt, her fingertips grazed his nipple. Her lips parted, and she looked at his mouth. "I could help you if you'd like."

Again, with no softening to his rejection, Joe said, "No." He took her wrist and removed her hand, fighting the urge to push her away. He pitied the poor bastard who planned to marry her.

"But—"

Joe closed the door in her face. God, it ate at him, thinking of a woman so cold and calculating playing caregiver to two young vulnerable kids. He was now glad that Luna had decided to step in. He'd help her get things in order; then he could convince her to move back home—where she'd be close at hand. If she wanted to bring the kids along, he'd deal with it.

Rather than unpack, Joe went to the patio doors to look out. The lake was beautiful with mature trees edging the shoreline and small ripples disturbing the surface. Sunlight glinted off the water like the finest diamonds, almost blinding it was so bright. Far off, a fish celebrated the sunny day by jumping out of the water, then landing again with a splash.

A rectangular, somewhat dilapidated building stood about forty feet off the shoreline. A storage shed? It looked too large for that and mirrored the styling of the house. An enormous crow circled the outbuilding, then landed on the roof.

Joe's chest expanded with some strange emotion. It felt like . . . contentment. Yeah, that was it. Despite his injuries, his disgust at the situation he'd walked into and Luna's continued rejection, he could feel himself relaxing more than he had in a year. Nature always had that effect on him. That's why he liked to fish. Whenever he was on the water, surrounded by woods, he felt at peace and right with the world. The fresh air and the sounds of birds and rustling leaves had a way of blocking out the uglier things that usually made up his life.

He turned back around to survey his new room. The cot was bare, so he'd need to rustle up sheets and a pillow somewhere. The dresser was rickety, but it'd hold his clothes. First things first, though. He opened the patio doors to let in the fresh air, then went about putting away his things. The door that he thought would lead to a closet instead led to a small bath.

Joe put away his shaving gear, splashed his face, and finally felt ready to face the barracudas. Luckily, Luna was just entering the kitchen at the same time. She gave him a sunny smile, and he noted that Julie Rose also appeared pleased. Apparently, they'd come to a mutual decision. That relieved him.

Joe held out a chair for each woman before seating himself at the only empty chair at the head of the table. Dinah passed around a platter of sandwiches and poured iced tea in tall glasses.

"This looks delicious," Joe said, determined to be polite. He took a bite of the chicken salad and started to nod in appreciation—and he felt a foot in his lap.

Joe choked.

Looking up from her food, Luna frowned in concern. "Are you all right?"

He nodded, wheezed, and felt a set of toes curl into his crotch before sliding along the length of this thigh, and finally leaving him.

Still a little stunned, Joe grabbed up his tea and took a long drink. Who the hell had . . . ?

Patricia, sitting to his left, leaned over to rub him on the back, saying sweetly, "My goodness, Joe. Are you okay?" Her hand drifted low, almost to his ass as she continued to stroke him.

On his other side, Dinah stood to hand him a napkin. "Here, let me help." She leaned into him, pressing her boobs into his ear.

Both women wore innocent looks, even while fawning all over him. Joe looked at Luna, hoping it might have been her toes he'd felt, but she just scowled at him for all the attention the other two gave him.

He glanced at Julie Rose with serious doubts. She raised her brows without much interest. "You really should chew your food."

"Uh . . ." To escape the women, Joe pushed his chair back in a rush and came to his feet. Patricia and Dinah backed up; Julie and Luna stared. "I've been sitting all day. I think I'll stand."

"While you eat?" Luna asked.

"Yeah." He picked up his plate and paced over to the counter. "Go ahead with your lunch. I'm fine."

Patricia seemed surprised by his behavior, but she rallied. "Well, as I was about to say, I had planned to leave within the hour. I'm anxious to meet with my fiancé again. He's in Illinois, waiting for me."

"Great," Joe said, at the same time Luna asked, "You're leaving so soon?" She glared at Joe, then added, "Don't you think the kids need a little time to get used to Joe and me?"

Dinah waved a hand in dismissal. "We don't want to hold Patricia up." She smiled at Joe. "Besides, I'll still be here, but really, it won't matter. The kids go out of their way to be difficult."

"They've never had a father figure," Patricia added. "No one even knows who their real father is, and no other man is willing to take them on."

"But they need a firm hand," Dinah added. "They're a bother to everyone in town. It's downright embarrassing how we're all treated by association."

Julie threw down her napkin. "That is not true. The children are simply—"

A door slammed, interrupting whatever Julie

might have said. Running feet sounded in the hall and seconds later a small, towheaded child slid to a halt in the kitchen. He was without a shirt and his bare toes were dirty. He stared up at Joe, his dark brown eyes huge, then looked at Patricia. "Who is he?"

Joe started to smile. The boy's too-big shorts hung low on narrow hips, his mop of fair hair was tangled by the sun, wind and water, and he was tanned a nut brown. The little ruffian really was cute. Then Joe noticed a small detail, and he felt his temper spark.

Beneath the dirt on the boy's face shone a fresh, swelling black eye. Someone had struck him, and all of Joe's protective instincts kicked into high gear.

Chapter Seven

Joe thunked down his plate and moved forward with a purpose. When he reached Austin, the boy backed up a pace before planting his feet apart and facing off. His defensive stance gave Joe pause. He hesitated, aware of the silence behind him. He touched the boy's chin, tilting his face. It wasn't easy, but he kept his voice calm and moderate. "What happened to you?"

The small chin lifted another inch, and the big eyes narrowed. "Nothin'."

Patricia came out of her chair in a rush. "Austin Calder! You've been fighting again, haven't you?"

Austin glared at her. "No."

Dinah made a rude sound. "Disobedient and a liar."

"That's enough." Luna pushed back her chair and went to Joe's side. She touched the tangled mop of hair. "Austin, I'm your cousin, Luna Clark. I'm glad you're here."

Austin shifted his hostile gaze to her. "Yeah? How come?"

She smiled at the challenge in his voice. "Because I want to get to know you, that's how come. Since we'll be living here together, don't you think that's a good idea?"

"I dunno."

A young girl stepped into the kitchen. Unlike Austin, she was neatly dressed, her long, straight blond hair smooth and untangled. She wore shorts and a tank top and sandals. Her eyes, however, were as dark and uncertain as her brother's.

Luna looked up in surprise. "Willow?"

The girl nodded and came into the kitchen, casting one quick, assessing look at the other people in the room. She stopped in front of her brother, and much as Joe had done, she tipped his chin, then made a tsking sound. "You never learn, Austin."

Austin shook a fist. "He's got more bruises than me."

Joe smothered a laugh. Damn, but the little guy amused him. Sort of reminded him of himself at that age. Austin was small for nine and skinny as a beanpole, but now that Luna was here, she'd put some meat on the boy.

Willow sighed. She took Austin's hand and led him to the porcelain sink, then went about wetting a cloth in very cold water. She wrung it out and pressed it to her brother's eye. He obediently held it in place.

Joe didn't know what to think about the girl. If Austin looked small for nine, Willow looked decidedly developed for fourteen. Imagining the job Luna would have keeping the boys away from her, he shuddered. She was a cutie, no way around it, and unfortunately, he knew how boys thought—having been that age once himself.

Willow eyed him. "Who are you?"

Gallantly polite, Joe held out a hand. "I'm Joe Winston. I came with Luna."

Her small hand was cool and soft, but firm. "You're her boyfriend?"

"I'm working on it."

Luna laughed too loud, giving away her discomfort with that particular topic. "He's a friend, Willow. You mentioned some trouble in the area and Joe is good at handling trouble."

"Much like your little brother here." Joe squeezed Austin's shoulder.

Patricia looked scandalized. "For God's sake, don't encourage either of them."

Julie muttered, "God forbid anyone be encouraging."

Joe liked Julie more and more by the minute. She was outspoken, stiff, and as genuinely concerned for the children as Luna. And at the moment, an ally seemed like a good idea.

Luna knelt down by Austin. "Okay, kiddo. Spill it. How'd you get the black eye?"

"Probably annoying someone," Dinah sneered, but she shut up when Luna fried her with a look from those golden brown eyes of hers.

Austin looked very undecided, and finally Willow took pity on him. "I was walking home when some guys decided to give me a hard time. Austin has a habit of trailing behind me, playing guard dog." She cast her brother a chastising look, which he pointedly ignored.

Joe crossed his arms over his chest. "Why does he need to guard you?"

She shrugged. "Ever since . . . since Mom died . . ." She glanced around the room, uncomfortable but determined. "Ever since then, the boys have decided I'm fair game."

"It's because she's led them to that impression," Patricia claimed.

The look of disdain Willow directed toward Patricia was far too cynical for a girl her age. "I dated a guy once, and he started bragging. Most of what he said was lies, but everyone believed him anyway." She again looked at her aunt. "Including Patricia."

Before Patricia could comment, Joe stated the obvious. "You're too young for dating."

"I'll be fifteen soon."

Joe nodded. "Too young."

Luna shushed him with a touch on his wrist. "So these boys came up to you and said something unkind, and Austin intervened?"

As if taking her measure, Willow studied Luna, then sighed again. "We might as well sit down if you really want the whole story."

Dinah objected. "You're interrupting our lunch, young lady."

Joe's mouth fell open, then just as quickly snapped shut. He'd had enough. "Dinah, I don't think we'll be needing your services. Luna is a great cook, and I'll be here to help her keep house."

Dinah sputtered. "I beg your pardon?"

Luna wasn't quite so tactful. "You're fired."

Dinah stared at Joe in blank surprise, then quickly transferred her gaze to Luna. "This is absurd!"

Joe waited to see if Luna would cast an evil spell on her or laugh. It was a toss-up which way she might go. She did neither, asking simply, "Do you need help packing?"

For one moment, Dinah's face turned bright red and Joe thought she might implode. Then she threw a mean, hate-filled look at the children and stalked out.

Patricia pressed a hand to her chest. "Oh, my. That was certainly unpleasant, and perhaps ill advised." She appealed to Joe, and he just knew that was going to set Luna off again. "Dinah can be pushy, I know, but she came to me highly recommended. She's here every day without fail, and only complains about the kids a little. You may not realize exactly how messy and disruptive children can be. Why, they track in mud from the lake and have endless loads of laundry, and they're forever hungry—"

"Yeah," Joe said, interrupting her while keeping a cautious eye on Luna. She could be so damn unpredictable. "You said you were in a hurry to go, too, right?"

Both children stared at him with owl-eyed expressions. Luna actually laughed, surprising him. She took Patricia's hand and patted it in sympathy. "It would be for the best. We'd like to get settled and spend some time getting acquainted with the kids. And you did say your intended was waiting for you. So really, why make him wait?"

Smug at the turn of events, Julie left the table. "Come along, Patricia. I'll see you out." The two women trailed away, leaving Joe and Luna alone with the kids.

Joe rubbed his hands together. Seeing Luna in action was pretty exciting. She was one surprise after another, and he enjoyed every moment. "Now. Let's figure out what the hell is going on here."

* * *

Luna wanted to hug Joe for backing her so completely. She'd first thought it might be helpful to have Patricia hang around, to acclimate the kids to yet another change. But it hadn't taken her long to see they had no real rapport, and that Patricia had no care for their sensibilities. They'd all be better off muddling through alone.

Joe nodded to both kids. "I feel better already. Either of you hungry? We can talk while we eat. Sit down and dig in." He dropped into his seat, tossed one tiny sandwich into his mouth, and smiled while he chewed.

Luna urged Austin into a chair. She didn't want to smother him with concern, but she couldn't help wincing at the sight of his black eye. "Does it hurt?"

"What? My eye?" His disgruntled tone let Luna know exactly what he thought of her concern. "Naw. It's nothin'." He ducked away from her hands, twisting in his chair.

Joe pointed a finger at him. "I know it's macho for men to deny pain—I do it all the time myself. But when you're around a woman who really cares, it's pretty cool to have her coddle you a little."

Austin made a face. "No way. That's for sissies."

Joe laughed. "Did you just insult me, boy?"

Austin looked so horrified by that prospect, Luna rushed to reassure him. "Joe here got beat up not long ago. He's let me take care of him."

Both kids blinked in surprise, looking first at Luna, then with skepticism at Joe.

Cautiously, Willow asked, "Because you really care about him?" which left Luna with an open mouth and not much to say. She did care about Joe, but admitting it to him would only encourage him.

Austin saved her by asking Joe, "You really got beat up?" and he sounded very dubious at that idea. Luna didn't blame him. The idea of anyone getting the better of Joe was pretty hard to swallow, with him so big and commanding and hard.

"Yeah." Joe stood and lifted his shirt. "Some sneaky thug got in a few sucker punches."

Austin whistled in awe. Joe's bruises had darkened to purple and black and pea green. "Wow, looks like a lot of sucker punches."

"That's because he passed out."

Joe threw a pickle slice at Luna. "I did not *pass out.* I got knocked out. There's a huge difference, woman, and I'll thank you to remember it."

Willow watched them with wide, cautious curiosity. "I think you're both nuts."

"Luna is definitely nutty, but it's part of her charm." Joe caught the pickle when she tossed it back to him, then he ate it. "Now, tell us what happened, okay? We want to help."

Austin came out of his chair in a rush, his small fist again in the air. "Some asshole called Willow a whore, and I slugged him."

Luna and Joe went mute at the passionate, colorful statement from the mouth of a nine-year-old.

Willow gasped, and her face bloomed with color. "Austin! Watch your language."

"He is an asshole," Austin declared. "I hate him. Next time I'm gonna break his nose."

It was all Luna could do not to laugh out loud. She cleared her throat and fought off her smile. "Yeah, well, if he called your sister that, I agree. But you still don't need to be saying such things."

Thoroughly disgruntled, Willow settled back in her chair. "Mom never let him talk like that, but Patricia mostly just ignores him."

Austin glared. "That's cuz Patricia is a—"

Interrupting what would surely be another awesome insult, Joe said, "You know what I like to call people like that?" He leaned back in his chair. "Besides thugs, I mean?"

Austin instantly became attentive. "What?"

"Worm, slime, bottom feeder—"

"Dicks," Austin offered.

Joe laughed again. He looked at Austin's innocent expression and laughed until he had to wipe his eyes. After she'd worked so hard to fight off her own chuckles, Luna glared at him. "Joe . . ." she said in warning.

"Sorry." With that slight grin still tipping the corners of his mouth, he said to Austin, "No, that's as bad as asshole, and besides the fact that you're way too young for that kind of language, it's also rude to talk that way in front of ladies. You don't want to be rude, do you?"

Austin peered at both females and gave a shrug of indifference.

"Of course you don't. So if you have to insult someone, use your imagination, okay?"

Scratching his ear, Austin concentrated for a moment, then said, "What about scab, toe jam or snot?"

Willow groaned, but Joe nodded, his eyes alight with laughter. "Perfect. See, you can be man enough to cut out the swear words and still put him in his place."

"But," Willow interjected, "you're not man enough to attack him every time he says something ugly to me."

"I'll find a big stick next time. Or maybe a rock. Or . . ."

Willow huffed in exasperation. To Luna, she said, "I walk to town every day and one way or another, the guys find me, even when I try to cut through the woods like I did today. They like to nettle me because Austin always gets so riled."

"They pester you cuz you're pretty and they want to do nasty things to you." Austin turned his shrewd gaze on Joe for confirmation. "Ain't she pretty?"

Joe's expression softened, and he gave a slight nod. "Very."

Satisfied, Austin turned back to Luna. "Willow looks like our mom."

Solemn, Joe said, "Then your mom must have been very pretty."

Both children became subdued, so Luna tried to move the conversation forward. "Why are you walking to town?" She no sooner asked the question than Willow got evasive and looked away. "Willow?"

"She takes piano lessons," Austin offered.

"Really?" Why did she act so secretive about it? Luna wondered. "So you're a musician? I'm impressed." No reaction. Luna sighed. "Why are you walking, Willow? Especially when you know there's likely to be trouble?"

"Because no one'll drive her."

Willow appeared ready to choke her brother. "I have a mouth, rodent, so quit speaking for me."

Austin turned to Joe. "Rodent is a good insult, too, huh?"

"Sure, according to how you use it. Your sister says it to you with affection, but if you say it to some bully, then it'd sound hateful enough."

Austin chewed that over. "Okay." His brow

scrunched up with suspicion. "But I don't think Willow meant it nice, either."

"No, I didn't." She reached for her brother's arm and gave him a shake. "Those boys are all too big for you to mess with."

Austin's small chin jutted forward. "I kicked his ass . . ." He glanced at Joe. "I mean butt."

"You kicked and then ran. But not fast enough." Willow tapped a finger against his bruised cheekbone beneath his eye, making him flinch.

Joe gently separated sister and brother. "How old are these boys?"

Willow retreated back into her seat. "Sixteen."

Luna watched Joe go on the alert, then saw outrage stiffen his spine. "The hell you say!" He was out of his seat in a heartbeat.

Austin raised his brows. "You're bein' disrespectful."

"What?"

With great accusation, Austin explained, "You said hell."

"Oh." Joe ran a hand through his dark hair, his expression sheepish. "Right. Sorry."

"That's okay. I don't mind." In fact, Austin looked faintly approving.

Joe looked to the ceiling for inspiration, but got no help there. "Where can I meet these young men?"

Willow eyed him, came to some silent decision, and rolled one shoulder in a show of unconcern. "They usually show up here not long after I get home. They always complain to my Aunt Patricia about Austin fighting with them, and she always grounds him."

It was Luna's turn to go rigid. "She does what?"

"Doesn't do her any good." Austin puffed up with pride. "I just sneak out anyways. I'm good at sneakin' out."

"God help us." Joe scowled, then pulled Austin out of his seat to face him. He kept his hands on the boy's bony shoulders, and while his tone was grave, it wasn't mean. "Here are some new rules, okay? First, your sister won't be walking into town anymore. Luna or I will drive her." He glanced up at Luna. "Right?"

"Absolutely." It made her stomach dip to think of Willow alone that way, with or without Austin trailing her. Luna had been on her own long enough to understand the perils that could fall on a young beautiful girl. She swallowed down her worry and addressed Austin. "If you ride along, fine, but you won't be making the trip alone either."

"How come?"

How come? Luna wondered if the children had had any supervision at all since their mother's death. "It isn't safe."

"I'm not afraid of those ass . . . uh, bullies."

"We know you're not." Joe squeezed his shoulders. "But there are other dangers, and neither Luna nor I could bear to see either of you hurt."

Willow's expression was carefully masked, her voice hollow, almost cold. "You don't even know us."

"That doesn't matter," Luna rushed out. "Adults are meant to protect children, and that's what we intend to do."

Willow turned away. Without saying a word, she made her skepticism clear.

Luna wished there were magic words she could

say to ease the pain. She wished she really were a psychic so she could know Willow's thoughts. She reached for the girl's shoulder. "Willow, we do know you a little now, and we like you both."

"Right."

Luna's heart twisted at the sarcastic comment. "I'll have you know, I'm very good at reading people."

"That's a fact."

Joe's quick agreement made her smile. "We already know that your brother is honorable enough to want to defend and protect you, even against guys older and bigger than him. And we know you're mature enough to want to make sure he doesn't get hurt while he's doing that. You're both very brave and considerate and loyal. Those are exceptional qualities, especially in someone so young. I know an awful lot of adults who don't possess them."

"Like Aunt Patricia."

Luna wanted to agree with Willow, but she wasn't sure if that'd be the right thing to do or not. Reaffirming to a child that her relative hadn't cared enough about her seemed counterproductive. "I don't think Patricia is cut out to be a guardian. We are what we are. I'm sure she did her best."

Austin peered at Luna. He looked hopeful and a touch scared. "Are you cut out to be a guardian?"

Luna's heart expanded. "I've never been responsible for anyone but myself. But I'm the type of stubborn person who refuses to fail at things. If I decide to do it, then by God, I do my very best. But I'm not perfect, Austin. When I make mistakes, I expect you and Willow to tell me, and we'll discuss them and see if we can't find a solution that pleases everyone. Okay?"

year at a rather prestigious, private school an hour east, but when I saw they needed summer school teachers here, I signed up."

"That's very generous of you."

She scoffed at Joe's comment, surprising Luna. "No, it's just that this is why I became a teacher, to relate to children, not to baby-sit the rich." She folded her hands together on the tabletop. "Besides, I needed some time away from my fiancé."

At that artless disclosure, Joe and Luna looked at each other in helpless confusion. Julie Rose, engaged? She'd sort of struck Luna as the spinsterish type. Perhaps Julie had hidden depths.

"I'm sorry if you're having problems . . ."

Julie waved away Luna's concern. "My fiancé is a real stick in the mud, but never mind that. My point is that it took me less than three days to find out that Clay Owen is a very misguided young man. In his own fashion, he works rather hard at getting Willow's attention."

"He called her a whore! He said nasty things about her."

Julie tilted her head at Austin, not the least put off by his language. "Yes, I know, Austin, and that's inexcusable, of course. But, unfortunately he hasn't been taught any better. If he misbehaves, his stepfather just covers it up and makes excuses for him."

"So he's the same young man who gave you the black eye?" Luna asked.

"He's a creep," Austin claimed. "He used to be Willow's friend. They played together all the time when Mom was still here. But now he makes her cry."

Willow gasped. "Shut up, Austin!"

Joe folded his arms over his chest. "He won't make excuses to me."

Joe nodded. "Same with me."

Luna blinked at him. What the heck was he promising? He wouldn't be around that long.

But Joe didn't seem concerned with that fact. "If anyone insults your sister in any way, or does anything to insult you, I want to know about it."

"Why?"

Luna hadn't realized that kids asked so many questions. Every time she or Joe said something, they questioned it three ways to Sunday. She waited to see what Joe would say.

Unlike Luna, he didn't seem the least unsure of his response. "Because I'm good at handling this sort of thing."

Willow fretted with the edge of her shorts. "How would you handle it?"

Luna was rather curious about that herself. If the offenders were grown men, Luna knew Joe would have no trouble dealing with them. But Joe couldn't physically intimidate a bunch of minors. As he'd just said, adults protected children. Sixteen-year-olds were on the verge of adulthood, but also young enough to be forgiven many faults. So what could Joe do?

"I'll have a long talk with the boys first, and if that doesn't work, I'll take it up with their fathers."

Ah, Luna thought, bypass the minors by going to the adults. That made sense. After all, it was the fathers' duty to see that their sons behaved. "Joe can be very intimidating." Which was why she'd brought him along.

Deflated by Joe's answer, Austin stared down at his feet and rubbed his dirty toes across the floor. "Their parents don't care none. They don't like us either."

Joe tipped Austin's chin back up. "And why is that?"

Austin shrugged. "Don't know."

"Liar." Looking far too old for her age, Willow sighed. "Austin's had a few scrapes here and there."

"Yeah? What kind of scrapes?"

Willow counted off the transgressions on her fingers. "He put dog doo-doo in the principal's chair, broke the librarian's car window with a rock, trampled the grocer's prized rose bushes . . ."

Luna stared at Austin in disbelief. Good God, how could a child who looked so sweet and innocent get into so much mischief?

Ready to defend himself, Austin propped his tight little fists on his hips and spoke to each person in turn. "I threw a rock at the car because the librarian's son spit on me when he drove past. I thought it was his car, not his mom's." And in a mumble, "I was hopin' it might make him come back so I could kick his ass . . . er, butt. But he just kept driving away, the big chicken."

Joe's eyebrows shot up. "He *spit* on you?"

Pleased with Joe's reaction, Austin gave a firm nod. "That's right. A big ol' glob. Hit me right in the side of the head. He needed his butt kicked, huh?"

Joe looked to Luna for guidance, but she only shrugged. If someone had spit on her, she would have done more than throw a rock. Seeing she'd be no help, Joe asked, "Did you tell Patricia?"

"She don't care. She'd have grounded me. That's what she did when I accidentally stepped on the stupid flowers."

"Accidentally?"

"Yeah. I was just tryin' to see in the window."

Luna almost hated to ask. "Why did you want to look in the window?"

When Austin didn't reply, Willow took his hand. She'd called him a liar moments before, but now she gave him her support. "They were having a party. All the kids were invited, except Austin."

"I didn't want to go to their stupid party anyway!"

The venomous words couldn't hide the hurt in his eyes. Dear God, this was getting worse and worse. Poor Austin. That must have crushed his feelings, but she couldn't condone his actions. This was exactly the type of situation she dreaded, because it made her feel helpless and ignorant. She finally decided the best thing to do was to get everything out in the open and decide how to handle it later. "And the stuff you put in the principal's chair?"

Trying to hide his wicked grin, Austin rubbed his nose, his ear. "He sat in it. It squished all the way through his pants to his underdrawers." A snicker escaped his pursed mouth. "You shoulda heard him howlin'. And the stink . . . It stuck to him all day."

Joe smirked, but quieted when Luna glared at him. She didn't know a lot about kids, but she did know that if Austin realized they were amused by his antics, there'd be no stopping him. "Let's hear it, Austin. Why did you do it?"

Both Austin and Willow pinched their mouths shut.

Julie stepped back into the room, dusting her hands off, indicating that they'd gotten rid of Patricia. "I can answer that." She came forward as if invited and reseated herself. "I've only been in town a few weeks. I teach throughout the school

Julie seemed less than impressed with Joe's confidence. "Men," she said with disdain. "If you want to get along in this town, Mr. Winston, you'll need to get along with Quincy Owen."

"And why is that?"

"He's clearly the town leader, very respected by most everyone in the area."

"Most?"

She sniffed. "I'm not overly convinced of his respectability yet, so I'm withholding judgment."

Willow was still disgruntled with her brother because of his disclosure, but she finally quit glaring. "Clay's stepdad runs fund-raisers for the fire department, and he's on the town council and the school board. He sponsors the high school football team and gives college scholarships. Everyone in town goes to him when they want something. Well, except us. He doesn't like us."

"He kisses all the babies and flirts with all the old women," Austin added in disgust.

"Quincy controls much of the town," Julie added. "He has a small mall that houses several shops, and he owns the factory, which means he employs most of the people living here in one way or another. They depend on him. Because of that, his stepson is given a lot of leeway."

"And so," Joe surmised, "the principal lets Clay slide when he does things he shouldn't do, like calling Willow names."

Julie shrugged with philosophical disregard. "Quincy Owen is not without influence."

The baring of Joe's teeth only faintly resembled a smile. "I have my own store of influence, trust me." Joe's cell phone rang just then, removing some of the impact from his statement. He fished it out of his pocket, flipped it open and said, "Winston."

Luna waited, breath held. Had the police discovered the man who'd been spying on them? She hoped so. It'd be nice to have one less worry now.

"Yeah?" Joe's jaw locked, and he growled. "You're sure they were fictitious plates? A stolen car?" And then, with barely contained frustration, "Shit."

Austin narrowed his eyes, saying to Luna and Julie, "He sure is disrespectful, huh?"

Rubbing his head, Joe paced away from the table, then back again. "Yeah, okay. Thanks anyway." He closed the phone and tucked it back into his pocket. "Sorry, ladies. That was disappointing news."

"Did someone steal your car?" Austin wanted to know, and damned if he didn't sound hopeful.

"Not quite." Joe's pale blue gaze locked on Luna. "The plates were stolen, so they can't help us. What's really odd is that the car fit a description of one that had been jacked, too, and because I called it in, my friend had a patrol car run by the area. They found a car matching that description in the area but with the original plates on it." Joe rubbed his chin. "I'm thinking the guy in the brown sedan is the same one I saw this morning. He just switched vehicles on us."

Julie sat in silent incomprehension. Austin and Willow were frozen in awe. Luna didn't want everyone to know just how lethal Joe could be. She brightened her tone and forced a false smile. "Well, we can talk about that later." She saw no reason to cause the others alarm. She was supposed to be an authority figure, not additional trouble. "Right now I'd rather figure out a schedule."

"What kind of schedule?"

It amazed Luna that one small boy could continually look so suspicious. "I want to make sure that your sister can fit her piano lessons in with summer school."

Willow leaned forward with carefully banked excitement in her eyes. "Summer school? Really?"

Displaying the opposite reaction, Austin groaned and staggered back a step. "*Summer* school?"

Luna chuckled at his antics. The way he tottered on his feet, it looked as if he'd been shot.

"I'd like you both to attend," Julie said. "You're a little behind in your regular classes, but that's not your fault. I looked over your scores, test grades and assignments. It's my conclusion that you weren't challenged as you should have been."

Austin clutched his heart. "I don't wanna be challenged! It just means more work."

"No. More work is just more work. You're ingenious enough to see through that ploy right off." She glanced to Luna. "They're both exceptionally bright."

Luna beamed, proud in spite of the fact she'd only just met them.

Very matter-of-fact, Julie continued. "Austin, did you know you have a natural affinity for math? In many ways, you're two grade levels ahead of other kids your age. You simply don't test well, but testing has never been my favored method of measuring success. There have been noted geniuses who perform poorly when tested. I believe with just a little direction, you'll find ways around that problem."

Austin stopped staggering and straightened with interest. "Really?"

"Absolutely. And I can show you how to use your

math skills to conquer other subjects. Math is a very versatile subject that applies in general concepts to our everyday lives."

"Then I can be ahead of the other guys in all ways." It was apparent that idea appealed to him more than anything else.

Julie nodded. "With hard work, it's quite possible. And I can see you're not averse to hard work."

Austin said, "Huh?"

Joe leaned down. "She's saying you're not a wimp."

"Oh. Yeah." He grinned. "I'm not."

"And, Willow, your vocabulary and grammar skills are astounding. I've been teaching for several years now, and it takes a lot to impress me, but I was most impressed with your essay on social standards. Very insightful and thought provoking. You managed to teach me several things with that paper because you convey your thoughts so well. With only a little instruction you could easily be high honors."

At first Willow flushed with pleasure and excitement, but seconds later, she lowered her head to stare down at her feet. Her fair blond hair hung like a curtain around her face, hiding her expression, but her tone was laden with unmistakable despair. "The principal doesn't like us. He called me a troublemaker, and he said Austin was a hoodlum. He even told Patricia that she should send us to a private, very strict school."

"You're not going anywhere, so don't worry about that." Luna curled her lips. "And as to those insults, why, I think I'll have a little talk with the principal."

Joe groaned at that prospect.

"Leave the principal to me." Julie put her hands on her knees and spoke with firm and reassuring conviction. "I can handle him."

Luna knew she could handle him, too, but Joe looked so relieved that she wouldn't have to, she smiled. "Thanks, Julie. We appreciate it."

"So that's decided. I'll tutor you both, and Austin, before you let out another dying-cow sound, I can promise it won't be like regular school. I'll even wager that you'll enjoy it. I have a knack for making school fun."

Luna watched both kids, knowing they found that hard to believe. After all, Julie did seem rather straight-laced and prim. But as Luna had said, she was good at reading people, and Julie Rose was a fighter. She'd keep the kids enthralled because she honestly loved children and her work. "I think it sounds wonderful."

Willow nodded. "I can take my piano lessons in the afternoon. That'd work out, don't you think?"

"Who teaches the lessons?" Luna wanted to find the person and offer thanks. At least Willow had had some constructive influence in her life. Hopefully, it could be arranged so that the schooling and the music lessons would all fit in.

Julie raised her brows. "Why, I do. And she's an excellent pupil."

"Aunt Patricia said we couldn't afford lessons," Willow confided. "Ms. Rose teaches me for free."

Amazingly, Julie actually blushed. To hide it, she grew even more prudish. "It's my pleasure. You're a delightful and talented student. What type of teacher would I be if I ignored that?"

Touched, Luna smiled at her. "You're obviously a wonderful teacher."

"Yes, I like to think so."

"And from now on, we'll pay."

Julie didn't argue the point. "That'd be fine." She tipped her head toward Willow. "I'm relieved I can still work with her, but it's always concerned me that she walked to and from town. I didn't like it at all. I decided today was the last time, which is why I drove directly here to discuss it with Patricia yet again. She refused to see it as a problem."

It was a good thing she'd sent Patricia away, because Luna felt volatile with anger. Smiling wasn't easy, but she managed. "I'm not at all like Patricia."

Julie eyed her colorful peacock earrings, her shimmering purple tank top and the numerous rings on her fingers. "Yes, I can certainly see that."

She didn't sound insulting, so Luna just nodded. "We'll make sure Willow has a ride at whatever time you think will work best."

"Wonderful. We'll start school next Monday, say nine o'clock? That'll give you all week to get acquainted with the children and to get settled in."

"Sounds perfect."

Julie stood. "I should be going now." She offered Luna her hand. "It's been a pleasure making your acquaintance."

"Same here."

Next, she stuck her hand out to Joe. "Mr. Winston. Thank you." After a brisk, man-to-man handshake, Julie headed out. Luna was relieved to see that other than a perfunctory farewell, Julie had no interest in Joe.

With only the slightest limp and a crooked smile, Joe walked with them to the door. On the way, they discussed Julie's fees—which Luna considered reasonable—and Luna invited her to come back at any time to visit. She had a feeling that even though Julie was new to the area, she could prove a good source of information.

On the front porch, Willow hung by Julie's side, anxiously asking questions about what they'd study, how much time they'd spend together. Austin still had reservations, until Julie told him they'd start with science, which included collecting and studying bugs from around the area.

Because she patiently answered all of Willow and Austin's questions, it was another fifteen minutes before Julie was able to leave. Her car had just disappeared from sight when a loud, sporty jeep turned down the driveway, kicking up gravel and dust and filling the air with loud music from the car stereo.

Willow glanced at the approaching vehicle, alert, cautious. Like a rabbit frozen in the headlights, she went utterly still. Her voice dropped to a near whisper. "That'll be Clay Owen and his buddies, Darren and Lee."

Luna put an arm around her. "The boys who bothered you earlier today?"

Willow nodded.

Eyes lighting up with anticipation, Joe rubbed his hands together. "Perfect timing." He went down the porch steps and across the yard to greet the young men.

Knowing Joe would likely do more cursing, Luna turned to the children. "You two should wait inside."

"No way." Austin leapt down the porch steps in one bound to land beside Joe. He attempted to mirror Joe's stance with his skinny legs braced apart and his arms folded over his bare chest.

Willow shook her head at her brother. "If I can keep him alive till he hits his teens, it'll be a miracle."

Both amused and sympathetic at Willow's awesome task, Luna hugged her. Willow stiffened, but she didn't pull away. Luna chose to see that as progress. "You've done an awesome job so far. But now that I'm here, maybe I'll be able to help."

"Maybe." The jeep came to a halt. After a contempt-filled glance at the boys, Willow went back to the door. "I'll wait inside." Without looking back, she said to Luna, "Good luck." The screen door closed with a bang behind her.

She'd need some luck, Luna thought, watching Joe smile in anticipation. She decided to join him and strolled down the steps to stand on Austin's other side.

Unaware of the pending confrontation, Clay Owen cut the engine. After the disruptive music, the sudden silence exaggerated the throbbing tension in the air. For several moments, Clay sat behind the wheel studying Joe with curiosity.

Luna had to admit he was a good-looking young man. Dark brown hair, a summer tan and an athlete's strong body probably made him popular with most of the girls. Like a prizefighter's belt, he wore his cockiness with a pretentious show of pride.

One boy sat in the passenger seat beside Clay, his long, muscular arms spread out along the seat back. The other boy was behind them, without a seat belt, his feet propped up on the seat beside his friend's arms. They were drinking colas, wearing dark aviator-style sunglasses and ball caps turned backward.

Finally taking his gaze off Joe, Clay glanced around, apparently looking for Willow. He opened the jeep door and climbed out. Shielding his eyes with one hand, he stared up at the house. "Is Willow around?" he asked of no one in particular.

Austin puffed up like a rooster ready to defend the hen house. "You're in big trouble, Clay."

He pulled off his sunglasses to reveal penetrating, dark green eyes. "That right, squirt?" He laughed and started to swagger toward the house, unconcerned with Austin's anger.

He drew up short when Joe casually moved forward, putting himself in the way. Clay stopped so abruptly, he spilled some of his cola. "Hey."

Clay was a tall boy with wide shoulders, but Joe towered over him, six feet, three inches of hard muscle. Clay took a hasty step back. "What's up, man?"

"My name is Mr. Winston, not man." Joe smirked at the disrespectful tone. "And you're trespassing."

Joe had sounded almost cordial, but still Clay looked worried. "Trespassing? Naw. Patricia doesn't care when I'm here."

"I care."

Clay swallowed. "Uh, where is Patricia?"

"Gone." Joe's grin epitomized evil delight. "From now on, you deal with me."

"And me," Luna said, unwilling to be cut out of the equation. "I'm Luna Clark, Willow's cousin." She held out her hand, making Joe frown.

Eyes wide, Clay accepted her hand in a brief, hurried shake. "You're here to take care of Willow and Austin?"

"That's right." Joe waited, not budging.

Clay again looked around. "I don't understand."

"It's simple enough." Joe raised his brows. "You were rude to Willow, and you put your hands on

Austin. That's unacceptable behavior. Until you learn some manners, you're not welcome here. Now I suggest you get in your car and leave."

His mouth fell open. He glanced back at his friends, who stared in shock. With obvious disbelief and a heavy dose of bravado, Clay faced Joe again. "You're threatening me?"

Luna rolled her eyes and laughed. "Of course not. Joe doesn't threaten children." Joe didn't bother replying.

Clay choked at being called a child. "But . . ."

Aware of the insult she'd dealt him, Luna fought off a smile. "The thing is, I don't want Willow insulted or Austin struck. Did you see his eye?"

Austin glared at Clay, the eye in question narrowed meanly.

Rather than answer, Clay pointed a finger at Austin. "That little weasle started the trouble this morning. I was only trying to talk to Willow when he jumped on my back."

"You called her names," Austin accused, his small body bunched to attack again.

With a nervous laugh, Clay said, "Nothing she hasn't heard before, and besides, we were just funning with her."

Joe caught Austin before he could move. He pulled him to his side and held him there. "Leave, Clay, and don't come back unless Willow invites you."

Clay looked undecided for only a moment before he straightened his shoulders and lowered his voice. "I want to see Willow first. I need to talk to her."

Luna shook her head. "Nope. She went in when she saw you drive up."

Frustration darkened his eyes. "Just call her out for a minute."

"She doesn't want to see you."

Clay cursed and threw down his can of cola. "Listen, if this is about the brat, I didn't mean to black his eye. He jumped me and got hurt in the scuffle. It's not my fault he got in the way of my elbow."

Shored up by Clay's foolish bluster, his friends again snickered.

Joe shook his head. He bent, picked up the half-full can of Coke, and tossed it into the driver's seat of Clay's car. It foamed out all over the expensive leather upholstery, sending Clay into a panic.

"Jesus!" He jerked off his shirt and ran to the jeep to mop up the mess. His two friends scrambled to assist him. They tried not to look worried, but Luna saw right through them. This was probably the first time they'd ever run across anyone like Joe Winston, and they didn't know what to make of him.

She'd had a similar reaction the first time she met him, so she understood how they felt. Joe inspired awe, fear and, if you were female, lots of interest.

With a total disregard for their disgruntlement, Joe joined the boys at the jeep. Austin kept pace with him, thoroughly enjoying himself. "Don't throw garbage in the yard and don't call Austin names."

Clay whipped around to face off with Joe, his sopping shirt held in his hand. "My stepdad is going to be majorly pissed about this, you just wait and see."

"Yeah? Good." Joe held the jeep door open for

him. "Maybe he'll give you a swift kick in the butt, like you deserve."

Comical outrage suffused Clay's face. "Not at *me*. At you!"

Joe nodded to the car. "Get in."

The cordial tone was long gone. Luna sighed. With no other apparent choice, Clay did as he was ordered. Joe pushed the door shut, then leaned in to say, "Tell your daddy to give me a call. I'll look forward to talking to him."

"He's my stepfather," Clay clarified.

"Whatever. In the meantime, I think I'll give the Welcome County police a call. I'm willing to bet you've broken a few ordinances here today."

Clay's gaze darted between Luna and Joe. He tried for a cavalier scoff that fell flat. "I have not."

"Loud music, speeding, no seat belts, profanity, littering . . . I could probably think of a few more. See, I used to be a cop, so I know the rules and I make a damn fine witness." Joe straightened and looked at each boy in turn. "If I make a complaint, they'll show up at your door to question you about it."

Clay drew a deep breath and frowned.

"You might just be fined, or they might take you out in handcuffs. Either way, you think your stepdaddy will like that?"

Clay remained silent.

Joe shook his head. "You know, Clay, you're old enough, probably smart enough, to try acting like a man instead of a punk. You'll find life is a little easier if you do."

Luna stepped forward. "But until you do, until you can visit without the foul mouth and nasty attitude, stay away."

Clay chewed his upper lip. After a moment, he

turned his head and stared toward the house. The seconds ticked by before he muttered a soft curse under his breath, then started the jeep and drove off. Luna noticed that he didn't speed this time, and he immediately turned the music down.

Austin kicked a small rock in their general direction. "Cowards."

With an expression like a thundercloud, Joe leaned down, caught Austin under his arms, and raised him to eye level. Knowing how bad Joe's ribs probably hurt, Luna fretted—but she didn't interfere. Joe seemed to be doing pretty darn good all on his own. His arms didn't shake, and he didn't appear to be straining at all.

"Listen, you," Joe said, all seriousness now, "real men don't gloat."

Austin hung limp in his hold, his feet dangling well off the ground. "What's that mean?"

"It means when someone is defeated, you don't kick rocks or call them names. To do so leaves you without dignity and makes you a coward, too."

"I'm not a coward."

"No? Then don't lower yourself to their level by acting like them. When I talk to the cops, I want to be able to assure them that you're on your best behavior. Any altercations will start and end with them, not with you. Understand?"

Serious and sincere, Austin nodded, but at the end, a big grin split his dirty face. "It was awful fun to watch, though."

Joe held his grim expression for three seconds more before he laughed. "Rodent." He set Austin down and ruffled his untidy hair. Dust flew up around him.

Joe looked at his hand, at the dust still floating in the air, and asked, "Do you think you could help

me unhitch Luna's car? Then maybe we can check
out the lake, swim and do a little fishing. What do
you say?"

"Sure! We'll have to dig up some worms for bait,
though."

Luna wrinkled her nose at that prospect until
Joe turned, caught the back of her neck, and
hauled her close for a kiss on the forehead. "Is that
okay with you?"

If he kept up with those casual, possessive touches,
Luna would soon be mush. Aware of Austin shifting restlessly beside them, Luna nodded. "That
sounds like a great idea."

Joe didn't release her. Instead he pecked her
mouth and smiled. "Wanna come with us?" And
then, near her ear, "I'd love to see you in a bikini."

Luna swatted his chest. "I think I'd rather get
the lay of the land. But you two go on. And have
fun."

"Spoilsport." With another kiss, Joe headed off.

Watching the two males saunter off side by side
did something funny to Luna's heart. She heard
Austin laugh, and felt like laughing, too.

Damn Joe Winston, did he have to be so good at
everything? Not only was he too sexy for words, but
he was kind and gentle, macho and brave, understanding and reasonable and . . . She swallowed.
He was everything she'd ever thought a man
should and could be.

But he wasn't for her.

She turned away to head to the house and saw a
curtain drop over the window. Uh oh. So, Willow
wasn't as disinterested in Clay as she'd claimed.
Had the young man seen her peeking out? Luna
had a feeling Clay wouldn't give up.

She winced. It didn't take a psychic to see that

this was going to be trouble. But at least this gave her and Willow something in common.

Caring about the wrong guy . . . Yup, that was right up Luna's alley. She and Willow could commiserate with each other. At least with Willow it was likely no more than infatuation.

For Luna, she knew it was much, much more.

Chapter Eight

High on a hill facing the house, mostly concealed by scrubby shrubs and weeds, the man shook his head. Careful to keep the sun from glinting off the lenses, he lowered the binoculars to the ground, then pulled the "big ear" headphones off and rubbed the bridge of his nose. Joe Winston appeared to be making himself right at home.

Following him hadn't been easy after all. Winston had spotted him early on, forcing him to put even more distance between them. He could have taken the time to switch cars, but then he'd have run the risk of losing them altogether. Besides, it wouldn't be catastrophic if Winston found out about him. It'd change his plans, but it wouldn't change the end results. Things were just easier this way.

For now.

He used his forearm to wipe sweat from his eyes. The damn summer sun was relentless, beating down on him in waves. Too bad he couldn't take a nice cool dip in the lake out behind the house, as Winston and the little boy planned to do.

He sat up, keeping his body concealed by the brush. The Smith and Wesson nine-millimeter pressed into the small of his back. It was hard, uncomfortable, but he always kept it on him. Like Winston, he was always prepared, but unlike Winston, he chose to carry a gun instead of a knife.

Being armed was only one of the many things they had in common. Being ruthless was another.

And a common enemy—now that made a third.

Maybe he and Winston were more alike than he'd first realized.

Impatient, annoyed, Dinah stood out back of the estate, hidden in the shadows of the small guest house next to the in-ground pool. It was risky coming here, but she'd never been fired in her life, and she didn't like it.

After a twenty-minute wait, he finally slipped out the patio doors and came to her. When he reached her, she started to speak, but he shushed her with one venomous look. His hard hand closed on her upper arm and dragged her farther away, deeper into the surrounding landscape until they were completely hidden behind a lush rhododendron in full bloom.

He grabbed her other arm and slammed her up against a sturdy trellis. They were of a similar height, but still he overpowered her. "What the fuck do you mean, coming to my house like this?"

Dinah's heart raced. Oh, God, she'd never seen him so angry before. She'd always considered him too suave and sophisticated for an outburst. Perhaps she'd made a mistake coming here. "I . . . I wanted you to know. I got fired."

His dark brown eyes seemed fathomless in the

dim night. After a heart-stopping moment, he dropped his hands. "The cousin fired you? Why?"

His fair, immaculately styled hair reflected the moonlight, forming a halo around his head. Dinah recovered her aplomb and straightened. "Who knows? She's ridiculous, very eccentric, just as you said. But she brought someone with her."

"Who?"

Dinah licked her lips. "Joe Winston." Just saying his name gave her delicious shivers. Talk about a real man. Because she asked for very little—sexual satisfaction, a few laughs—few men had ever turned her down. Yet Joe Winston had looked at her with contempt. She wasn't giving up on him, though. Not yet. "I assume he's her lover. They're not married, I know that much."

He stepped closer to her, crowding her back, his breath hot and angry, though his voice now remained cool. "What did you do, Dinah?"

"Nothing."

"Bullshit." His mouth tilted in a sneer. "Did you come on to him? Did you throw yourself at him?"

Dinah wished the question wasn't so humiliating. Usually men were easy to get, but there was nothing easy about Winston—and unfortunately, that only made him more appealing. He'd told her no, and meant it.

Just as this man had.

She couldn't continue to meet his gaze and looked away. "They both took exception to the truth about the kids. I was explaining how they are, the trouble they cause, and they fired me."

Almost without thought, he brought her face back around to his, causing her heart to race and her womb to tighten. He stared into her eyes, but spoke more to himself than her. "That doesn't make any sense. Those brats are nothing but trouble."

"I know." He'd been generous with her, getting her the job, paying her extra on the side, in exchange for a little worthless information. He did everything under the guise of responsibility to the town, to his family. Dinah knew better. He cared only about himself. "What am I going to do now? I need a job."

His dark gaze narrowed, then he stepped away. "Give it a week. By then they'll see what they're up against, and they'll either be at your door, begging you to return to help keep the kids in line, or they'll have given up and agreed to move away. It's only a matter of time."

"I know. Patricia was ready to leave with the kids until that idiot man asked her to marry him."

"Jealous?"

He just stood there, damn him, impassive, detached, probably amused. Few people ever saw this side of him, but he could be such a cold bastard at times.

Dinah thrust her breasts out and lowered her voice to a purr. "I can get any man I want."

He laughed softly. "Not me. And apparently not this Joe Winston fellow."

Anger roiled through her. "Within a week, he'd have been in my bed."

"But you didn't get a week, did you?" His smile was malicious. "You didn't even get a whole day."

It did her no good to fight with him. She'd realized from the first that he held no special reverence for women. To get what he wanted he'd trample over man, woman, or even child. "No, I didn't, and now I'm out of a job. What am I going to do while waiting for Luna Clark to come to her senses? And what if she doesn't? What if she decides she likes it here?" She pouted—but it had no effect on him. "I need money to live on."

He pulled out a wallet, flipped through several twenties, and handed them to Dinah. "Maybe I'll speak to Mr. Winston. I'll reason with him, and then we'll see."

Dinah curled her fist around the money. "That might be harder than you think. I got the impression that Winston isn't an easy man to reason with."

He gave her an indulgent grin. "Every man has his weakness. I'll find his, and then you'll see just how easy it is."

Dinah watched him walk away, that damn opalescent moonlight still framing his pale head. She snorted. The halo was very misplaced. Beneath that blond hair, she was sure he hid horns, because God knew, he was as close to the devil as a man could get.

Luna came into the kitchen with a list. It was nearing ten o'clock, and she'd just tucked the kids into bed after they'd both said good night to Joe. That had been nice, Joe thought, sort of domestic and comforting.

It had taken him by surprise.

After swimming in the lake, Austin claimed to be clean enough. The lake water had knocked the top layer of dirt off the boy, but the ground-in grime had remained, so Luna insisted he shower, too. It hadn't been an easy battle, but Luna had set out to win, and in the end, Austin had proved no match for her.

When Austin later sidled up to Joe to say good

night, he'd smelled good, sort of like soap and little boy and innocence. Austin hadn't exactly hugged Joe, but he had gotten close, looking shy and uncertain. Joe rubbed his back, messed his freshly brushed hair, and sent him to bed with a gentle thwack on the shoulder.

Willow had come to him next. She'd worn a faded blue housecoat over her nightgown, and her long blond hair was loose, freshly brushed. She looked adorable and far too wise for her years. Joe had waited, letting her decide what to do. He wasn't quite sure if one went about messing a young lady's hair.

Willow stared at him a long time, then nodded. "Thank you."

Joe's brows rose at her grave tone. He pulled off his reading glasses. "For what?"

"For coming here." Then she'd walked away, breaking Joe's heart and forcing him to fight the urge to draw her back for a tight hug. He'd already decided not to smother the kids, to let them get used to him naturally.

But it wasn't easy.

He wanted to pull them both close and promise that nothing and no one would ever hurt them again. He wanted . . .

Shit.

Luna sat down beside him. She, too, was freshly showered, and that played havoc with his libido. He could smell her, all soft and female and sweet. He wanted to rub his nose against her neck, her breasts, her thighs. His abdomen tightened.

She leaned forward to look at the papers he had spread out in front of him. "What are you working on?"

She had a lot on her mind, too much to have to

deal with his lust, too. Joe tugged on his earring. "These are the accounts for the lake." His voice was a little hoarse, but he ignored it. "Do you realize how prosperous it was? Why the hell Patricia shut it down, I can't imagine. Especially since there wasn't that much cash left to the kids."

"You've been looking into the money situation?"

"It seemed pertinent. Now don't frown. I'm not snooping. You asked me to come along to help set things right. Well, you'll need money to keep things afloat, but there doesn't appear to be any."

"The house is paid for."

Nodding slowly, Joe looked around. The kitchen was immense, beautiful, not overly dated, but certainly not modern either. "You've never cared for kids, Luna. I remember my mother complaining about the laundry that had to be done for Alyx and me." He regarded her, knowing she was strong and more than capable, but perhaps a little naïve about what she faced. "Hot water bills, gas and electric, taxes, insurance . . . Groceries alone are a large monthly bill. Figure everything you spend on yourself and quadruple it. That's the cost of kids, and it's endless."

Her exotic eyes narrowed. "You're suggesting I give up already?"

"Hell no." He leaned back in his seat and laced his fingers over his middle. "But you'll need some form of income. There's the interest on what's left in the bank, but I can think of better ways to work that money to get a higher return. That's something you ought to take up with an accountant."

"The stock market?"

"Or mutual funds, something like that. But in the meantime, the lake might be a solution. It was making money. Your cousin Chloe did a helluva job with it. So why did Patricia shut it down?"

Luna shrugged. "My guess is she didn't want to be bothered with it. She struck me as a lazy, self-indulgent bitch."

"Yep. Not very nice at all." Joe remembered the foot in his lap, and he shook his head. He still didn't know if it was Patricia or Dinah, but it didn't matter. Either one was unacceptable.

No reason to tell Luna about that now. Pulling himself back to the table, he put his head on one fist and again lifted a paper. "If you don't mind, I could check into this and see how difficult it might be to get things going again."

"Sure." Beneath the light centered over the table, Luna's lashes looked long and soft and left shadows on her cheekbones. After her shower, she'd changed, and she now wore a breast-hugging, spaghetti-strap cotton shirt with loose, opaque harem pants. Her makeup was gone, and she had removed all her jewelry. Even in the comfortable clothes, she managed to look flamboyant, sexy and exotic.

This was likely how she'd look the morning after making love.

That thought warmed him. Joe liked sitting with her in the evening, discussing things. They were almost like a family, and while that should have worried him, instead it made him feel . . . necessary.

Ha. What the hell was he thinking? Nonsense, all of it. He shook his head, drawing a funny look from Luna. He pushed another paper toward her. "It's the only big lake in the area, and with school out and the temperatures climbing, I bet plenty of people would be happy to renew their memberships. It might be a nice cash flow."

She picked up a flier on seasonal activities. "There's more involved than just swimming?"

The fresh scent of her hair and the indescribable fragrance exclusive to Luna filled him. Joe drew a deep, uneven breath. If he didn't have her soon, he'd become a halfwit. "The shed down by the lake used to be a shop of sorts. There's an enormous freezer that might need a little electrical work, but otherwise seems to be in good order. Austin told me their mom used to sell ice creams and colas, bags of ice and chips and snacks to the people who visited the lake. And there's a vending machine for bait, though I haven't found the records yet on where to order the bait. There were rentals on floats, canoes, fishing equipment. Pretty much anything you could think of that could be used in or around a lake. Austin tells me the stuff is still stored here, most of it in the shed but some in the attic and basement."

"Huh." Luna leaned back in her seat, and the shirt pulled around her breasts, practically outlining her nipples. "You know, there's a computer in Willow's room. In this day and age, maybe most of the records are on it."

Joe forced his gaze to her face. "Good idea." It wasn't easy to concentrate on what she said when his beleaguered brain wanted only to think of sex. "So I'll check into it, agreed?"

She smiled at him, and it was so sweet, so trusting, Joe felt every muscle in his body tighten. "You're awfully enthusiastic about all this."

I'm enthusiastic about you. No, he wouldn't say that to her, damn it, not until he had more time to think about it himself. But Luna had impressed him. From the moment they'd arrived, she'd had one problem after another thrown at her, yet she hadn't lost sight of why she'd come—to care for the kids. For a free spirit moon goddess, she'd done a terrific job of reassuring Willow and Austin, of making them feel more secure.

Joe reached for her hand. "So far, I'm having fun."

That made her laugh, and even her damn laugh turned him on. Better get his mind back on track, he decided. He nodded to the list she held. "What have you got there?"

She lifted her brows and sighed. "I'm trying to figure out everything we need to get. The list is getting pretty long, though. Austin's clothes are almost all secondhand, some too big, some not big enough. His shoes should have been replaced ages ago. Willow's wardrobe isn't quite as bad, but she tells me that's because she's done growing, so clothes from a few years past still fit her. She hasn't had anything new in far too long."

It was difficult for Joe to consider such a petite female done growing, but Willow was almost as tall as Luna, just very slender with only adolescent curves. "Boys are slower to mature, I hear. Plus I'm willing to bet that Austin is a whole lot harder on his clothes than Willow."

"Exactly. She told me Patricia refused to buy him anything new because he just got it dirty or torn anyway." Her hand curled tight. "She also said Patricia claimed Chloe was a fool for not naming the father and making him pay support. Apparently she grilled the kids endlessly about possible fathers with the intent of filing a suit herself."

Joe sympathized, but said, "He should be paying, Luna. They're his responsibility."

"I know it. I'm not making excuses for him,

whoever he is. But it's not right to drag the kids into the middle of it, especially with the way their lives are right now. And I have to assume Chloe had her reasons for not including him. I just . . . I wish I'd known about them from the start."

Joe considered that and frowned. If she had known of the kids, she would have been long gone before his visit to his cousin, Zane. He never would have met her, and that thought formed a vise around his lungs. "Were the others as bad as Patricia, do you think?"

"They left them, so they couldn't have been great."

She looked so eaten up about what the kids had gone through, Joe tapped the list she held and changed the subject. "So you're planning a shopping spree?"

Her lashes again lowered as she reviewed her list. "Hopefully this weekend. I'd like them to have new clothes before they start summer school. We'll need groceries, too. There's hardly anything here that the kids like to eat. It was pure luck that we found that hamburger for dinner."

Because he couldn't stop himself, Joe lifted her hand and kissed her knuckles. He would have liked to work his way up her arm to her elbow, then her throat, until he reached her breasts. To stifle a groan, he said, "The spaghetti and meat-balls were perfect." He kissed her knuckles again, then dipped his tongue between the crease of her ring and middle finger. He heard Luna catch her breath, and he murmured, "For a psychic's assis-tant, you make a damn fine cook."

The paper in her other hand trembled. "Thanks."

Joe leaned closer to peruse her list. "Looks like you're planning an all day trip for this."

"Looks that way." She drew a shuddering breath, bit her bottom lip, and pulled her hand away. "You want to come along?"

"*Want to*, no." Here he'd been seducing her when he'd just decided not to. He wanted to give her a few days to get acclimated to things before he pressed her. "I'm not big on shopping. But since I planned to buy a bed, I suppose I'll tag along."

Luna did a quick double take. She'd had her pen poised to write down his request, but now she just stared at him. "You don't have a bed?"

"Not a very good one." Joe also wanted to keep an eye on them all. He couldn't be sure that they'd lost their tail when they arrived in Visitation. He hadn't seen anyone following, and he'd taken extra efforts to make following them difficult, but Joe left very little to chance. And added to that, he didn't trust Jamie Creed. The man had spooked him, and that wasn't an easy thing to do.

He eyed Luna, wondering how long it would take him to work his way into her bed. "I'd like a king size, but it'd never fit in that cramped room, so I guess it'll have to be a double. With a thick mattress."

Luna still looked floored when the phone rang.

Joe twisted to reach for the kitchen phone on the wall. "Now, I wonder who that could be this time of night."

Luna rolled her eyes, detecting the note of cynicism in his tone that he didn't bother to hide. They had both been expecting the call from Owen all day.

" 'Lo."

There was a moment of silence, then, "This is Quincy Owen. With whom am I speaking?"

"Quincy? 'Bout time. I was almost ready to turn in."

"Excuse me?"

Joe wasn't surprised that Quincy Owen would be inconsiderate enough to call so late. According to Julie, Quincy owned most of the town, meaning he could pretty much do whatever he pleased with immunity. "You're Clay Owen's dad?"

"His stepfather, yes. And you are?"

"Joe Winston. What can I do for you, Quince?"

"It's Quincy," he replied with an annoyed clip to his tone, "and you can start by explaining to me what happened earlier at the Calder house."

Joe tipped the chair back on two legs, at his leisure. "Clay was disrespectful, obnoxious and rude. Since I don't tolerate that type of behavior from adults, much less kids, I told him to leave and not come back."

Another strained silence. "Perhaps you don't know who I am."

Joe was aware of Luna watching him with bright-eyed satisfaction. "I was apprised of your influence, Quince. Thing is, I just don't give a damn. Teach your stepson some manners and maybe he can try calling again."

"*How dare you.*" The calm had been replaced with anger. "Maybe you aren't aware of everything those Calder brats have done, but—"

Joe put the phone back in the cradle.

Luna blinked. "He hung up?"

"No. He was still talking." Joe grinned. "I just didn't like what he was saying."

The phone immediately rang again. Joe snatched it up, and as if he didn't know exactly who would be on the line, he said, " 'Lo?"

"I'll assume we had a bad connection."

"You can assume whatever you like. But if you insult Willow or Austin again, the bad connection will return."

Several seconds passed while Joe had the feeling Quincy gathered a volatile temper. "Mr. Winston, I didn't call you to argue."

"Glad to hear it. Not that there's much to argue about anyway. I witnessed the whole thing, and I can tell you, man to man, that Clay was out of line."

"The Calder children provoked him. It's happened before."

"I have my doubts about that, but it definitely wasn't the case this time. Willow went inside the second she saw their car drive up, and Austin— who is only nine, by the way—was sporting a black eye thanks to Clay." Joe paused to let that sink in, then added, almost as an afterthought, "Makes him sound like a bully, doesn't it?"

The sound of teeth grinding came through the phone. "Clay told me the boy jumped him."

"Did he tell you why? Surely not, because I can't believe any man would condone the use of that language toward a young lady. Austin did what any honorable brother would do when someone is being a jerk to his sister. Talk to Clay again, Quince. And teach him what it means to be a man."

"Are you issuing orders to *me?*"

"Just some well-meaning advice. From Clay's behavior, I'd say you could use it."

"Just who the hell are you anyway?"

"I already told you." The chair legs hit the floor with a resounding thud, and the smile left Joe's face. "I'm Joe Winston."

"And?" Quincy jeered. "You say that like it should mean something to me."

"Yeah. It means I'm looking out for Willow and Austin now, and I take my responsibility to heart. That's something you're going to want to remember."

"We have that in common then, because I, too, have my responsibilities. It would behoove you to learn more about the trouble the Calder children have caused. Perhaps then you'll see that it'd be best for all concerned to move them to another area."

"Nope."

The voice lowered to a growl. "I'm thinking of their best interest, I assure you. The children could use a fresh start elsewhere. In Visitation, everyone knows they're illegitimate as well as orphaned. There's nothing here for them."

"I'm here. That's all the fresh start they need."

"You're taking on a task of monumental proportions, given their past behavior. They're hooligans with no breeding and no respect for—"

"Let me worry about it, Quince, okay?" Joe again hung up the phone. Damn, he felt good.

He turned to Luna, opened his mouth to speak—and she launched herself at him. *"Joe."*

"What the—" Her body landed against his with enough impact to make him catch his breath in a gasp of pain. But with Luna touching him everywhere, the pain was quickly relegated to the back of his mind. Joe wrapped his arms around her, cradling her closer and struggling to keep them both in the chair.

"Hey, you okay?" He tried to tip her back to see her face, but she hugged his neck in a strangle hold.

"Thank you." She landed a tickling kiss on his ear, his chin, his jaw. Every touch of her soft, damp mouth burned him, teased him, until Joe wrapped a hand in her hair and managed to take control. His mouth covered hers, hungry and hot. He sank his tongue in, and she gave a small, sweet moan of acceptance, then went utterly still except for the racing of her heartbeat against his chest.

"That's it," Joe whispered, savoring her taste, the softness of her tongue, her sighs. He tightened his arms and her breasts pressed more firmly into his chest. Spreading one hand wide on her behind, Joe scooped her closer still. He could enter her like this, he thought, in a chair, with her legs around him. He groaned low and took her mouth again, rapacious, hungry, all thoughts of giving her time long obliterated.

By small degrees, Luna pulled back to stare at him. Breathing hard, a pulse racing in her throat, she licked her lips and whispered, "Joe?"

"Yeah, babe?"

She touched his jaw with a shattering gentleness. "You are the most remarkable man."

"Whatever I did," Joe rumbled low, so hot he saw her only through a haze, "remind me to do it again." He kissed her throat, her shoulder. She was so soft against him, he just naturally cuddled her behind through the silky harem pants, tracing the deep cleft with his fingertips and driving himself insane. "You have such a fine ass."

Luna went still, then laughed. She treated him to another suffocating hug and an avuncular pat on the shoulder. She pressed away from him and stood. Her hands curled tight at her sides, but her voice was shallow and soft. "I better get to bed."

Joe stared. "What?" It sounded as though she planned to leave him in the kitchen. Alone. With a raging boner.

"I have so much to do tomorrow and so much to think about still tonight." She started to turn away but paused. "Do you think we'll have more problems with Mr. Owen?"

Joe, too, stood. He watched her, waiting for any sign of indecision. "I'm betting on it."

Nodding, Luna took a step back, inching toward the doorway. "I'll, uh, see you in the morning."

No way. "Luna . . ."

"No."

His head threatened to explode. "You say that entirely too damn much."

"Not easily." Her gaze dipped over him, once, fast. Her eyes shone bright when she again looked at his face. "You're very, very hard to resist, Joe Winston. You know that. But it's our first night here, and the kids might still be awake and . . ." She gave him a floundering, helpless look. "No."

Knowing she was right didn't make it easier to swallow. Taut with need, Joe growled, "Then go now before I try to change your mind. I'll lock up."

She hesitated.

"*Go.*"

Luna turned and fled the kitchen as if she, too, had to fight the urge to give in.

Damn, he hurt. Why in hell did he have to want—*need*—this one particular, difficult, loony woman? Joe waited until he heard her footsteps overhead before going through the downstairs, room by room, checking to make sure every window was latched and the doors were securely locked. The security inspection helped to take his mind off his burning need, but it didn't remove it. Nothing would except burying himself inside Luna for a long, hot, leisurely ride.

It was a large house, and by the time Joe finished, the clawing need for sexual satisfaction had diminished enough to allow other, more rational thought.

He realized that the locks were old and flimsy, and even the most inept burglar would have no problem breaking in. The house was isolated, making it prime pickings for the nefarious element of society. Before he left Luna and the kids here alone, he'd make the house more secure.

After shutting off all the interior lights, Joe went into his room and silently closed the door. The tiny, narrow bed didn't look the least appealing, so he went to the patio doors to stare out. A half moon hung low in the sky, surrounded by a blanket of stars. It was a bright night. A romantic night.

A night that stirred a man's blood.

He paced away, dropped onto the bed with a groan—and heard an indistinct thump. Stilling, Joe listened and caught a faint creak. He left the bed and went to the door to again look out, but saw nothing. It was an old house, and he was unfamiliar with the sounds it made as it settled for the night. But still . . . The niggling suspicion gnawed at him until he left his room and made his way to the stairs. Yep, he heard it again. Someone was moving around up there when he thought everyone had gone to bed.

Navigating the stairs in the dark, Joe reached the landing without a single sound. It was quiet now, but a light shone from beneath Willow's door, so he paused there to listen. He heard Luna's voice and crept closer. The door was slightly ajar, and Joe could just barely see Luna sitting on the side of Willow's bed while Willow sat at a desk.

"Can't sleep?" Luna asked her.

Willow shrugged.

"You can talk to me, you know."

With only one desk lamp on, shadows dominated the room. But Joe could see Willow's eyes, huge and sad. "I don't want to bother you."

"Oh, honey, you won't bother me. I promise. I want to help. That's why I'm here."

"You're here because we don't have anyone else." Willow sounded guilty. Joe wanted to walk in, to tell her that young girls weren't supposed to be burdened with so many worries. But he held back, trusting Luna to handle it.

"No." Luna reached for her hand. "I'm here because we're family. And I really want you and Austin to confide in me and to like me. I've never had a real family before, so this is as important to me as it is to you."

Joe stiffened. What the hell did that mean? Of course Luna had a family. Everyone had a family.

Willow looked as stunned as Joe felt.

"It's true." Luna smiled. "I was never very close with my folks. They argued a lot whenever they were together, then they were separated off and on before finally divorcing. I stayed with my dad. My mom left to get remarried, and I hardly ever saw her after that. I have two half brothers that I barely know."

"You don't visit them?"

"They live pretty far away. I went to see them once, but it was awkward."

Joe remembered her saying that her family was scattered around the country. He hadn't realized . . .

"What about your dad?"

"He worked a lot after Mom left. When I graduated high school he remarried, and so I have a stepsister, too. But she and I don't have much in common, and again, they live pretty far away."

Willow pushed her hair behind her ears. "I don't have a dad at all. That is, I never met him."

Luna just nodded. "I know."

"Because I never met him, and don't even know who he is, I don't miss him. Not like I miss my mom. But you must miss your dad a lot."

Shrugging, Luna said, "I never think about it that much. It's just how it's been for a long time. But now I have you and Austin, and I want to do this right. I want to stay."

"Things are pretty much a mess," Willow warned.

"We'll work it all out, I promise. In the meantime, you can come to me whenever you have a problem. I can't promise to have all the answers, but I can promise to always try my best and to listen."

Willow seemed to think that over, then blurted, "Patricia said she couldn't afford to stay here anymore. She was going to move us away before that guy proposed to her."

Luna sighed. "Willow, honey, I'm not Patricia. I'm not going to leave you. I promise."

"But you're talking about buying us clothes."

Joe could hear the hope and the fear in Willow's voice, and it broke his heart. How long had it been since she'd had anything new?

"That's right. Don't you want new clothes?"

"It's just that there's not much money left."

Willow fretted with the papers on her desk. "I was looking at things, and I'm not sure . . ."

"Shhh. Willow, I have money."

"You can't use your own!" She sounded appalled at the thought, making Joe grit his teeth. Hell, he had money, too, and he wasn't using it for anything important.

"Why not?" Luna reasoned. "I'm living here now, saving on rent. What's mine is yours. Besides, I'm really looking forward to our shopping expedition. It's been a while since I got to shop with another woman."

The rigidity left Willow's shoulders, and she even smiled. But when Luna reached past her to pick up a newspaper clipping on the desk, she stiffened again. "That's nothing."

"It's an article on Clay Owen." Luna skimmed it before handing it back to Willow. "He won athlete of the year?"

Scrunching up her face into a frown, Willow nodded. "Yeah. He gets good grades, and he's the quarterback for the football team and a pitcher for the baseball team. Everyone thinks he's perfect."

Cautiously, Luna said, "He's very cute."

"I guess."

"Do you like him, Willow?"

Her eyes flared and her voice lowered. "No, I hate him."

As if she hadn't answered, Luna said, "Because if you did, I could understand it."

Willow shook her head hard. "We used to be friends. Even though he's a little older, we always got along great. I've known him since second grade." Her eyes darkened. "But now he's always mean to me."

"Some guys are pretty clueless." Luna smoothed Willow's hair behind her ears with a maternal touch. "There's no good excuse for being mean to someone else, but Julie said he does it because he's trying to get your attention."

Willow still sounded mutinous. "He used to like me okay, I guess. But then the rumors about me started, and he got ugly and nasty."

Very gently, Luna asked, "But you still like him, huh? It's okay. I understand all about liking the wrong guy. Common sense tells you one thing, but your heart tells you another."

Joe's muscles, mind and gut all pulled into a tense knot. Who the hell did Luna like? If she was talking about that damn spook, Jamie Creed, he'd . . .

Willow tipped her head. "Joe?"

"Yeah."

What? Joe slumped against the wall, and the furious racing of his heart slowed to a dull thud. Well, hell. Since when did he become the wrong guy?

But he already knew the answer to that question: he'd never been the right guy. Not for a woman like Luna.

"He's a wonderful man," she said, and to Joe, it sounded like she meant it. "One of the very best. But Joe doesn't ever want to settle down."

Now she was speaking for him when she didn't know what he wanted. Hell, *he* didn't know what he wanted. He used to know—but that was before he met Luna and she started driving him crazy.

"And you do?"

Luna nodded. "I didn't use to, or maybe I just didn't know it before now. But I'm jazzed about the idea of staying here with you and Austin forever. And Joe will have to go back home pretty soon, so there's definitely no point in liking him too much when I know it won't—can't—last."

"So if it wasn't for us . . ."

"No." Her laugh was soft, full of self-derision. "Even before I heard from you, I was saying no to Joe."

Joe could damn well testify to *that*.

Willow sounded startled by that disclosure. "But why?"

Her sigh was long and drawn out and too damn dramatic to do anything other than insult Joe. "Because there are some guys in this world sure to break your heart. Joe is pure heartbreaker. He wallows in his bachelor status, so I can't see him ever marrying. Did you know he has four male cousins who've married? Joe's close with them, and I guess he's happy for them, but he sneers at the idea of tying himself to one woman."

"He's real popular?"

"With the ladies?" This time Luna's laugh was definitely mocking. "Oh, yeah. Very. But Joe's not a guy you can just date for the fun of it, and then become friends. He's too dynamic for that. It's better not to get too close to him at all."

Willow slanted Luna a look that made her appear quite mature. "I think you're already pretty close to him."

"Yeah, you're probably right." Luna looked both resigned and sad at that disclosure. "But as long as Joe doesn't know it, I'm okay."

Joe gave a smug smile. So, she'd hoped to keep that from him? Ha! Now he knew, and he sure as hell wasn't likely to forget. One way or another he'd sort everything out, and he'd use whatever information he could to his advantage.

"That's sort of how I feel about Clay. I think

about him all the time. When he's around, I try to just ignore him, even though that's pretty hard to do. But Austin makes it impossible." Her hands curled into fists in her lap. "I told Clay if he ever hurt Austin again, I was going to beat the crap out of him."

Joe grinned. Willow was so small and delicate, he couldn't imagine her hurting anyone.

"Hopefully, we've dissuaded him from pestering you."

"I doubt it. He'll be back. I just know it."

Eyes warm with sympathy, Luna cupped her chin. "And even though you wish it was different, you're sort of glad?"

Willow groaned. "Yes. I'm glad."

"It won't be easy for him to be mean now," Luna pointed out. "You won't be walking into town alone. If Clay wants to see you, he's going to have to come here. And that means he's going to have to be polite."

Willow said nothing to that, and finally Luna stood. "Why don't you get to sleep? Things always seem clearer in the morning." Luna gave a bright smile. "I thought we'd work on our shopping list more tomorrow. I'd like to figure out everything we'll need, then we can go into town on Saturday. We can make a day of it, have some lunch. Maybe even see a movie."

"A movie, really?"

Even through his distraction with all that Luna had revealed, Joe heard Willow's excitement. By God, if she liked movies, then he'd add a VCR to the list and rent her one every night of the week. She deserved some fun, and he intended to see that she have it.

Willow pushed out of her seat with new purpose. "The house needs to be cleaned, too. I haven't had a chance because walking to town for my piano lessons took so long, and Dinah and Patricia didn't seem to care."

"But I thought Dinah was a housekeeper?"

"Yeah, right." Willow snorted. "She cooked occasionally, but mostly she just snooped around."

Snooped around for what? Joe wondered.

"You didn't like her?"

Willow shrugged. "I tried to just stay out of her way. She could be really hateful."

Hearing that, Joe's heart almost broke. When Luna spoke, he detected a strain in her voice as well.

"I promise never to be hateful, okay? And we'll clean the house together. Joe and Austin can help."

"You want Austin to clean?" Willow stepped away to turn down her bedding, but she shook her head as she did so. "Good luck. Austin's much better at making messes."

"Just because he's male doesn't make him helpless. Besides, I have a feeling Joe will insist on helping, so maybe Austin will want to, too."

Smiling, Willow plumped her pillow, then hugged it to her chest. "Joe's different, isn't he?"

"I sure don't know any other men like him."

"My mom used to say to me that you can't tell about men just by looking at them. She said a guy might look well-mannered and kind and smart, but when you got to know him, he could be an egotistical snake."

Joe frowned. Had Chloe been speaking from experience? Had she maybe even been referring to Austin and Willow's father? It'd make sense, seeing that the man left her alone to raise two kids.

"Do you think Joe is a snake?" Luna asked with surprise.

"No." Willow's smile lingered. "I think it's just the opposite. When I first saw him, he looked sort of . . . I don't know. Big and dark and mean, like he could chew nails and enjoy it. I was . . . worried. Especially with Austin cursing and acting like such a brat. But as soon as I saw how he handled Austin, I knew he was okay."

Luna neither confirmed nor denied his meanness. "Are you still a little afraid of Joe?"

"No." Willow chewed her lip, then ventured into very adult ground. "But I think you are."

"I trust Joe more than anyone I know."

"You don't trust him not to break your heart," Willow reminded her. "But as my mom said, you never can tell."

Luna plastered on a very false smile. "We can talk about it more tomorrow, okay? Right now I really think you should get some sleep."

"All right." Not the least fooled by the diversion, Willow climbed into her bed with a sigh. "Luna? Thanks."

"Thank *you*. I enjoyed our talk." Luna kissed her cheek, turned out her light, and headed for the door.

Joe drew back down the hall and ducked into a bathroom. Damn. Why couldn't Willow be the average fourteen-year-old girl? Did she have to be a philosopher? *Was* Luna afraid of him? If so, she sure as hell hid it well.

He peered around the door frame. Luna came into the hallway, quietly pulled Willow's door shut, then went into her own room. Her light flicked off.

Joe let out a breath. Maybe he could sneak in there and reassure her. At least kiss her good night. He could tell her how proud he was of her, how he wanted to help.

Convinced of his altruistic motives, Joe was just about to leave his hiding spot when he felt breath on his back. His eyes widened in shock, and he whirled around. A small, pointy elbow connected with his ribs, right over a bruise.

"*Damn it.*"

In a whisper, Austin said, "You talk way worse than I do."

Joe froze. He saw his plans for Luna—not so altruistic after all—evaporate into thin air. "What the hell?" He reached out, caught Austin's upper arm, and said, "Shh. What are you doing here?"

"I was gonna take a walk."

Every hair on the back of Joe's neck stood on end. "Take a walk *where?*"

"Around the lake."

His heart almost stopped. He felt sweat pop out on his brow. "God help me."

The scrawny muscles in Austin's arms bunched as he braced his hands on his hips. "If you tell on me, I'll tell on you."

"What are you talking about? Tell on me for what?"

"For spying on Luna."

For a brief moment, Joe wondered if he should awaken Luna to help him with this predicament, but he decided against it. She had her hands full, and surely, he could handle one very determined little boy.

Besides, he didn't want her to know that he'd been skulking around in the hallway, eavesdropping on her private conversation. She might be embarrassed. He knew for certain he'd feel like an ass.

And she might doubt his sincerity when he set about proving to her that he wouldn't break her heart.

How he'd prove that, he didn't have a clue. But he'd come up with something.

Joe stuck his head out the door and saw that no one had been alerted by their whispered conversation. "Come on," he told Austin, and kept his long fingers around the boy's arm as he led him back to his room. "In you go."

They stepped inside together, and Joe slipped the door shut. Now that they had some privacy, he spoke a little louder. "Do you have a night light?"

"Night lights are for sissies."

"You're obsessed about this sissy stuff, aren't you? All right, never mind. There's enough moonlight to see." He pulled Austin's drapes open, and pale bluish light spread into the room. "Now. Let's me and you talk."

"Are you mad?" Austin seemed a little worried about that possibility.

"No." Joe lifted him and sat him on the foot of the bed. "I'm concerned. That's an altogether different thing."

"How's it different?"

Joe didn't have an answer to that. "Austin, surely you know you can't go walking around alone at night."

"I do it all the time."

Joe's brain throbbed. Damn Patricia and her earplugs. "Well, no more, my boy." He gingerly seated himself beside Austin. That elbow had left

an ache in places that were just starting to feel better.
"First, I want you to know that I don't keep secrets
from Luna. Ever. So don't try blackmailing me."

"You were listenin' in."

"I was," Joe admitted, "but only because I was
worried. I didn't announce myself because I didn't
want to intrude." Good. That sounded entirely
plausible.

"You're going to tell Luna you were listenin'?"

Hell, now he'd *have* to. "In the morning. And
I'm going to tell her that you thought to take a
moonlight stroll."

That had Austin frowning in disappointment
and anxiety. "Will she be mad?"

"No, like me, she'll be concerned. Once Luna
puts you to bed, she expects you to stay there."

"What if I have to use the bathroom?"

"You can get up for that."

"What if I need a drink?"

"That's okay, too."

"What if I—"

"You can't leave the house, Austin. All right?"

Austin kicked his feet, hemmed and hawed and
finally said, rather grudgingly, "All right."

With as much sincerity as he could muster, Joe
said, "Thank you. I appreciate your cooperation."
He stood. "Under the sheet now."

Austin turned and crawled up to the top of the
bed, then slipped beneath the sheet. Joe draped it
over him. "Should I shut the curtains again?"

"Yeah. Moonlight is for—"

"Sissies. I know." Despite himself, Joe chuckled.
"You do what you want to do, but I intend to leave
my drapes open. I like looking at the stars when I
go to sleep. And don't you dare call me a sissy."

"I wouldn't." Silence, then, "I reckon I like lookin' at the stars, too."

"Then we'll leave them open." He ruffled Austin's shaggy hair. "Good night."

"Night, Joe."

Joe was still grinning a few minutes later when he sank into his own bed. Naked except for his boxers, he propped his arms behind his head and did, in fact, look out at the stars. He had a lot to think about, so much, in fact, he barely noticed the thin, lumpy mattress or the way his ankles hung over the foot of the bed.

With all that he'd overheard from Luna, things had just gotten doubly complicated. Her words left him a little confused, and that didn't sit well with him at all. Confusion led to indecision—something he'd never before allowed.

Because of the jobs he'd held, the way he lived on the edge, he'd always been forced to snap judgments. Shoot or be shot at, take a dangerous case for money or find a simpler one. Fight, or walk away.

He trusted his own instincts, so that method of deciding things had naturally carried over into his private life. Anytime he saw a woman he wanted, he either took her to his bed so they could both have a little fun or he'd recognize her need to nest and walk away from her before things got complicated—as they were now.

Snap decisions . . . But he'd stood behind them all. He'd made the decision to have Luna almost from the first moment he'd seen her, but hell, who could have predicted all this? Now he had to re-think things, and he damn well didn't want to. He wanted to go upstairs and crawl into bed with her and love her silly, until she forgot her reservations and that nonsense about him being a heart-breaker.

Disgusted, Joe sighed and closed his eyes. At least he'd gotten Austin to stay in his bed.

Or so he thought.

Chapter Nine

Only half awake, Luna stood at the sink pouring herself a cup of freshly perked coffee when Joe's door opened. Still bleary-eyed, she glanced up, and slowly, her gaze focused on him leaning in the door frame. She wouldn't have minded seeing him like that every day for the rest of her life.

The cup of coffee held suspended in her hand, she took in his mussed, inky black hair, his sleep-heavy blue eyes, and the very dark shadowing of beard stubble on his austere face. His chest was bare, and as she watched, Joe idly dragged a hand over his wide, sleek shoulder to his flat, hard stomach, rubbing a little, scratching a little—*turning her on.*

Around a deep yawn, he asked, "What time is it?"

Her vision blurred even more, and she clutched the countertop for support. Joe wore only his boxers, and she hadn't yet gotten used to seeing him like that. She doubted she'd ever get used to it. He was just so . . . male. So incredibly macho.

"Almost ten." Luna lifted the much-needed coffee to her mouth and gulped, burning her tongue in the process.

Talking with Willow last night had only succeeded in bringing her feelings for Joe to the fore. She'd thought about him and ached in so many ways, sleep had been impossible. He was by far the most appealing man she'd ever met, yet he never intended to get seriously involved with her, much less with two kids.

Would she be foolish or wise to let him walk away without ever knowing how it felt to be naked with him, to have the memory of that broad, hard chest pressing down on her, to feel his mouth touch her in secret places.

To feel him inside her, as close as two people could get? Just thinking of it made her shiver in need.

Throughout the long night, she hadn't been able to find an answer. Now her head throbbed, and her eyes burned. Stupid, stupid, stupid. Shoring herself up, Luna forced herself to look at him again. "Coffee?"

Joe groaned, but the groan stopped in midrelease as she faced him fully and he gave her a sexually oriented once-over. "Damn, woman."

Confused, Luna looked down at herself. The shirt she'd slept in was now badly rumpled. The harem pants had been exchanged for shorts because of the morning heat. She didn't wear a bra, but then, Joe had seen her without a bra before. And her hair . . . Because she'd tossed and turned all night, it had gotten horribly tangled, and she probably resembled a deranged witch.

She held the coffee cup with one hand and touched her hair with the other. "I needed the coffee so bad, I didn't take time to . . ." Her words trailed off as a fire lit behind Joe's eyes. He started toward her with sensual purpose. Uh oh. He didn't look half asleep now.

"Joe," she protested, but the protest sounded weak even to her.

"I'm not at my sharpest in the mornings," he told her in a low voice, "or I might have been able to deal with this. But I went to sleep last night thinking about you." His hands slid to her waist, then around her, one going up her back to her nape, the other dipping low, just above her rear. "About this. Hell, I woke up wanting you, and now here you are, looking so damned sexy and soft and sweet." That last word was growled, just before his mouth nuzzled into her throat. He eased her closer, and she felt his erection against her belly through the barriers of boxers and her tee.

Feeling wobbly, Luna quickly set the coffee on the counter and braced her hands against his wide, hard shoulders. She didn't push him away. The feel of his sleek, hot flesh intoxicated her. Her fingers curled inward, leaving indents in the thick muscles.

Joe grunted, in pleasure, in pain. "I can't take much more of this, babe." He kissed her throat, the top of her shoulder. His warm breath fanned sensitive nerve endings, making her tingle. His whiskers abraded her cheek, her throat. And his hands . . . They continued to caress and entice and tease. "I don't know what's right, honey, I just know I have to have you."

Luna shook her head, not in denial but in confusion. She stroked his chest, enthralled by the silky, crisp hair there. "Joe . . ."

"Tell me you want me, too." He nipped her bottom lip. "Tell me."

Her eyes started to drift shut again. Having him do this now, on the morning after she'd struggled so much, put her at a disadvantage. "I do."

The breath left her when his thick arms tightened in reaction, and then his mouth closed on hers. He tasted morning warm and musky, his breath coming fast, his touch almost urgent. One wide hand opened on her bottom, lifting her to her tiptoes. He ground her against his erection. Their breathing became choppy, urgent.

"Oh, gross."

Joe released her so fast, Luna almost fell. Almost as one, their heads jerked around and they stared at Austin as he opened the refrigerator and started to pull out a two liter of cola. His blond hair stood on end and his shorts were so loose, they were about ready to fall off of him.

Other than his initial comment, he paid them no mind at all.

Joe said, "Uh . . ."

Luna looked from Austin, who went to the cabinet for a glass, to Joe—who had an erection. Her eyes nearly fell out of her head, and she shoved him hard. *"Joe,"* she hissed in a frantic whisper. "Go get dressed."

He turned to her, his face comically blank—until he heard Willow coming down the stairs. Then he moved faster than she'd ever seen a man his size move. His door closed with a thud.

In a semi state of shock, Luna stood there for two seconds before the hilarity hit her, and she burst out laughing. Austin looked at her, rolled his eyes, and she laughed even harder. She had to hold her sides to keep upright. It was a safe bet that Joe had never had a nine-year-old boy interrupt his seduction. He'd looked so stupefied, so utterly lost as to what to do. She snickered again.

Willow walked in, saw Austin with the cola, and made a beeline for him. "What's so funny?" she asked Luna even as she snatched the tall glass from her brother's hand before he could get a drink.

Austin made a face. "Joe was smoochin' up Luna and then he ran off."

Willow gave Luna a woman-to-woman look and smiled. "Is that right?" She set the glass in the sink.

Austin said, "Hey! Give that back."

"No Coke for breakfast, Austin. You know better."

Luna peered at Willow. No Coke for breakfast? Why not? Was this one of those motherly rules that no one had ever told her about? Austin reached for the glass in the sink, and Willow smacked his hand.

Luna pulled herself together. She was supposed to be the guardian; she was supposed to relieve Willow of some of her burden. "Austin, Austin, Austin," she chided as she crossed the floor to them, trying to sound as though she knew what she was talking about. "Willow's absolutely right. Coke for breakfast won't work. Why don't you drink some juice?"

"We don't have any." Then he thought to add, "Patricia didn't care what I drank."

Luna really didn't either. In fact, a cold Coke sounded good. But . . . "I'm not Patricia. Milk?"

"I hate milk."

Willow poured him milk anyway. "Drink it."

"No. It's gross." Then, looking sly, he said, "Almost as gross as seeing Joe slobber on Luna's face."

Willow shoved him. "Stop being so obnoxious, you little rodent."

An argument ensued, leaving Luna lost. This situation was as new for her as it was for Joe. She needed time to wake up in the morning, time to gather herself. Instead, she was faced with a fast-growing battle of insults and shoves and spilt milk.

She looked from one child to the next, but all she could really see was the horrified expression on Joe's face. She started snickering again.

From in his room, Joe called out, "It's not that damn funny."

Austin paused in his argument with his sister to yell to Joe in a gleeful, singsong voice, "You're bein' disrespectful again."

Luna heard Joe's growl and struggled to get her chuckles under control. She turned to both kids, hoping to end the conflict before they came to blows. "How about pancakes?" she asked over their traded insults.

They paused and eyed her. Austin wore his patented expression of skepticism. "You're going to cook for us?"

"Breakfast?" Willow clarified.

Luna rolled her eyes. Did she look too incompetent to handle it? "Yes, it's this greatly honored American pastime. Pancakes, and maybe some bacon." Thoughtfully, more to herself than the kids, she murmured, "I think I saw bacon in the refrigerator."

Austin went very still. For a boy who'd just been calling his sister atrocious names, he somehow looked very sweet, and heartbreakingly vulnerable. "Mom used to cook us pancakes every Sunday."

Nodding, Willow added, "And even sometimes during the week, instead of cereal." Her voice was soft, nostalgic. "Patricia didn't like to cook much, especially not early."

The mood in the room had just changed, leaving Luna at a loss. The kids were subdued, maybe even a little sad. She couldn't bear it. "Well, I like cooking, but only if I have hungry people to feed."

Joe yelled out, "*I'm* hungry," making Luna chuckle again.

Willow stared at her a moment more, then moved to the refrigerator. She opened it, rummaged around and finally pulled out a package. "Yes, we have bacon."

"Great. Then how about I get cooking?"

Austin sized her up. "Can I have Coke with my pancakes?"

Both Luna and Willow said, "No."

Austin turned his cannon on his sister again. "You ain't my boss."

"Aren't your boss," Luna corrected, then frowned at herself in confusion. God help her, she was starting to sound like a mother. Mostly under her breath, she mumbled, "At least, say it right."

"What?"

Luna gave up. "Wait here. I'll get the food going in just a minute." She went to Joe's door and opened it the smallest bit. Joe was pacing. He wore jeans now and had his arms up, his hands locked behind his head. His hair was even more mussed, his movements hard, rigid. He looked to be in pain.

Luna took a moment to appreciate the sight of him, the way his enormous biceps bunched in that position, how his wide chest expanded with each deep breath. With the dark, silkier hair under his arms visible, he looked more masculine, more macho than ever.

She sighed and stepped in, pulling the door shut behind her. "You okay?"

Pausing, Joe glared at her. He nodded down at a still impressive erection pressing at the front of his jeans and gave her a what-do-you-think look.

Luna smiled. "I'm sorry."

"You do not look one damn bit sorry, Luna, so don't patronize me." His chest expanded, and once again, he took a visual survey of her body. "God Almighty. You being in here isn't helping, babe."

It made no sense to Luna. She had to look a wreck with her wild hair and lack of makeup and sloppy clothes.

As if he'd read her mind, he said, "You look like a woman who spent a sleepless night in bed."

She nodded. "I did."

Joe swallowed. "Me, too."

Shaking herself, Luna tried to smooth her hair. "I've got terrible bed head."

Several seconds passed, then Joe dropped his arms and drew a deep breath. He tugged at his ear, pressing the small earring there. "Since I suppose we're going to find ourselves in this situation more than once, I'll promise to ignore your hair if you'll ignore my morning wood."

She slanted a look at his lap. "I don't know. That's pretty hard to ignore."

"Don't." He squeezed his eyes shut. "If you talk about it, it'll come back."

Laughing, Luna back-stepped for the door. "All right. I'll give you five more minutes to do . . . whatever you do in the morning, then you can join us in the kitchen."

He glanced at her face, noting the touch of

whisker burn, thanks to him. "Make it ten, and I'll shave."

"Deal."

Luna reentered the kitchen to find both kids sitting like silent angels at the table. She paused. "What's this?"

Austin fidgeted in his seat. "Want me to set the table or somethin'?"

"I can help cook," Willow offered. "Or we could just have cereal like we usually do so you won't have to bother."

Luna looked from one solemn, sincere face to the next. "All right." She put her hands on her hips and tapped one bare foot. "What's going on?"

Willow shrugged. "Nothing."

But Austin wasn't one to remain quiet for long. "Willow said you and Joe were arguing cuz of us and we don't want you to get mad and go away so we promise to be good and help out around the place and I won't even drink Coke in the morning or make faces when you and Joe are smooching or argue with Willow—if she doesn't try to tell me what to do—and I won't sneak out at night anymore." He drew a long, starved breath after all that.

Luna stared. "That was a pretty impressive speech, Austin."

He beamed.

"But I'm not going anywhere." Absently, she replayed Austin's whole diatribe through her mind. Her eyes widened. "Sneak out at night? What in the world are you talking about?"

Willow scowled and reached over to punch her brother in the arm. He winced, and his face scrunched up as he concentrated on not rubbing it.

Luna felt like pulling out her hair. "Willow, please don't hit your brother."

"He's got a big mouth."

"He's nine years old, honey. He says what's on his mind, and that's good. But, Austin, what's this about sneaking out?"

Joe's door opened, and he walked into the kitchen, a little stiff legged and still wearing his whiskers. "I was going to talk to you about that."

While Joe poured himself a cup of coffee, Luna waited. "Tell me about what?"

He sat beside Austin. "Houdini's antics."

"Who's Houdini?" Austin asked.

"Someone who was better at escaping than you," Willow informed him, which prompted Austin to stick his tongue out at her.

"Joe, what's going on?"

Joe stretched out his legs, took his time sipping his coffee, then sighed. "I caught Austin trying to slip out of his room last night."

"To go where?"

Joe raised a brow at Austin, who flushed, looked down at the table and mumbled, "Just out."

"He goes to the lake," Willow told them. "When I hear him, I follow him. But he's good at being quiet."

"Not good enough," Joe told her. "I caught him three times last night."

The monumental task ahead of her finally sunk in. Luna swallowed, looked at both kids, and wondered how in the world she'd ever handle them. She knew nothing of children, of what motivated them or how they thought. And these two weren't your everyday carefree kids. She stared at Austin, trying to think what to say to reach him.

His small shoulders stiffened and his face colored, not with embarrassment but with determination. Luna knew she had to do or say something, right now.

"Austin—"

He twisted toward Joe and pointed an accusing finger. "He was listenin' in on you and Willow last night."

That drew Luna up. Swamped in confusion, she looked to Joe. "What?"

Austin inhaled to continue, but Joe held up a hand, silencing him. His gaze locked on Luna's like a laser, watchful, intent, as if he somehow wanted to convey some silent message to her. "I heard Austin moving around last night and went up to investigate." He searched her face, and his brows drew down in an expression of conviction. "You were in Willow's room chatting. I didn't want to interrupt, so I didn't announce myself."

"He listened!"

Words, images, flashed through Luna's mind. Her chest tightened, and mortified heat rushed to her face.

"I did," Joe confirmed, still watching her too closely. "First, because I was worried about Willow. Then I found Austin and I put him back to bed, only he didn't stay there. I ended up putting him back to bed a few more times. This morning, I think he should be punished."

Deflated, a little desperate to redirect the attention, Austin turned to Luna. "Aren't you mad that Joe was listenin' in?"

Luna felt stiff. Mad? She was humiliated, wounded. He'd heard all her nonsense about him being a heartbreaker. Oh, God. She couldn't even remember all the awful things she'd confided in her efforts to share with Willow and to get her to open up in return.

Her face burned with the memory of it. But with both children peering at her and Joe gauging her every reaction, she swallowed her hurt and addressed the most important problem. "Even if I was mad at him, Austin, that wouldn't change what you did. After I've gone to bed, you can't leave the house for any reason."

"But I—" A knock sounded on the front door. Both children jumped, turning to each other as if expecting the hounds of hell to enter.

Joe took in their curious reactions. "I'll get it."

"I'm going to my room," Austin blurted and started to push back his chair.

"You," Joe told him, "are staying put until we're done discussing this."

Austin slowly sank back into his seat. His eyes were huge and fretful, and Luna couldn't bear it. Was he that worried about being punished? She moved behind him and put her hands on his shoulders. "It'll be all right, Austin. We'll figure everything out."

But a minute later when Joe came into the kitchen with a deputy, she had her doubts.

"Coffee?" Joe offered the man.

"Thanks." He held out a broad, work-rough hand to Luna. "Deputy Scott Royal, ma'am. I'm sorry to disturb your morning."

"Deputy." Luna shook his hand—and noticed how he gave each child a familiar, censuring glance. "I'm Luna Clark."

"The new guardian, I know, Joe explained already. Nice to meet you, Ms. Clark."

"Please call me Luna." She gestured at the table. "Make yourself comfortable, Deputy."

Joe handed Scott his coffee. "Luna, you remember me telling you that I knew some of the law officers in Welcome County? Well, Scott's the one who invited me back to visit after I returned their guy."

Scott pulled out a chair and sat. He removed his hat and put it on his knee. Luna liked him on sight. He had sandy brown hair, gentle blue eyes, and a quirky smile. "We were this close," Scott said, holding up his finger and thumb to indicate less than an inch, "to catching that rascal a dozen times, but he always slipped away from us. I'd about given up hope, when one day Joe calls and says, 'Hey, you guys missing someone down there?' He was so cavalier about it, I almost didn't believe him at first."

Austin stared wide-eyed at Joe. "You caught a criminal?"

Scott nodded. "He caught a bunch of them. Joe's one of the best bounty hunters in the country."

"Not anymore," Joe corrected. "I gave it up."

It was Luna's turn to blink. "I knew he'd been a bounty hunter, but I didn't know . . ."

"That he was so good? Yes, ma'am. Damn good. Had a reputation a mile long, both with the law and with the criminals, though I dare say they didn't share the same sentiments about him."

Austin opened his mouth to reprimand the deputy on swearing, but Joe said, *"Austin,"* and he relented, slumping down in his seat.

Scott turned to the boy. "So, Joe tells me you were in all night last night."

"Yeah." Austin said it cautiously, as if unwilling to commit himself until he knew why Scott had asked.

"That's a good thing, Austin, since I have a few people complaining that you vandalized their property last night."

Austin perked right up. "I didn't! Joe wouldn't let me leave. I tried, but he kept sneakin' up on me and grumbling and making me go back to bed." He turned excitedly to Joe. "Ain't that right?"

Scott almost laughed, but he pulled together a frown instead. "Glad to hear it. If I'd caught you again, I'm afraid I'd have had to haul you in."

Again? Now Luna understood why the kids had looked so alarmed by the early morning caller. Was a visit from the local deputy routine? Luna felt sicker by the moment. "What happened?"

Scott pulled out his notes. "A lot of stuff. Flowerbeds trampled, car windows broken, dog doo-doo on the front steps." He slanted his gaze on Austin. "All the earmarks of an Austin operation."

"Wasn't me."

Scott closed his notes. "Because I've caught you myself a few times, Austin, I'm afraid I wouldn't be able to take your word for it. That's the bad thing about getting into trouble. Once you do it, it's tough to prove you're not doing it again. But I know Joe, and I do trust him. He tells me you were in bed, so I believe him."

Austin seemed to go boneless in relief. Watching him, Joe reached over and put a big hand on his shoulder.

But Willow's voice was cold when she spoke. "Like you said, Deputy Royal. It had all the earmarks of an Austin operation."

Scott nodded. "I'm afraid so."

"That means someone was trying to make it look like Austin did it."

Luna hadn't considered that, but she saw that both Joe and Scott had already come to that conclusion.

"It's possible," Scott said. "But those things are typical pranks that we see from time to time."

Joe glanced meaningfully at Luna. She knew he wanted to pass some silent message, but she didn't quite understand. He cleared his throat. "I think I'll put up some motion lights and detectors, maybe a security camera, and the house definitely needs new locks."

"Not a bad idea." Scott sipped his coffee while looking at each person in turn. "It'll ensure that everyone stays in who should stay in, and everyone stays out who should stay out, so you can get a little sleep." He raised his coffee cup to Joe in a salute. "I don't mind telling you, you look like hell."

Joe laughed. "Yeah, no kidding. It's been a rough couple of weeks."

"Maybe we can get together one night and you can tell me about it." Scott propped both elbows on the table and leaned forward. "But first I have to go pacify a bunch of people who were more than ready to let Austin pay for repairs. They won't be happy to know he didn't do it. That's if I can convince them."

"I'm sure they'll want the real culprit caught," Luna insisted, feeling sorry for Austin with his long face.

Scott looked skeptical over that, but only shrugged. "You'll need to drive into the city to get the stuff you need. I can give you the address of a good place. It's two hours away, but worth the trip."

"Thanks."

"The rest of you should be more careful, just in case it was a setup. And, Austin, I hope you see how serious this is. If you hadn't had Joe for an alibi, you'd be in the back of my car right now."

Luna wasn't certain if that was true or if Scott only wanted to impress upon Austin the importance of staying in at night. Because he *did* look impressed, she could have kissed the deputy's feet for his well-timed intervention. "Thank you, Deputy."

"Call me Scott. Any friend of Joe's and all that." He finished off his coffee and stood to leave.

With another long, meaningful look, Joe gave Luna's hand a squeeze, then walked Scott to the door. The children were subdued in his absence, and that bothered Luna. She was faced with the monumental task of reprimanding Austin for his own good and reassuring him at the same time.

She put the bacon in the frying pan, all the while thinking. Finally she leaned back against the counter and considered him. "Why do you leave the house, Austin?"

His head dropped forward, and she heard the shrug in his tone. "Just to walk and think about stuff."

Luna recalled being nine once herself, and like Austin, she'd taken walks to think. Her parents were forever arguing, saying vicious, cruel things to each other. Getting away from them had made her feel better.

She'd go around the block to an empty baseball field, and she'd circle it, taking her time, feeling the sun on her back, the dust in her face. She didn't think about her problems when she took her long walks. Instead, she tried to imagine what a normal, happy family might be like.

Could it be the same for Austin? While she had enjoyed the sun, perhaps he enjoyed the moon. Luna broke three eggs atop the pancake mixture, added some milk, and offered impulsively, "You know, Austin, if you ever feel that way, maybe you could wake me up and we could walk together?"

Joe stepped back into the room. "No one is walking outside at night."

Luna rolled her eyes. "Of course not. I would never risk Austin that way."

"Then take your walks during the day."

Joe's autocratic tone had her bristling. "Austin doesn't want to walk during the day, now does he?"

Austin said, "No. I like it at night."

Hands on his hips, Joe stared down at Austin. "Why?"

"It's quiet. Everyone else is asleep. There ain't anyone to yell at me."

It was an amazing thing to watch Joe Winston soften. Luna smiled. "Joe's right that it isn't safe to be outside at night. Especially not right now while someone is pulling pranks. But maybe we could just walk around the house. We could talk and I could keep you company. Or if you want, I could just be quiet and you wouldn't even know I was there. What do you think?"

Austin's brown eyes regarded her for several heartbeats. "Yeah. Maybe."

There was that suspicion again. Luna knew it'd take time for him to trust her, to relax with her. But when she thought of all he'd been through, it hurt and made her impatient to help put his worries behind him. "Great. Then that's what we'll do."

Willow propped her elbows on the table. "So you used to be a bounty hunter?"

With both kids watching, Joe casually kissed the side of Luna's neck. She stiffened, but he patted her back, whispered, "It'll be all right," and then went to the table. "I gave it up a year or so ago."

"How come?"

"Lots of reasons, but mostly because I got tired of traveling so much. Bounty hunters run anywhere from five to fifteen cases at a time, which meant I was always on the road."

"Tracking?" Austin asked with wide eyes.

"That's right. And when you're working, you don't have any set hours. Because you can't turn your phone or pager off, you get calls—tips—in the middle of the night. When a tip is good, you follow up on it, even if that means crawling out of bed after only two hours of sleep. I got to where I wanted some personal time to myself. So I quit."

Luna poured perfect circles of batter onto a hot griddle while listening. So Joe wanted personal time? Alone? And here she'd dragged him to Visitation with her, right into the middle of two troubled kids and mass chaos. Worse, he was still injured and not up to snuff. She'd been incredibly selfish, and it made her stomach churn.

"What do you do now?" Willow asked.

"I was acting as a bodyguard. Luckily I'd finished a job before I got beat up, and then your cousin showed up at my door and invited me along to meet you two, so here I am, hanging out in Visitation."

"Do bodyguards carry guns?" Austin asked.

"They do. But only to protect the person they're working for. I'm good with my hands," Joe bragged, holding them up and flexing his fingers. His fists were enormous, his arms bulging with strength. Austin's eyes widened even more.

"Make a muscle," Austin insisted, and Joe, with a grin, did just that. Austin used both hands and still couldn't encircle Joe's biceps. "Wow."

Luna's reaction was different, more feminine. She remembered how Joe had tackled that intruder in his apartment, the ease with which he'd gained the upper hand, and she sighed in awe. Joe Winston was all superior male, and as a woman, she couldn't remain immune to him.

"Strong and in shape is important," Joe said, "because whenever possible, I use nonlethal force."

"Meaning you don't shoot people?"

"Meaning I don't even like to hurt people if I can help it. Other times . . . ." He shrugged. "My last case was to protect a young woman who was turning evidence on her husband."

Willow tipped her head. "Turning evidence. What does that mean?"

"It means her husband was a really bad man who mistreated her and other people." Luna heard a distinct edge in Joe's tone now. She glanced at him—and found him watching her with too much intensity.

"In order to put him in jail, she had to testify in court against him. He didn't want her to do that, so he tried to intimidate her."

Willow leaned forward, engrossed in the story. "How?"

"By threatening her, intimidating her physically. Hurting her." Joe's voice roughened. He gave his attention back to the kids, releasing Luna. "He tried to sneak into her house one night." Joe paused, flexing his knuckles, building the expectation. And then, with satisfaction, "I caught him."

Austin blinked in awe, and his voice lowered to a reverent whisper. "What did you do?"

Luna was rather curious about that herself. She forgot the breakfast long enough to turn and listen.

Joe bared his teeth in that familiar, triumphant smile, but she knew his reply was censored for the kids. "I . . . *detained* him until the cops showed up."

Willow snorted. "What'd you do to him?"

"In my mind, he was about the lowest scum imaginable. He liked to hurt anyone smaller than him, including women."

"I bet you were bigger than him, huh?"

Not averse to bragging, Joe said, "A lot bigger. I trussed him up in handcuffs, leg irons and a belly chain." Before the questions could commence, Joe explained that a belly chain connected the restraints between hands and feet. "All he could really do was flop around on the floor and whine. I gave him to the cops that way. They locked him up. After that the trial went smooth and he got eight years in jail."

"Wow."

Joe laughed. "Now, if you want to hear about an interesting job, you should talk to Luna. Do you know what she does for a living?"

Both kids shook their heads.

Grinning, Joe leaned back in his chair and put his arms behind his head. Prominent muscles swelled and bunched, making Luna sigh again. No man should be so mouth-watering in so many ways.

"Well, kids, let me tell you about Luna, Goddess of the Moon." He sent Luna a wink and said in a ridiculously theatrical voice accompanied by wiggling fingers, "Luna knows all, sees all."

Luna hadn't seen this, she thought, amused at Joe's antics and amazed at the ease with which he dealt with the kids. She'd known that he'd be better with them than she was, if for no other reason than that he had more experience dealing with children because of his extended family.

But she hadn't counted on Joe being so comfortable in the role or apparently enjoying it so much. For a confirmed bachelor, for a bounty hunter extraordinaire and bodyguard badass, he'd taken right to the company of children.

If a woman didn't know better, she might think Joe Winston enjoyed playing house. She might even be led to think he would enjoy playing husband to a loony ex-assistant and father to two needy children.

Luna did know better, though.

Feeling touched, she listened with only half an ear as Joe entertained Austin and Willow with stories of where she used to work at a popular psychic shop. He included tales of his outrageous cousin Zane and his gypsy wife, Tamara, who owned the shop. With Austin and Willow hanging on his every word, he expounded on some of the more colorful characters that frequented the shop. He shared stories of Tamara's relatives, who all claimed to be free spirits.

Both kids were again filled with endless questions, so over pancakes and bacon, Luna read palms, explained about astrology, and shared some trade secrets to the psychic business. Despite the rocky start to the morning, the meal was fun and filled with camaraderie.

They were just finishing up when Austin surprised her by asking, "Are you like Jamie?"

Joe stiffened. "You know Jamie Creed?"

"Of course we do. He visits sometimes," Willow explained. "Patricia liked him and always tried to get him to stay, like some of the other men would."

A frown of concern passed between Joe and Luna.

"But Jamie would only stop in every now and then, and he never stayed long." Willow bit her lip, undecided about something, then shrugged. "You should probably know something, Luna."

Now that sounded serious. Luna tilted her head at Willow, encouraging her. "And what's that?"

"Jamie . . . Well, he's the one who told me to call you."

Chapter Ten

Luna dropped her fork. "But . . . I don't know him."

"Jamie knows everyone." Austin nodded hard when both Joe and Luna stared at him in disbelief. "He does. And everyone around here knows Jamie. Some of the people are afraid of him cuz he's so quiet and he doesn't act like everyone else."

"But most like him." Willow grinned toward Joe. "The guys are sometimes jealous because the women all get moony-eyed over him. I've heard Patricia say that he's so mysterious and quiet he gives her chills."

Joe scowled at Luna as if he'd just caught *her* being moony-eyed.

"He's an interesting man," Luna said with as much detachment as she could muster, given the fact she found Jamie more than merely interesting.

"He came here one day when Patricia was talking to Mr. Owen. Patricia sent us out to the lake so we wouldn't bother her, she said. We'd taken the canoe and were just rowing around, looking for turtles and stuff, and then suddenly Jamie was there, standing on the shore. When we came in, he crouched down on the dock to talk real quietlike to us. He told me that Patricia would leave soon, but I shouldn't worry. I should just call my mother's cousin. I didn't know who he meant, but he told me that if I started calling relatives, someone would remember a name."

Austin nodded. "And sure 'nuff, Patricia told us she was leavin'. She said we'd have to move away, to a foster home or something because she couldn't stay here anymore."

"She said it'd be best for us, because the town doesn't like us." Willow looked down at her hands. "It wasn't easy to not be upset. Especially since Austin was really scared."

"Was not!"

"But I did what Jamie told me to do. I called everyone I could think of to ask them if they'd want to come here and live. No one did." She drew a deep breath and looked back up at Luna. Her eyes were big and sad and far too serious, making Luna's throat tight with emotion. "They kept giving me numbers of other family members, and finally someone mentioned you and . . . Here you are, just as Jamie said."

Luna wasn't a weepy woman. She was strong and decisive, and she prided herself on living life to her own specifications. Much like Tamara's relatives, she considered herself a free spirit. She liked to tease and laugh, and she didn't believe in wasting time on things she couldn't change.

Despite all that, she had a hell of a time swallowing down her tears. If only she had come to Austin and Willow sooner. If only they'd been spared . . .

She jumped when Joe laced his fingers through

Austin glanced at Luna, shrugged, and said, "I guess so."

Joe crouched down in front of him. "It's okay to be cautious. I'm a cautious sort myself. In time, you'll trust Luna, just like I trust her. But until then, it'd sure make things easier on everyone if we didn't give Deputy Royal any reason to call other than a friendly visit. Agreed?"

"Yeah."

"So will you give me your word that you won't leave the house without our permission?"

Finally he nodded. "I promise."

"Great." Joe straightened. "I'm going to shower and get ready to go. Maybe later on today we can go for another swim?"

Austin brightened like a Christmas light. "I can show you how to get mussels off the bottom of the lake."

"Really? I can hardly wait."

Luna's heart swelled. "Kids, go on upstairs and get washed up and dressed. We've got some work to do today."

They went off with smiles and a lighter step, filling Luna with hope that maybe, with time, things would work out.

Joe caught Luna's hand and brought her around him. "Mad at me?"

"For what?"

"Eavesdropping."

Oh, shoot, she was, but she'd forgotten about it the middle of the other confusion. "You shouldn't listened in, Joe."

hand curved around her nape beneath her he felt his warm, hard fingers stroking, and ombined with the interest in his heated gaze, er tingle.

hers and held her hand tight. He teased her about being a psychic, yet at that moment, he was the one reading minds to know that she needed his touch so much.

Luna drew strength from his touch, enough to keep her voice steady. "You don't know for sure that Jamie meant me."

"He did." Austin nodded. "Jamie knows everyone."

"He said you'd be here, and you are." Willow sounded very philosophical about it.

Deciding the kids wouldn't be swayed otherwise, Luna broached a new topic. "You said Patricia had men over?"

"She flirted with everyone. I think she liked every man she met."

"She was always slobbering on them," Austin interjected with exaggerated disgust. "Like Joe was slobbering on you."

"I do not slobber," Joe said.

He sounded so indignant, Luna laughed.

Willow nearly shoved her little brother off his chair. He quickly righted himself, and Willow, while casting glares at Austin, continued. "I guess most of them liked her, too, because they came back often enough. But not Jamie."

"And not Deputy Royal." Austin made a face. "I saw Patricia licking his ear once, but he pushed her away. She was real mad about that."

Joe narrowed his eyes. "What about Quincy Owen? Did Patricia ever kiss him?"

Luna gulped. Owen was obviously married, but perhaps that wouldn't have mattered to a woman like Patricia.

With the mention of Clay Owen's father, Willow clammed up. Austin eyed his sister, shrugged without much sympathy, and picked up the verbal ball. "He visits here lots. Sometimes just to complain about me or Willow, but sometimes he's here when we haven't done anything. I haven't seen them smoochin', but probably they have. Patricia smooches on everyone."

Willow heaved a breath. "And when Patricia wasn't mauling a man, Dinah was."

Joe rubbed his chin. "Interesting."

"No, it's gross."

Pulled from his ruminations, Joe surveyed Austin. "So, Luna, what do you think should be Austin's punishment for not staying in his bed last night?"

Austin drew up, both afraid and defiant.

Willow slid out of her chair to stand beside her brother. Seconds ago she'd been shoving him out of his chair, but now she put one hand on his shoulder, providing a united front.

They amazed her. They'd been emotionally neglected yet were still so loyal to each other. To her mind, that said a lot about her cousin Chloe and the loving job she'd done raising them before her death.

Luna watched Austin while speaking to Joe. "I think maybe Deputy Royal's visit might have helped Austin to see the error of his ways. If he's out at night and more vandalism happens . . . Well, as Scott said, Austin might be a prime suspect, even if he's innocent. But, Joe, you're the one who has experience dealing with criminals. What do you think?"

Austin turned such a woeful look on Joe, Luna knew he wouldn't be able to resist it. Big and tough as Joe might be, he wasn't immune to a little boy's silent plea—and that only made him more loveable in her mind.

Joe put on a stern expression. "I think a man is only as good as his word. If Austin tells me he won't do any more sneaking around, I'm willing to give him the benefit of the doubt. Austin?"

He ducked his head, silent and withdrawn.

Tilting up his chin, Joe made him look at him. "Austin, you don't ever, for any reason, have to be afraid of me or Luna, okay?"

"You were gonna punish me."

"Yeah, that means maybe doing yard work or being grounded in your room." Austin seemed confused by that. "What did you think we'd do?"

"Send me away. Or maybe give me to Deputy Royal."

Luna's heart hit her feet. "Oh, Austin, honey, no. I will never send you away, I swear."

Austin puckered up even more. Joe sighed. "Well, in the first place, Deputy Royal doesn't want the likes of you. He'd have to be forever checking his seat for dog dung."

Austin's mouth quirked at that, but he re-mained silent.

"He only takes criminals, and as Luna s? know all about them, so I can safely say you one."

Austin peered up at Joe, still a little dish

"Scott likes you. Willow, too. When about Clay and the other boys, he pr keep an eye out for you, to make s don't bother you or Willow again."

"He did?"

"Of course he did. Scott is a k means he dislikes bullies as muc

Luna slipped her arm arou do you understand that I'm h care about you?"

He brought her mouth up close to his. "If I say I'm sorry, will it help?"

"Maybe." She was already half breathless and he hadn't even kissed her yet. "If you promise not to do it again."

A wry smile tilted his sexy mouth. "No can do. It seems the only way I can figure you out is to listen in on private conversations." His voice lowered and he touched his mouth to hers. "I would never deliberately hurt you, honey."

Her face burned. Damn him, she wanted to push him away, but she could feel his heavy heartbeat against her breasts and feel the gentleness of his hold. "Hurt is hurt, Joe, doesn't matter if it's deliberate or not."

His hand slid from her nape to her chin, and his thumb kept her face still for a brief, melting kiss. "Maybe," he whispered against her lips, "I'll surprise you."

Luna thought of how he'd dealt with Willow and Austin, and she gave a groan of acceptance. "You already have."

"Yeah?" He tilted back to smile at her in satisfaction. "Well, that's a good thing, right?"

"No." Luna slowly disengaged herself from his arms. "That's not a good thing at all. You're confusing me and I don't like it."

"What does that mean?"

"Give me time, Joe, okay?" While Joe frowned at her in confusion, she stepped around him, hoping to put some space between them. Not that it would do her much good, because she was already in too deep.

Regardless of the dictates of common sense, she'd done something very stupid.

She'd fallen in love with Joe Winston.

* * *

Joe waited until he was in his truck driving away from the house, then he flipped out his cell phone and dialed his sister.

On the third ring, Alyx answered, sounding sleepy and grouchy. "What?"

Joe shook his head. "Hell, Alyx, it's going on noon and you're still in bed?"

"Joe? 'Bout time you called. Mom's been worried."

"And you haven't been? I'm wounded."

Joe heard the creaking of bedsprings, some rustling, then a yawn. "Yeah, wounded in the head." She snickered at her own joke. "So how's it going? You all settled in?"

"Getting there. You got a pen and paper handy?" He gave her the phone number for the house, just in case of an emergency. For most calls, she'd use his cell phone number.

After she'd scribbled down his number, grumbling that she wasn't awake enough to see straight, she asked, "Is your *wife* still with you?"

Alyx would wear that joke out before she quit, Joe knew. Refusing to let her bait him, he said simply, "Of course she is. This is her family, remember, not mine."

"Hey, you didn't object to the wife thing. Strange. I expected you to be tired of her already. This must be a personal record for you, huh?"

"Brat. I'd swat you if you were close."

"Ha. You'd *try*."

Joe grinned. They sounded almost like Willow and Austin, and that amused him. Even though he knew Alyx was joking, he felt compelled to say, "Luna is different from most women."

"Yeah, how so?" A new alertness had entered Alyx's tone.

"For one thing, she doesn't trust me."

"Smart woman. I like her already."

Joe hesitated only a moment before admitting, "She doesn't really want to get involved with me either."

Alyx whistled. "Maybe you should marry her for real. She sounds special."

"Don't be a smart-ass." Joe squeezed the phone hard. "I just told you she doesn't want to get involved."

"In casual sex, right? But one has nothing to do with the other. Women rule out casual sex when they know they might fall in love with a guy. It gets too risky then."

Narrowing his eyes, Joe said, "You sound like you know an awful lot about this casual sex business."

She laughed. "I'm twenty-eight, Joe. Wise up."

Twenty-eight, beautiful, smart and stubborn. Joe had no doubt his sister could have her pick of men, but that didn't sit well with his protective instincts. "I don't want to hear this."

"Good. So let's talk about Luna." There was more rustling, and Joe assumed she'd left the bed to pace. Alyx continually paced when she thought. She had more energy than Austin, which meant she always had to be moving. "You're so smart, why don't you see what's right there? She loomed over you at your apartment, chasing off other women. I know because she tried to run me off, and that smacks of jealousy no matter what she called it. She played nurse for you, so she must care, because God knows you're a bear to be around when you're sick or hurt. And she invited you along on this little trip of hers, so obviously she does trust you, right?"

Joe held the phone away from his ear to stare at it a moment before returning it to his ear. "Damn, Alyx. I wake you out of a sound sleep and you immediately start analyzing. Amazing."

"Aren't I, though?"

Joe laughed. "Okay, so since you've got all the answers, how do I get her to quit pushing me away?"

"Duh. Ask her to marry you for real."

Joe choked, and for only a second the truck swerved. When he caught his breath again, he cursed. "Jesus, Alyx, you know I don't want to get married."

"No, you don't want to marry those vacuous and vain females you've previously dated. Luna's different, you said so yourself."

She sounded so sure about that, Joe grunted. "You don't understand."

"I understand that she's got you scrambling. That makes her okay in my book."

"I'm hanging up now." Of course, he wouldn't.

"Coward." She *knew* he wouldn't.

"Knock it off, Alyx. I'm not marriage material and you damn well know it."

"Who says so?"

Luna does. But he didn't want to admit that, not to his sister, not even to himself. "Everyone knows it," he grumbled. Hell, he'd spent his whole adult life making sure everyone knew where he stood on the issue of matrimony.

"Well, they obviously don't know you the way I do. Deep down, you're a big softie. Granted, you have to dig pretty deep . . ." When Joe growled, she laughed, then said quickly, "Okay, wait. Don't hang up yet. Talking about marriage reminds me, Mom wants to know what she should tell your other women who keep calling looking for you."

"What other women?"

"Oh, my, you do have it bad if you can't even remember them."

"Alyx . . ."

She said on a long sigh, "Mostly Amelia."

Well, hell. He thought Luna had run her off. "Amelia doesn't believe I'm married?"

Alyx snorted. "She's a leech, Joe, not an idiot. Besides, she claims you told her you'd never marry."

"Yeah, I did." Hell, he told almost every woman that. "But she was okay with it."

"You believed her? Sheesh. And here I thought you were smart." Alyx made an irritating tsking sound of disapproval. "I bet she thought she'd eventually wear you down."

"Well, now she knows different." Joe would have felt like a real heel, except he'd been straight with Amelia. Not once had he ever lied to her, and not for a second did he think she really loved him.

"Mom told her you left town. She wants to know where you went."

Joe stilled. God, all he needed was for another woman to show up . . .

"Don't worry. Mom didn't tell her—not that she knows exactly where you are anyway. But Amelia says she's worried about you because you were so beat up."

"She was with me the night it happened," Joe explained, but his mind was churning.

"Don't worry about it, Joe. I can handle her."

Joe blew out a breath. The idea of his sister playing

defender was an awesome and terrifying thought. "Don't tangle with her, Alyx. Just tell her I'm married and leave it at that."

"Do you think if you keep saying it, everyone will eventually believe it, and then you won't even have to ask Luna? You could just go on pretending—"

"I really am hanging up this time, brat."

"No, wait. I want to know how you feel. Zane said you were pulverized."

"I'm feeling better. Much better." Joe realized it was true. Hell, he'd barely winced at all this morning, except for when he'd gotten caught making his move on Luna.

The memory of that nearly brought him to a blush. Kids showed up at the damnedest times; that meant he'd have to be extra cautious. Getting Luna in his bed would be even harder than he'd first considered, because he not only had to convince her, he had to find the right time. And good timing would be scarce with two kids running around.

Alyx drew him out of that disheartening revelation. "All joking aside, I'm relieved to hear that, Joe. I don't like knowing you're hurt." Her voice hardened and became mean with conviction in an oh-too-familiar way. "It really ticks me off that anyone would dare sneak up on you like that. If I ever get my hands on the guy who did it, you can bet I'll—"

Joe had been hearing that particular tone from Alyx since she was five years old. At thirteen, he'd been unable to scuffle with the other boys when she was around, or she'd jump into the middle of it and try to defend him, never mind that they were only playing.

It had scared him then, worrying that she might get hurt. It scared him even more now. The thought of Bruno Caldwell touching his family—his baby sister—filled him with rage. It would never happen. He wouldn't let it happen.

Interrupting Alyx's awesome and unlikely threats, Joe said, "You got everything at my apartment taken care of?"

Distracted, she switched gears, taking offense that he'd even ask. "Of course I did. Why do you think I'm still in bed? Zane and I were there till late. All your important stuff has been moved in with me."

"Thanks, hon."

"You owe me. Anything else?"

"Yeah." Joe grinned, considered her reaction, then said, "I love you."

Alyx went silent. "You sure you're okay?"

Usually it was Alyx who came to Joe for advice or help, and he enjoyed doing what he could for her. But this time it felt nice to get her input. His baby sister had a pretty good head on her shoulders—when she wasn't playing his protector. "Yeah, I'm fine."

"Well, all right, then." She didn't sound entirely convinced. "Is that it?"

He started to hang up, but hesitated. "One more thing."

She gave an exaggerated sigh of impatience. "Yeah?"

Joe swallowed hard. Introspection was a real bitch. "Don't date any guys like me, okay?"

Alyx's husky, teasing laughter sounded in his ear. "I can promise you that, big brother." Then, very sweetly, "Luckily for womankind, there are no other guys like you."

She hung up, leaving Joe chagrined, but with an ear-to-ear grin on his face.

His conversation with Alyx had lasted him right through to the outskirts of the small town. He reached the sharp bend in the road, going upward and to the right this time. A little way ahead, he saw the sign for Visitation. From this side, it said, *Be Sure To Visit Visitation Again.*

He was almost to the spot where he'd first met Jamie Creed. Joe no sooner thought of the mysterious man than he saw him lounging there on the side of the road, his arms crossed over his chest, one shoulder propped against a tall boulder. Jamie looked as though he'd been waiting on Joe, which didn't make any sense at all. But nonetheless, Joe pulled the truck up beside him and stopped.

Joe was rolling down his window to speak when he realized Jamie had circled the truck to the passenger door. He opened it and slid in.

Jamie's jeans were so worn they were threadbare in the knees. His gray T-shirt hung loose but couldn't disguise a lean, hard musculature probably achieved through hard work, not a gym. His dark hair had been pulled back into a ponytail, making his beard more prominent. A shave wouldn't hurt him at all.

One brow raised, Joe stared at him. "Excuse me?"

In idle interest, Jamie gazed around the interior of the truck. "I'll ride with you. I need some more stuff from the security warehouse myself. Some tapes and special batteries and a new lens that an animal must have broken." He slipped on his seat belt and then waited.

Indignation rose. "Who says I'm going to a security warehouse?"

Jamie glanced up. "Deputy Royal."

"Oh." So he hadn't just divined it? Joe shook his

head at himself. He didn't believe in that non-sense anyway. "Why don't you drive yourself?"

"Don't have a car."

Don't have a . . . "Why the hell not?"

"Can't get it up the mountain."

Joe considered that—and came to the conclusion that Jamie Creed was certifiably weird. What grown man didn't have transportation? What grown man lived alone on a mountain? "You could order your stuff on-line."

Enigmatic black eyes surveyed him. "Then I'd be deprived of your company. And we should do some talking, don't you think?"

Knuckles flexing on the steering wheel, Joe said, "Oh, yeah, I think we should talk." He had a few prime things to say to the man, particularly where Luna was concerned.

Jamie slowly nodded. "It's a puzzle."

Giving up, Joe put the truck into drive and pulled away. "What's a puzzle?"

"All of it." He lifted the fold-down center arm-rest that Joe used as a business console. While peering at Joe's stored laptop and a few CDs, Jamie said, "You have women troubles."

Joe scowled. Damned snoopy bastard. He snapped the console shut and growled, "The hell I do." Things between him and Luna weren't perfect, but he'd work them out. Somehow, he'd get Luna in his bed, and the experience would be nothing but pleasure, not heartache. He had to believe that or he'd go nuts. If Jamie thought he could sneak in and try to usurp his relationship, he'd . . .

"No, not Luna. But there's danger, and it's all mixed up, hard to decipher." He started tinkering with the finger-touch reading lamps, turning them on and off, as if fascinated. "Unclear."

Joe drew a deep breath that didn't help worth a damn. "I may just beat the hell out of you, Jamie."

"No, you won't."

That had Joe's brow cocking and his masculinity bristling with challenge. "You don't think I can?"

Unaffected by Joe's snarling tone, Jamie shrugged. "Maybe." Then with a slanted, black-eyed perusal, "Though I'm not a slouch myself, so don't presume it'd be easy. It's just that you wouldn't hit me without a reason, and no reason exists. Ergo, no beating."

Ergo no beating, Joe mimicked in his mind. "I want you to stay away from Luna."

That appeared to amuse Jamie, though he sure as hell didn't smile. It was just something in his eyes, something condescending and indulgent. "I'm not competition."

"Damn right, you're not."

"The big question," he murmured, ignoring Joe's ire while deep in thought, "is who's following you?"

Joe's gaze automatically hit the rearview mirror, the side mirror. He didn't see another single soul on the long, empty road. "No one is, damn it." Joe was certain he'd lost the tail before entering Visitation.

Stroking his beard, Jamie stared out the windshield without appearing to see anything. "Things are muddled in my mind."

"Yeah, no kidding." Muddled minds were the trademark of every lunatic wandering loose.

Joe's sarcasm went unnoticed. "There's someone watching you. But . . ." He shook his head. "One person, two, a damn dozen. I don't know. There are angles involved, slanted perceptions . . ."

Despite his skepticism, Joe heard himself ask, "Bruno Caldwell?"

"I don't know names. One minute it's black and

sinister, toward you, toward Luna, sometimes even toward the kids." His eyes squeezed shut, showing Joe that he did, in fact, care about the kids. "I don't know. I don't like it."

In the face of so much mumbo jumbo, Joe's brain throbbed. "Just who the hell are you, Jamie Creed?"

Jamie opened his eyes, but his gaze remained shuttered. He looked distant, alone, apart from Joe and everyone else. It gave Joe chills to see such a desolate look. "I'm no one. I don't exist."

Fed up, Joe's temper snapped. "Just what the fuck is that supposed to mean?"

Jamie's head bowed, his gaze narrowed on something internal that Joe couldn't see. Voice very low and eerie, he said, "It means you're forcing me to show myself, and that's dangerous to me. But the kids . . . There's a tangled web around you, Joe Winston. I've spent years disappearing, but I'll help if I can."

Joe clenched his teeth.

"But you'll have to believe." Jamie lifted his head to pierce Joe with that portentous gaze. "And you'll have to listen."

Though he hated to, Joe finally nodded. "Yeah, what the hell. Let's hear it."

Luna stood beneath Joe, steadying the ladder. "That's all he said?"

"He said a lot of insane junk that made me want to smash my fist in his face. But damn it . . ." Joe tightened the last screw on the PIR camera. "Jamie sounded so positive, he spooked me. I don't trust him at all, but I do trust my instincts, and they tell me something is going on. Maybe Jamie's even in on it, and playing some deep game by tipping me off."

The PIR, or passive infrared detector, hid a high-resolution black-and-white video camera. When it sensed motion, it would start a time-lapse VCR. It would be turned on at night, or whenever they were away from the house.

Luna assumed Joe had spent a great deal of money on all the equipment, though she didn't know exactly what such things cost. When she'd mentioned it, wanting to pay him back, Joe had shrugged and said he could afford it.

"No, Jamie's okay."

Joe made a sound of disgust. "Luna knows all, sees all?"

"Don't be snide. You have instincts and I have mine. My instincts say he's okay."

"Yeah, well, you're the one who thought a woman was trying to kick my ass, if you'll recall. I'd say your instincts are a bit skewed."

Much as she was starting to adore him, Joe could be infuriating at times. "Why do you dislike him so much?"

"Jamie? I don't know him well enough to dislike him, but I don't trust him worth a damn." Joe adjusted the camera to face the front of the house. It could tilt up to ninety degrees and had more than seventy degrees field of view—not enough, Joe had said, but better than nothing. "He said a lot of cryptic stuff to me, and judging by the high-tech equipment he bought, his mountain is a fortress. What the hell is he hiding up there anyway?"

"Did you ask him?"

Joe snorted. "Yeah, and I got more obscure comments. Something about the blackness inside us all."

While Luna held it steady, Joe climbed down the ladder, then dusted off his hands. A sheen of sweat glistened on his face and bare shoulders and the sunshine showed blue-black depths to his hair. He swiped a powerful forearm over his eyes, then surveyed the camera with hands on hips.

He stood so tall and straight, strong and protective. In contrast, Luna felt very feminine beside him. Her heart gave a silly pitter-patter as she stared up at him.

God, she had it bad.

Because Joe had just noticed the way she watched him, she blurted, "I think Jamie has the sight."

Joe sneered. "He's got a case of lunacy, if you ask me."

"But you bought the camera."

"Yeah." Irked, Joe began picking up packing boxes. "A camera for front and back, motion sensors, new locks, door and window alarms . . . As I said, he spooked me. Spending so much time in the truck with him was an experience, I can tell you that."

Luna sighed. "I wish I'd gone along."

Joe whipped around to blast her with a look as dark and turbulent as a thundercloud. "You," he said with stark emphasis, "will stay the hell away from him."

She rolled her eyes. "Don't be a jealous ass, Joe. He's interesting, that's all."

"A jealous ass?" Joe rocked back on his heels, and his eyes flared. "Is that what you think? That I'm *jealous?*"

Willow meandered up. "That's probably what all of Visitation thinks with the way you're yelling. I'm sure at least half of them have heard you."

Joe rumbled a feral growl, and Luna wouldn't

have been surprised if his hair stood on end. "I want you and Austin to steer clear of Jamie Creed, too. The guy is certifiable."

Willow walked up to Joe and hugged him. He looked stunned for a moment, his arms stiff at his sides, then he drew her close in a gentle embrace. Seeing his sturdy, darkly tanned arms gently enfolding Willow touched Luna's heart.

"You see," he boasted over Willow's head to Luna, "she appreciates my concern."

Willow leaned away to laugh. "No, I just wanted to thank you again for the VCR and tapes. Austin is in heaven." She patted his chest in absent affection.

Luna thought Willow was the one in heaven. Her eyes had widened in undiluted glee when Joe unearthed the gifts earlier. Austin had jumped around in joy, but Willow considered herself too mature to gush, so she'd demurely thanked Joe while hugging a copy of *The Mummy*, with Brendan Frasier. She and Austin had immediately set up the VCR and started a tape. Joe had also bought *Dr. Doolittle* with Eddie Murphy, and two Disney cartoons.

As naturally as if he'd been doing so for years, Joe kissed Willow's forehead. "My pleasure, sweetie. I checked on the way home and there's a rental place where we can get more movies. I wasn't all that certain what you and Austin might like."

"The ones you bought are perfect. Austin is all settled in for a marathon."

Watching Joe interact with Willow left Luna all but speechless. He just kept doing wonderful, unexpected things that made it impossible *not* to love him. Willow felt it, too. She'd already warmed to him, and Austin had become his shadow—except that Joe couldn't compete with *The Mummy.*

When she'd first asked Joe along, it was with the knowledge that sexually, he'd be a temptation. She hadn't realized he'd tempt her heart as well, that being near him would fill her with such a jumbled mix of emotions she wouldn't be able to withstand his appeal.

Pulling herself together, Luna shook her head. She was supposed to be supervising the kids, not mooning over Joe. "Austin can watch one a day, but that's all. I don't want him to become a couch potato."

"Austin?" Joe snorted. "Not likely. He reminds me of my sister Alyx, constant explosive motion. Besides, I'll keep him busy."

For the rest of the day, that proved true. Joe had Austin help him install the new door and window locks; then they cut the grass and did some weeding. At first, Luna fretted that Joe was overdoing, but he claimed the physical labor felt good to his sore muscles, so she and Willow pitched in and it turned into a family affair.

Eventually they all ventured inside to work on the house. By the time they finished, everything was freshly cleaned and looking much better. The house desperately needed a new coat of paint and roof repairs, but those would have to wait awhile.

After a simple dinner of grilled steaks and potatoes, Willow and Luna decided to go through the closets in anticipation of their upcoming shopping spree. While the women went off to take more notes, Joe and Austin headed for the lake. They swam for hours before dragging back to the house exhausted.

Luna knew Joe's intent. He hoped to wear Austin

out enough that he'd go right to sleep. Well, it worked for Joe. At ten that night, he was practically asleep on his feet and even though Austin appeared equally beat, he found one excuse after another to stay out of his bed.

Despite his assurances that he was fine, Luna insisted that Joe turn in for the night. "I know you're feeling better, Joe. I can see that. But your ribs are still pretty colorful, and I'll feel better if you get more rest."

Because the kids were both upstairs, Joe caged her up against the kitchen sink. He angled his hips in, pinning her body in place. "I'd sleep better if you were curled up beside me."

The low, husky words sent a wave of pleasure through Luna, weakening her knees and her resolve. She'd already come to the conclusion that she couldn't resist him forever. She knew her own limitations. Saying no to Joe just wasn't natural. It got harder and harder every hour, so she'd rather surrender on her own terms. That way, she stayed in charge.

Deciding to have Joe Winston, and telling him so, were two very different things. She drew a deep breath to shore up her resolve.

Her hands on his chest, Luna stroked him, reveling in the solid evidence of his strength and anticipating how much nicer it'd be to stroke him with no barriers. "The kids will be at summer school for three hours on Monday."

Joe froze. His hand snaking down her back stopped at her waist. He quit nibbling on her ear and jerked back to see her face. Blue eyes quickly heating, he rasped, "Are you saying what I think you're saying?"

He appeared so stunned, Luna blushed, and

that annoyed her enough to add a touch of sarcasm to her tone. "Don't act so shocked. That's what you've been after, right?"

"Among other things."

Now what the hell did that mean? She started to ask him, but he dipped down to see her averted face. "You want me now, do you?"

Forcing herself to look directly at him, Luna nodded. "I've always wanted you, Joe. You know that."

He tangled his fingers in her hair and touched his forehead to hers. "You've done one hell of a job hiding it."

Luna didn't want to get into the reasons she'd felt compelled to say no. The reasons still existed, but they just didn't seem as important anymore. "Do you think you can hang on till Monday?"

"Oh, I'll hang on." His eyes burned brighter, and a slight, sensual smile appeared. "I'll die waiting, but wait I will. Monday huh?" He pressed his face into her throat. "Three more days. Seventy-two hours. More minutes than I can count in my head . . ."

"Joe."

He touched his mouth to hers, and his voice went husky and deep. "Kiss me to tide me over."

The heated command worked the same as a physical caress. "Yes." Luna slowly inhaled and went on tiptoe to reach him. The kiss was filled with sweetness, with timid promise—until Joe slanted his mouth over hers and took over. He pressed his pelvis into her belly with a groan. His tongue licked into her mouth, deep, devouring. His breath fanned her cheek, choppy and hot. His hands stroked down her back to her bottom, gripping her, moving her against him.

Luna held on, breathless in an instant, but then, this was Joe, and when he kissed her, she became aware of so much: his heat, his scent, the tempered strength in his hands, the unyielding hardness of his body.

His heartfelt groan trembled between them. "I've been wanting you forever, Luna."

"A few months," she corrected around her panting breaths.

"Feels like forever." Joe kissed her again, voracious, hungry. Their bodies touched from chests to knees and she felt him trembling, heat pouring off him. "God, this is difficult." His long fingers contracted, then released her bottom with an effort. "I want to touch you everywhere," he growled, "but I just know if I do, Austin will appear."

Luna tilted back to see him. Arousal shone in his face, in the glittering of those vivid, heavy-lidded blue eyes, the dark flush on his cheekbones, the flaring of his nostrils. Seeing what he felt made her feel it, too. "Feel me where?"

He stared down at her, his gaze incandescent. "Your nipples, your belly. And especially between your legs, where I just know you're nice and wet for me." He closed his eyes as if in pain.

It took Luna a shuddering breath before she could say, "I would like that, Joe."

An arrested expression fell over his features, then he groaned. "Aw hell." He wrapped his arms around her and rocked them both. "You can't say things like that to me, babe."

"You brought it up."

"Because of you, it's been up." He laughed, nibbled on her earlobe, teased inside with his tongue, then in a hoarse whisper, "And you expect me to go to bed now to sleep? I'll be up all night. And yeah, I do mean *up*."

Luna nodded. "It won't be easy for me either, you know."

Sexual arousal hardened his features, making his cheekbones more prominent, his jawline sharper. He started to lean down to her, and they both heard the sound of footsteps on the stairs. Joe fell back with a groan. "You see? Kids have radar. I better disappear into my room since my condition isn't suitable for an audience." He tipped up her chin. "Don't let him wear you out, okay? If you need me to step in, let me know."

Joe didn't tell her to just put Austin in his bed and forget about him. He didn't tell her to threaten the child with punishment. Like Luna, he seemed to understand that Austin's late night adventures had to do with more than the mischievous antics of a child.

Her heart expanded until her chest ached. She kissed him again, quick and light on his mouth. "I can handle it, Joe. Get some sleep."

With the sound of Austin fast approaching, Joe started backing up. "Promise me you'll wake me if you need me."

"We'll be fine."

He stood in his bedroom doorway, one hand on the doorknob, one on the frame. "Promise me, Luna, or I'm not going to bed."

Austin poked his head into the kitchen, saw they were several feet apart, and sighed in relief. "I'm hungry again."

Luna laughed. "I promise, Joe. Now, good night."

He saluted her, winked at Austin, and closed his door.

* * *

Joe was still awake an hour later when he heard Luna and Austin take another turn through the kitchen. That was their forth time around, and he could hear Austin droning on in quiet, sincere conversation. Joe's damn heart felt too big for his chest. Everything inside him seemed crowded and uncomfortable and out of place—because of Luna.

No other woman had affected him this way, and he wasn't at all certain he liked it. But then, he'd never played guardian to two small, very needy children either.

He got up, listened at the door until Austin and Luna left the kitchen, then slipped out. He could hear Luna say, "Everyone has bad dreams, Austin. Even when you're awake, they can still bother you sometimes, right?"

"Yeah, 'specially when they seem real."

"Like the dream you keep having about Willow?"

Joe crept up behind them, again eavesdropping and not giving a damn. Most of the lights were turned out, but the front porch light shone through the windows and a pale stair light had been left on.

Austin had his small hand tucked in Luna's and the two of them padded barefoot around the perimeter of the dining room, their gait unhurried, both their heads down as they walked.

Austin nodded. "Yeah. I dream that I can't find her, and then a stranger comes and tells me she's gone, like my mom was gone and . . ."

His small voice got kind of rough there at the end, and he fell silent. Joe squeezed his eyes shut, hurting with Austin, smote clear down to his soul at the emotional torment of one small boy.

Austin swallowed, breathed a little too loudly.

Luna waited. Finally, in a tight little voice, he said, "I *hate* that stupid dream."

"I would, too."

"I miss my mom a lot." He made a fist and roughly rubbed his eyes. "I don't want to miss Willow like that."

Luna stopped at the staircase and sat on the bottom step. She and Austin stared at each other a moment before Luna shrugged. "I'm sorry to insult your masculinity, Austin, but I need a hug really, really bad. Do you think that'd be okay?"

Austin hesitated, shifting from one foot to the next. Then he shocked Joe by crawling right into her lap and wrapping his scrawny arms around her neck. Luna squeezed him tight, her shoulders shuddering a bit. Joe heard a hiccup, a small sniff, but didn't know if it was Luna or Austin. He wished he was part of that hug, because God knew, he needed it, too.

"Mom used to hug me like this," Austin admitted in a whisper. "She liked huggin'."

Joe's own eyes got damp, and he retreated to the other side of the wall before they heard him. Head back, Joe squeezed his eyes shut and tried to calm the drumming of his heart now lodged in his throat, choking the hell out of him.

It was emotion overload, damn it. First Willow embracing him earlier, then Luna admitting she finally wanted him, and now this. How the hell was a badass scoundrel supposed to hold up under all that?

"I know I'm not your mom," Joe heard Luna say, "but if you wouldn't mind, I'd like lots of hugs like this."

Sounding watery and uncertain, Austin whispered, "You're gonna stay, huh?"

"A team of wild horses couldn't drag me away."

"And Joe, too? Will he stay?" Before Luna could answer, Austin said, "I want him to stay."

Joe clenched his teeth and swallowed, but damn it, it didn't do any good. His throat closed up and he knew his eyes were getting misty. Hell, he hadn't got misty-eyed since . . . He didn't remember the last time. Must have been before grade school.

Luna sniffed. "I can't speak for Joe, honey, but I know he likes you an awful lot. Even if he leaves, he'll come back to visit, I promise."

Damn right, he would, Joe thought.

"He likes the lake, huh?"

"Yes, he likes the lake. But he likes you and Willow even more."

Several seconds ticked by, then Austin mumbled around a yawn, "I'm tired. I think I'm ready to go to bed now."

The stairs creaked as they both stood. "I'll tuck you in if you don't mind."

"Cuz it's something girls like to do?"

"That's right. And if you have any more dreams, you'll come and get me, okay?"

"Okay, then."

When he heard them overhead, Joe moved to the bottom of the stairs. He stood there with his hands on his hips, his thoughts churning in every direction. He had some decisions to make, the sooner the better.

But one thing was certain—he wasn't about to budge any time soon. As Luna had said, wild horses couldn't drag him away from here now. He'd wait to tell Luna his change in plans. She'd fight him, he just knew it, but it wouldn't do her any good at all. Austin wanted him to stay. Maybe Willow did, too. Eventually, he'd convince Luna.

He'd never considered himself a family man, but now . . . He wanted to try it on for size. He wanted to make a difference in their lives. He wanted—well, a lot. And so he'd stay and that was that.

The decision lightened the heavy weight on his heart. It'd work out. He'd see to it.

Chapter Eleven

The late night visit between Luna and Austin seemed a turning point for them all. Over the next few days, they worked, played and talked together. With no more visits from Deputy Royal, things settled down and the kids started to relax. Willow was still reserved, but that just seemed an integral part of her nature. Once when Joe had been wrestling on the floor with Austin, she'd sat on the sidelines and laughed, egging them on.

Luna, however, joined in. From one second to the next, Joe got rolled to his back and both Luna and Austin attacked him. His injured ribs were all but healed, but with Luna bouncing on him, he'd felt a twinge of pain that was more sexual awareness than physical injury.

He needed her.

With every day that passed, he grew more impatient for Monday and the minutes when he'd finally have her alone, in his bed, ready to put him out of his misery. He didn't let the time pass without notice. No, Joe used every opportunity to ensure she'd be ready for him.

If he caught her alone, he copped a quick feel, kissing her neck, her ear, cuddling a breast, patting that delectable behind that had gotten him into trouble with her in the first place.

Only now she didn't complain.

It made Joe crazy the way she accepted his attention, even seemed to revel in it. He considered their private, secretive touching as extended foreplay, and no way in hell would he give it up, even though it kept him taut and on the edge. Luna, the tease, deliberately provoked him.

It got to where if he was in the room, she watched him with her exotic, slanted eyes, practically challenging him to come to her. She sashayed around in her sexy little outfits: short shorts that made his blood boil, strapless tops that exaggerated the swells of her breasts, hip-hugging skirts. And her shoes. Joe shook his head.

Though they were now situated in a country setting, Luna hadn't resorted to sneakers or boots. Her high heels and sexy wedges were as unique in Visitation as Luna herself.

More than once Joe had taken a dip in the cool lake, just to regain control.

He'd also used the days to plan for a reopening of the lake. As Luna had suggested, there were plenty of business related details on Willow's computer. Between that and details the kids had shared, things were under way. All he really needed now were the permits. If it worked out as he planned, the lake would be open and operational in less than four weeks—in plenty of time to take advantage of summer.

The kids had really gotten into the idea, helping in any way they could. For as long as they could
remember, the lake had always been opened year-
round for a variety of events. Only since their
mother passed away had it been shut down, and
they missed the familiarity of it.

Discussions of the lake often led to discussions
of Chloe. Sometimes they laughed over stories,
sometimes they shed a few tears. But the kids enjoyed talking about their mother, so Luna and Joe
always listened. Joe had a feeling no one else had
bothered.

He was at the kitchen table Saturday night, going
over a few last minute details while Luna and Austin
took their nightly stroll around the house. Joe could
hear the low drone of their voices, the squeak of
their feet on the floorboards. Their walks were now
as routine as a bedtime story, but their conversation
was no longer wrenching. In fact, sometimes they
turned the walk into a game. One minute they'd
be chatting, then they'd be racing.

Twice now, they'd gotten into pillow fights when
Luna attempted to tuck Austin into bed.

Joe wondered if Austin would eventually out-
grow the need to talk before sleeping, not that
Luna seemed to mind. Joe knew she enjoyed the
nightly ritual as much, maybe more so, than Austin.
Perhaps, because of her background, she needed
the comfort as much as Austin did.

It seemed Luna would now have the family
she'd always wanted—and damn it, Joe wanted to
be a part of it.

He already knew that she adored his cousins
and his cousins' wives—who had become family
the minute they married a Winston. Luna would

also adore his crazy sister. Alyx could be a real pain in the ass, but then, that was something she and Luna would have in common.

That thought had him grinning.

When Joe heard Luna and Austin upstairs, he rose from the table. Just as they made a habit of walking, he'd made it a practice to double-check every lock before turning in.

Judging by the upstairs light, Luna was still in Austin's room when Joe checked the dead bolt on the front door. Satisfied that all was secure, he started to turn away—and then he heard the sound in the yard.

Nerves prickling, he moved to a window and pushed aside a curtain to search the area. There, close to where the vehicles were parked, a shadow moved. It could have been anything—the shifting of a tree limb, an animal.

Joe knew better.

Like a live wire down his spine, his instincts shouted a warning, and everything inside him went on alert.

"Son of a bitch," Joe growled low. There would be only one reason for someone to skulk around in the dark of the night. Whoever was out there, they were up to no good.

It didn't matter that he was barefoot, that he was without a shirt, or that they were virtually isolated on the outskirts of town. Since the day Scott Royal had visited, Joe kept his balisong knife tucked into his pocket as a nightly precaution. It was the only weapon he needed, but as he'd told Austin, he was good with his hands, too.

Incensed, Joe silently turned the locks.

"What's going on?" Luna appeared at the top of the stairs, her hands griping the railing.

Beside her, Austin said with fear, "Joe?"

Damn it, he'd hoped to take care of this without her even knowing. "Stay inside, Luna." Joe pierced her with one fast, searing glance that brooked no arguments. "I mean it."

She started down the steps in a rush. "Of course, I'll stay inside. What's the matter? What are you doing?"

With no time to waste, Joe ignored her questions and opened the door just enough to slip out, then skirted fast into the deepest shadow. Breath low and even, muscles tensed and ready, he stared toward the cars. And he waited.

After only a moment, his patience paid off and he saw one lengthy shadow that didn't belong in the night-shrouded yard. It shifted, gained form, until Joe saw that a man crouched by his truck. Other than the reflection of moonlight on his blond head, he seemed indistinguishable in black clothes.

Blond. Rage welled inside Joe; he well remembered the man who'd been watching as he and Luna packed for the trip to Visitation. Apparently, he had followed them just as Jamie Creed had said.

With incredible speed Joe bounded across the porch and down the steps, hitting the hard-packed ground in a flat-out run. His knee objected, stiffening up and sending shards of pain to radiate throughout his thigh and hip. But that was an old, familiar pain now, one he'd long ago learned to live with—thanks to Bruno Caldwell. If this was one of his henchmen, well then, it'd take more than a little pain to keep Joe off him.

At the sound of Joe's thundering approach, the man jerked upright. Shock held him immobile for only a moment of time, then with a panicked screech he high stepped it around Joe's truck toward the wooded area adjacent to the property. The trees and shrubs there shielded the access to the main road.

Knowing he likely had transportation hidden there, Joe pressed himself, determined to catch him. With silent, acute concentration, his long legs ate up the ground, drawing him nearer, nearer. He could feel the blood rushing through his veins, the throbbing of his own heartbeat. His bare feet registered every small rock and piece of debris on the ground. The sonorous breaths of the man he chased mimicked their crashing footfalls.

They reached the blackened woods filled with concealing shadows and foliage. The ground was a trap of twisted roots and fallen branches, sharp brambles and prickling weeds. Joe cursed to himself and stretched out one arm, his fingertips almost there. He lunged—and snagged the back of a black shirt.

Issuing a ridiculously high-pitched scream, the body twisted, striking out, kicking. A clumsy fist landed on Joe's jaw, barely dazing him, and a foot caught him in his sore ribs.

He hung on.

In a wild tangle, they both went down into a bed of sharp-pointed twigs. Joe landed mostly atop the intruder. The man held his arms over the face while kicking and thrashing. In a red haze of rage, Joe drew back his fist, intent on smashing the man's nose. At the last second the man turned his face and the punch landed on his temple. He grunted, his arms fell to his sides and he went limp with a rumbling groan. Joe took quick advantage, drawing back to deliver a knock-out, immobilizing blow.

Willow shouted behind him.

There was no mistaking the fear in her voice. Had Joe miscalculated? Were there two men? He was on his feet in an instant, holding his captive with a hand twisted in his shirtfront. Fear washed through him as he turned toward the house—and he saw a small fire burst to life next to his truck.

It was only a moment of distraction, but the body he held bucked and lunged free. Cursing, Joe reached for him again and stepped on a fallen tree limb. His bad knee crumpled, causing Joe to grit his teeth in pain as he went down. *"Goddammit."*

Frustration bit into him, adding to his fury. He was back on his feet in a heartbeat, but already the intruder had disappeared from sight, swallowed up by the black night. Deep into the woods, Joe could hear the lumbering, quickly receding footsteps, but he couldn't see a thing. He stood undecided for only a moment, knowing he'd never catch the bastard now, not barefoot, not without light. He was sick at the idea of letting him get away. *Again.*

Then Luna was there, her flowing white nightshirt billowing in the evening breeze.

"Joe?" She frantically stroked her hands over him, his face, his chest. He heard the trembling in her tone and felt it in her touch. "Are you all right? Damn it, Joe, answer me."

"I'm fine." Still tight with anger but determined to reassure her, Joe threw an arm around her, dragging her to his side so he could see beyond her to the fire. "Shit."

In a hobbling gait, he started forward. Luna braced her shoulder under his arm, offering her slight support. "You are not all right! You damn fool," she raged. "How dare you do that? How dare you run off into the dark without a weapon—"

Disgusted, Joe said, "I needed shoes, not a weapon. Besides, I had my knife. I just wasn't sure I wanted to stick anyone tonight, especially without knowing who it was."

She glared at him. "Look, Joe, I know I came here to take care of the kids, and I know they come first. That's a given."

Thank God. At least if she was worried about the kids, she wouldn't be dogging his heels.

"But I'm not very good at hanging back while you go off to probable danger. In fact, I don't like it at all. I waited this time until I saw the guy run off, but in the future—"

"In the future, you'll do the same." Through an open window on the porch, Joe could see the pale, alert faces of Willow and Austin where they huddled together. Someone had frightened them. No way in hell would Joe tolerate that.

"*I* called Deputy Royal," Luna told him in a short voice filled with censure. "Which is what *you* should have done before charging off like a vigilante without an ounce of sense—"

"Wives can be such a bother." Joe kept his gaze on the fire. It was small, but too damn close to his truck. His steps became more hurried. He saw a gas can tipped to the side and quickly moved it farther away. If he hadn't interrupted things when he had, would his truck have been torched?

At his side, Luna huffed. "I'll go get an old blanket before it spreads." She hurried away.

Willow unlocked the front door to let Luna in, then stepped outside. She had her arms wrapped around herself, her long hair drifting in the damp evening breeze. "There's a hose at the side of the house, Joe. Want me to get it?"

He shook his head. "It's a gasoline fire, hon. That might make it spread."

Joe's bare feet felt shredded from his chase across a field grown wild with thorny weeds. His knee throbbed. Bloody scratches marred his bare chest and arms from where he'd fallen, and rage burned like acid in his stomach. But he wasn't about to react to any of that yet, not when the kids were watching him so closely.

Luna reappeared with two tattered blankets, and Joe went about smothering the flames. When only smoke remained, he put his truck in neutral and pushed it several yards away, closer to the house and the light of the porch. It was as he left the truck that he saw the deeply etched message on the side.

Take the tramp and leave, before someone gets hurt.
Joe's eyes narrowed and his teeth locked.

He felt a small hand on his bare biceps and twisted to see Willow's wide brown eyes staring at the message. "They mean me."

"You don't know that," Luna said beside her. "They could mean me."

"You?"

She shrugged, but her gaze never wavered from the truck. "I imagine Dinah has told everyone how I fired her." She had Austin's hand in hers, and all three of them seemed spellbound by the obscene message.

Joe stepped in front of them, blocking it from their view. "All of you listen to me." Three pairs of eyes locked on his face: hopeful, expectant, still dark with anger and fear. Protectiveness erupted, so strong Joe wanted to shout with it. He drew one breath, then another, but Jesus it didn't help.

"You're mine now," he told them, and he knew his voice was hoarse, trembling with furious conviction. He hadn't meant to rush Luna, to spill his guts so soon. He'd meant to give himself time, to give her and the kids time. But he couldn't hold it in. "All of you. I protect what's mine. No one is going to hurt you, and no one is going to run us off. I'll find the son of a bitch, I swear it. And when I do, he'll pay."

Luna's eyes, narrowed with rage only a moment ago, now softened with an expression far too close to concern. She gave a reluctant nod and spoke very softly. "All right, Joe."

He had the awful suspicion she agreed more to soothe him than because she believed what he said.

Willow swallowed, nodded, then gave him a trembling smile. "All right," she said, agreeing with Luna, and she, too, seemed to want to comfort him.

Women.

Austin launched himself forward, hugging himself around Joe's knees and hanging on tight. Joe almost fell over. He felt as though he'd been stomped on already, his muscles, his mind, his deepest emotions. Hell, he hadn't known he *had* deep emotions until the kids and Luna had dredged them from a dark, empty place.

He wasn't all that steady on his feet, and Austin hit him with the impact of a small tank. But it was more the punch to his heart than the impetus against his legs that threw him off balance.

Joe touched the tangled mop of blond hair. "Austin?"

Austin squeezed him, then said against Joe's knees, "Okay." He finally tipped up his face to give Joe a crooked, admiring grin. "I sure like it when you're disrespectful."

That ridiculous comment lightened Joe's mood, and he laughed. "Rodent."

Beneath the moonlight, with the scent of smoke thick in the cool evening air, they stood there. A retired bounty hunter, a psychic's assistant, and two needy kids—a mismatched family, but a family nonetheless. Though it seemed to have happened at Mach speed, Joe accepted it. He needed them, as much if not more than they needed him. No one would hurt them. He wouldn't allow it.

Joe reached for Luna and Willow and gathered them close, relishing the warmth and love and odd sense of security that he hadn't realized had been missing from his life. He felt Luna's warm breath against his bare shoulder, felt Willow's tear-damp cheek on his chest. And Austin, clinging like a scrawny monkey to his legs. Deep inside him, something expanded—and this time there was no doubt, no hesitation. It felt right, filling him up with satisfaction.

He was a marrying kind of man after all, it seemed. Now the hard part would be convincing Luna.

Seconds later, flashing lights and shrill sirens split the night. Joe looked up as Scott Royal pulled into the yard with a lot of fanfare. When he saw them all congregated outside in their sleep clothes, he turned off the noise and climbed out of his car.

He did not look happy.

Both admiring and amused, he lowered the night-vision goggles that had allowed him to watch the unfolding drama as clearly as if it had been pure daylight.

It had been a real pleasure, watching Winston do his thing. He had that deadly combination of speed, agility and stealth. There was no way *not* to admire him.

He lifted the goggles again and tracked the re-treating figure as it wisely left the woods and headed toward a car on the side of the road. The guy ran like a turkey. A terrified turkey. 'Course, Winston was a big bruiser, and if the guy hadn't gotten free, Winston would have pulverized him. Too bad that hadn't happened. He was so bored right now, he'd take any form of entertainment he could get.

Not that he disliked Visitation. The small town had started to grow on him. At night, the damn sky was so clear, so laden with stars, it fair took his breath away—and here he'd always considered himself a cynical bastard unmoved by things like starry skies. He snorted. Maybe once this was fin-ished, he'd buy himself a spot of land and put up a little house. Visitation would be a right fine place to settle, or at least visit when the bullshit got to be too much.

He smiled, wondering if Winston would enjoy having him for a neighbor.

But first, he had a job to do. And he couldn't very well do it if things stayed so complicated. So maybe he should help Winston sort it out a bit.

From this distance, he couldn't make out the plates on the retreating car. The night-vision gog-gles weren't good enough for that. But he saw it was an older hatchback. What would Winston do with that information if he had it? Maybe, when the time was right, he'd share it with him, just to see.

Yeah, he'd do that.

When the time was right.

Luna felt ridiculously nervous Monday morning. She'd be alone with Joe today, and that was enough to make her hands shake and her body flush in anticipation. Loving him as well as wanting him made for some pretty intense sensations.

But she was nervous, too, because Joe was different now. Some of the changes she'd noted were subtle, like the way he looked at her, how he touched her. Every kiss and caress still reeked of possessiveness, but there was a new tenderness, too, in the way his gaze lingered on her, the way his hands held her. It thrilled her, but also left her confused.

Other changes were less subtle.

Since the deliberate fire and the damage to his truck, Joe looked more like a badass than ever. He appeared bigger, more imposing, too. And he positively heaved with menace.

The tape from the surveillance camera had shown nothing more than the top of the man's head and his dark clothing. The feed was good, but they didn't have one single shot of his face. He'd stuck close to the shadows, making height and weight difficult to estimate.

Deputy Royal was still checking the gas can for prints, but the can was old and rusty, so they weren't very hopeful. Other than knowing that the man had blond hair and, as Joe put it, screamed like a girl, they didn't have a thing to go on.

Luna thought Joe might want to cancel their shopping trip that next day. But Joe had refused to rob the kids of their outing. Instead, he'd stuck close to them and kept a watchful eye on everyone. Luna had driven into town with the kids in her car, and Joe had trailed behind them in his truck. It'd be a week before the body shop could remove the scratches from the side panel, so Joe had covered it with strips of opaque plastic to spare Willow and Austin from seeing it again.

Joe's vigilance had never been more apparent than while they shopped. People had given him wary looks and walked a wide berth around him. Not that Luna blamed them. Even while in the relative safety of the mall, Joe had surveyed everyone and everything with burning blue eyes and sharp suspicion. His expression was so forbidding that only Willow and Austin had seemed immune.

To Luna's mind, the shopping spree had turned into an odyssey of excitement for Willow, but mind-numbing torture for Joe and Austin. Within half an hour, Joe had chosen a bed to be delivered the next day. It was bigger and better able to accommodate his large frame.

They'd then spent several more hours deciding on a multitude of clothes and shoes and underwear for the kids. With every shirt, pair of shorts or jeans purchased, Willow glowed. Even new socks had her sighing in pleasure—and Luna loved it. She could have shopped the rest of the day.

Austin, however, had carped and complained and dragged along with a bogus limp that hadn't garnered him one speck of sympathy from Willow, but had obviously amused Joe. Getting him to try on clothes proved nearly impossible, so Luna finally purchased what she thought would fit him and spared him more torture. Austin's complaints got on everyone's nerves and for a while there, she had expected Joe to pull up lame, too. But with

Willow's excitement so plain, Joe had sucked up his objections, juggled the packages she piled in his arms, and encouraged Willow to continue shopping.

What a great guy.

Now, thanks to Joe's patience, the kids were decked out in all new clothes and shoes for their first day at summer school. Luna looked over at Joe as he drove, but he kept his eyes on the road, sparing her little attention.

She didn't like being ignored. She'd deliberately worn a new dress, a stretchy tan sheath that clung to her body. The dress itself was simple, but she'd adorned it with long loopy earrings, several silver and gold bracelets, and a woven belt that hung low on her hips. She thought she looked rather nice in the outfit, but Joe had only given her one quick, cursory glance.

The kids were in the backseat of her Contour, subdued in their anticipation of school. Joe, however, seemed very disgruntled as he constantly scanned the area with a threatening scowl.

Luna leaned to look into the backseat and was struck anew at how much the kids had come to mean to her in such a short time. Austin's hair, freshly brushed just that morning, had already sprung back into an impossible tangle, thanks to his open window. Willow nervously fiddled with a new bracelet, quietly introspective in that special way of hers. Though Willow looked very delicate and Austin appeared as rugged as any nine-year-old boy, the similarities in features couldn't be denied.

"You have Joe's cell phone number, right?"

Since she'd asked that several times already, both kids made faces and said, almost in unison, *"Yes."*

"I'm being a pain, aren't I? I always swore I wouldn't be a pain."

"You are not a pain," Joe rumbled without looking at her.

Austin just rolled his eyes, much aggrieved, but Willow smiled. "Mom was worse. She fretted over everything."

Luna asked, "So you're used to it?"

"Yeah. But we'll be fine. Ms. Rose won't let anything happen."

Austin thrust up his small chin. "If anyone tries anything, I'll—"

Joe cut the threat short. "You'll call me. Understand?"

His tone left no room for arguments, and Austin subsided with a mulish grumble that was neither agreement nor denial.

"I mean it, Austin."

He glared at the back of Joe's head, then nodded. "All right. I'll call ya."

When they pulled up in front of the small school, Julie Rose was there, waiting at the door with a smile. She wore a prim summer suit of pale green with sensible brown pumps. Joe paid her no mind, but Luna smiled and waved. She adored the woman for caring about the kids.

After they parked, they got out to walk the kids to the door. Luna was about to greet Julie when Austin pointed across the street. "There's Clay."

Willow's reaction was immediate. She blushed with pleasure, then almost as quickly frowned in forced dislike. "Don't look at him, Austin." She grabbed her brother's upper arm and prodded him along. When they reached the school door, she said in passing, "Ms. Rose," and hustled on inside.

Julie shook her head. "Relax, Mr. Winston. I'll watch the kids closely, I promise."

Joe nodded toward Clay. "Will he be at summer school, too?"

"No. He and his friends always hang out in town during the day. If you ask me, they should have summer jobs. I'm told they used to spend all day at the lake, until Patricia closed it."

"We're thinking of reopening it," Luna told her. "Joe's been checking into it. Sometime this week we'll talk to the county commissioner to see what permits we'll need."

Julie raised a brow. "You'll need to talk to Quincy Owen, too. He's on the board of trustees, and from what Patricia told me, he pushed to have the lake closed."

Joe's head jerked up. "Why?"

"I have no idea what his reasons might have been, but according to Patricia, it was too much work. Of course, she only told me this in passing. Most of my discussions with her centered more on the children's schooling."

"Well." Joe rubbed his hands. "Since we're already here, maybe I'll just ask him right now."

Luna didn't think that boded well for anyone. And the idea that Joe wanted to prolong their trip to town was something of an insult. After all, they planned to spend some very special time together once they returned to the house.

She knew Joe still wanted her—that hadn't changed. She saw it in his every look, his every touch. Joe watched her with the heated intent of a lover, though they'd yet to sleep together. And if his looks were hot, his touch was even more so. He'd used every available moment to build the tension between them. If he found her alone in a room, he kissed her nape, fondled her backside, murmured suggestive compliments, and basically drove her insane.

But since the fire, he'd also been distracted, dark and calculating. The rage inside him seemed barely suppressed and served as a testament to his strength of character; though a volatile confrontation was imminent, he remained gentle and patient with Austin and Willow.

Luna made plans with Julie on when to pick up the kids, then followed Joe across the street to where Clay leaned on the front of the jeep. The young man straightened as Joe neared, his gaze watchful.

Luna stepped in front of Joe, saying quickly, "Good morning, Clay."

Her jovial greeting threw him, but Clay couldn't seem to pull his gaze away from Joe. Luna cleared her throat. "It's nice to see you again."

Staring at her with the same caution he might give a bear trap, Clay finally swallowed and murmured, "Ms. Clark."

Today Clay wore loose-fitting jeans, a long-sleeved tee, and a baseball hat—set on his head the correct way.

Joe put his hands on Luna's shoulders and gently, forcibly, moved her to his side. "We had some trouble the other night."

"I heard." Clay shifted, defensive and defiant. "I'm glad no one was hurt."

"Know anything about it?"

Clay scowled at the blatant accusation. "Only what I've heard around town."

Luna elbowed Joe hard, earning a grunt and a frown. To make up for Joe's bad manners, Luna smiled sweetly. "Clay, we were hoping to discuss a

few things with your stepfather. Where might we
find him?"

Trying to determine who was in charge, Clay
looked between the two of them and finally settled
his gaze on Luna. "Usually he's in the offices above
the shopping center. But he's home sick today."

"Nothing serious, I hope?"

Clay shrugged. "He was in his room when I left."

Joe said, "I'm going to assume you're *not* waiting
here for Willow."

Silence.

Luna started to elbow Joe again, but before she
could, he caught her arm and held it.

"If you are," Joe continued, "I expect you to be
polite and to make damn sure anyone with you is
polite."

Luna relaxed, because after all, she expected
the same. As long as Joe didn't order Clay to stay
away, Luna figured Willow could handle herself.
She was a very resourceful young lady.

Clay screwed up his courage, rearranged his ball
cap, and then faced Joe with as much pride as a
male his age could manage. "I was going to apologize."

Joe's dark expression cleared. "S'that right?"

"Yeah." He looked at Luna, and color brightened on his cheekbones. "Maybe I could stop by
and see Willow sometime?"

"That would be up to Willow," Luna told him,
but deep inside she was so pleased she felt like
laughing out loud. She had a feeling Willow would
make Clay work for his forgiveness, and that was as
it should be. "But if she's okay with it, then I have
no problem."

"She's too young to date."

Joe's unconditional statement fell hard into the

middle of the pleasantries, causing Clay to gulp and infuriating Luna. Through her teeth, she said, "She's almost fifteen and it depends on the date, Joe." Then, more sweetly to Clay, "Let's take it a day at a time, okay?"

Relieved, Clay nodded. "Thanks."

Before Joe could burn the young man with his bluster, Luna said her farewells and dragged Joe away. And she *was* dragging him, she realized, because he still had his watchful gaze surveying the area, and he seemed in no real hurry to leave.

Which meant he was in no real hurry to be alone with her.

Her vanity pricked, Luna punched his rock-solid shoulder the moment they were ensconced in the car.

Joe glared down at her. "What the hell was that for?"

She crossed her arms and glared right back. "I know you're concerned about things, Joe. And of course, that's why I brought you along, as a safeguard for these situations."

Joe started the car and pulled away from the curb. "Uh huh. That's why you brought me along."

The way he said that gave her pause. "Joe, I *do* appreciate your . . . enthusiasm."

"My enthusiasm?"

Luna waved a hand. "The way you're so grim and threatening and watchful. You're so tense right now, you look like you could explode at any second."

"That's about it," he agreed.

"Well . . . good. I mean, I want you to use your experience to keep the kids safe and protected. But I thought . . ." She trailed off. How did she say that she wanted him blind with lust? For her?

Joe made a rough sound of amusement. "I *am* tense, Luna."

"I know." She sighed, realizing how silly she was being. The kids were her number one priority. If Joe could help keep them happy and safe, that's what mattered most. "This whole thing of being harassed and not knowing who it is—"

"I'm tense," Joe interrupted, "because I'm so damn hot for you I can barely draw breath."

Luna stared at him.

"You think I'm stiff legged with anger? No way, babe. The best way to fight is to stay loose, limber and ready. And believe me, I know how to fight." He reached across the seat and slid his palm over her bare thigh. His fingers just barely went beneath the hem of her dress. "But I don't know how to deal with wanting you so much I can't see straight most the damn time. Until I get you under me, I'm going to stay tense, so it's a damn good thing you're finally ready. Once we spend an hour or two burning up the sheets, then I can bend my mind around figuring out who the hell is bothering us. And when I do, I'll take care of it. I promise you that."

His hand slid higher, making her catch her breath, teasing at the edge of her panties. His voice lowered, smoky and deep. "But first things first."

Luna swallowed, drew two breaths, and then nodded. "Yes, okay. But, Joe?" When he glanced at her, she whispered, "Drive fast."

Chapter Twelve

They made it back to the house in record time. Luckily, there hadn't been any traffic, any mysterious appearances by Jamie, and not too many stop signs. Joe barely had the truck in park before Luna was out and hustling her sexy ass toward the porch. Knowing she was in a hurry made him doubly anxious.

He reached the door only seconds before her. He unlocked it and pulled Luna inside a little more forcefully than he intended. Not that Luna complained. The second they were inside, she was in his arms, burrowing close, her hands sliding up his shoulders, his neck, to furrow into his hair.

"Luna," he said, and she turned her face up to him. From the moment he'd met her, he'd been filled with constant grinding sexual need. He detested being out of control, but around Luna, he had no choice.

Joe took her mouth too hard, too fast, but she was open, hot, just as eager, and it made it impossible for him to slow down.

He pinned her up against the wall and closed one hand over her breast. The clinging dress and bra posed no barrier. He could feel her nipple against his palm and it made him wild.

Pulling her mouth free to gasp in air, Luna arched into him and groaned. Her eyes were closed, her head tipped back.

Enjoying that response, Joe growled, "I can feel your nipples, Luna, already puckered and tight. You like this?" While kissing the soft flesh of her throat, he dragged his thumb back and forth over her, and when that wasn't enough, he dipped down and closed his mouth around her, sucking at her through her dress and brassiere.

"*Joe.*" Her hands clenched in his hair.

"You wore this damn killer dress today to tease me, didn't you?"

She shook her head, but whispered, "I don't know."

When he'd stepped into the kitchen that morning, only half awake but with a full morning erection, he'd taken one look at Luna and known he was a goner.

Playing a sexy Martha Stewart, she'd already made coffee, had fragrant waffles cooking for the kids, and was fully dressed and made-up. The sight of her had hit him on so many levels, Joe knew he couldn't deal with it, not that early, not before coffee.

Without so much as a "good morning," he'd escaped to the upstairs bathroom and a long, cold shower that had only served to temper the lust rather than diminish it. Since then, his need for her had throbbed and swelled until he felt savage with it.

Joe thrust one leg between hers, forcing the sinful dress high. Her pale thighs enclosed his denim-clad leg, practically riding him. He wished she was naked already so he could feel her and only her against his thigh.

Spreading his fingers wide on her fanny, Joe dragged her up close and tight to his groin, pressing her to his swollen erection, moving her against him in a tantalizing rhythm.

A moan blossomed from deep in her throat. Joe took her mouth, obliterating the sound with the thrust of his tongue. She tasted so sweet he had to fight to stop kissing her long enough to say, "You've got too damn many clothes on, woman."

Her hands tugged at his T-shirt. "So do you."

Their gazes clashed, his bold, determined, hers soft, willing. Joe bent at the knees and scooped her up.

"Your ribs!"

"What ribs?" He carried her to the stairs.

Arms around his neck, Luna asked, "Where are we going?"

"To your bed. It's bigger." His double bed was much more comfortable than the cot, but Luna had a queen-size mattress, and with the ride he intended, the more room, the better.

He bounded up the steps with her cradled in his arms, and Luna murmured, "How romantic."

"Tease." He kicked her door open and practically tossed her on her bed. She immediately came up on one elbow, then watched while Joe stretched one arm over his back, grabbed a fistful of his shirt and stripped it off over his head. He threw it to the floor and toed off his shoes.

He saw Luna surveying his chest. Her gaze

tracked the recent scratches he'd received the
night of the fire, a few lingering bruises from his
attack, and numerous old scars.

"Joe." She sounded sad and concerned, but Joe
didn't want her distracted with any of that.

Bracing his knees on either side of her hips, he
came down over her, and his hands immediately
snagged the hem of the dress to lift it. He got it as
high as her breasts before the sight of her bared
body stalled him.

Chest laboring, muscles trembling, he looked at
her soft lace panties, so tiny they barely covered
her mound. Oh, God. He could see the triangle of
curls beneath and it pushed him, destroying his
last thread of finesse.

With a groan, Joe bent and kissed her navel,
nuzzled her belly, took a gentle love bite of her
hip. "Luna." He could smell her, warm and female
and *his*. He released the dress to spread her legs
wide apart.

"Joe, wait," she protested, attempting to draw
her thighs back together.

Big hands holding her immobile, Joe fixed her
in his gaze. "Don't. Don't tell me no, Luna. Not
now."

She drew a low, shivering breath. "I won't. *I
can't.* But—"

Her body bowed when Joe put his mouth against
her. He breathed deeply of her erotic scent, filling
himself up, hurting with his need. He pressed with
his tongue, only barely able to taste her through
damp lace. It wasn't enough.

With a low growl, he straightened, adjusting her
legs to strip the panties off her, then positioning
her around him again, spread wide, totally visible.

Joe allowed himself a leisurely study of her. She wore sexy sandals with ties around her ankles. Joe left them in place, liking her this way, her dress bunched around her ribs, legs open to him. He stared at her face while threading his fingers through the tangled curls, lightly probing.

Her hands knotted into the bedding; her eyes grew heavy and vague. Joe could barely breathe. Watching her, he used his middle finger to part the slick, swollen lips—then pressed in.

So wet. So damn hot.

Luna's eyes sank closed while her lips parted on a gasp. He watched the tightening flex of muscles in her thighs, the way her soft, smooth belly sucked in, how her rib cage expanded on a huge breath.

He had to see all of her.

Withdrawing his finger, he grabbed her upper arms and hauled her upright on the bed. Startled, she looked at him, but he already had her dress swept up and over her head. He tossed it over the footboard, then tackled the front clasp on her bra. It, too, was stretchy lace, but with sexy little rosettes stitched on as a border.

The bra opened, and Joe peeled the cups out of his way.

Her taut nipples were soft brown, begging for his mouth. Joe groaned and, with his hands under her armpits, lifted her level with his face so he could close his teeth gently around her left nipple.

She cried out and her hands locked on his head. He was still on his knees between her legs, and she naturally wrapped her thighs around him for balance. Keeping her in place with one arm, Joe drifted his other hand down along her graceful spine to the flaring of her softly padded hip, then lower, cupping one warm, supple cheek. He kneaded that wonderfully female flesh while teasing her nipple with his tongue, circling, flicking.

Luna panted, kissed his ear, then whispered hotly, "Joe . . ."

Licking her nipple with lazy enjoyment, he said, "Tell me what you want, babe."

"Quit teasing me."

"I'm not." But he knew he was. He needed her to catch up and the best way to get her there was to build the pleasure, the anticipation.

"Joe . . ." Frustration laced her tone, and her thighs tightened, squeezing him, before she pleaded, *"Suck on me."*

The wanton command fired his blood. He drew her deep, locking her to him with one arm across her back, the other braced under her ass. He could feel her wet vulva against his abdomen, grinding into him.

With a harsh growl, he lowered her flat to the bed. His arm behind her kept her breasts raised and made it easy for him to continue tasting her, first one breast, then the other, while Luna twisted and tightened and made soft, incredible sounds of need. Almost there, he thought, but he wanted more. He wanted everything.

Working his way down her body, Joe kissed her ribs, her navel, the soft flesh of her belly. This time her legs fell open without his instruction. Joe hooked his arms under her thighs to hold her motionless while he looked at her.

Her sex was swollen, flushed a darker pink, glistening. His heart clamored in his chest, his muscles rippling with need. Wanting to devour her, he pressed his face into her and licked, slow, hot, flicking over her clitoris once before prodding, sliding his tongue deep into her.

She cried out; her hips shifted, seeking more. But Joe was content to tease for a while first, so other than that one playful lick, he avoided her clitoris—until her fingers again locked into his hair with stinging, insistent force.

"Damn you, Joe."

He almost smiled. "All right, baby." He closed his mouth around her and very, very softly, he suckled.

Her reaction was immediate and mind-blowing. She started coming, wild and hot. Spasms shook her and she sobbed, the sounds real and raw as she gave herself to the pleasure. Joe didn't ease up, wanting it to last, pushing her until she grew hoarse in her pleas, twisting to be free.

In an instant, he was over her, taking her mouth despite her weak protest and kissing her hard, long, sharing her taste with her. He cupped both breasts and tugged at already sensitive nipples.

Luna panted and groaned. "Oh, God."

Joe drew back. "I'm going to last about two seconds, but I swear I'll make it up to you."

Eyes heavy, her lips swollen, she smiled and languidly touched his clenched jaw. "All right."

Her easy agreement only added to Joe's urgency. He'd been waiting months to be with her and now his control shattered. He jerked free and shucked off his jeans in record time. Before tossing the pants aside, he removed the cell phone from his pocket and put it on the nightstand, then tore open a condom packet and rolled on the protection.

Luna's golden brown eyes glittered and her face

was flushed. Low, in a near soundless whisper, she murmured, "I want to look at you, Joe."

He groaned. She looked like a wanton angel reclining across the bed naked. He adored the sight of her lush hips and rosy breasts, those still-puckered nipples. "No, not right now." He stretched out over her, holding her face and kissing her gently, softly. "I need to be inside you, Luna." His voice shook. "Right now."

She bent her knees and lifted her legs alongside his hips. Giving him a slight smile, she nodded. "Ready when you are."

Joe held her gaze, loving the smoldering response mirrored there as he reached down and stroked her sex with his fingertips. Despite just coming, her eyelids grew heavier and her pulse quickened. She didn't look away. They both breathed too hard, too fast. Using his middle finger, Joe parted her, spread her wetness to make his entry easier for her, then pressed his hips forward, nudging the head of his cock inside. Her inner muscles immediately clamped down on him.

Her eyes closed. His jaw locked.

"Eyes open, sweetheart," Joe rasped. "I want to see you."

She drew two deep breaths, swallowed, and lifted her lids again.

"That's it." His muscles twitched. "Do you have any idea how good you feel?" He rocked back and forth, gliding his cock just barely inside her, easing her, teasing them both by refusing to go deep yet.

She tried to lever up closer, and Joe caught both her wrists, pressing them to the bed beside her pillow. "I've thought about this so many times, how it'd be, how you'd be. I wanted to fuck you about two minutes after you said hello."

Lips parted, a glistening sheen of sweat on her upper chest, Luna said, "Me . . . me, too."

His eyes flared. Now there was an admission guaranteed to destroy his discipline. "This is more than fucking."

She stared at him, but damn it, he needed her to know, to understand, that this had grown into something more than just the physical. He emphasized his point by thrusting a little harder, going deeper, stretching her.

Her body arched—in pleasure, acceptance. She moaned.

Joe held himself firmly inside her and reached down to hook his arms behind her knees. Her eyes rounded in uncertainty. "Joe . . ."

"Shhh. I want everything, Luna." He spread her legs wide and high, leaving her vulnerable.

Her pupils expanded until her eyes looked almost black. Her breathing became shallow, then jerky when he eased forward all the way, filling her up, touching her womb. He growled at the way Luna squirmed beneath him, how her teeth sank into her bottom lip, how her body squeezed him like a fist, milking him, urging him on.

He withdrew, then reentered her with a forceful thrust that shook the bed, jiggled her soft breasts, made her gasp and cry out. Her head tipped back, her fingers grasped his biceps as if to ground herself. A red haze of blinding pleasure rose up inside Joe. He saw her nipples, painfully tight, and lowered his hairy chest to lightly abrade them. The new position tilted her hips even more, buried him impossibly deep.

Luna moaned—and to Joe's amazement and satisfaction, she began to come again.

It was enough. It was too much. Joe pressed his

face into her throat and drove into her over and over again. Her legs were strong, straining against the hold of his arms. Her nails bit into his shoulders, leaving half moons. She screamed out her climax—and Joe came with her, his mouth open on her shoulder, his growls barely suppressed against her soft skin.

Seconds ticked by, the silence in the room broken only by their still-gasping breaths. Joe rolled to his back, one hand limp on his abdomen, the other possessively holding her thigh. His legs still tingled, his heart continued to thunder, and his mind felt like mush.

The rich, musky scent of sex permeated the air; they were both damp with sweat.

It took some effort, but Joe pulled himself upright and removed the condom, wrapping it in two tissues from Luna's nightstand. Braced on one stiffened arm, he turned to look at her. Her eyes were closed, her hair wild, her legs slightly parted. Her nipples were soft now, but her chest still rose and fell with her deep breaths. What he felt for this one particular woman couldn't be measured or put into words. She was so incredibly beautiful to him—her body, her spirit, her heart.

"You ready yet?"

She swallowed, got her eyes half open. In a croak, she asked, "Ready?"

"You didn't think I was done, did you?"

Her eyes widened and she choked. "But . . ."

Joe turned and lowered himself atop her. Her breasts made a nice soft cushion that immediately fired his blood. "Not by a long shot. You put me off for too long for me to finish this any time quick. Maybe after a week of gluttony I can calm down enough to take you just once or twice a day. But we don't need to get the kids for a couple of hours, I have plenty of rubbers, and you look good enough to eat. Again."

Her eyes darkened and she swallowed hard. "Well . . . when you put it like that."

During the rest of that week, they fell into a routine that suited Luna just fine. Each morning they drove the kids to school, then came home to make love. Every time with Joe was hotter, longer, more intimate. He was insatiable and undeniable. He took her in ways she'd never considered, but always left her screaming in pleasure. Luna felt addicted to his scent, his big, gorgeous body, and his exciting touch. The longer he stayed, the more she loved him, and the more she wanted him to stay forever.

She knew that was impossible, that eventually he'd head back to his apartment and his family and his sexual variety. But danger awaited him back home, so until Bruno Caldwell was caught and put behind bars, Luna prayed he would want to stay. So far, he'd shown no signs of wanting to leave.

They spent the late afternoons tending to chores, and now the yard looked better than ever. Dinner was definitely a family affair with lots of conversation, joking, and the inevitable bickering between Willow and Austin. Afterward, they played or watched a movie together until the kids went to bed. Austin had no qualms about curling up at Joe's side and talking through half the movie, but other than Willow grousing, they persevered.

Once the kids were tucked into bed, Joe would settle at the kitchen table and go over plans to reopen the lake, crunching numbers and figuring strategies for hours. He'd already applied for permits, so things were under way.

He also worked with Luna on setting up a budget, determining what it would cost to get the exterior of the house in order and keep it that way. Luna had never before been responsible for more than one—herself—and she appreciated his efforts. It amazed her the lengths Joe went to in trying to help out.

Whenever any of them left the house, Joe insisted on going along. Though nothing more had happened, he claimed his instincts told him to be on guard, so by God, he'd be on guard, and that was that. They were getting along so well, and Luna trusted him enough, that she didn't make waves just because he was overly protective.

In fact, she understood how he felt, because she had her own store of protective instincts now—for Austin, for Willow . . . and for Joe. She tried not to let Joe know. He wasn't a man who would tolerate coddling. Joe was arrogant enough in his ability to protect that he set himself in the path of danger to shield total strangers. It was what he did, who he was as a man.

And now he'd taken them all on as his responsibility. She hadn't meant to do that to him, to burden him with her worries. Knowing he would willingly risk himself kept her awake at night. The damn bruises on his body were finally gone, but they'd been replaced with the web of tiny but deep scratches on his neck and arms that he'd gotten wrestling in the brambles.

None of the scratches were serious, and they were already fading, too, but Luna still remembered the awful panic she'd suffered watching Joe foolishly rush out the door into the night to face an unknown threat. The man had no sense of self-preservation. She'd wanted to clobber him for scaring her like that, yet his actions had made a startling impact on the kids, reinforcing the fact that they mattered and that they were loved.

Austin's evening walks were shorter now. He wore himself out chasing behind Joe and just being a kid, playing hard and enjoying himself.

Willow found more reasons to smile, especially whenever Clay called—and he called often. Luna almost felt sorry for him because Willow hadn't yet reciprocated Clay's interest, was, in fact, downright cold to him. Luna knew it couldn't be easy on her, because she did like Clay. But despite everything that had happened to her, Willow had a strong sense of self-respect, and she wasn't going to be quick to forgive Clay for his unkind treatment. Luna was very proud of her, and she loved her more with each day.

Luna was beginning to relax in her role as guardian when on the forth morning, as they were preparing for school, Austin noticed a message left on the shed down by the lake. Standing in front of the window, he shouted for Joe, bringing them all together to read the hateful comment.

Dark red paint, dripping down the side of the shed like fresh oozing blood, made an incongruous picture against the serenity of the calm lake. The rising morning sun reflected off the placid surface with a myriad of colors. Birds chirped, happy to start another day. A duck glided across the surface. Leaves rustled in a warm breeze.

But those calming effects of nature couldn't soften the message: *Trash Go Away.*

"*Why?*" Willow cried out, holding her middle and backing away from the window. Big tears glistened in her eyes. "Why can't they just leave us alone?"

Alarmed by Willow's upset, especially since the girl was usually so contained, Luna put an arm around her and gathered her close.

Seeing his sister's tears, Austin stiffened up and shouted, "I'll stomp him into the dirt!"

"Him *who?*" Willow said, now clinging to Luna. "We don't know who it is."

Joe still faced the window, but his quiet voice soothed them all. "I know he's a coward, not worth your tears, not worth Austin's anger."

Luna rubbed Willow's back and at the same time reached over to the stove to turn off the scrambled eggs. She was so furious she could spit. "Joe's right, you know. Only a complete sniveling coward leaves messages in the dark. He wants you upset, and he's succeeding. Don't you let him win, honey. You're so much better than that."

Willow pushed away. "No we're not." Her lip quivered, and tears still swam in her big dark eyes. "Everyone knows we're bastards, that we've never had a daddy, that Mom was never married."

Austin turned his cannon on his sister. "Shut up, Willow!"

"It's true," she shouted right back. "That's why they want us to leave. That's why they hate us. Our own father didn't want us."

Joe caught Austin and pressed him into a chair. "That's enough."

"I'll say it is." Luna kept her voice firm, her gaze direct on Willow's tear-ravaged face. "People are not judged by their parents, Willow. And thank God for that, because mine didn't care much about each other, or about me."

Joe's sharp gaze jerked toward her, and Luna

felt him watching her so intently, her skin prickled. Through their physical intimacy of the last few days, their emotional intimacy had also grown. Luna hadn't expected that. She'd thought, or maybe feared, that once Joe got sexually sated, he'd tire of her and be on his way. Instead, the opposite was true.

He just seemed to grow hungrier, and the more they made love, the more he wanted to talk, to know about her. Yet, she shied away from sharing her background with him. They were so different, and like Willow, she hadn't wanted him to judge her by her past. She wanted everyone, including Joe, to see her as a strong woman, not a wounded one.

"They weren't good parents, Willow, and that means we didn't have much of a family. I've pretty much felt alone since I was Austin's age. But you, well, your mother was a better single parent than many couples are. She loved you and Austin and that made you a family, the best kind of family, with or without a father around. If anyone did judge you by your mother, they would already know how wonderful you and Austin are."

Willow glanced at her little brother, dashed away a tear and nodded. "She did love us."

"I know. That's plain to see anytime I think about how special you and Austin are."

Willow looked at Luna a long time, then whispered, "She did a lot of the stuff you do. Talking with us, hugging us when we don't expect it."

Austin nodded. "All that mothering stuff. Patricia never did it, but I'm glad. I didn't like her anyway."

Luna just knew she was going to start bawling. If she looked at Joe, she'd lose it, so she turned away to the stove. "Well, it was Patricia's loss. And your father's, too, because he's missing out on some pretty special kids."

"Maybe he has other kids now. Like your father got other kids."

Austin scrunched up his face. "Do you think maybe he does? Do you think we'll ever meet him?"

Luna's heart slammed into her chest, but she managed a credible shrug. "I don't know. Do you want to?"

Willow said immediately, "No. He wasn't here for my mom, so I don't care if I ever meet him."

Austin frowned. "Me either."

Knowing they both lied, that their hurt probably went bone deep, Luna turned back to them and did some of that hugging they'd accused her of. "Maybe someday you'll change your mind. But for now, if anyone is stupid enough to judge you only because your mother didn't marry, then they aren't anyone you need to be concerned with. Okay?"

Joe kept one hand on Austin's shoulder while reaching out to stroke Luna's head. Very gently, he tucked her hair behind her ear. When she chanced a quick glance at him, he smiled. Before she could decipher that smile, he turned to Willow.

"I will find the guy harassing us, honey, I promise. His shenanigans will end, but in the meantime, don't let him know he got to you. I want you and Austin to go on with your business, heads high, showing him that he can't hurt you, that he's not important enough to be bothered with. Okay? Do you think you can do that?"

"I can," Austin bragged, nodding hard.

Willow sighed. "Me, too." Then, in a small voice, "But I wish it'd end."

"It will." Joe tipped up her chin. "You have my word."

And if it didn't, Luna thought to herself, well, then maybe she should consider moving the kids away.

She met Joe's gaze and knew he was thinking the same. They loved the house, but the important thing was that they'd have a home, stability, and less worries. "I need to finish breakfast so we won't be late."

"I'll call Scott and fill him in, then go down and wash the paint off the building." Joe turned toward his room but was stalled when Austin jumped up.

"I'll help you."

Minutes later, Willow watched Joe and Austin heading toward the lake. She stood there, silent in her thoughts, eyes still wounded. Then she shook her head and turned to Luna with a heartbreaking smile of determination. "I'll help with breakfast."

They were both so special, Luna had to wonder how she'd gotten so lucky. She was no longer alone, because she had Willow and Austin. She glanced out the window one last time and saw Austin take Joe's hand as they trekked across a grassy field. Was Joe hers, too, or was he only on loan?

It didn't really matter to the moment. For right now, for as long as he wanted to be with her, she'd take what she could get.

Chapter Thirteen

It hadn't been easy to look for clues with Austin dancing around him, talking like a chatterbox. Joe had known kids, plenty of kids. But he'd never realized the strength of their individual natures. They were complex little people, and he found he enjoyed uncovering and understanding each facet of their personalities.

It hadn't taken him long to conclude that Austin used bold statements whenever he felt threatened. Bravado masked his biggest fears, those of losing Willow and being left alone. He was pugnacious when riled, loud when uncertain, and forever bursting with questions about everything and everyone.

He was a proud little guy, refusing to admit to insecurities.

Willow reacted to her worries just the opposite. She said what she thought and felt, and when she wasn't comfortable doing that, she said nothing at all, closing up tighter than a clam and keeping to herself.

For two years, she'd had the weight of the world

on her frail shoulders, but she'd handled it like a trooper and kept her priorities straight. Circumstances had forced a level of maturity on her normally expected of someone five or six years older, yet she still had an adolescent's vulnerability.

She'd broken down that morning—and crushed Joe's heart in the process. How anyone could deliberately hurt that little girl was beyond him. Like Austin, Willow was very special to him now. She was family, damn it, and Joe protected his family.

He thought about Luna's comments in the kitchen—and he felt like a pig. He'd been in such a rush to get her into bed, not once had he ever really asked her about her life. Now his brain was bombarded with questions. If she wasn't close with any of her family, where did she spend her holidays? Alone, eating Lean Cuisine? Just the thought of that made his stomach cramp and nearly suffocated him in tender thoughts. He'd be willing to bet that no one did anything special for her on her birthday—hell, he didn't even know her birth date. But he'd find out. In a thousand different ways, he'd make up for her losses. She understood the responsibility of family; now Joe wanted to show her how fun family could be.

While cleaning the paint off the shed, Joe carefully inspected the area. Footprints remained in the loamy, dew-wet ground, showing large, adult-sized feet. Surprisingly, the tread wasn't that of a sneaker or athletic shoe, but rather a smooth-bottomed dress shoe.

The prints were fresh, and they weren't Joe's.

Bent weeds and crushed wildflowers left a very visible path. Whoever had painted the vile words had come across the same bramble-laden field where Joe had gotten scratched up after the last incident. It served as a prime location to leave a car while approaching the property.

A hidden camera at the road would be a good idea. He'd see to that first thing today. Joe no sooner had that thought than he shook his head.

A trip to the security store would be second on his list of things to do. First came Luna. He wanted to make love to her, to continue his daily campaign to win her over. She hadn't realized it yet, but he'd staked a claim. Not a temporary claim, either. No, Luna was his, and she was staying his.

She'd figure it out soon enough when he refused to leave.

Willow meandered outside, not really looking for Clay. *She wasn't.* But Ms. Rose had given her a break while she and Austin worked on bugs. Ick. She didn't even want to be in the same room with the creepy things, so Ms. Rose said it was okay for her to go out to the playground as long as she didn't leave the fenced-in area.

Since her first day at the summer school, she'd seen Clay hanging around outside. She'd deliberately ignored him. He hadn't been with his friends, but stood outside alone. Waiting. For her?

As she stepped away from the building, Willow glanced around and there he was, leaning over the chain-link fence that surrounded the playground as if he'd known she would come. She hated him.

She was so glad to see him.

The second his gaze settled on hers, Willow put her nose in the air and turned away, purposely snubbing him, wishing she could hurt him as much as he'd hurt her.

Apparently through with waiting, Clay jumped over the fence and started toward her. "Willow!"

She whipped around, stunned at his persistence—and secretly pleased. "Go away, Clay. I don't want to talk to you."

"Then just let me talk." His long legs ate up the distance between them.

"I don't want to listen to you either."

He drew up short, frustrated, embarrassed. "C'mon, Willow. You won't take my calls, you won't visit with me." His face was red, but he continued, determined. "I . . . I want to tell you that I'm sorry."

Shock rippled through her, but Willow did her best to hide it. She crossed her arms and glared. "For what?"

He scowled right back, his hands on his hips, his gaze direct. "For everything. For . . . being mean and saying nasty stuff to you."

Willow's heart raced, shaking her so badly she sneered, "Why did you?"

"I dunno." His gaze was locked on hers, troubled by her loss of control. He shrugged in helpless confusion and took two more cautious steps toward her. "You went out with that guy and—"

"And he told lies on me." She took two steps toward him, squaring off. If he insulted her again, she'd pop him right in the nose. "And *you* believed him, Clay Owen." Then, choking on her hurt, she added, "I hate you."

His shoulders fell. Very softly he said, "No, you don't." He inched closer until he stood right in front of her. He had his hands tucked into his pants pockets, his head down. She heard him swallow. "I'm sorry, Willow."

Willow turned her back on him. "Fine. Apology

accepted." She sniffed, hating the stupid tears. They'd never gotten her much. They certainly hadn't gotten her mother back or returned their lives to normal. For the longest time now she'd faced each new day with grim acceptance, just wanting to get through it but not quite enjoying it. She'd hated Patricia, but she'd been afraid to say so. Dinah had often told her that if she and Austin didn't behave, they could be split up and put in foster homes. Patricia didn't abuse them; for the most part, she just ignored them. And Willow had considered that better than some of the alternatives.

But there'd been no love, and she felt so hollowed out inside, it sickened her.

And Clay . . . He'd deliberately added misery to her life when she couldn't understand why. The tears clogged in her throat, and she started away from him, refusing to let him see.

He caught her arm. "Willow."

He sounded ready to cry, too, but she didn't care. "Let go." Darn, her voice had been all wavery, not at all earnest.

"No." Very gently, he brought her around to him. He tried to see her face, but Willow kept her head lowered, her face averted. "I've been an awful jerk, Willow. I don't blame you for not wanting to talk to me. I was just so jealous, and I liked you so much . . . more than any other girl I know."

A humorless laugh erupted. "Good thing you didn't hate me then, huh?"

"I could never hate you." He tucked her long hair behind her ear. "Can we start over, Willow? Please?"

Filled with suspicion, Willow forced her head up. "Why?"

"Why what?"

"Why are you being so nice now?" She didn't understand his sudden turnaround, and she sure didn't trust it.

His mouth twisted in a wry grin. "I got the impression that big guy at your house would never let me near you again otherwise."

"Joe? You're being nice to me only because of Joe?"

"No." He hurried to reassure her, stumbling on his words. "I was really mad when he told me to get lost, and I was thinking of ways to get to you, how I could still see you without him knowing. And that got me thinking about *why* I want to see you so bad that I'd risk getting in trouble with him." Clay cleared his throat. "He's kind of an intimidating guy."

"I know. But he's real nice. At least to me and Austin." She wasn't ready to let him off the hook and added with a hint of menace, "I don't know how he feels about you."

Clay's Adam's apple did a dive when he swallowed hard. "You know, since your mom died, everyone has said bad things about you and Austin. Everything changed and I hated that." He chewed his bottom lip, thinking. "I guess I, um, took it out on you."

Clay had been one of the few familiar things that remained in her life, and he'd so easily destroyed that. "Real nice of you, Clay. Thanks."

He tipped his head back and groaned. "God, I'm sorry, Willow. Really." He held both her hands. "Please give me another chance."

Still not trusting him, she asked, "A chance for what?"

"We could just be friends—if that's what you want."

He sounded as if he wanted a whole lot more, but Willow wasn't about to forgive him so quickly. Still, she wanted, needed, a friend more than anything else. Her chest hurt, but she said, "Yeah, all right. But you'll have to be nice to Austin, too."

He grinned, and Willow felt her heart flutter and her stomach flip. He was just so cute. "Can you keep him from pounding on me?"

"As long as you're nice, Austin will be nice. At least, I think so. He doesn't like you much more than Joe does."

Still grinning, Clay said, "I'll win Austin over."

"What about your friends?"

"To hell with 'em. If they're mean to you, then they can get lost. I don't care."

Happiness started to bubble inside her. A smile twitched, but she bit her lip to hide it. "What about your stepdad?"

Suddenly Clay looked older than sixteen. He straightened his shoulders like a man and turned serious. "I'm sorry that he's never liked you. I don't understand it except that he takes his duties to the town real serious, and he thinks the fact that you and Austin don't have a dad is a bad influence or something. But he's wrong about you, Willow, and I don't care what he thinks anymore."

"He might get mad at you if he knows we're . . . friends."

Clay shook his head. "He doesn't have to know, but even if he does find out, it won't matter." He tugged her closer, dropping his forehead to hers. "We've been friends a long time, Willow. You're the only one that matters."

He started to kiss her, but Willow turned her head and his mouth brushed her cheek. It was enough to make her flush, to cause her toes to curl inside her new sandals. Very few guys had ever kissed her, but she felt ready to give it a try. *After* she knew for certain that Clay was sincere. "I should go back in."

Clay released her. "Okay." He drew a big breath. "If I call you later, will you talk to me?"

"Sure." Willow started backing toward the school. Though she tried to contain her smile, her cheeks hurt. Things seemed so different now, better, promising.

And then she saw the scratches on Clay's arms. Her stomach dropped into her feet and she swayed.

"Willow?" Clay trotted toward her. "What is it?"

He started to touch her, but she reeled back, sickened by a barrage of suspicion. "Your arms."

He glanced down. "My arms?"

"How did you get those scratches?" She stared at him with accusation, with fresh heartache. "How, Clay?"

"They're nothing." He stared down at the scratches with indifference. "Quincy brought a stray kitten home and it's still trying to get comfortable settling in. It's more wild than not—sort of reminds me of Austin if you want the truth." He tried a teasing grin that only made Willow feel more hollow.

"A cat?" Disbelief swept through her. Quincy Owen was not a pet lover. Willow didn't know how she knew that, but she did. "You expect me to believe that your stepdad brought home a cat?"

Now Clay frowned. "Why would I lie about it?" And when she still frowned at him, he shrugged. "Come by the house and see for yourself. We made it a real nice bed in the mudroom. I'm going to take it to the vet's tomorrow for shots and stuff."

She hated the pleading in her tone when she whispered, "Don't lie to me, Clay."

"I'm not." He searched her face, worried, sincere. *I won't.* I swear it, Willow."

She stared at him a long time, and finally believed him. "All right." Her heart still raced, as much with hope as dread. Should she tell Joe? God, she just didn't know and she felt sick with trepidation. "I . . . I have to go in now."

"Wait." He reached out for her, but she ducked away. "Willow, why were you asking about—?"

Willow didn't let him finish. She turned and ran for the school. She believed him, she really did. But . . . What if Clay was lying? His scratches looked an awful lot like the ones Joe had. What if Clay was the one who'd done those awful things to her home, taunting her, trying to force her to move away? What if he was the one calling her trash? His stepfather disliked her; everyone in town knew that.

Shaking from the inside out, Willow ducked inside the school and leaned back on the wall. *Please don't let it be Clay. Please.* But she knew she had to tell Joe. Whoever it was, they not only hurt her, but Austin, too. And she couldn't allow that.

If it was Clay, she had to know.

But maybe it wasn't. And then one small part of her life could return to normal.

Luna curled into Joe's side, replete, exhausted, madly in love. Damn, he was good. With his hands, his mouth, his whole body. She shivered with a small aftershock of pleasure and kissed his chest.

Joe raised his head from the mattress and glanced down at her. "Now what was that for?"

"What?"

"That small shiver."

"Oh." Luna smiled at him while smoothing her hand through his dark chest hair. His muscles glistened with sweat and he still breathed too hard, yet he'd felt her shiver. Joe stayed so aware of her that she couldn't sniff without him noticing. She'd never known a man to be so attuned to a woman. It was both comforting and disconcerting to have all that masculine focus directed her way. "I was just thinking how incredibly talented you are."

"In bed?"

She nodded.

He grinned and dropped his head back with a groan. "Glad you noticed. And for the record, I get better with age, okay?"

That made her laugh and feel a bit melancholy. She wouldn't get to sample Joe as he aged; he'd be long gone by then, working his magic on numerous other women. The cad.

"I'm sure you will. I can see you even as a grandpa, tottering around and grabbing for some poor woman's behind."

Eyes closed, expression composed, he murmured, "Well, your ass is so fine, babe, I don't doubt it for a second."

It was Luna's turn to rear up and stare at him. He said that as if *she* would be growing old with him.

Joe slowly opened his eyes, revealing smoldering heat and sexual intent. His attention dipped to her breasts.

"Come here." His gravel-deep voice almost made her lose track of her thoughts. When Joe wanted her, it made her want him, too.

"No wait." Luna attempted to hold him off. Surely, Joe didn't think he could drop a suggestive statement like that, hinting at a future for the first time, then just carry on as if he hadn't said it? "What did you—"

"I thought you were done telling me no." With laughable ease despite her efforts, Joe brought her forward until her breast was close to his mouth. "We can talk later."

"But, Joe . . . *oh, God.*" His mouth was hot, gently tugging, speeding her toward arousal. She closed her eyes and relished the pleasure.

Joe idly licked her before switching to the other breast. "I love how you taste, sweetheart. All over." He caught her hips and levered her over him. "Come on top so I can get my hands on this sweet ass we've been discussing."

"You've been discussing it, not me." But Luna found herself sprawled over him, her legs open around him, his greedy mouth back at her nipple while his hands squeezed and palpated her behind. Already Joe grew hard, and she knew what that meant. Since she'd said yes, he'd been unstoppable and insatiable.

For days now, he'd generously overwhelmed her with so much pleasure she hadn't had a chance to reciprocate. But Joe had such an incredible body that she wanted her turn at giving. She wiggled free and scooted down his chest to his washboard abdomen. Fingers spread wide, she reveled in the textures of crisp body hair, sleek flesh over hard bones and bulging muscles.

Before she could move too far south, Joe's hands clamped on her waist in protest. "Come back here."

Luna raised up on stiffened arms. "Hush, Joe." While speaking, she visually explored his body. His small copper nipples were drawn tight, barely visible beneath his chest hair. His shoulders glistened with sweat. His inky black hair was mussed.

She stroked his chest down to his hipbones and smiled. His penis, soft only minutes ago after a grinding release, was now long and hard again, twitching for attention. "Just lie there and enjoy yourself for once, okay?"

His nostrils flared; his gaze brightened until the blue of his eyes burned like a flame. In a sexy, very interested rumble, he asked, "What are you going to do?"

"Nothing that you haven't already done to me."

A long, husky groan escaped and he squeezed his eyes shut. "Lord, help me."

Powerful and in control, Luna laughed. "A big, strong guy like you can handle it, right?"

He twisted his head to glance at the clock. "We have two hours till we have to leave to get the kids. I'll need at least one of those hours to recoup, okay?"

Joe had such a dry, sincere sense of humor that he kept her grinning. "I'll keep that in mind."

She moved to the side of him, then rested one hand high on his thick, hair-roughened thigh. "Where to start?"

Sounding choked, Joe asked, "Do I get to make suggestions?"

Using one fingertip, Luna traced the length of his cock. "Here?"

"Oh, yeah."

She laughed and swatted at him. "Turn over."

"Turn over?" He slanted a very dubious, cautious glance her way.

"You look just as uncertain as Austin with that expression."

Joe grunted and rolled onto his stomach. "I am never uncertain in bed." Arms folded beneath his head, he attempted to look relaxed, but Luna saw the stiff set of his wide shoulders, the tensed muscles in his legs. Oh, Joe Winston was far from relaxed. "Have at it, woman."

"Have I ever told you that for some insane reason, I kind of like it when you call me woman?"

Momentarily distracted, he said, "Yeah?"

"That's right." Luna dragged her fingertips down the long length of his spine. His back was broad, silky smooth and taut. Well-defined muscles at either side of his spine caused a deep groove that she found ultimately male and appealing. "I like butts, too. Course, with this silly tattoo on yours . . ." She again read the words, *I Love Lou*, and shook her head, bemused.

"I'll have it removed."

"I thought you said that'd hurt?" She stroked the colorful design on his firm bun and felt her breath catch. "It doesn't bother me."

Joe twisted to his back again. "Yeah, well, it's starting to bother me."

That surprised her. "Why?"

He rolled his eyes and growled. "Are you going to keep teasing me or are you going to get down to business?"

Biting back a smile at his impatience, she snaked her hand lower and cupped his testicles. They pulled tight. "You're so hot."

"You're in bed naked with me," he rasped. "What did you expect?"

She continued to fondle him. Very softly, she asked, "Is this the kind of business you anticipated?"

"Oh, yeah."

Without warning, she curled her fingers around the very base of his erection to hold him steady, bent down, and drew the broad, sensitive tip into her mouth. Joe went rigid on a long, vibrating groan.

It was a heady thing, pushing big, badass Joe Winston past his control. She drew him deep and was rewarded with another, harsher growl. He smelled delicious, of heated male flesh and the unique smell of Joe. This close to his sex, his scent was intoxicating. She moved her tongue around him, teasing the underside of the head where he was most sensitive, then slowly drew back.

Joe's hips lifted off the bed, following her retreat.

"Relax, Joe."

He grunted, but his hands went behind his head, locked there, and his biceps swelled and hardened and flexed as he visibly restrained himself.

Pleased with his efforts, Luna treated him to a long, slow lick. "You look in pain, Joe."

"Yeah," he rasped, eyes squeezed tight and teeth on edge, "it feels so fucking good I almost can't stand it."

"Perfect," Luna purred and drew him in again while cradling his balls, gently kneading. She fell into a satisfying rhythm, taking him deep, slowly withdrawing, licking the head and then swallowing him deep again.

Among raw groans of encouragement, Joe started to tremble. After three minutes, he was stiff enough to break. "I ain't gonna last, babe." Every big, hard muscle in his body wound tight. *"Luna?"*

She loved the desperation in the way he said her name.

With a curse, Joe halfheartedly tried to pull her away. He caught her hair and tugged gently, but Luna made it plain that she wanted all of him. Finally, with a long moan of surrender, Joe came.

He still held her head, showing her what he needed, gently guiding her. His tempered strength was exciting.

Luna waited until he collapsed back against the mattress, laboring for breath and still giving low, sated sounds of pleasure, then she cuddled up to his side again. A limp arm came around her, but other than that, he didn't move.

"Joe?" She touched his chest, stroked his crisp hair, then flattened her palm over his galloping heartbeat.

"Yeah?"

I love you. No, Luna wouldn't do that to him, wouldn't make him feel awkward during the time he remained with them. She knew how Joe felt about settling down, so she swallowed the surge of emotions and kissed his right pectoral. "Thank you for everything you've done and everything you're doing. We all appreciate it."

His breath held a moment, then he shrugged. "S'no problem."

He still sounded winded, making Luna chuckle. "The kids adore you, and they're so impressed by you."

The limp arm around her tightened in a slight hug. "I feel the same about them. They're incredible and smart and so damn cute." He shook his head and got his eyes open to look at her. "And you." He kissed her forehead. "For a free spirit, you've got the best maternal instincts I think I've ever seen. The kids might like me, but they trust in you. In such a short time, you've reassured them enough to make a huge difference."

Luna sighed and rested back against him. "We could make so much more progress if we didn't have all this stupid harassment going on. Every time I think it might be over, something else happens."

Joe shook his head. "I can't understand how anyone could mistreat those two. And to think that their father walked out . . . on them . . ." Joe sat up and stared at Luna.

"What?" She, too, sat up. "What is it?"

"Do you have any idea who their father might be?"

"No." Luna saw the wheels churning and knew Joe was busy working something out in his head. "No one seems to know. From what I understand, he's never been a part of their lives."

Joe swung his legs over the bed and stood. "I want to check something."

As he left the room, Luna trotted after him. He went to the kitchen and picked up the stack of papers he kept atop the microwave. They were records of the lake and the business that Chloe used to run before her death. He'd been going over everything nightly while figuring out all they'd need to do to make it profitable again.

Joe shuffled through the papers until he found the original records. Being he was naked, he didn't have his glasses on him, so he held the paper back at arm's length and squinted. "Well, what about that."

"What?" Luna tried to see over his shoulder, but he was too tall.

He glanced down at her, his expression thoughtful. "Did you know that your cousin got the lake and all this property fourteen years ago?"

If there was significance in that, Luna didn't understand it. "So?"

"So that's when Willow was born. How would a single, pregnant woman afford all this? Even minimizing property values because of the area, it's still one hell of a set-up. The house alone is worth a bundle, and it's not exactly small. Why would a single woman with only one baby even want it?"

Luna shook her head. "I don't know what you're getting at."

"I think Willow's father gave it to her. I think the son of a bitch knew she was pregnant, that maybe he bought her off with the house."

"But why? Lots of men get women pregnant and don't marry them. This is a new age—single mothers are everywhere. And how do you account for Austin? Because, Joe, they were born five years apart, yet they look exactly alike."

"Like Chloe?"

"I suppose. Austin said Willow looked just like their mom, and he looks like a smaller, masculine version of her with the big dark eyes and fair hair. That's not a real common combination. Usually someone so blond has blue eyes, or someone with eyes so dark has dark hair also."

"True. They have very striking looks."

"But wouldn't different fathers have some influence on appearance? And if they have the same father, why would the guy buy Chloe off, then still come around enough to get her pregnant a second time?"

Joe lifted one brawny shoulder. "I don't know. Maybe he was already married, so paying child support would've given him away. This would be easier, support but without anyone knowing. He could enjoy Chloe's company, keep her happy with the property, and still keep everything secretive. It'd be a lot easier to hide one land purchase than to cover up weekly payments."

"Maybe Chloe loved him too much to deny him, even though he wouldn't marry her."

"Maybe. I think I'll find out where Chloe used to work. Maybe that'll give us a clue as to who she—" A knock sounded on the kitchen door behind them, startling them both. Joe's gaze shot up, and he cursed. Luna ducked behind him, trying to hide.

A woman they didn't recognize stood there. She started to put her face to the door window to look in, and with a horrified yelp, Luna dashed into Joe's bedroom with him hot on her heels.

They stood on the other side of the door, staring at each other wide-eyed. Joe started to laugh. "Busted."

Luna punched him in the shoulder. "It's not funny. Who is she?"

"How the hell should I know?" He peeked out the door, saw the woman peeking in, and jerked back. "Damn, I think she saw me."

Luna groaned. "Put on some pants. You can answer the door, and I'll slip out behind you to go upstairs and get dressed."

"Whatever you say, darling." Joe stepped around her to the rickety dresser and pulled open a drawer. He shook out a pair of jeans and stepped into them. "Quit looking so guilty. We're both adults. We're allowed to have a nooner if we want."

Luna held her head. "She saw us, I just know it."

Joe tipped up her chin. "So what? If she didn't want an eyeful, then she shouldn't go around peeking in door windows." He kissed her forehead, then turned her with a swat on her naked derriere. "Ready?"

Rubbing the stinging spot on her cheek, Luna groused, "Paybacks are hell, Joe Winston."

Not in the least threatened, he opened the door, blocking her from view with his body, and Luna made her escape. She raced out of the kitchen to the sound of Joe's chuckles, then hurried up the stairs.

As she dressed, her thoughts were more on how Chloe had gotten the property than on their impromptu visitor. She assumed the woman to be a neighbor, or perhaps someone ready to complain about Austin. Not that she'd let anyone insult him because she knew for a fact he'd been on his best behavior. Unlike Patricia, she didn't let the kids out of her sight except at school, and she trusted Julie to watch them closely while they were there. The rest of the time they stayed close at hand, so she knew they hadn't done a single thing out of line.

But when Luna reentered the room, freshly dressed in a long cotton summer dress of iridescent blue and aqua with silver sandals, she got the shock of her life.

Joe was at the counter, his chest and feet bare, making coffee. He cast one quick look her way, then said with great sobriety, "Luna, this is Ms. Grady—with CPS."

While Luna went mute, her rushed entrance now comically frozen in the doorway, the woman stood. Her demeanor was pleasant enough given the circumstances. She held out a hand.

"I did knock on the front door first, but no one answered, so I ventured around back just to see if you were in the yard."

"Oh. We were . . ." Luna swallowed and let her voice trail off. They were upstairs making love and she'd been so involved in Joe's body, nothing else had intruded. But she couldn't tell Ms. Grady that.

The woman nodded, amused, as if she quite understood without Luna's explanations. "As required by Children's Protective Services, this is a routine surprise visit to see the family situation." She laughed a little, still holding Luna's hand as her gaze slued toward Joe. "And it does appear that I've taken you by surprise."

Chapter Fourteen

Joe handed Ms. Grady a cup of coffee, then seated himself. "The kids aren't here right now."

"Oh?" Ms. Grady swept a long, skinny gray braid over her shoulder and sipped at her coffee. "Delicious. And where did you say the children are?"

Luna fumbled with her own cup. "They're at summer school. Julie Rose, their teacher, tells me they're really bright, but unfortunately a bit behind, so we all agreed that it'd be best if they—"

Hating to see her babble in nervousness, Joe interrupted. "We're due to pick them up in about half an hour."

"Well, I won't keep you, then." Her kind brown eyes surveyed first Luna, then Joe. She fought a crooked smile, cleared her throat, and said in all seriousness, "We got an anonymous call that the two of you had an illicit arrangement that could be detrimental to impressionable children."

Joe set his back teeth, refusing to appear embarrassed by looking away from Ms. Grady, and refusing to acknowledge Luna's groan of despair. "Whoever called you is misinformed."

She again sipped her coffee. "What is your arrangement here?"

Luna's mouth opened, but Joe beat her to it. "Luna is a wonderful guardian. The kids adore her and she adores them."

"And you, Mr. Winston?"

"Joe is—"

"What's not to adore?" Joe asked. "As I said, they're terrific kids."

Because he'd again interrupted her, Luna glared at him.

Ms. Grady laughed. "So do you intend to stay on here?"

Joe set his cup down hard and stood, which prompted Luna to surge to her feet also. She looked panicked and said his name in warning. Joe shook his head. "Ms. Grady, I don't know who called you, but—"

"Funny, we don't know who called either. But she seemed to think the fact that you two aren't married would cause quite a stir."

Joe stiffened. This wasn't quite how he'd planned things, but he'd be damned before he let Luna be second-guessed. "Are you saying we need to be married for Luna to keep the kids?"

Luna's eyes rounded and she fell back into her chair. "Married?"

Disliking the appalled way Luna sputtered that, Joe leaned on the table, facing Ms. Grady. "Because if that's the case, then I'll—"

Ms. Grady cut short Joe's grand sacrificial offering by chuckling again. "Obviously you two have no understanding of how we work. As to that, your anonymous caller doesn't either or she wouldn't have wasted her time. Please, sit down and compose yourselves. There's no reason for all these theatrics." She turned to Luna. "I don't suppose you have a cookie or something to go with this coffee?"

Luna's behind had just touched the chair seat, but with the woman's request, she shot back to her feet again. "Yes. Oatmeal and raisin. Willow and I made them yesterday. Austin tossed in the raisins. That is, he tossed in the ones he hadn't eaten . . ."

"Wonderful. I'll take two."

Joe had never seen Luna so flustered. She'd thrown food at him and raised hell with him when most people wouldn't dare. She'd faced off with Dinah and Patricia without blinking an eye. She'd taken on two emotionally troubled kids and treated the feat as if it were the most right thing in the world to do. But now she was stammering and blushing. He didn't like it.

He said, "Excuse me," and went into his room to get a shirt. He'd face this inquisition properly dressed, if nothing else. Part of Luna's discomfort was no doubt because of him. He didn't qualify as anyone's idea of the proper male guardian, not by a long shot. He knew he was too rough edged, and the damn earring didn't help.

Thank God Mrs. Grady hadn't seen the tattoo on his ass. That would have clinched his inappropriateness.

When he came back out, his upper body now covered, Ms. Grady smiled. "So you sleep down here, do you?"

The woman seemed awfully calm for an interrogator. "That's right. And Luna sleeps upstairs."

Joe felt his left eye twitch. He was too damn old to be explaining himself. "We're very discreet in front of the kids."

"It's really none of my business, you realize, but with the caller . . . Well, I did think it might be a propitious time to stop by. Not because the two of you have a relationship. These days, we see just about every type of family situation you can imagine. And believe me, from my perspective, the most important thing is that the children are well cared for."

"They are," Joe assured her. "Not that everything is perfect, but we're working on it."

"Yes, I heard there's been some trouble? That information came from the anonymous caller as well."

With an unfortunate clatter, Luna set a plate of cookies in the middle of the table and joined in. "Willow and Austin are still dealing with the loss of their mother. That's natural, I'm sure. They haven't had uninterrupted time to grieve, not with so many guardian switches and the problems with some neighbors."

Ms. Grady chose a cookie, then asked, "Neighbors?"

Joe sat back and let Luna explain. She was calmer now, concise, impressive. She detailed the scrapes Austin had gotten into, all the while defending him and singing his praises. She went on and on about how mature Willow was, then shared her concern that she hadn't had time to just be a young girl.

She also told of their plans to reopen the lake, and eventually do repairs to the house. She wanted the kids to understand that they planned for the future because the arrangement was permanent.

She hoped that with that emotional security, they could quit fretting about things that no child should have to worry about.

Joe was so proud of her. His loony Luna understood the kids better than even she realized, and the second he looked at Ms. Grady, he knew she saw it, too. His little moon goddess had made quite an impression on the social worker by just being herself.

When it was time for them to leave for the school, Ms. Grady stood. "I'm sorry I missed the children, but I feel very reassured that things are going well." She laced her hands together over her middle and looked at Joe and Luna in turn. "Only one thing concerns me."

"The trouble in town?" Joe ventured.

"That's right. We don't take any negative feedback lightly. The fact that someone called us anonymously in the hopes of putting you in a bad light is more alarming than what they had to say. The action suggests that one of you has made an enemy here already, and that could affect Willow or Austin or both."

"I'm working on that," Joe told her. "Deputy Scott Royal is aware of the problems. Also, I've put in a security camera to catch anyone who tries to sneak onto the property, and we have new alarms and locks. We keep the kids under pretty close watch, and soon, I'll be able to figure out exactly who's been behind the vandalism."

Ms. Grady allowed Joe to lead her to the door. "I want to be kept aware of what goes on." She handed Luna her card. "If things worsen, if I feel the children are in danger here, it may be necessary to move them to a safer place until the problems can be worked out."

Luna went pale. "I'd do that myself if I thought it necessary. But I'd be going with them."

Her obvious upset infuriated Joe. "That won't be necessary. I'll take care of it."

They stopped at Ms. Grady's car. She tipped her head and smiled. "I do believe you will, Mr. Winston." She shook both their hands, then got into her car. After starting the engine, she said, "Oh, one more thing."

Luna said, "Yes?"

"I didn't see the housekeeper, Dinah Belle."

"Dinah's not here anymore." Hoping to remove that stricken look from Luna's face, Joe took her hand and gave her fingers a reassuring squeeze. "We fired her."

"I see." Mrs. Grady's smile spread until she started to laugh. "A wise decision, as far as I'm concerned. I never did care for her manner. But it does give rise to speculation, now doesn't it?"

Luna raised both brows.

"The anonymous caller was a woman." She nodded. "Perhaps you already know who your enemy is."

Luna stood mute for fifteen seconds after Ms. Grady's car disappeared from sight. Joe knew just what she was thinking, and it annoyed him.

"Damn it, Luna, it wasn't Dinah that I tangled with the night of the fire."

Though she didn't say so, Joe knew she was unconvinced. She gave him one long, telling look, stepped around him, and headed for the house.

Joe stomped after her. "It was *not* a woman. Why in hell you keep wanting to think it is, I have no idea. But if a woman can outrun me and outwrestle me, then just shoot my ass now because I'm giving up."

Luna stopped on the porch to spare him a pity-ing glance. "A tattoo *and* a gunshot wound? Your poor behind."

His teeth locked. "I'm telling you, I know the difference between a man and a woman."

A slow smile appeared. Luna looked him over with bold sexual interest, then murmured, "Yes, you do." She crossed her arms and met his out-raged gaze. "But you refuse to see that a woman could very well be involved."

"All right, peripherally maybe." He waved a hand. "In the planning, maybe, just maybe. But that was not a woman in my apartment. The punch I landed on that guy would have knocked a woman out."

Frowning, Luna agreed. "You're probably right."

"And," he stated, now that she was ready to see reason, "that was not a woman who started the fire. I had my hands on him a couple of times, and bone structure alone told me it wasn't a woman." He drew a breath and looked at her squarely. "Know who I think is doing the vandalism here?"

Her expression arrested, her lips barely moving, Luna asked, "Who?"

"Willow and Austin's father."

Luna's mouth fell open. "Their *father*?"

Joe's cell phone rang before he could expound on his theories. Unfortunately, he'd left it inside in her bedroom. Fearing it might be the kids, that something might be wrong, they both went still.

Luna unglued her feet first. She dashed inside and up the stairs at top speed. She heard Joe thun-dering up the steps behind her. The phone was on the fourth ring when she snatched it up and pushed the button. "Hello?"

There was a pause, then a feminine voice in-quired, "Is this Luna?"

"Yes." Practically panting, Luna demanded, "Who's calling?"

"Alyx, Joe's sister. But hey, you sound . . . winded. Am I interrupting anything?"

Luna collapsed to the side of the mussed bed. Joe stared at her, concern bringing his brows low. She shook her head at him. "Hello, Alyx. No, you're not interrupting. We were downstairs, but Joe left his phone upstairs, and so I ran . . ."

"Left it by the bed, huh?"

Luna said, "Well . . ." and heard a snicker.

With the same irreverence Joe often displayed, Alyx said, "Yeah, that's my brother. I'm glad to hear things are going so, uh, well."

Perhaps outrageousness ran in the family. "If you want to speak to him, he's right here."

"He's looming again, isn't he?" Alyx had a penchant for theatrics, given the aggrieved sigh that sounded in Luna's ear. "Joe always looms when he's feeling protective. Believe me, I know it well."

Luna couldn't help but laugh. "I'm sure you do."

Beside her, Joe crossed his arms impatiently. His thick lashes were at half-mast, giving him that sensual, in-charge look that so appealed to her. She shrugged. Alyx seemed in no hurry to speak to him.

"Well, I'd as soon talk to you, Luna, so tell Joe to get lost."

"Easier said than done."

Proving her point, Joe sat on the bed next to her and said loudly so Alyx could hear, "What do you want, Alyx? We're in a hurry here." As he spoke, he picked up his shoes and socks and began pulling them on.

"A hurry, huh? He's such a bad influence on me."

Again, Luna laughed. "No, he doesn't mean in a hurry for that."

"Don't I wish," Joe grumbled, and Alyx started laughing again.

Luna rolled her eyes. Brother and sister were *too* much alike. "I don't mean to be rude, Alyx, but I only have a few minutes. We have to go pick up Austin and Willow."

"Ah, the squirts. How's Joe taking fatherhood?"

"Oh, no, he's not . . ." Luna glanced at him, then stalled. Actually, Joe was as comfortable, as loving as any father could be. "He's doing great. The kids love him."

" 'Course they do. Who wouldn't love Joe?"

Such a loaded question. Luna stared helplessly at Joe and shrugged. She sure couldn't resist loving him.

Alyx took pity on her silence and cleared her throat. "Luna?"

"Yes?"

"Tell Joe I'm coming for a visit. In fact, I'm already on the road. Thing is, I need some directions."

Luna's eyes widened. "Oh." She turned to Joe. "Your sister is coming for a visit."

"Yeah?" He grinned and leaned toward the phone so Alyx could hear him. "What prompted this, or should I even ask? You know, that curiosity of yours will get you into trouble one day."

"Hey, Trouble is my middle name."

Luna gave up. She handed the phone to Joe. "Your sister needs directions."

Joe took the phone and paced to the sliding doors that led to the wraparound porch. He stared out at the lake while playfully haranguing his sister and alternating giving her directions.

Luna didn't know if she was ready to meet Joe's family. Doing so hinted of a more binding relationship, though Joe had never said anything of the sort. She had him on temporary loan, and she really didn't want to get more entwined emotionally.

Joe disconnected the phone and slid it into his pocket, then looked up at Luna. "Hey, what is it?"

Realizing that she stared at him with longing, Luna dredged up a smile and shook her head. "Nothing."

"Luna." He came to her and took her shoulders. "I know you better than that. You're fretting. Did my goofy-ass sister say something to upset you?"

"No, of course not." And in an effort to change the subject, she said, "Alyx sounds really nice."

Joe took her arm to lead her out of the room. "She's a pain in the ass, but I love her. You'll love her, too. I promise."

They went down the stairs together. Because they were running a few minutes late, they didn't say more until Joe had them on the road. Luna kept checking her watch, until Joe said, "Quit worrying. If we're a few minutes late, no big deal."

"It's irresponsible."

"No, it's human. Get used to it. Little mix-ups are bound to happen on occasion. You can't be perfect."

Luna was just disgruntled and worried enough to say, "Why not?"

Joe laughed. "It's not part of the job description. The wisest people in the world are the ones who know they'll make mistakes, especially when dealing with kids." When Luna looked away, Joe said, "Hey, what's with the long face? You still worried about the social worker?"

"What if I don't do a good job, Joe?" The day had been crazy enough to really hit her on a gut level. What if the kids got uprooted again because Ms. Grady found her lacking? "Joe, what do I know about kids? Nothing. Not a damn thing."

He reached over and brushed a knuckle along her cheek. "It doesn't matter how much experience you've had, babe. You're a terrific person."

"Yeah, right." She lifted her arms and waggled her fingers, saying with mystic drama, *"Luna the loony. Luna knows all, sees all."* Disgusted, she dropped back in her seat, groaned and covered her face. Not since she was a young girl had she suffered such insecurities. She'd long ago accepted herself, and under normal circumstances, she liked herself, too. "I'm an ex-psychic's assistant, for crying out loud. And you know what I did before that?"

Joe looked back to the road. "No, what?"

Luna twisted in her seat to face Joe. "I bussed tables. Before that, I sold lingerie in the mall. And before that, I modeled the stupid lingerie for a small company."

Joe's expression warmed with interest. "No shit? Got any pictures left?"

Luna slugged him, and despite her worries, she felt her spirits lift. "No, and even if I did, I wouldn't let you see them. That was back when I was skinny and young."

"As opposed to being older and . . . what?" He shot her that killer grin that made her stomach tingle. "Not skinny?"

"Nicely put, Winston."

He laughed and gripped her thigh. "I love the way you look, Luna. Haven't I proven that already?"

The *L* word threw her for a second there, but she quickly recouped—even though her heart remained in her throat. "Thank you." God, she sounded like a sick frog. "The point is that none of those jobs have qualified me for trying to raise two kids."

Joe didn't remove his hand; instead, his fingers started roaming, teasing, stroking. They slid a little higher, scooting the material of her dress along her thigh in the process. "Regardless of what some overqualified children's specialists might say, the only thing that'll ever qualify you for raising kids is raising kids. And even then, you'd need to finish the job and see how well you'd done to be able to call yourself experienced."

Luna only half heard him. It hadn't been that long since they'd made love and she was still warm and soft from the pleasure of it.

"So," Joe continued, unaware of her distraction, "you're as ahead of the game as anyone. The important things that you need, you have in spades."

Luna deliberately tried to block the effect of those strong, rough fingers. "Such as?"

"Sympathy, understanding, compassion and concern."

"How could anyone not have compassion for Austin and Willow? Look at all they've gone through."

"Exactly." He sent her a smile. "And there's loyalty and responsibility. They know they can count on you."

"Of course they can. We're family."

Joe smiled. "Patience. You're giving them time to adjust to us, listening no matter how many questions Austin asks or how much the two of them bicker."

"They're just working things out," she said, dismissing his compliments because they were nothing. The bickering could be tiresome, but she supposed all kids carried on in that way. She knew Joe's cousins, the Winston brothers. They were grown men, and yet they were forever twitting each other. And when Joe was involved, too, they seemed to take berserk delight in trading insults. Why should a nine- and fourteen-year-old be any different?

Joe squeezed her thigh to regain her attention. He kept his tone low, warm. "You also have plenty of love to go around."

Damn it, there was that *L* word again. Cautiously, not quite sure where he was going with his remarks, she said, "You think?"

He nodded slowly. "You're the most loving woman I've known."

Luna drew a blank. No response came to her beleaguered mind.

"That's all anyone really needs, right? Security and love and understanding." He patted her leg and released her. "You give them all that and more. Trust me, you're doing a terrific job."

The compliments, especially coming from Joe, filled her up and gave her the reassurance she needed. "I hope you're right."

" 'Course I am." He pulled down the street to the school. "Would you mind dropping me off to pick up my truck? It's ready today, and no offense to your car, but there's not near enough leg room for me. I wanted to visit the security supply store again, too, and I'd rather make the trip in my own truck."

"No problem." After all that love talk, she could use the time away from him to regroup.

"The thing is," he continued, "I'm still worried

about something happening. I want your word that you'll go straight home and stay in the house until I get there."

She didn't mind his protective nature, but that was going a bit far. "Joe, no one has bothered us during the day. Our troublemaker only strikes at night, remember?"

"I know he's only struck at night so far."

Joe looked so determined, Luna gave up. "Yes, I'll stay in the house. I have to get dinner started anyway, and I'll put the kids to a few chores. You won't be too long, will you?" Joe wasn't the only one who worried. She hated for him to be off alone.

"No, I'll make it quick, I promise."

Knowing Joe, he wouldn't be comfortable away from them, so Luna believed him.

The kids were sitting on the front steps with Julie when they arrived. Joe parked next to the curb, then, staring at the teacher, murmured to Luna, "What the hell did she do with herself?"

Luna had been wondering the same thing. Julie's hair was half up, half down, giving her a wanton, somewhat appealing appearance. Her dark eyes glittered with laughter, and a bright, sweet smile lit up her face. A becoming flush heated her face and left her skin dewy. She had one arm around Willow, but her attention was on Austin.

"She looks . . ." Luna felt at a loss for words.

"Sexy." Joe grunted in surprise. "Imagine that."

Luna gave Joe a quick glance, saw he was more surprised than interested, and shrugged. "Yeah. I never thought of her that way."

"I doubt anyone would have. She's usually so nondescript." Joe climbed out of the car and circled the hood. "Everything okay?"

Austin jumped up and ran toward him. "Look. I got an earring like yours!"

Luna joined Joe on the curb, saw the mangled paperclip pinching Austin's earlobe, and started chuckling. "Just what is that supposed to be?"

"Ms. Rose wouldn't let me pierce it for real. She said the paperclip would have to do for now."

Still with her arm around Willow, Julie came toward them. After bending a fond look on Austin, she said, "It's been a rather hectic day." The top button of her blouse was undone and she'd removed her suit jacket and rolled up the sleeves of her blouse.

Austin bounced next to them. "Can I get a real earring like Joe's? Can I?"

Feeling a little conspicuous with the way Julie raised her brow, Joe tugged at his earring. To Austin he said, "Yeah, sure. When you're forty."

"Are you forty?"

"Close enough."

"But I don't wanna wait that long."

Julie sighed heavenward, blowing a long tendril of brown hair from her face. She was a tad sweaty, limp, and she seemed very real and approachable. "Austin, you're forgetting your bug collection inside."

"Oh, yeah." Exhibiting boundless energy, Austin ran off for the school while Willow grumbled under her breath and sent a killer glower at her little brother.

Julie gave a fond chuckle. "Austin's been more interested in telling me all the ways he intends to emulate Mr. Winston than doing any actual work. Earrings, knives, fighting lessons . . . He's been a handful today."

"He's been a brat," Willow corrected.

Luna fretted, especially when Julie didn't disagree with Willow. Why had Austin been misbehaving so badly? "I'm sorry. I'll talk to him."

Julie nodded. "All in all, he's been amusing, if somewhat wild. We ended up in a game of chase, and I don't mind telling you, he's fast."

"You had to chase him?"

"I chose to chase him. It was a game, nothing more. Don't worry. Boys his age can only keep that energy contained for so long before the young male animal inside breaks free." She smiled, letting Luna know she wasn't overly concerned. "I actually enjoyed myself. I like to play every now and then, too."

Joe choked, then quickly cleared his throat and started surveying the sky, the parking lot, anywhere rather than look at Julie.

"I didn't mind Austin's antics, but Willow isn't feeling well."

For the first time, Luna noticed that Willow had her arms folded around her middle. "What is it, Willow? Are you sick?" She put her hand to Willow's forehead, but she didn't have a fever.

Willow glanced at Joe, then away. She stared down at her feet and tightened her arms around herself. "No, I'm okay. Just a stomachache."

Austin raced out of the school with a cardboard square covered with bugs. Luna promptly backed up, and Willow threatened to flatten him if he got too close—which apparently he'd been doing off and on while they were at school. Joe moved in for a closer look and in the process shielded Willow with his body.

Luna watched him, amazed. His instincts as a guardian of young children were much more natural than hers.

"We only used dead bugs," Julie explained, "so some of them are pretty smashed. But he found some very interesting specimens."

At the top of the cardboard square was a big red-eyed locust, making Luna cringe. "It's going in the trunk."

"Thank you," Willow said with feeling.

Joe stowed the collection, then scooped Austin up like a sack of potatoes, holding him under one arm. "Why don't you ladies drop me and the Great Bug Hunter off to get my truck? After we go to the security store, we'll pick up a pizza for dinner."

Willow made a show of putting her hands together in gratitude, but she still seemed pale and pinched. With Austin held almost upside down under Joe's arm, screeching in hilarity, Luna quickly agreed to that plan.

They bid Julie goodbye. She'd already begun dragging herself back to the schoolroom and sent a feeble wave toward them.

On the way to the body shop, Austin remained outrageously obnoxious and loud. Despite Luna's repeated requests to calm down, he continued to harass his sister until Luna said with grave meaning, "I better take him home with me, Joe. I don't think you want to have him in stores while he's acting like a wild animal."

Rather than giving him pause, Austin started begging and complaining and making outlandish promises of angelic behavior. He even kicked the back of Luna's seat once.

Wide-eyed, Luna stared at him. She was a little aghast at his verbal velocity and volume. So far, she hadn't had anything like this to deal with. Sure the kids got loud. They were kids. She wondered if Austin's awesome display meant he no longer feared

she'd send him away. Was he now comfortable
enough with her to test her a bit?

She wished she had some answers. She wished
she had more experience. He kicked her seat again,
and without thinking about it, she said, *"Austin."*

He quieted long enough to blink at her. It was
the very first time she'd yelled, and Luna was as
honestly surprised as Austin appeared to be. She
tangled a hand in her hair, harried, confused. Joe
patted her leg to encourage her, and damn if he
wasn't wearing a small smile.

After an indrawn breath, Luna said, more calmly
this time, "Show me you can quiet down and behave,
and maybe, *maybe*, I'll still let you go with Joe." If
she didn't let him go, she'd only be punishing herself, so she prayed her tactic worked.

Thankfully, it did. Luna was so relieved as
Austin made a subdued exit from the car, she felt
as limp as poor Julie had looked. Joe surprised her
by stopping her as she went around the hood to
slide in behind the wheel. He caught the back of
her head, tipped her face up, and kissed her
square on the mouth, lingering for a heart-stopping
moment before he pulled away.

Still close enough that she could feel his breath,
he said, "We'll be back as soon as we can."

Luna peeked around. Austin stood next to Joe,
his face frozen in repelled consternation. In the
backseat, Willow had her nose to the car window, a
half smile curling her mouth.

"Yes, well." Luna cleared her throat, patted Joe's
chest, and said, "Drive careful."

Always ready to copy Joe, Austin reached up for
her. When she bent down, he hugged her neck
and planted a loud kiss on her cheek. He hitched

up his shorts and said, in a manful voice, "We'll be careful. Don't worry."

Stupidly, tears stung her eyes. Willow climbed out of the backseat and went to Joe. Without saying a word, she gave him a hug, then went around to sit in the front seat and put on her seat belt.

Joe looked very pleased with himself. "Come on, Austin. We've got stuff to get done."

Austin skipped beside him toward the body shop entrance. "Women worry, huh? That's why we kiss 'em goodbye."

"Yep. They worry." Joe put a hand on his head. "Plus it's just nice kissing them."

"It wasn't bad," Austin admitted, but he looked pained saying so.

The sigh of contentment blossomed inside Luna. Together, the four of them made a family—a wonderful, complete family. And whether Joe Winston had intended it or not, he was in the center of that family.

Austin adored him, Willow admired him, and Luna loved him more than she'd ever realized possible. Joe might not want to admit it, but he felt the same about the kids. Maybe he even felt the same about her. All she had to do was find a way to make him realize it. Well, she was done playing fair.

One way or another, she'd get him to love her, because no way did she want him to go.

Chapter Fifteen

Joe's head was ready to explode by the time they returned to Visitation. Austin talked nonstop, and while they were in the security supply store, he'd grown three extra arms—or at least it seemed that way. Joe had to stay right on top of him to keep him from damaging some pretty expensive equipment. Finally, Joe bought him an inexpensive pair of field glasses to keep him busy. Austin spent the rest of the time staring at everyone in very close perspective.

On the way out of town and on his way back in, Joe subconsciously watched for Jamie Creed, until he realized what he was doing, then he scowled at himself. Hell, he didn't believe for a second that Jamie just seemed to know when to show up. That sort of mystic crap was Luna's thing, not his. All of Joe's beliefs were grounded in reality and experience.

He was still pondering Jamie—and his natural dislike for the man—when his cell phone rang. Austin gave up his perusal of the passing landscape through his field glasses long enough to try to take Joe's phone on the seat between them. Joe got to it first.

"This is Joe."

"Joe? Hi. It's me, Willow."

Alarm slammed into him. "What wrong?"

"Nothing!" She hesitated, then said, "I . . . sort of need a favor."

They had just entered the town proper, so Joe pulled over to the side of the road, then had to grab Austin by the collar of his shirt when he released his seat belt and started to open his door. "What is it, hon?"

She cleared her throat, again hesitated.

"Willow?"

"Can you stop at the drugstore for me?"

More alarm. "You're that sick? Maybe you need to see the doctor."

"No, I just . . . need something."

Relief rolled through Joe. "Something for your stomach?"

"It's, well, not my stomach."

"Okay." She had him at a loss. He'd never been any good at twenty questions. "Then what do you need, Willow? Just tell me."

She rushed out an explanation. "I was going to ask Luna to call, but she got in the shower after I lay down, and I was afraid if I didn't call now, you'd already be through town. I didn't want anyone to have to make a trip back there. I hate to ask, I really do, but . . . ."

Hoping to soothe her, Joe said, "Whatever it is, I'll get it. Just tell me."

"Tampons."

Joe stalled. Tampons. But she was only . . . well, fourteen. He had no idea when young ladies needed such things. He said, "Uh . . ."

"I know," she all but wailed. "I'm sorry. But there aren't any here, and you're already there."

"Yeah, of course." He glanced at Austin. "No problem at all, hon." He swallowed. "Any particular kind?"

She gave him a brand name, then quickly hung up.

Joe took a fortifying breath. He'd known plenty of women, but they took care of those things without any help from him. Never in his life had he bought feminine products. Alyx had tried sending him to the store for some once, but he'd refused and had instead driven a girl he dated, and she'd gone into the drugstore while Joe waited in the car. Course, he'd been in his early twenties then, not in his late thirties. Hell, he could kick ass on felons, play bodyguard and bounty hunter, so surely he could buy a stupid box of tampons.

He glanced at Austin and found the boy studying him through the field glasses. Joe opened his truck door. "C'mon. We'll order the pizza first, then go to the drug store for your sister." Poor Willow. No wonder she'd looked miserable. He hadn't met a woman yet who wasn't a little grumpy and uncomfortable during that time, at least for the first day or so. It figured Austin would be at his most intolerable, just to make her feel worse.

It was as they were leaving the pizza place that Austin, still with the stupid field glasses up, said in a mean voice, "There's Mr. Owen."

Joe pulled Austin to a halt. "Where?"

Austin pointed across the street to a tall, slender man dressed in a full suit despite the smothering heat. Joe made note of two things—Quincy's blond hair, and his dress shoes.

He was already getting into an expensive black

Mercedes, so Joe just watched, his gaze icy, his gut tight with cynicism, his lip curling in automatic, intuitive dislike. As Quincy checked traffic to pull out, his attention slid over Joe, then jerked back. His expression went blank, then startled. After several seconds, his dark gaze drifted to Austin, narrowed, then shot back to Joe. He nodded once, curt and brief, then drove away.

Austin's hand slipped into Joe's. "I don't like him."

Joe didn't like him either, but rather than say so, he asked, "How come?" He started Austin toward the drug store.

"He always looks at me like that. He's not a nice man."

"Like what?"

Austin shrugged, kicked a pebble with his toe. "Like I'm dirty or something."

Damn the man. Joe squeezed Austin's shoulder and growled, "Remember what I told you?"

" 'Bout puttin' my head up?"

"Your chin, yeah. He's not worth your notice, Austin, if he can't be nice."

" 'Kay." Austin stuck his chin so high in the air, he couldn't use his field glasses.

Joe's thoughts churned, shifting, sorting and piecing together ugly suspicions. A bell chimed as they entered the drug store, and a portly man with impossibly thick gray hair looked over his wire-rimmed glasses from his position behind an old-fashioned counter. "Austin Calder. I haven't seen you in ages." The pharmacist took off his glasses and set them aside. "How are you, son? And your sister?"

"Willow is sick."

The pharmacist glanced at Joe. "I'm sorry to hear that. Anything serious?"

To Joe's consternation, heat rushed up his neck. "Uh, no. She's okay. Just a little under the weather."

"Can I help you find anything?"

No. If he was going to buy the damn things, he didn't want or need help. "We'll browse, thanks." Belatedly, Joe reached across the counter to offer his hand. "I'm Joe Winston. I'm here with Austin's cousin, Luna Clark."

Through a hardy handshake, the older man said, "Marshall Peterson." And then in a smiling whisper, "He's eyeing the candy already. Used to come in once a week before his mother passed away. Chloe always bought him the red shoestring licorice, but I haven't seen him much lately."

Joe had to admit to some surprise at Marshall's friendly disposition. From everything he'd heard, he'd fully expected to face strong dislike from most of the townsfolk. "Did Willow have a favorite, too?"

"Cordial cherries. As I recall, she'd eat one and save the rest for later. Said they were special, and she wanted to appreciate them."

Joe grinned. "That sounds like Willow. We'll take two dollars' worth of the licorice and a box of the chocolate-covered cherries."

Marshall nodded in approval. "Good man."

While that was being bagged up, Joe made his way to the *female* aisle. They passed several people who said hi to Austin with no animosity whatsoever. Austin took it all in stride, so Joe knew it wasn't uncommon. He found himself going through one good-natured introduction after another before he was finally left in peace to make his purchase.

In front of the tampons.

He'd had no idea of the variety he'd face. He frowned, put on his glasses to read a few labels, then gave up and just grabbed a box. He had planned to pick up more condoms, too, but now that he'd met so many people, it didn't seem like a good idea. He should have bought them some-place nearer the security store—away from prying eyes.

He thought about making love to Luna without a condom, feeling her and only her, the soft, wet clasp of her body, and a rush of heat assailed him. Damn. Because he'd never once considered set-tling down with any particular woman, he'd never considered making love without protection. He'd sure as hell never considered himself fathering a baby.

But he looked down at Austin with his fair hair forever disheveled, his small hands holding the field glasses while he peeked between shelves, watching customers. Joe noted the way he planted his narrow feet apart, how his knees looked too big for his skinny legs.

Joe smiled—and he wished Austin were his.

Once he started thinking of kids and babies and sex without condoms, his thoughts progressed at an alarming rate. It wouldn't be right to spring a new baby on Austin and Willow. Hell, it wouldn't be right for Luna either. Taking over as guardian was a huge upheaval in her life. But things should be fairly set in a few years. And he wouldn't be forty for four more years. Surely, that'd give them enough time to . . .

Joe drew up short on that lofty thought. Good God, he was planning additions to the family when he wasn't yet an official family member. First, he

had to tie Luna to him. But given the way she'd reacted during Ms. Grady's visit when he mentioned
marriage, it wouldn't be easy. She'd damn near
swallowed her tongue. Not a promising reaction at
all.

Every day, things seemed more settled. The kids
were doing great, and other than the vandalism,
Joe had seen no signs of any serious threats. Before
Luna could decide he wasn't needed after all,
she'd get the brunt of his attention. She'd be left
with no doubts to what he wanted from her.

He'd just started toward the checkout when
Dinah Belle stepped in front of him, blocking his
path and insinuating herself into his personal space.
With thoughts of Luna still crowding his brain, Joe
almost plowed over her.

Today her blond hair was loose to her shoulders, her makeup overdone, her blouse so low she
displayed an impressive amount of cleavage. Joe
hadn't seen her since the day she'd been fired,
and again, he expected some animosity.

Instead, Dinah greeted him with the affection-
ate familiarity of a long-lost lover. *"Joe."*

Before he could stop her, she threw herself
against him and locked her arms around his neck.
Her large breasts flattened on his chest, a rounded
belly pressed into his abdomen, plump thighs
shifted against his.

With great alacrity, Joe freed himself, but already
other shoppers were giving them disapproving
looks. To be safe, Joe held her back with one hand
wrapped around her upper arm. He would have
used both hands if he hadn't held the tampons.

"Dinah," he said without much inflection or ex-
uberance. He was already missing Luna, dumb as
that seemed, and he was anxious to get back to

her. The last thing he wanted was a full-body rub-down from Dinah.

She tipped her head in coy regard, staring at him through heavy eyes. "I was afraid you'd be gone by now."

"Now, why would I leave?" Joe was beyond grateful that she'd accosted him at the back of the store, rather than up front where any number of shoppers might have witnessed the spectacle.

She glanced down at Austin—who promptly curled his upper lip and thrust his chin into the air in snooty disdain, just as Joe had instructed. "I assumed a man like you"—she looked him up and down as she drawled those words—"would tire quickly of the domestic routine."

"Actually, I'm enjoying myself." Joe glanced down at Austin, who raised the field glasses to Dinah's face. With an exaggerated wince, the little imp pretended to gag. Joe almost laughed. He shared those sentiments, but he didn't want Austin to be so rude. "Behave," he said in an aside to Austin, and took the glasses from him.

Unfortunately, that meant he had to let go of Dinah, and she immediately pressed close again.

"It's so kind of you to want to help them." She splayed a hand over her chest, attempting to draw Joe's gaze there. "It's just that I hate to see you get caught up in such a mess."

"What mess?" Joe wondered how much Dinah knew about their situation.

In deference to Austin, she just barely lowered her voice. "I've heard of the trouble. Everyone has. It's obvious that they've alienated themselves from the town by their behavior. Why, they've caused so much trouble that sooner or later they'll be gone, either put in foster homes or in juvenile. And then you'll be—"

"They're not going anywhere."

His tone was ferocious enough that Dinah backed up a pace. "Well." She twittered a nervous laugh. "It's not up to me, of course."

"No, it's not." Joe started to walk around her when a thought occurred to him. Taking her by surprise, he said, "Who hired you as their house-keeper, Dinah?"

Her face went blank, then bloomed with color. "Patricia, of course."

Joe looked into her deceitful eyes, knew she was lying, and said to Austin, "Go on up front and wait for me. The pharmacist has some licorice for you."

"All right!" Austin took off at a run, darting around customers and aisles alike.

Joe moved closer to Dinah, closer and closer until she held her breath and her eyes widened and a frantic pulse fluttered in her white throat. She was a vision of shock, wariness and extreme interest.

Joe counted on the interest—he needed it to get what he wanted.

Standing close, Joe gently fingered a lock of hair lying over her shoulder, close to her left breast. Voice low, he asked, "What were you doing, working for Patricia?"

Her lips moved twice before words emerged. "What do you mean?"

Breathless. Good. "Just as you said you can't picture a man like me going the domestic route, it doesn't quite fit a woman like you, either." Joe looked at her trembling mouth and allowed a small smile. "You, Dinah Belle, are much too much woman to be keeping house."

Her eyes turned soft, smoky and adoring. "I . . . I needed the job."

Stammering. Even better. Luna never stammered around him. It was nice to see he hadn't entirely lost his touch. "Surely Patricia could see you weren't a frumpy housekeeper. She wasn't blind."

"I had a good recommendation."

"Yeah? Now what fool would recommend you for such a demeaning job?" Joe dragged the back of his hand lower until his knuckles brushed the plumped-up flesh of her breast.

Heat washed over her face and her eyes closed. "Quincy Owen."

"Ah." Joe dropped his hand and stepped back from her. The sensual undertones disappeared from his voice. "You two know each other well, do you?"

Blinking fast, Dinah brought herself back to reality. Confusion over what had just happened kept her expression vague. "No. That is, we're acquaintances." And almost as an afterthought, she added, "Quincy is happily married."

"With a stepson."

"Yes." Knowing she'd been used, Dinah huffed. "He's a good man."

"Yeah, right. And he sent you to Patricia out of the goodness of his heart, huh?"

A frown marred her brow. "He wanted to be helpful, yes. He knew she had her hands full with those two. They'd been running wild and with no father around to keep them in line—"

Joe turned his back on her and made his way to the checkout. Dinah stayed on his heels until Joe had paid for the tampons and candy, and stepped outside. Ignoring her, Joe looked up at the sky and saw that dark clouds had moved in. The air smelled thick with an impending storm that suited his current mood just fine.

Hoping to get home before the downpour hit, he started toward his truck but he'd only taken two steps when he saw a man in dark glasses and a hat glance toward him, duck his head and hurry away. Beneath the hat and above the collar of the man's shirt, Joe could just detect the hair.

Blond.

Fury, suspicion gathered.

Not Quincy. No, this man was too tall, too broad shouldered, too solid. Joe watched as he disappeared around the corner of the lot at a fast clip.

By instinct alone, Joe started to go after him. He would have him this time, and he'd beat him to a pulp. Adrenaline rushed through his veins, making his breath come fast, his vision narrow with purpose. He started forward—and Austin tugged on his hand, asking, "Can I have some of the licorice now?"

Shit. *Shit, shit, shit.* Austin stared up at Joe, hopeful, innocent, too young to be left alone on the sidewalk while he chased after a damned nut case. Joe felt impotent, and that pissed him off.

Dinah chose that inauspicious moment to demand Joe's attention. "What are you going to do?"

Frustration riding him hard, Joe cut her with his gaze. "About what, damn it?"

Her mouth fell open at his acerbic tone. "About what I told you," she hissed, aware of passersby on the sidewalk around them. "About Quincy."

Attention divided, Joe looked back at the street just in time to see the brown sedan that had followed them into town. It pulled out of a parking lot close to where Joe had left his truck, then drove away. Had Bruno Caldwell sent a henchman? Bruno was such a small-time Neanderthal creep, Joe doubted he could afford that. No, Bruno tended to do his own dirty work. Who was the blond man?

Austin said, a little worried now, "Joe?"

Absently, torn between responsibilities, Joe ordered, "Eat your licorice, Austin."

He didn't need to be told twice. Austin nearly tore the bag open in his haste to get the candy.

"Joe?" Dinah's tone was far more whiny than Austin's had been.

Joe turned to her, his fury barely contained. "Tell Quincy I've had enough, Dinah."

Her eyes widened.

Joe took Austin's hand to hurry him across the street. "Tell him I'm coming to see him."

She looked paralyzed by the mere thought. She called his name twice, but Joe had just noticed a folded slip of paper on his windshield and didn't spare Dinah the time.

When she realized he wouldn't reply, she yelled, "Damn you, Joe Winston!" and then, with several spectators looking on, she got into her car and squealed away.

Was she going to Quincy? Joe would find out. Somehow, he just knew the two of them were well acquainted.

Careful to touch no more than one corner, Joe pulled the small square of paper from beneath his wiper and shook it open. He didn't need his glasses to read the bold, masculine scrawl: *Your firebug drives a hatchback. Just thought you'd want to know.*

Joe's head snapped up. Dinah's taillights came on briefly as she made a pretense of obeying a stop sign, before she again burned rubber in her haste to get away.

In a hatchback. The stupid bitch.

Luna answered on the first ring. "Hello?"

"Hey, honey, it's me."

"Joe?"

He rolled his eyes and steered around a pothole in the road. The sky was getting darker by the moment, and the wind had picked up, whistling around them, bending trees. "Is there another man who calls you honey? If so, tell him to get lost."

She laughed, and with the way Joe felt at the moment, even her laugh could send him into an oblivion of tenderness and lust. "Sorry, you just took me by surprise. Are you almost home? I don't want you to get caught in the storm."

Home. The more he heard it, the more Joe liked it. He'd lived in numerous apartments, but they'd only been places to bed down. They'd never been permanent. They'd never been home. "The pizzas should still be warm when we get there."

"Pizzas, as in plural?"

"I can eat one myself, so I got three."

"Oh."

"I just wanted to make sure you're staying inside. I spoke with Willow before, but she said you were in the shower."

"Willow is napping and I was fussing with my hair."

Joe groaned past an indulgent smile. "What color is it now?"

She sniffed. "I never said I changed the color."

"It's okay, honey. I'm surprised you held out this long."

She went silent only a second or two before saying with a shrug in her voice, "Okay, so it has red streaks now."

"Red, huh?"

"Very red. Like almost purple. But it looks great."

Joe laughed. "I'll get to see for myself soon." This was probably the longest Luna had gone without changing her hair. Deep inside, she was still the free spirit who'd first attracted him. And he was glad. He never wanted her to change. "Lock the doors and don't let anyone in but me."

"Joe?" A new attentiveness laced her tone. "What's going on?"

Joe said to Austin, "Don't get your sticky fingers on my leather seats, son. Here." He handed him a napkin.

Austin looked more asleep than awake as he swiped his fingers over the napkin. One long piece of licorice still hung from his mouth and his eyelids were drooping. Joe grinned, eased the candy away and that easily, Austin slumped against the door and started snoring.

"Austin is listening?"

"Maybe. I think he might've just fallen asleep, but I'm not sure." Austin shifted around to get comfortable, folding one hand beneath his cheek. His lips were cherry red, matching his fingers.

"Then just tell me—is something wrong?"

"Possibly. Remember the brown sedan? I spotted it in town."

"Oh, God."

"Now, don't panic." The last thing Joe wanted to do was scare her. "I'm going to call Scott right now. He'll check into things and put the word around to watch for the car." Two cars, Joe reminded himself, taking Dinah's hatchback into account. "I also

ran into Dinah, and she had some interesting things
to tell me. I'll clue you in tonight, okay?"

"Promise me you'll be careful, Joe. Do *not* go
chasing anyone, do you understand me?"

Luna always got demanding when she worried.
There was a time when a woman fretting over him
would have been annoying, and no way in hell
would he have allowed a woman to issue orders.
But with Luna, he liked it. "I've got Austin with
me, remember? I'm not going to put him at risk."

"Joe?" She said his name softly, the way females
did when they got emotional. "I . . ."

Joe waited, everything male within him standing at attention. When the silence dragged out, he
prompted her with, "Yeah?"

But she only said again, "Be careful."

"Right. Talk to you soon." Joe refused to face his
disappointment over the lackluster goodbye. So,
she hadn't said anything profound. She would.
Eventually.

He dialed the sheriff's department and asked to
be put through to Scott Royal. Seconds later, Scott
accepted the call, saying right off, "Tell me there
hasn't been more trouble."

"Nothing tangible." Joe knew he had to go carefully here. Scott might be a friendly acquaintance,
but he was still a lawman. Having been one himself, Joe knew that they didn't like outsiders coming onto their territory and running the show. "I
have some questions for you, and maybe a favor or
two."

"Shoot."

"The favor first. Can you keep an eye out for a
brown sedan?"

"The guy you thought was following you here?"

"I saw him today in town. I couldn't go after him

because I had Austin with me, but he was hanging around near my truck. I found a note."

"A note?" The question was sparked with new interest. "Do you still have it?"

"I have it. You can come by the house tonight and pick it up, but it's not anything threatening. It just said that my firebug drives a hatchback." Joe paused, building to his point. "You know who has a car like that?"

Judging by the sounds he detected, Scott had just relaxed back in his chair. "I know a rhetorical question when I hear one."

"Dinah Belle. She cornered me at the pharmacy and damn near molested me in an aisle." Thankfully, Austin slept on. "She left in a huff, driving a hatchback. Coincidence?"

"Shit. As I recall, you don't believe in coincidences."

"Not often, no."

"And I don't believe in chicken-shit notes. If the guy has information for you, why not just come up to you and tell you so?"

Though Scott couldn't see him, Joe shrugged. He'd asked himself the same question a dozen times already. "Why lie about it?"

"Let me get this straight. Some asshole who followed you here leaves you a note, and now you think Dinah is the one who set that fire and scratched up your truck?"

"No, that was definitely a man. But how well does Dinah know Quincy Owen?"

Joe got the expected reaction to that question. There was a thump and a muffled curse. "Ah hell, Joe, you're not going to blame Quincy, are you?"

Joe laughed at Scott's woebegone begging. "You don't think he's capable of it?"

"Apparently you do." Another groan. "And I have to assume you have your reasons, which I'm just dying to hear, by the way, because the surveillance tape you left with me didn't show a goddamned thing."

"It gave us blond hair." Even as he spoke, Joe considered different angles and possibilities. "And this morning, after that nasty paint job on the shed, I saw smooth-soled shoe prints in the ground. Those two things fit Quincy."

"And a hundred other people in town. He's not the only blond businessman, you know. And besides, I thought you decided the guy following you from your home was a blonde. He's here in town, skulking around and leaving you notes. He's damn well up to something."

"I agree. But he didn't set the fire."

"Who says?"

"I do. I saw him today. He's a hell of a sight bigger than the guy I wrangled with the night of the fire. Hell, he's damn near my size. But now Quincy . . . I saw him for only a moment today, and physically, he could fit the bill."

"You can't be sure of that. It was pitch-black outside, and other than a twenty-second match, you never touched him."

That reminder had Joe grinding his teeth. It wasn't often that someone got away from him. But then, it wasn't often that he had to worry about children too near the action. "I yanked him around like a rag doll. He had no power behind his punch, and he screamed like a girl. Believe me, he's a wimp, but the guy leaving a note on my truck wasn't."

"Fuck." Scott huffed for a few seconds, very put out, then finally groused, "You know, for a guy who doesn't believe in coincidences, you're sinking your teeth into this one. Just what do you think the odds are that you've got two blond thugs after your ass?"

"I have a gut feeling on this one, Scott."

"Jesus, Joe, you used to be a cop. You know I can't work on your instincts. I need more than that."

"I'll get you more, but in the meantime look around for that brown sedan, okay? I'd really like a chance to question that guy up close and personal."

"You and me both, and since I'm the law, I get to go first. Understand?"

"I know how it works, Scott. I was an officer once myself, remember?" Joe flexed his knuckles on the steering wheel and smiled. "If he puts up his hands and turns himself in nice and pretty like, then I'll have no reason to beat him into the ground."

Since a passive surrender was about as unlikely as Joe just handing him over, Scott gave up. "Anything else?"

"Yeah. Do you happen to know who Chloe used to work for before she bought the lake property?"

"That's before I transferred here, but odds are it was either the factory or the mall, since those two places do the most hiring."

And they were both run by Quincy Owen.

"I can ask around. Dare I ask why?"

Scott sounded so wary, Joe laughed. "Let me know if you find out anything and I'll explain then." And before Scott could protest that, Joe added, "I need to get home to Luna and Willow. I don't like leaving them alone there. I have a feeling when this rain hits, the roof is going to leak."

"You know, Joe, it really seems like you're into

the whole home and hearth thing. You planning to stay with us awhile?"

"Damn right." Then he thought to add, "But Luna doesn't know it yet, so don't say anything to her."

"Gonna surprise her, huh?"

"I thought I'd ease her into the idea." And once he got entrenched in her and the kids' lives, hopefully she'd start to understand that he was around to stay. He'd prove to her that her heart was safe with him, and then she'd stop saying no, once and for all.

Chapter Sixteen

The steady drizzle started just as Joe pulled up in front of the house, and judging by the thunder, it'd turn into a full-fledged downpour at any second. He saw a curtain drop on the front window and knew Luna had been watching for him. It was a unique thing, to have someone waiting for him, but damned if he didn't like it.

She opened the door and stepped out onto the porch, her arms folded against the chilling breeze. Joe scooped Austin's small, compact body into his arms. He didn't awaken, despite the rain sprinkling his face. Joe lightly rubbed his chin against the mop of fair hair. Austin smelled little-boy sweet and looked too peaceful to be the same wild hellion of that afternoon.

Luna held the door open as he dashed across the yard and up the porch steps. "Is he okay?"

"Just ran out of gas." Joe noticed the bright streaks of scarlet in Luna's hair and paused to press a warm kiss to her mouth as he passed her.

"Hello," he murmured against her soft lips. "I missed you."

Bemused, Luna touched her mouth and stood there mute.

Joe liked taking her off guard. "Should we wake him, do you think?"

She glanced at a tall clock in the hallway. "Maybe. If he naps much later, he won't go to bed at all tonight."

"Right." Joe headed into the family room with Austin tucked close to his chest. He placed him on the couch and gently shook him awake. It was only five o'clock, but already the sky was as dark as midnight. Just as Austin got his eyes open, the storm started in earnest.

He bolted upright in alarm.

"Hey, it's just a little rain," Joe told him, taking a moment to sit beside him and rub his back. "You hungry after all that candy you ate? I'm going to run out to the truck now to get the pizza."

Austin yawned and stretched, then turned and gave Joe a brief hug.

He'd never get used to it, Joe thought. It was almost too damn nice. He smoothed Austin's hair, touched by the boy's easy affection, then looked up in time to see Luna standing in the doorway with a misty smile on her face.

If only things could be as simple with her as they were with Austin.

She came into the room and tugged Austin to his feet. "Hey, sleepyhead. Why don't you go clean your face and hands, then head to the kitchen, okay? Ask Willow if she's ready to eat, too."

Still dragging a little, Austin started out of the room. He turned back to Joe. "Where's my spy glasses?"

"Right here." Joe slipped the strap from around his neck and handed the glasses to Austin. He clutched them in a fist, then ran off to clean up.

Joe headed to the front door, followed by Luna. The rain now came down in impenetrable sheets. "I hope like hell my sister gets off the road. I'd hate to think of her in this mess."

"She should be here pretty soon. Don't worry." Thunder shook the floor beneath them. "Maybe we should wait a few minutes, to see if the rain lets up. You'll get soaked to the skin if you go out there now."

"It doesn't look like it's going to blow over any time soon." Joe glanced out at the stinging rain and wanted to curse. The house needed a garage that opened to the interior. Maybe that was an addition to think about, after they got the lake opened. "Besides, I won't melt."

Luna said, "Oh, I don't know. Willow told me that you stopped at the store for her." Wearing a teasing grin, she caught his arm and turned him around. "You're awfully sweet."

Joe was about to protest that silly description when Luna went on tiptoes to lick his bottom lip. "Mmmm," she purred. "Very sweet."

The suggestive lick sent a wave of heat through Joe. "Tease." He caught the nape of her neck and held her still for a real kiss, and this time when he felt her tongue, he drew it into his mouth. Luna made a small sound of pleasure and pressed up against him.

She'd changed into a pair of leopard-print leggings and a long black tee. He allowed himself one quick, casual grope of her sexy behind. The thin material was no barrier to her supple flesh. With a groan, Joe released her before he got carried away.

Luna stared up at him, her eyes warm and mellow, her cheeks flushed. She was barefoot, and her toenails had been painted to match the new color in her hair. They curled against the floor, proving she wasn't unaffected by the kiss either.

"If I don't go now," Joe growled, "I'll evaporate when I step into the rain."

She stroked his chest. "Feeling warm?"

"Scalded." He kissed her forehead and dashed outside.

When he came back in this time, his shirt stuck to his back and his jeans clung to his thighs. He'd shielded the pizzas with his body as much as possible, but the boxes were still damp. He handed them to Luna so he could kick off his shoes and peel off his shirt. He caught her boldly admiring his chest.

Using the edge of his fist, he tipped up her chin. "Keep looking at me like that, and I'm going to sneak into your room tonight for sure."

A heartbeat passed; then she said, "Promise?"

Damn. She sounded serious, as if she wouldn't object to that at all. "I would love sleeping with you, babe." He stepped closer, his voice going husky and warm with just the thought. "I'd love feeling you next to me all night long."

In nervousness, she licked her lips and stared at his chin. "Would you love waking with me in the morning?"

"Yes."

Her gaze lifted; they stared at each other. "You'd get quickly bored, Joe."

"Not a chance." He smiled into her beautiful golden eyes, wanting her to know he meant it. Wanting her to trust him. "Not with you."

Luna looked undecided, anxious, then ventured carefully, "Maybe we should talk about this."

"Yeah?"

She nodded. "About . . . us."

Joe was more than ready to convince her when Austin yelled from the kitchen, "Hey, I can see the fishes in the lake with my glasses. Come and look, Joe."

He needed privacy to tell Luna how he really felt. Hell, he'd never told a woman that he loved her and he damn well wanted to do it right.

"Tonight," he told her, and she nodded.

Joe hauled up the packages in one hand, slung his other arm around Luna, and went into the kitchen with the kids. Luna set the pizza boxes on the counter and got out plates and glasses.

Willow was at the table, her chin propped on a fist while she stared into space. She looked very morose, making Joe frown. Was she feeling that bad? He didn't know much about the whole monthly thing, other than that it could be damn inconvenient. But he knew he didn't want Willow to feel bad in any way.

"Here you go, hon." He handed Willow her package still in the pharmacy bag.

She blushed. "Thanks, Joe."

He flicked the end of her nose. "Anytime." Then, more seriously, "I mean it, Willow. You can come to me with anything, okay?" He gestured, feeling a little awkward. "Even with stuff like this."

She bit her lip, nodded. The storm seemed to have dampened everyone's mood, except Austin's. Luna frowned to herself as she set out plates, and Willow fidgeted nervously. Only Austin remained animated as he watched the storm through the kitchen windows.

"Joe?" Willow straightened in her chair. "There is something I wanted to tell you."

Joe had been about to go change into dry clothes, but now he stalled. "All right." Willow looked so worried, he forgot that his clothes were dripping all over the floor.

"I saw Clay today. He was at the school, in the yard, and I talked with him."

Joe's shoulders knotted in dread. "Did he say something to upset you?"

"No, he apologized, and he was real nice." She glanced at Austin, but he was busy dragging a chair to the window so he could better see outside. He wasn't paying their conversation much attention. "The thing is, he had some scratches."

Luna turned from the counter, a pizza cutter held in her hand. "Scratches?"

Willow came out of her chair and walked to Joe. Very lightly, she touched the top of his shoulder and neck. "Like these." She swallowed hard. "Not quite as thick as your scratches were, and maybe not as healed up. But . . . Well, I don't know." She looked from Joe to Luna, her eyes dark and sad and resigned. "Do you think it could have been Clay who set that fire?"

She appeared devastated by that possibility. Joe cupped her shoulder and shook his head. "No, honey. It wasn't Clay."

She desperately wanted to believe him, Joe could tell. "But how do you know? His scratches looked an awful lot like yours."

"For one thing, the guy who set the fire had blond hair, remember? Clay's hair is brown. Also, I found footprints down by the lake after the paint job on the shed. They were smooth-bottomed shoes. Doesn't Clay wear athletic shoes?"

Looking hopeful, she nodded. "That's all I've ever seen him wear."

"How did he say he got the scratches?"

"He said his stepfather brought home a kitten. I just . . . I didn't know if I should believe him. Quincy Owen doesn't seem like the type of man who'd want a pet. Especially not a sweet little kitten."

Joe's eyes narrowed. "No, he doesn't, does he?"

A flash of lightning illuminated the dark sky in a burst of light, followed instantly by a rippling crack of thunder that made the house tremble. The storm had to be right overhead.

Startled, Austin flailed away from the window with a shout, almost falling before Luna caught him.

"He's here!" Austin yelled, pointing and struggling away from Luna. "He's here!"

Joe strode to the window. "Who's here?"

"The man who did it." Austin chattered and danced around in nervous excitement. "I seen him. Outside! When the lightning flashed, I could see him with my glasses. He's down by the lake."

Austin dashed to the window again, but Joe snatched him back. "All of you stay away from the windows and doors. Luna, lock up behind me."

Willow jerked around to face Joe. "What are you going to do?"

Luna surprised him by saying with firm conviction, "He's going to go get him, of course."

Joe stared at Luna, saw the guarded way she held herself, and said, "That's exactly what I'm going to do." He headed for the front door.

"Willow, Austin, do as Joe says and get away from the windows." Luna rushed after him. He was just about to open the door when Luna said, "Joe, I changed my mind."

Joe froze. What the hell did she mean, she'd changed her mind? If she thought to send him home, if that was the reason she wanted to talk to him tonight, she could damn well think again. "Too late for that, babe." He pulled the front door open. Rain blew across the porch and into the house.

Luna reached out to him. "Joe?"

His temper snapped. "Damn it, Luna, I don't want him to get away this time."

"Neither do I," she shouted back. Then she looked over her shoulder at Willow. "Call Deputy Royal."

Willow rushed to obey. Austin stood there, eyes wide and confused. Luna stared up at Joe, then drew a deep breath. "I lied, to myself and you. I brought you here because I wanted to be with you."

Joe stared at her, stunned. "Jesus, you know how to take a man off guard."

"I'm sorry." She swallowed hard, her breath fast and low. "I don't mean to insult your abilities. God knows you're more than capable of holding your own."

"That's right. I am."

She patted his bare chest. "Go and get him. Hit him once for me. Just . . . be careful doing it. That's all I'm asking. Much as you like to think otherwise, you're not invincible."

Austin raised a fist. "Hit him once for me, too!"

Joe nodded, said, "Stay inside," and then with no more time to spare, he ducked out the door and slammed it shut behind him.

Rain stung his bare shoulders as he jogged around the house, keeping to the shadows, thankful now for the heavy sheets of rain that helped to hide him. Sure enough, as he sprinted across the field that led to the lake, he could see a masculine figure bent to the handle on the shed door, attempting to break the lock with a crowbar.

His footsteps muffled by the pounding rain, Joe crept closer and closer until he was a mere two feet away from the intruder. Vibrating with menace, unmindful of the downpour and resounding thunder, he straightened to his full height and stared at the man with blond hair and slick-bottomed shoes.

His voice as mean as he currently felt, Joe rumbled, *"Quincy."*

The man screeched the same way he had the night of the fire. Flapping about in a panic, he slipped on the wet ground and fell hard. The crowbar dropped from his grip.

"You sniveling mother fucker," Joe whispered, and grabbed him by his collar to haul him back to his feet. Joe rattled him with a firm shake. "I've got you now."

Quincy Owen attempted to straighten, to jerk free. "What do you think you're doing," he blustered. "How dare you attack me."

"Attack you?" They each had to shout to be heard over the fury of the storm. Heavy waves slapped against the shoreline. Joe shook Quincy again. "You're lucky I don't rip you in half. The only thing saving you is that Scott Royal wants to arrest you himself." Joe narrowed his eyes on Quincy's face, then released him. "Give yourself up, and I won't beat the shit out of you."

Quincy backpeddled a step. "Give myself up? For what?" He sounded hysterical. His sodden windbreaker hung on his shoulders, and his dress slacks were now caked with mud. "I'm only here for a . . . a neighborly visit."

"Is that why you were breaking into the shed?"

He shook his head hard. "Don't be ridiculous. What could you possibly own that I'd want?"

Loathing burned the back of Joe's throat. "I'm thinking it's what you don't want. Convincing Patricia to close down the lake. Setting fires. Painting insults." Joe had never been able to stay unemotional when dealing with the scum of the earth, but this man sickened him more than most. "You want the kids gone."

Alarmed, Quincy's dark brown eyes shifted, looking for an avenue of escape. But with Joe in front of him, the lake behind him, he had nowhere to go. "What kids? I don't know what you're talking about."

Joe stalked him, forcing Quincy to back up in circles. "You bought this place for Chloe, didn't you? You thought it'd keep her happy and conveniently close. But what happened, Quince? The kids starting to look too much like you now? You afraid everyone's going to figure out who their daddy really is? And when they do start noticing the resemblance, your sterling reputation will be shot to hell. That's it, isn't it?"

"Shut up."

"Your wife might not like that, huh? God knows the town will be so disappointed. Not only did you father two illegitimate children, but you failed to live up to your responsibilities to those kids."

"Shut your fucking mouth," he shouted.

"Platinum hair and dark brown eyes. Poor Quince. They look just like you, don't they?" Joe maneuvered him into the side of the shed, boxing him in so that he could no longer retreat. "They're your flesh and blood, and you've wanted only to rid yourself of them. You've spread nasty rumors and made their lives hell. It was Dinah who called the social worker, wasn't it? And it was her car you used to sneak onto the property."

"Lies! All lies."

"You're a miserable, insufferable little worm, and when people find out, they'll wash their hands of you."

Like a cornered rat, Quincy struck out. He pulled back a fist and swung. Joe took the blow on the chin. In comparison to the disgust he currently felt, the pain was negligible. "There you go, Quince." His grin spread in tandem with his anger. "You struck first—which leaves me free to retaliate."

Joe's blow to Quincy's gut doubled him over, making him heave and gag. He wrapped his arms around his middle and sank to his knees, struggling for air.

"What were you going to do to the shed?" With Quincy momentarily immobilized, Joe reached inside his windbreaker. His fingers finally closed on several flares tucked in an inside pocket to keep them dry. "Ah, another fire, huh? How redundant. No imagination at all. But then, as long as mishaps keep occurring, we can't very well invite other people onto the property, huh? In fact, with you spreading rumors, you probably think everyone will blame Austin."

"Go to hell."

"You hoping to slow us down, Quincy? I mean, if we successfully reopen the lake, there'd be no reason to move, huh?"

"No."

Joe pulled the collar of the windbreaker aside. "Scratches, just like the ones I got, only worse, because the last time we tangled, your ass was on the ground. Your stepson said you got a cat. Was that your clever way of explaining the marks left by brambles and brush? You really tried to cover the bases, didn't you? Did your wife believe that pathetic story?" Joe shook his head. "Don't worry, I'll set her straight just as soon as I see you locked in jail."

Cautiously, with one arm still squeezed tight around his stomach, Quincy staggered upright. "Why do you care, you son of a bitch? Patricia was ready to leave. She'd have taken the kids away from here, and everything would have been fine. Then you and that other bitch showed up."

Joe whispered, "Do you want me to kill you, Quincy? Is that it?"

Panicked, Quincy said, "Why don't you just leave?" His eyes narrowed maliciously as he plotted his next offer. "You can take the kids with you. I'll even pay you to go. Just tell me how much it'll cost me."

"You don't have a single thing I want, Quincy." *Except for your children.* But Joe wouldn't admit that to him. Then he saw Quincy's eyes shift to the side and widen with new alarm.

Joe held Quincy immobile with a hand tight on his throat while jerking around to face the new threat. He got a surprise. Not twenty feet away, between him and the house, stood the man he'd seen in town.

Also blond. Also trespassing. Not nearly a wimp.

Well, fuck. He just hated coincidences, he really did.

Joe had only a moment to gauge the situation, but he figured he could take the other guy. He was of a similar size to Joe, and judging by his limber, ready stance, he knew how to fight. But Joe had the adrenaline rush on his side. Even with Quincy to contend with, he could hold his own.

Hell, he was even looking forward to it.

That is, before he saw Luna creeping up on the other man with a shovel in her hands.

"Goddammit, no!" Joe shouted out the warning at the same time that the other man heard her approach. Taken off guard, he reacted automatically. With a swiftness that Joe might have admired in any other situation, the man turned, caught Luna by the shoulder and elbow, and literally threw her over his head. The shovel dropped from her hands, and she screamed as she went sailing, then hit the ground flat on her back with a resounding thump that could be heard even over the storm.

"Luna." Joe meant to yell her name, but it emerged as a weak whisper.

She held perfectly still, not even breathing, then her eyes closed on a rasping, broken groan.

Fury roared through Joe, erupting in a shout of primitive outrage.

Cursing, the other man shrugged a satchel off his shoulder and moved to stand over Luna. His muscles were still bunched, his posture aggressive. He started to crouch down.

Joe didn't take a single moment to think. Through messing with Quincy, he did the expedient thing and brought his elbow back in a sharp sweep. Quincy's head snapped back against the shed. He didn't even have time to grunt before he blacked out. Joe let him sink to the muddy ground with no regard for any additional injuries he might sustain.

The man near Luna stood and backed up. "Hey. Easy now, Winston. She's okay, just winded." He held up both hands. "I'm here to help you."

"You're fucking dead."

Exasperation showed on the other man's features, and he growled, "Bruno Caldwell is here, you damn fool."

Joe kept advancing until he was within range, then he moved so fast that his fist was a blur, striking against the man's jaw. With all the fury Joe possessed behind the blow, the man went sprawling on his ass—but he didn't stay there. He was back up in an instant, shaking his head to clear it, backing up again. Joe smiled in anticipation. At least this guy wouldn't be as easy as Quincy. He'd offer a little challenge.

Luna sat up slowly, holding her head. "Joe?"

"Sit still," Joe ordered her without taking his eyes off the man. Then, with evil intent, "I'll be done here in a minute." Judging by the tone of her voice, Luna was no more than dazed, but Joe wasn't willing to risk it.

The other man's expression darkened with anger as he worked his jaw and continued to back up. "I don't want to fight you, Winston."

Joe laughed, taunting him, wanting him close so he could do more damage. "I'm not giving you a choice." And Joe swung again, landing a punch in the ribs that bent him double. Just as quickly, Joe brought a knee up and into the man's chin. He collapsed back into the mud, and this time he didn't bounce back.

Braced on the ground, he wiped blood from his mouth and then spit. "Didn't you hear me?" he yelled over the storm. "Bruno is *here.*"

"I heard. That's the only reason you're getting my fists instead of my knife. I want some answers." Joe looked him over. "You working for Bruno, is that it?" Joe kicked out, oblivious to his bad knee, his only cognizant thought of Luna lying on the ground, thrown there by this man. His booted foot landed on a thigh, and the man rolled to the side, cursing in pain.

Luna struggled up to her knees. "Stop it, Joe. Don't hurt him." She started to rise.

Hobbled by pain, the man shoved himself to his feet and, limping, again faced Joe. "That's it, damn it. I gave you your chance, but it's over. If you're so anxious to let Bruno kill you, then—"

A bullet ricocheted off the shed and both Joe and the man moved with incredible speed. The man grabbed his satchel and ducked for cover behind the shed, close to Quincy. Joe threw himself over Luna, shielding her with his body.

Frantically, she pushed against him. "Joe!"

"Stay still," he ordered.

"My name's Bryan Kelly," the man shouted in a rush. "I've been hunting Bruno."

"Why?" Joe crawled right on top of Luna, folding his arms over her head and nearly smothering her shouts of outrage.

"I'm a bounty hunter." He levered one hip off the ground and dug into his pocket to produce a gold badge that read, "Bail Enforcement Agent."

Another bullet zipped past, kicking up mud far too close to Joe. He gathered Luna against him and in a crouching run joined the others behind the shed.

Bryan was already stripping off his lined jacket as Joe scrunched down beside him with Luna in his arms. She was shivering, her hair muddy and hanging over her face in clumps, and still she said, "I'm okay."

As if she hadn't spoken at all, Bryan draped the jacket around her shoulders. "We have to move or we're all dead. Bruno may be a cowardly little creep, but he's toting a tactical rifle, which outshoots my nine-millimeter all the way to hell and back."

"Unless he's been practicing a lot, Bruno is a sloppy shot. He'll have to get closer if he hopes to hit us." Joe was busy arranging the jacket around Luna and tucking her arms into the sleeves. "By the way, how the hell do you know all this?"

With the comfortable familiarity of someone well used to firearms, Bryan pulled his own weapon from his waistband and held it in his right hand. "I've been watching you from up on the hill." He stood, crept to the edge of the shed, and peeked out. A bullet immediately clipped the wood near the shed's roof. "Shit."

"If you're lying, I'll kill you."

Bryan glanced down at Joe, saw how he protected Luna with his body, and nodded. "I know you'd try." Shielding his eyes from the rain, he surveyed the area. "I saw him heading this way, then I saw you wasting time with this other fool." He paused a moment, rubbed his head in disgust. "I hadn't planned to let anything get in my way this time, not women, not innocent men. But you've got two kids here, and some goddamned remnant of conscience kept gnawing at me until I decided I had to do something." And then, with a rueful glance at Luna, "I didn't particularly want to see her hurt either."

"Coulda fooled me."

Bryan shrugged off Joe's comment. "Bruno is probably moving into position right now. All he has to do is keep shifting until he has us in range. With this damn rain, I can't see a thing."

Luna groaned again, but Joe had the feeling it was in worry, not pain. He cuddled her, kissed her forehead; then, because he was still pissed over the way Bryan had handled her, he reached out with his left hand and slugged him in the ribs.

Bryan cursed luridly and turned a hot, vicious glare on Joe. "One more, and I swear to God—" His gaze landed on Luna. Looking beyond wretched, she rubbed the back of her head and winced. Bryan's predatory eyes suddenly filled with sympathy. "Damn it, I'm sorry," he bit out. "I wasn't expecting you, and your hair is different . . . I thought you were Amelia or Dinah, and I don't mind telling you I wouldn't feel a second's remorse if one of them got tossed."

That perked Luna right up, and it was Joe's turn to groan. "Amelia? Dinah?" she asked.

While continuing to survey the area with dark, narrow eyes, Bryan nodded. "Amelia is working with Bruno." He slanted a glance at Joe. "Seems she wasn't too pleased that you didn't want to marry her, so when Bruno showed up looking for you, she decided on some revenge. She's a bitch, but to her credit, she doesn't know Bruno intends to kill you. She thinks you'll get beat up a bit more, affording her the opportunity to take care of you."

"That bitch!" Luna stiffened, but Joe immediately shoved her head back down. "She was in on the beating, then," Luna said, her voice muffled against Joe's chest. But not so muffled that he couldn't hear her gloating overtones. "I *knew* it. And she wasn't taking care of Joe anyway. All she did was fondle his butt."

Bryan appeared intrigued by that disclosure.

Joe ground his molars together. He thought about hitting Bryan again, just for giving Luna that information. She'd never let him hear the end of it now. "Wanna tell me how you figured all this out?"

Bryan shrugged. "I had tracked Bruno the night he jumped you in the parking lot, but the bastard got away. Again. Then Amelia showed up, and I figured that was a little too pat—"

"I told you so," Luna crowed.

"—and I started watching her. Sure enough, she had several calls from Bruno that I picked up with a listening device. They planned to follow you, so I planned to follow you too. Hell, you're easier to keep an eye on than Bruno."

"So you've been spying on me all this time?"

"Good thing, too." Bryan prodded Quincy, who was wide awake and aware now but staying silent out of a healthy sense of self-preservation. "This bozo has been working with Dinah Belle. I didn't know that till today by the way. I just saw the car leaving the night of the fire and knew it was a hatchback. When I saw her get out of a hatchback at the pharmacy, then saw her feeling you up in the aisle, I knew she was in on it."

Luna knotted a hand in Joe's wet hair and pulled his face down to hers. In a voice as low and mean as any criminal's, she said, "Feeling you up?"

"Bryan exaggerated." Joe gently disengaged her tight fingers, then said to Bryan, "I didn't see you in the drugstore."

" 'Course not. I didn't want you to see me. And besides"—he winked at Luna—"you were busy fending off Dinah."

"But you figured out she and Quince were together, so you left me that damned note?"

"It was the only thing I could think to do. I knew Bruno was in the area. If I'd told you outright who I am, you'd have gone after him yourself." He levered an implacable look on Joe. "But he's mine."

"Big payoff?" Joe asked with sarcasm.

Bryan shook his head. "No, our association is more personal than money."

"How so?"

"None of your damn business." Bryan took aim and fired into a line of trees. Shots were immediately returned and they all scampered to the other side of the shed.

"I bet it involves another woman," Luna whispered far too loudly.

"Doesn't matter now," Bryan complained, "the dumb ass is complicating the hell out of things by pulling this stunt. No way the local police are going to want to let me have him."

Joe pondered that for a moment. If he didn't press charges, and no one else witnessed Bruno's attack, Bryan could still take him in. It'd simplify things a lot if Joe didn't have to deal with him. He didn't want to further disrupt the kids' lives. Things were going to be complicated enough dealing with Quincy.

Somehow, he'd make everything right, and to that end, he made a sudden decision.

Joe knew what he had to do, just as he knew how Luna would react. He dreaded upsetting her, but he really had no choice. He clasped her shoulders, drew a breath, and said, "I'm going to go get him."

Luna straightened. "But he has a gun."

"Tactical rifle," Bryan muttered, earning a shove from Joe. "Sorry."

"It won't be safe here for much longer," Joe reasoned. "And then what happens to the kids?"

Bryan looked at Joe with speculative admiration. "You going to sneak up behind him?"

"That's the plan."

Luna punched Joe's chest. "At least let Bryan go along for backup."

"And leave you here alone with Quincy? No."

"Then I can go for your backup. I can shoot a gun. How hard can it be?"

Bryan snorted.

"You," Joe told her with a firm shake, "are going to keep your sexy little ass right here, without moving, until Bryan tells you otherwise, do you understand me?"

"This is a stupid plan, Joe."

"Don't push me, Luna." Despite her insults, there were tears in her eyes, and seeing Luna upset did awful things to his gut. He buried that reaction, which could dangerously weaken and distract him, beneath firm resolve. "You're already in it deep enough for leaving the house."

Her anguished gasp blasted him. Annoyance replaced some of the wrenching terror in her golden gaze. "I saw him creeping up on you! You were busy with Quincy. What was I supposed to do?"

"Trust me?" Joe narrowed his eyes, knowing he fought dirty but unwilling to risk her involvement. "But no, that would never occur to you, would it, Luna? You don't trust me at all, not with your safety, and not with your heart."

Bryan looked away with a whistle. Quincy just stared between them, his eyes darting this way and that.

"Of course I trust you."

"Then you'll damn well stay put." He released her and slipped his knife from his pocket. With a quiet *snick-click*, it was open. He asked Bryan, "You got any restraints?"

" 'Course." Bryan pulled disposable hand and foot ties from his pocket. "These ought to do it."

Joe accepted the configured, woven nylon cords.

"Keep him busy while I run into the woods behind us. I'll circle around and find him."

"You good enough to do that without getting your ass shot?"

"Yeah." Joe stared at Luna. "I'm good enough."

Luna sat there, silently miserable, her eyes narrowed and her mouth flat. The rain finally slowed, but they were all soaked through, and Joe was without a shirt. He barely felt the icy chill in the air. All his concentration was on keeping Luna and the kids safe.

Bryan leaned back against the shed wall. "I have a feeling I'll have my hands full with her." He kicked the toe of a boot against Quincy. "What do I do with this jackass if he moves?"

Joe looked at Quincy, and without hesitation, slugged him again in the jaw. Obligingly, Quincy slumped into another dead faint. "Glass jaw, the cowardly bastard."

Bryan actually laughed, which infuriated Luna.

She thrust her chin up and glared. "You're both idiots." And then to Joe, "I swear to God, Joe Winston, if you get hurt I'm never going to forgive you."

"No faith at all." Half smiling, Joe cupped her cold, wet, dripping cheek, gave her a quick kiss, then disappeared from sight. The odds of him actually getting hold of Bruno were fifty-fifty. But if nothing else, he'd draw the fire away from Luna. If he caught a bullet, he could live with that. But no way in hell could he live with her getting hurt.

It would have been helpful if the rain had continued to mask his footsteps, but at least this way he could see. And just as Bruno might hear him move, he would definitely hear Bruno.

Bryan's gun fired into the surrounding woods, giving Joe the distraction he needed to advance and helping him peg Bruno's location when Bruno fired back. Like a bull elephant, Bruno moved without an ounce of stealth. Of course, he thought he had them covered. He thought he had the upper hand.

For a good five minutes Joe crept through the woods, barely making a sound. He circled the shore, constantly gauging the direction of each shot Bruno fired.

And finally, Joe found him.

Chapter Seventeen

Luna had never known such numbing fear. Bryan Kelly, damn him, seemed unconcerned. In fact, every so often he grinned, especially whenever he fired his gun. Or maybe that was a grimace. She wasn't sure. In some ways, he reminded her a little of Joe in his ridiculous enjoyment of the lethal game.

He glanced back at her, noted her agonized expression, and shook his head. "Quit fretting, woman. Winston knows what he's doing."

"Of course he does," Luna said, but she knew that even Joe couldn't fight a bullet.

Quincy groaned and held his head. His face was bruised, swollen, covered in blood that had run from his nose down his chin. He looked like hell. But it was his fault Joe had gone outside in the first place, so Luna couldn't find any sympathy for him. For the most part, she ignored him and his measly complaints. If Joe got hurt, she'd add another punch to his assorted bruises.

Luna watched Bryan as he swiped a forearm

across his face, pushing his wet hair aside and wiping away the rain. Like Quincy, he had blond hair, only Bryan's was darker, long and unkempt, boldly streaked from the sun. He also had brown eyes. But where Quincy's were dark and fathomless like Austin's and Willow's, Bryan's were as light as honey and framed by long, dark lashes spiked from the rain. Joe had left a few bruises on him as well, but somehow they seemed to go with the man.

"I am sorry if I hurt you," Bryan muttered distractedly while tracking her face. "Instincts are a bitch sometimes." He turned away to watch for Bruno. "When you came up behind me like that, I just assumed it was one of the other women."

Luna glared at him. "If this is your way of asking for forgiveness, you can't have it."

"No?" He didn't smile, but she could tell her refusal amused him.

"You let Joe go out there alone."

That made Bryan laugh. "Hell, did you really expect me to try to stop him?"

Suddenly it grew quiet. No more shots. No noise at all. Luna's heart leapt into her throat and lodged there. She shoved herself to her feet and started to step around the shed, but Bryan caught her arm and held her at his side.

They both peeked out.

Foliage rustled. Bushes parted. And into the clearing, Joe emerged, tall and straight, head high. He limped slightly, favoring his bad knee, but then, he had a large, trussed-up man slung over his shoulder. A long, black rifle hung from his other hand. Luna stared at him in disbelief as his long legs brought him steadily forward.

"Well, I'll be damned," Bryan muttered as he walked away from the dubious safety of the shed.

Luna dashed out across the clearing, her feet splashing on the sodden ground. *"Joe."*

Lingering electricity crackled high in the pewter sky with a dramatic strobe effect. In the distance, thunder grumbled, mimicking the stern look of Joe's harshly carved features. The air was thick and dark and dismal, miserably cold.

Joe didn't bow under the weight he carried. In fact, he had that ominous, threatening aura about him again, as if he could tackle a pride of lions without breaking a sweat.

Luna noted the start of a black eye, a few more scrapes on his bare chest and shoulders, but what she noticed most of all was the triumphant satisfaction in his beautiful blue eyes. He'd enjoyed himself, and for that reason more than any other, she wanted to clobber him.

Luna stopped at Joe's side, her eyes wide. "Is this Bruno, then?"

Joe gave one sharp nod and strode past her, heading for the house. The man slung over Joe's shoulder resembled a burly bulldog in both appearance and tone. He grumbled and growled, but couldn't say much, not with the way Joe had gagged him with a piece torn off his shirt.

Luna hurried after Joe. "What are you going to do with him?" She worried for Joe's knee, for the outcome of it all, and for her heart. Foolishly, she'd held out a small hidden hope that Joe would decide he liked Visitation, and that he loved her—enough to stay. But how could he ever be content in Visitation when he so obviously enjoyed taking risks?

"I'll turn him over to Scott," Joe said with a surprising amount of indifference. Of course, Bruno looked as though he'd already been a recipient of revenge, so perhaps Joe had gotten it out of his system.

"Bruno is *mine.*"

Joe paused, turned to look at Bryan over his shoulder, then with a satisfied shrug, he dumped the portly man to the wet ground. Bruno kicked and screeched, and Luna imagined that if he weren't gagged, his foul curses would have filled the air.

"Fine." Joe put his hands on his hips. "Then you haul his ass to the front of the house."

Luna gasped. "Fine? That's it, *fine?* Just like that, you'll give him over to Bryan? You don't care? Since the day I first heard about Bruno, you told me *you'd* be the one to get him."

"I did get him," Joe reminded her.

"But I . . ." Her words trailed off as possibilities jumbled her thoughts. She shook her head. "I thought it was personal to you, that you wanted to take him back in yourself."

"It's personal to me," Bryan stated with unequivocal insistence. "I didn't sit up on that damn hill night after night watching your place just to let someone else have the satisfaction of putting Bruno back behind bars."

Joe ignored Bryan. "I don't give a damn what happens to Bruno as long as he stays out of our lives." Very gently, he cupped the back of Luna's neck and waggled her head. "I just wanted to make sure you and the kids were safe, babe. That's all that matters to me these days."

"That's all?" Luna's voice quivered, along with her lips.

"I can guarantee Bruno will be out of sight for a good long while." Bryan knelt down next to the fallen man to loosen the hobbles on his ankles so he could walk. Bruno's torn shirt was bloody, and his face looked much like Quincy's, with the obvious signs of battery. "You gigged him," Bryan said, recognizing the knife wound in Bruno's right shoulder.

"He was going to shoot me. I had no choice but to disarm him."

Luna staggered back, dumbfounded at the casual way Joe disclosed a close call on his life.

He shrugged his shoulders to relieve the tension now that he wasn't burdened with Bruno's considerable weight. "He'll be okay. I'm damn good with my knife. I know how to wound without killing." And then, looking beyond Bryan, he added darkly, "Want me to demonstrate on old Quince?" The lethal blade appeared again in his hand.

Quincy, who had been silently creeping away, froze in horror. He whipped around to face Joe and looked ready to faint.

Joe crooked a finger. "Let's go, Quince. Scott's gonna want to talk to you, too."

Quincy looked very undecided about whether or not to go quietly, or to try running for it. Luna looked up at Joe. "Why was he breaking into our shed?"

Joe's mouth flattened and his eyes darkened with renewed fury. His expression was enough to make up Quincy's mind; he rejoined them without a word.

"He's Willow and Austin's father." Joe slipped his arm around Luna's waist and hugged her. "He wanted to run the kids off because they're starting to look like him. It wouldn't have been too long before people noticed the similarities, and that would have shot Quincy's reputation all to hell."

Quincy wrapped his arms around himself and turned away. "I have a wife, a stepson, a life here. If people found out . . ."

Luna's heart ached for what the kids would have to face, yet Quincy was their father, and he didn't seem to even care. "They have a life here, too, you bastard." Joe pulled her back before she could reach him. She would have said more, but she didn't get the chance.

Into the silence, another woman's cheery voice intruded. "Brother, you just can't keep out of trouble, can you?"

Almost as one, they turned toward the side of the house and there stood a tall, slender woman, her feet braced apart at the very edge of a messy mud puddle. Her long, wet, and badly tangled black hair danced in the wind. She wore muddy black jeans and a shirt that had probably once been white, but was now soaked and stained and torn. One whole shoulder and part of her bra showed. She had her hands propped arrogantly on slim hips. An enormous smile dominated her face.

Bryan straightened, checking her out with curious, masculine appreciation. "And this is?"

Joe pinched the bridge of his nose, as if in pain. "My little sister."

Alyx swaggered forward, then peered down at Bruno, who lay curled on the ground, silent and still. She nodded at Joe. "Excellent job. Is he dead?"

Bryan pulled back in astonishment. His interest changed to wary disbelief. "Bloodthirsty female, isn't she?"

Bruno attempted to grunt and wiggle his way into a sitting position now that Bryan had loosened his tethers. Alyx almost appeared disappointed at the signs of life.

Joe scowled at Alyx. "What the hell happened to you? Are you all right?" He closed the space between them, but not before grabbing Luna's hand and hauling her along. "Did you have a damn car wreck?"

"Of course not." Alyx went on tiptoe to kiss Joe's cheek. Luna watched, bemused, until Alyx next drew her into a tight embrace. "I ran into an incredible guy named Jamie Creed on this old winding road. He just sort of came out of nowhere, as if he knew right where to find me. Very spooky event, I don't mind saying."

Joe closed his eyes. "Oh, God."

Alyx looked at Luna and bobbed her eyebrows. In a dreamy voice, she said, "He's delicious, isn't he? So dark and mysterious and—"

"Alyx."

She heaved a sigh at her brother. "*Anyway*, he told me there was trouble here and that we had to hurry. He was so convincing, I naturally believed him."

A muscle twitched in Joe's jaw. "You let a strange man into your car?" His voice had dropped to very threatening tones.

"And a good thing I did, given the drama going on here! But, ohmigod, Jamie drove, and I have to tell you, the man is a complete maniac."

Joe snarled. "No kidding. Is there a point to this story?"

Alyx absently patted her brother's chest. "Don't be so testy, Joe. We got here in time to see Amelia sneaking around the property. When I asked her what she was doing, she tried to hit me, so I hit her first." Alyx rubbed her knuckles with glee, which left Luna bemused and Bryan shaking his head. "Just like you showed me, Joe. Pow, right in the nose. She dropped like a stone."

Luna had never met a woman like Alyx Winston, and she was naturally speechless.

"I'm not sure what she was up to, but it kept her from trying to get inside the house, I can tell you that." Alyx grinned.

"The house is locked up," Luna finally said after finding her voice. "Willow knew not to let anyone in except me, Joe or Deputy Royal."

"She let Jamie in." Alyx appeared worried. "The kids seemed to know him and trust him, and he acted very familiar with them. I hope that was okay?"

Luna said, "Yes, that's fine," at the same time Joe pronounced, "No, it is not okay."

Alyx only listened to Luna. "Great. By the way, the deputy is already here, too. He pulled up while I was"—she gave a not so subtle cough—"restraining Amelia, and when he got in the middle of it, he sort of got knocked down, too." To Joe, she hurriedly explained, "I didn't *know* he was a deputy, now did I? If I *had* known, I wouldn't have hit him as hard as I hit Amelia. But boy, has he ever got a foul mouth. He started cursing and carrying on something awful. Singed my ears, I don't mind telling you. Unfortunately, he pulled me off Amelia or I'd have knocked her out, just as you taught me to do."

Joe looked very harassed. "Exactly where is Scott? You didn't hurt him, did you?"

Luna stared at Joe. He said that as if Alyx was ca-

pable of hurting a grown man trained as a law official. It wasn't like Scott was a slouch. No, he wasn't
Joe, but he looked big and strong enough to Luna.

"Scott's the deputy?" Alyx grinned. "He's okay.
He just has his hands full locking Amelia into the
back of his cruiser." And as an aside to Luna,
"She's not a very nice woman, but then, Joe dated
a lot of losers before now."

At that precise moment, Scott stomped around
the side of the house. He looked beyond furious,
and he wore twice as much mud as Alyx. It covered
his chest and most of his legs and one whole side
of his head and face.

With a resigned sigh, Joe crossed his arms and
waited. Luna moved closer to him. She was so relieved that he wasn't seriously hurt, she couldn't
stop shaking and she couldn't stop touching him.
Joe felt solid and strong, and she needed the reassurance that he was truly unhurt.

Scott's hard-booted stride splattered more mud
around as he stormed straight toward Alyx. *"You,"*
he roared, pointing a finger, his face dark red with
anger, "are about to get your ass handcuffed, too."

Mocking him, Alyx cocked out a hip and asked,
"Can you handcuff an ass? How clever."

Scott's eyes widened more, and his color deepened to near purple. Issuing an animal sound of
rage, he ran a hand through his muddy hair, knotted his fingers, and pulled. He turned his furious
attention to Joe. "She hit me. She knocked me
into the damn mud."

"You were in my way," Alyx explained with pre-
posterous calm. "And besides, how was I supposed
to know you're a deputy?"

Bryan hauled Bruno to his feet, surveyed both

Alyx and Scott, and laughed. When everyone looked at him, he laughed some more. "Never a dull moment around here, is there, Winston?"

Scott's jaw clenched so tight, it appeared his teeth might crack. He glared at Alyx and bellowed, "The sirens? The lights on the car? My uniform? What the hell did you think, that I'm a freakin' Boy Scout?"

Alyx smiled and even dared to smooth a hand over his mud-caked uniform shirt. "As soon as I noticed the uniform, I stopped fighting."

Scott was unappeased. He caught her wrist and flattened her hand on his chest. "Not before bloodying my lip." He thrust his chin toward her, showing the lip that was now swelling.

Alyx stared at his mouth. "Ah, poor baby got a boo-boo?"

Snarling, Scott hauled her up against his chest. Luna wasn't at all sure if he planned to kiss her or choke her.

She decided someone should regain control before more blood was shed, and it might as well be her. "Scott, I really hate to interrupt this tirade, but can you call for some backup or something? I need to check on the kids and I have to thank Jamie for his help, but I want these idiots gone first, before one of them hurts Joe."

Silence fell everywhere. Even the wet trees seemed to stop dripping. The crickets all hushed. No one breathed. As if in slow motion, Joe pivoted around to glare at her in incredulous wonder. "Hurt *me?*"

Luna looked up at him. His blue eyes, now filled with indignation, were bright and compelling in the remaining drab daylight. His black hair hung limp over his brow and his slightly crooked nose had mud across the bridge. He was by far the most beautiful man, inside and out, that she'd ever known.

She didn't mean to say it. If she hadn't been so emotionally rattled, so fearfully overwrought, she *wouldn't* have said it. But her heart still ached and her stomach still twisted in knots and the residual fear hadn't yet abated. Before she knew it, the words just tumbled out on their own. "I love you, you big lug, so I don't want to chance it."

Joe's mouth opened, ready with more arguments, then abruptly snapped shut. His brows lifted high and he rocked back on his heels. "What the hell did you say?"

Appalled at the unmeasured words that had left her mouth, and his demanding response, Luna shook her head.

"Luna?" Joe's voice dropped to that familiar, sensual drawl she'd come to recognize whenever he felt amorous. How he could feel amorous now, she couldn't fathom.

"Oh, no." Luna shook her head again, feeling like a complete and utter idiot. "I'm not saying it again, so forget it."

Alyx clapped her hands. "Well, I heard her plain as day the first time. She said she loves you. Hallelujah. Finally I'll have a sister-in-law, and a good one, too."

Luna knew she'd just made an utter fool of herself. Not once had she ever told a man that she loved him, and here she'd gone and shouted it at Joe. And not in private, as would be appropriate for a declaration of love, but with an unruly audience of friends, family and reprobates. Her face grew hot until she realized Joe was the only one paying her any mind.

Both Scott and Bryan gave their undivided attention to Alyx, watching her with the same wary regard they might have afforded a beautiful but deadly viper.

Laughing, Alyx shooed them. "Come on, boys, let's get busy. No time to stand around in idle chit-chat. Scott, did you call for another car? I think you're going to need it since it looks like Joe has two miscreants this time. And while they both look very disreputable, I wouldn't sentence them to the backseat with Amelia." She shuddered in exaggerated dread. "Heaven forbid such a fate."

"I know what I'm doing," Scott snapped.

Alyx nodded. "Great. I'll take that to mean another car is on the way. Thank you."

"Don't thank me for doing my damn job."

"Men get so surly when they're agitated." Alyx turned to Bryan Kelly and held out a hand. "Bryan? Nice to meet you. My, you're a big one, too, huh?" She didn't give him a chance to reply. "Would you like to haul one of these fellows up front? That's a good man. We'll be all organized in no time."

Fascinated, Luna watched Alyx quickly prod both men into doing her bidding. "She's dangerous."

Joe pulled Luna close and nuzzled her ear. "So are you, sweetheart. I think you stopped my heart with that damned announcement of yours."

Luna burrowed closer, loving his scent, his warmth and his strength. "What declaration?" she asked, which made Joe laugh. There'd be no denying it now, but at least he wasn't pushing her in front of everyone.

Scott cleared his throat. "Damn, Joe, much as I hate to interrupt this tender moment you're indulging in, in the middle of the carnage, we need to talk."

Alyx hooked her arm through his. "About what?"

Scott ignored her, but he didn't free himself from her hold. He just pretended she wasn't there. "You've got Quincy beat to a pulp, this other fellow hog-tied, and a muddy cat fight to explain."

"In a nutshell, Quincy was caught breaking into the shed. He swung first, so I hit back."

"That's a lie!"

"I'm a witness," Bryan volunteered, interrupting Quincy's denials. "I can testify that Winston acted in self-defense after he confronted Quincy trying to pry his shed door open."

Luna nodded. "Me, too."

Quincy whined, "I need a damn ambulance. I think my nose is broke."

Scott rubbed his eyes tiredly, then removed handcuffs from his belt and snapped them onto Quincy's wrists. "There's an ambulance on the way. They can look you over before I haul you off to jail."

"You'll need to pick up Dinah Belle, too. She was working with Quincy to set up all the little mishaps and vandalism."

Scott hung his head and groaned. "All right. I'll see to it." He stabbed Joe with a meaningful look of disgust. "Looks like the jail is going to be damn crowded tonight."

Bruno made a few muffled sounds through his gag, but Bryan said, "I've got this under control. His wound is superficial. He'll live—which is a damn shame."

Scott scowled. "I really hate to inquire, but just who the hell are you?"

Bryan flashed his badge, then handed Scott an authorization to arrest order. "Joe manhandled him, not me." His smile was not a nice thing. "I'm playing by the rules so there won't be any slipups."

"If that's so, then get that damn gag off him."

"Soon as I have him alone," Bryan promised, then he began prodding Bruno toward the front of the house. The big man had to take tiny steps with the cords still around his ankles. "I'll need a lift to my car so I can transport Bruno back. But we'll wait up front. I have a few things to say to him." Bruno didn't like that idea, given the way he fought Bryan, but he got taken around front all the same.

"This is a nightmare," Scott groaned. "All that's left to figure out is the cat fight."

Alyx chuckled and hugged Scott's arm to her breasts, rendering him mute.

Joe made a gruff sound of exasperation. "Damn it, Alyx, turn him loose and behave. Here, Scott, you can have Bruno's rifle. And, Quincy, quit your damn sniveling." He glared at Scott. "I want Luna to change out of her wet clothes before we do any more talking. And God help me, I need some aspirin and ice. I'm definitely too old for this shit."

Scott looked as though he would refuse, then he threw up his hands. "Yeah, sure, what the hell." He stared down at Alyx for a long moment, scowled darkly, and finally muttered, "I'm in no hurry."

They turned around and almost ran into Jamie Creed. His deep, intelligent brown eyes seemed to take in the entire scene without really moving. There was no smile on his face, no discernible expression at all.

The stormy breeze opened Jamie's well-worn flannel and molded a gray T-shirt to his hard abdomen. His hair was loose, hanging to his shoulders.

Willow and Austin flanked him, their expressions uncertain.

Jamie nudged them forward with a hand at their backs. "Go on now, and remember what I told you."

The kids nodded.

Jamie studied Luna a moment. He tipped his head and said with sage consequence, "Everything's going to be okay now."

"Here we go," Joe muttered.

Luna shushed him before turning hopeful eyes on Jamie. She needed a promising boost right about now. "You really think so, Jamie?" She glanced at Joe. *"Everything?"*

"Yes. You can quit your worrying."

Alyx whispered, "I feel a swoon coming on," and she leaned into Scott for support.

Joe scowled. He brought Luna's face around to his with a fist beneath her chin. "I tell you not to worry, but do you listen to me? Hell no." He glared down at her, taut with irritation. "Yet some strange character drags down off a mountain, and you hang on his every damn word."

"Joe!" Luna worried that he'd insult Jamie.

Joe had no such qualms. "I swear, Luna, if you tell me you believe Jamie's mumbo jumbo when you won't believe me, I'll . . ."

Luna waited, but the threat remained unspoken. "You'll what?"

Joe stared at her a moment more, then kissed her hard. "I don't know. I'll think of something."

Snickering, Alyx said, "Maybe Jamie just has more influence with the ladies than you do, Joe."

"Good God." Scott rolled his eyes and forced Alyx to stand on her own. "I could have guessed you'd buy into that nonsense, too. Hell, half the women in town are in love with Jamie Creed. They've got him built up to be some mysterious and ethereal romantic figure, and Jamie, damn him, drifts in and out of town just often enough to keep that impression thriving."

"It doesn't hurt that he's tall, dark, and handsome," Alyx teased, but when she turned to give her flirting comments directly to Jamie, he was gone. "Hey, where'd he go?" There was no sign of him anywhere.

Willow looked behind her, frowned and shrugged. "I don't know. He was right here just a second ago."

Luna stared around in wonder. "Wow, he's really good at that disappearing stuff."

"He'll show back up," Scott grumbled, and Joe muttered, "Unfortunately."

"I think you're both jealous," Luna told them, which immediately incited grave indignation.

"Maybe he went around front." Alyx started in that direction, toting Scott along with her. He bellyached, but he followed, which meant Quincy had to follow since Scott had the key to the handcuffs.

Willow sidled up to Luna. Her eyes were huge and dark. "Are you both okay?"

"We're fine, honey." Guilt hit Luna. "I'm so sorry I left you alone. That wasn't right, and I just didn't really think—"

"I'll say you didn't." Joe put his arm around Luna, softening his censure, and herded everyone toward the back door. "You should have stayed inside."

Willow looked at Joe, then at Luna. "She couldn't.

She loves you, so of course she couldn't leave you out there alone. That's what Jamie said."

"He did, huh?" For once, Joe didn't fuss over Jamie's perception.

Luna stroked Willow's long fair hair. "I love you and Austin, too, you know. I hope you weren't too scared."

Surprisingly, Willow smiled. "We were fine. You made sure we were inside with all the doors locked, and I'd already called Deputy Royal. We were safe."

Realizing that Willow, rather than being upset, was comforting and reassuring her, Luna blinked. "You believe that I love you?"

"Yes. Jamie said you were very loving, and that he knew you were here to stay, that you'd never leave us."

Joe growled, but didn't say anything.

Skipping, Austin moved in front of Joe and continued backing toward the house. "Jamie said you were staying, too, Joe. He said things were on their way to being set right, thanks to you, and that now you wouldn't want to leave."

Joe nodded. "Like Luna, I'm rather fond of you both. I'd miss you something terrible if I didn't see you every day."

Austin grinned. "Yeah. Jamie said you were here for good."

Joe tugged on his earring. "Yeah, well, this time he's right."

Luna stopped inside the kitchen doorway and stared at Joe in surprise. "He is?"

Joe moved very close to her. A puddle formed around them on the kitchen floor. "*Now* you're going to start doubting Jamie? Or are you doubting me again?" He didn't seem too happy with that possibility. "After all this time together, did you really think I'd leave?"

"Well . . ."

Joe caught her by the back of the neck and kissed her until Austin hung on his leg and moaned as if in mortal pain. Grinning, Joe said against her mouth, "You love me, I love you, the kids appear to be okay with it." He paused and eyed them both. "Are you okay with me hanging around?"

Austin whooped. "Will you teach me how to use a knife like yours?"

Joe said, "Uh . . ."

"You'll be like our dad, huh?" Austin stared up at Joe, his small brow puckered. "I don't like Quincy much. I don't want him to be my dad. I'd rather it be you."

Emotion got a strangle hold on Joe's throat. "You both know?"

Willow looked down at her feet. "Yeah, we overheard some of it through the window, and then Jamie talked to us about it." She lifted her gaze and gave him a very adult stare. "He said any man can father a child, but only a special man can be a dad."

Joe looked shattered. He swallowed twice. "I'd love to be your dad."

Willow wiped her eyes and put her arm around her brother. Her smile wavered, but it was there, a smile of relief and acceptance. She gave a delicate sniff, then half laughed. "It's okay, you know. About Quincy, I mean."

Luna wanted to cry, too. Willow was so damn grown up for a teenager.

"At least now we understand why he hated us so much. It wasn't anything we did. He's just a very shallow person. In a way, I feel sorry for him. And I really feel sorry for Clay."

Luna took a deep breath and swallowed down her tears. She had a feeling that if she started crying now, they'd all be bawling in moments. "Clay strikes me as a very intelligent, resourceful young man. He's strong. He'll get through this."

Austin hung on Joe. "Maybe you can help him, too."

Joe said, "I'd be happy to try, now that you've all invited me to stay."

Willow smiled her serene smile. "You'll have to marry Luna. She wants to settle down, to have a family and stuff."

Luna's face went hot.

"If that's what it takes," Joe said with mock gravity, and laughed when Luna slugged him. In a gallant display, Joe lifted her hand and kissed her knuckles. His voice was soft, compelling. "Will you marry me, Luna?"

Her stomach twisted for a whole new reason. "Do you really love me?"

He grinned. "Yeah, I really do. So damn much, it's almost scary."

Austin scoffed. "Nothing scares you." He punched the air twice. "You're too tough."

"How little you know about women, my boy. They're all terrifying, but Luna more so than the rest. I knew the day I met her that my bachelor days were numbered."

When Luna still stood there, a little stunned by how things had transpired, Joe drew a long breath. "Okay, let's try another angle. Think of the shock it'll give Zane. He'll probably faint. Now, won't that be fun to watch?"

"Who's Zane?" Willow wanted to know.

"My cousin and a real nice guy. You'll meet him at the wedding, along with the rest of the Winston clan. That is, if Luna will put me out of my misery and say yes." He eyed her, saw she was still dazed, then continued. "You know, Luna, if you really want family, I have plenty to spare. They could bring a whole passel of cousins to Austin and Willow and we'd have to do those really large holidays and family get-togethers. Once we have the lake open, I just know they'll all want to vacation here, so they'll be forever under foot, and I swear I think Alyx is already contemplating moving in. Between what the lake makes and our combined savings, we should be pretty well set—"

Luna threw herself against his chest. "Yes."

With a great sigh of relief, Joe pressed his face into her shoulder, locked his arms around her, and squeezed her tight. After only a moment, he blindly reached out and pulled Willow and Austin into the embrace.

Damn it, she was going to cry after all, Luna realized when she felt tears track down her face. But this time they were happy tears.

Joe kissed her temple. "Hey, it's okay. Remember, Jamie told you so."

She laughed, pinched him, and said, "I believe it because *you* told me so."

"Ah. Now we're getting somewhere."

Late that night, a knock sounded on the front door. Willow went to answer it, followed by Joe. It had finally quieted down a few hours ago, but Joe had been hovering. Alyx claimed it was a habit, that Joe always fretted like an old woman whenever he was worried. Willow didn't mind. She felt so much better about things, knowing why Quincy always treated her and Austin with contempt, and knowing that finally they'd have some peace. Joe and Luna would stay, and she'd be part of a family once more. Thank God, Quincy wouldn't be part of that family.

Even before Willow opened the door and saw Clay standing there, his hands in his pockets, his shoulders hunched, she'd somehow known it was him.

Her heart twisted at the hurt she saw in his eyes. Her life was finally straightening out, but his had just been turned upside down. "Hi."

Clay drew a deep breath. "Hi." He glanced at Joe. "Would you mind if maybe . . ."

Willow opened the screen door and stepped out. "He doesn't mind." The look she gave Joe told him to get lost. She knew Joe had as much compassion for Clay as he'd had for her and for Austin. Despite his forbidding appearance, he was pretty terrific.

Without either of them saying a word, they went off the porch together, wandering a small distance into the yard. Clay kicked at the ground, tense, silent.

Willow touched his arm. "I'm sorry."

He laughed and turned his face up to the sky. "That's what I was trying to figure out how to say to you." He turned to face her, and Willow saw his agony. "I swear, Willow, I didn't know. I remember you asking me about that damn kitten, how upset you got. If I'd known . . ."

She put her fingers to his mouth. "It's okay. You're not responsible for what Quincy did."

He caught her wrist and pulled her hand to his side. "You're not mad?"

"Not at you."

His head dropped. "Thanks." More silence, more tension, then Clay muttered, "I'm so damn embarrassed."

Willow didn't know if it was the right thing or not, but she stepped up against him and gave him a tight hug. His shoulders were wide and hard, his chest solid. It felt good to be so close to him, even if she only wanted to offer him comfort.

Clay went rigid, but only for a second, then he hugged her back, lifting her right off her feet. She felt him shaking and was afraid he might cry. But he didn't.

"Mom is leaving Quincy." He spoke against her neck, sounding disgusted. "Not because of what he did, but because he caused so much scandal getting caught. Everyone is talking about it already. All my friends have called."

Willow smoothed his hair, then leaned away to see his face. He set her back on her feet. "She's not going to move away, is she?" Willow hated the thought of yet another loss.

"I don't think so. Right now she's just talking about making Quincy pay."

"I'm glad. I'd hate it if you weren't my friend."

Clay stared down at her. Moonlight filtered through the trees, dappling his skin and adding very mature shadows to his features. He bent and pressed a warm, gentle kiss to her cheek. "You'll be fifteen soon, right?"

"Yes. Another month."

"Then . . . Maybe, once everything is calmed down again, we can be more than just friends."

Very slowly, Willow smiled. "Maybe."

* * *

Bryan, Scott, Jamie and Julie Rose came to the wedding three weeks later. Other than those special friends, it was a family affair, held outdoors at the lake. Joe hadn't wanted to wait for a more formal ceremony, and when he'd hesitantly asked Luna what she wanted, she'd wrinkled her nose and said, "I can't imagine me in fussy white lace. No, I'd rather just have fun." She'd compromised on the white lace by replacing the red streaks in her hair with some very pale blond highlights.

Alyx had agreed to stay with the kids while Luna and Joe took a mini honeymoon for five days. They would stay in an isolated cabin in the woods with nothing to do but love each other. That suited Joe just fine. They'd return home in time for the grand opening of the lake, which would be launched with a kids' fishing derby.

Joe had special events planned at the lake for the rest of the summer, then more seasonal events for the remainder of the year. Already they'd had numerous membership renewals, and Joe had had the lake restocked with bluegill, catfish, walleye, bass and crappie. Soon the field would be cleared to accommodate first-come, first-serve campers. All in all, he was pretty damned satisfied with his progress.

Luna had been stunned with the size of his bank account. Combined with hers, they had a nice nest egg to use for improvements to the house and some investments. The first thing Joe had bought was a king-size bed for their room.

Seeing that Luna was preoccupied with his sister, Joe headed over to talk to Bryan. The bounty hunter leaned negligently against a sturdy tree trunk in isolated splendor. Dressed in a suit, he looked like an entirely different man except that he was still quietly alert. His predatory gaze constantly scanned the numerous picnic tables scattered about the yard, filled with food and surrounded by guests. Joe could appreciate Bryan's wariness in a crowd, since he'd once been the same.

"You look miserable in that tie."

Bryan acknowledged Joe with a nod. "Hate the damn things." He accepted the drink Joe handed to him and continued to survey everyone and everything. "It was a nice wedding."

"The weather cooperated, even if my rowdy family didn't."

Bryan gave a crooked smile. "They're a boisterous bunch."

"Yeah." Joe studied Bryan's drawn expression and sighed. "You know, you look like a man who needs a vacation. You're welcome to come visit anytime. I might not have acted real hospitable that day we met, but—"

Bryan shook his head. "Forget it, Winston. I threw your lady to the ground. You reacted. No hard feelings." Bryan tossed back the rest of his drink and said quietly, "Just know that I didn't fight back that day. I let you pound on me because I figured I had it coming for using you to get Bruno. But if you ever tried it again . . ."

Laughing, Joe thwacked him on the shoulder, almost knocking him over. "If either of us gets bored, we'll have to test the outcome of that. But for right now, I'm too damn happy to start taking a chance on getting bruised up again."

Bryan found Luna in the crowd and smiled. "I can see that." He hesitated a moment, then narrowed his eyes. "Thanks for the invitation to visit, but I don't think it's necessary. I got used to the place while I was waiting for Bruno to act." He looked undecided, studied Joe a minute, then admitted, "I bought some land. It's a few miles south of here, just an acre, but it's secluded, near a stream. Nice and quiet."

Joe was surprised. "You going to build here?"

"I have some business to take care of first, then I'll think on it."

"Hunting up another bail jumper, huh?"

Bryan shook his head. "No, not this time." His fists clenched and unclenched. "My brother needs a little help."

Luna and Alyx joined them in time to hear that last comment. "You have a brother?" Luna asked.

"Does he look anything like you?" Alyx wanted to know. She leaned close and smoothed Bryan's lapel. "You certainly are handsome in a suit."

Joe caught his sister's arm and hauled her to his side. Bryan just smiled. "Actually, Bruce is the spitting image of me. See, we're identical twins. But looks are where the similarities end."

"Oh?" Joe smiled, and just to harass Bryan, he asked, "He's a nice guy, is that it?"

"Real nice. A preacher actually." With everyone momentarily speechless, Bryan straightened away from the tree. "Speaking of my brother, I need to get going." He gave Luna a hug, shook hands with Joe, then said to Alyx, "Scott is headed this way. Your ploy to make him jealous worked."

Alyx grinned. "What makes you think I wanted him jealous?"

Bryan's eyes narrowed. "Because otherwise a princess like you would never flirt with me. You have to be too smart for that." He saluted Scott on his way to the back door.

Joe laughed at his sister's stunned expression. "Well, Alyx, that trick fell flat."

She recovered quickly. "No, it didn't. If you look at Scott and the way he's fuming, you'll see that it worked just fine."

Just then, Scott appeared. He stood in front of Alyx, his nostrils flared, his eyes bright.

A mournful tone in her voice, Alyx said, "Bryan had to leave. But where's Jamie? I haven't seen him in hours."

Without a word, Scott wrapped his fingers around her wrist and tugged her away. Alyx looked over her shoulder, gave a tiny wave of triumph to Luna, and then went along quite willingly.

"Your sister is something else."

Joe stood behind Luna. He bent and kissed her nape, her ear. "This dress is something else. I do love your sense of style, babe." She'd chosen a long, cream-colored sheath. It was strapless, leaving her shoulders completely bared, and gathered just a bit between her breasts. The design was simple but elegant, and quite understated for Luna. She carried a small bouquet of daisies, carnations, and baby's breath tied with long ribbons.

"Do you love me?"

Joe growled. "Let's get out of here and I'll show you how much."

They heard Austin let out a shout and looked across the yard to where he sprawled on a quilt, arm-wrestling with Chase Winston, Joe's quieter cousin. With a lot of fanfare and heckling, Chase allowed himself to lose. Zane boosted Austin up to his shoulders, and they heralded him as a champ.

Julie Rose sat to the side, cheering as loud as anyone. She and Zane's wife, Tamara, seemed to be hitting it off. Though Julie Rose claimed to be an engaged woman, she'd come to the wedding and reception alone. But she didn't look sad about it. No, prim Julie Rose acted like a full-time partyer, given half the chance.

"Where *did* Jamie go?" Luna asked, looking around for him.

"I'm sure he's evaporated into the mists or magically transported himself somewhere. Who knows? More importantly, who cares?"

Luna slanted him a teasing look. "I can't believe you're still jealous."

"I'm possessive, not jealous." Joe started to nibble on her ear.

"Well, that's good. Because Jamie likes you. Before he left, he told me you had a really special wedding gift for me."

Joe froze. Very slowly, he lifted his head to stare at Luna. "The hell you say."

"Was he wrong?" She appeared a little deflated by that possibility. "I swear he almost smiled when he told me about it. The corners of his mouth curled up just the tiniest bit."

"That son of a . . ." Joe's soft exclamation trailed off. "Come on. Let's get out of here. I'll show you your gift once we're all alone."

"Well, now I'm doubly curious."

Joe lifted her into his arms and, at the same time, called out, "To anyone who's interested, she's throwing the bouquet so we can get on our way."

Alyx immediately reappeared, her hair a little mussed, her cocky smile in place. Julie Rose lined up alongside her, along with Willow, and Mack's daughter Trista, and a few other single relatives in the extended family.

Joe twirled Luna twice, making her laugh, then

said, "Throw it," and she pitched the bouquet into the air. Rather than soar toward the line of women, it went in the opposite direction.

Bryan had just come back around the corner. "Hey, my car is hemmed in by someone's mini-van—" The bouquet hit him square in the forehead, and like the combat machine Joe knew him to be, he staggered back, recovered, and caught the damn thing.

Not two seconds later, he got tackled by every single woman in the yard.

Joe was still chuckling about Bryan's fate when he carried Luna into the cabin and kicked the door shut. They were less than two hours from home, but for all intents and purposes, they had privacy.

"Finally," Joe said, keeping Luna in his arms while heading straight for the posh bedroom. From the moment she'd said, "I do," he'd been struggling with such a powerful sense of possession and pride and love, it was all he could do to keep being cordial.

Joe laid her on the mattress and followed her down, blanketing her with his body and sealing their mouths together before she could say a single thing. He cupped her face, licked into her mouth, and groaned with contentment.

"Joe," she whispered when he pulled the top of her dress below her breasts and began kissing his way down her throat. "Where's my gift?"

"It's coming." He gently drew one nipple into his mouth, all the while thinking how nice it would be to get to sleep the entire night with her. They'd kept to their discreet routine of nooners while the kids were in school. Luna might be a free spirit, but she took her responsibilities to the kids seriously, and that meant being what she considered a good example.

He slid his hand up her thigh and into her panties to palm a warm cheek. "Tell me you love me."

"I love you," she moaned, already wiggling against him.

"Good. Then let's get these clothes off you." Joe sat up and efficiently stripped her. Once she was bare, he had to touch her everywhere, and when that didn't suffice, he had to kiss her, taste her, everywhere.

Luna didn't ask about her gift again, but she did demand that he strip also. "Take your clothes off, Joe. I want you. Now."

Anticipating her reaction, he stood and yanked his tie away, then quickly unbuttoned his dress shirt. He wadded it up and threw it across the room. Luna came up on one elbow to watch as he kicked off his shoes, bent to remove his socks, and then, with a smile, turned and dropped his pants.

There was a moment of stunned silence before Luna started to laugh. "This," she asked, giving his tush a swat, "is my gift?"

"Yeah." Joe turned and crawled into bed beside her. "You like it?"

"I thought you said it'd hurt too much to have it lasered off."

"It hurt like hell. But, babe, you're worth a little pain. Besides, I only had to remove a few letters."

"And add a few more?"

Joe grinned. "I lost an *ou*, but gained a *una*." His tattoo now read, *I Love Luna*.

Luna crawled up onto his chest. "You're branded as mine, Joe Winston. There's no turning back now."

"Not a problem." Joe pulled her mouth down to

his and began to nibble on her lips. "I've been yours since the day you threw food at my head."

She teased his chest hair thoughtfully a moment before meeting his gaze. "You promise you won't get bored? You won't miss the excitement?"

Joe's eyes widened, and he laughed. He rolled Luna beneath him, felt her soft curves, the perfect way she cradled him. "Honest to God, you're about as much excitement as I can take, Luna. The only way I'd go back to one of my old jobs is if I needed the break, and I know I'm not a spring chicken anymore, but, honey, I ain't *that* old." This time when he kissed her, Luna was laughing and kissing him back. "Believe me?"

"Yes, Joe." Then she smiled. "Saying yes to Joe Winston—it has to be one of the smartest things I've ever done."

Joe growled as he entered her. "Beats the hell out of no any day, that's for sure."

Read on for two samples of more sparkling romance by Lori Foster.

First, please enjoy

TOO MUCH TEMPTATION,

available now!

Grace was so furious with herself, she felt like spitting. The near-torrential rainfall didn't slow her down as she splashed her way up the sidewalk to Noah's building, her every step punctuated by a passionate rage. Eight days. Eight hellish days she'd been away, probably when Noah had needed her most. She'd expected to come home to a list of things yet to be done for the wedding, because Agatha did love to give her lists.

Instead, she'd come home to the tail end of an uproar.

She swiped away a tear of fury that mingled with the rain dripping down her cheek. It was always that way. Hurt her, insult her, and she was fine. She'd summon up calm dignity and deal with it. But let her get really mad and look out—she cried like a baby.

Damn her car for breaking down, damn Agatha for being a hardheaded matriarch, and damn everyone for ever doubting him.

Poor Noah. Poor honorable, loyal Noah.

He *needed* her.

Spurred on by her convictions, Grace hurried on. She slipped as she jerked the foyer door open and bounded inside onto slick marble tile. She'd have landed on her well-padded behind if it weren't for Graham, the doorman, catching her arm and wrestling her upright.

"Here now!" Graham said with some surprise, maintaining his hold on her arm as Grace started to dart past.

It took him a moment to recognize her with her hair hanging in long, sodden ropes in her face and her clothes saturated through and through, making them baggier than usual. When he did recognize her, his old eyes widened.

"Ms. Jenkins! What in the world are you doing out in this storm?"

Grace forced herself to slow down. "Sorry, Graham. Is Noah in?"

"Yes, ma'am. He's with his brother."

Thank God. Grace would rather have had her visit with Noah in private, without Ben as an audience, but at least Noah was home. Besides, she should have known Ben would be close at hand. He very much respected his brother, and always offered unconditional support.

Grace was relieved that Noah hadn't been all alone during the ordeal.

"My stupid car broke down a few blocks from here," she told Graham. "I'll call Triple A from Noah's."

"Should I announce you?"

Noah had a standing rule that his family was always welcome. Grace was in no way a blood relative, but as his grandmother's personal secretary, Noah granted her the same importance. She'd known Noah for three years. She'd loved him just about that long.

Not that she would ever tell anyone, especially not Noah.

"No, I'll go on up. But thanks."

The doorman shook his head as she turned away, probably thinking she had less sense than a turkey to go running through the stormy weather. But she simply hadn't possessed the patience to wait in her car for a cab. A little rain wouldn't melt her, and since hearing what Agatha had done yesterday, how she'd treated Noah because of the breakup, Grace had been filled with a driving urgency to reach him, to let him know that at least one person still . . . what? Still believed in him, still trusted in his innate honor?

The elevator moved so slowly, Grace couldn't stop tapping her foot, which jiggled drips of rainwater from her body onto the elevator floor. She now stood in a puddle.

The second the doors opened, she leaped out, then had to leap back in when she realized it was the wrong floor. The woman getting on the elevator gave her a funny look but said nothing, even when she had to step around the soggy carpeting.

Grace chewed her thumbnail. It was a disgusting habit—as Agatha had often told her—but she couldn't seem to help herself.

This time she checked the floor before getting

off. Every step she took caused her feet to squish inside her pumps and left damp tracks across the carpeting. When she reached Noah's door, she drew a deep breath to fortify herself, pushed her long, wet hair behind her ears, and rapped sharply.

Nothing.

She knocked again, and even pushed the door-bell a few times, but still there was no answer. Refusing to give up, Grace tried the door and found it unlocked. She crept inside, calling out, "Noah?" but no one answered. And then she heard voices coming from the balcony.

Grace hurried through the apartment, noticing empty beer bottles everywhere, as well as pizza boxes and chip bags thrown about. A mostly empty, dried-up container of sour-cream-and-chive dip was half tucked into the sofa cushions.

The cleaning lady would have a fit.

Grace wondered if Noah had thrown a party, if he had actually celebrated the breakup. It seemed unlikely. For many years now everyone had expected him and Kara to marry and then be blissfully happy in their picture-perfect lives. The breakup had naturally thrown everyone for a loop, Grace especially.

She finally located him.

Noah sat on the covered balcony with his brother, and together they made such an impressive sight they stole Grace's breath. Oh boy, there were some outstanding genes running through those two. No wonder Agatha had put her pride aside and sought out her deceased son's illegitimate offspring. Noah was a man to make anyone proud.

The two brothers were talking, oblivious to

Grace's presence, and she studied them. Their large, bare feet were propped on the edge of the railing, getting rained on. Both of them lounged back in chairs, Ben with his tilted on its back legs.

Noah had a long-necked bottle of beer dangling between his fingers, his other hand resting limply on his hard abdomen. He wore faded jeans, a gray sweatshirt with the sleeves cut off, and nothing else. His silky, coal-black hair was rumpled, his face shadowed with beard stubble. His entire body bespoke weariness.

He was the sexiest, most appealing man she'd ever known.

And don't miss

JUDE'S LAW,

available now!

He blamed May Price for his new affinity toward lush curves. Before meeting her damn near a year ago, he'd been more than satisfied with willowy models and leggy starlets.

Now, Jude Jamison couldn't get the voluptuous Miss Price, or her very sexy body, off his mind. He wanted her. He *would* have her.

But so far, she hadn't made it easy for him. Hard? Yeah, he stayed plenty hard. When it came to May, nothing went as he intended. Thanks to his fame and acquired fortune, he usually only needed to make himself visible and women were interested.

He liked it that way—or so he'd thought before May challenged him with her resistance. She didn't care about money or fame. No, May liked his interest in art. Specifically, she liked his interest in the art she sold in her gallery.

Trying to make headway with May brought back memories of his youth, when getting laid made the top of his "to do" list and occupied most of his energy. He'd worked hard on sex back then, and he'd had the time of his life.

He still enjoyed sex, but without the chase, it didn't seem as exciting. Hell, it had almost become mundane.

May made it exciting again.

In fact, she made everything exciting. Talking with her left him energized; laughing with her made him feel good; just looking at her gave him pleasure—and often had him fantasizing about the moment when she'd give in, maybe loosen up a little, say yes instead of shrugging off his interest as mere flirtation.

He'd turned thoughts of that day into a favorite fantasy—May out of her restricting clothes and her concealing glasses, with her hair loose and her expressive eyes anxious, seeing only him.

He adored her dark brown eyes with the thick fringe of lashes, the way she looked at him, the way she seemed to really see him, not just his image.

But before he could make moves toward getting her in his bed, he needed to go the route of casual dating. She was different from the other women he'd known. More old fashioned. In no way cavalier about intimacy. And she had a big heart.

He appreciated those differences a lot, but thinking of his failed come-ons left him chagrined.

She took his best lines as a joke. Added sincerity left her unconvinced. And at times, she didn't even notice his attempts at seduction. Yet subtlety wasn't his strong suit. She left him confounded, and very determined.

May wasn't an insecure woman. She wasn't shy or withdrawn. Open, honest, and straightforward—

that described May. But no matter what Jude tried, she found a way to discount his interest.

He decided the local yahoos in Stillbrook, Ohio, were either blind, overly preoccupied, or just plain stupid when it came to women. For May to be so oblivious to her own appeal, they sure as hell hadn't given her the attention she deserved, the attention *he'd* give her—in bed.

It had to happen soon. With his financial status and number of investments, not to mention the propositions from two other factions, a slew of daily business details demanded his attention. But until he had May, he couldn't concentrate worth a damn.

Hands in his pockets, shoulder resting on the ornate door frame of May's small art gallery, Jude watched her with the piercing intensity of a predator.

Time for new tactics. She hadn't reacted to compliments and innuendos, so he'd spell things out for her instead. After tonight, May would have no delusions about what he wanted with her.

As she bustled across the floor, bouncing in all the right places, he visually tracked her, soaking in every jaunty step, each carefree movement. She hadn't yet noticed him, but she would. Soon.

Anticipation curved his mouth.

No matter the location, no matter the occasion, May always became aware of him within seconds of his entrance. She could deny it all she wanted, but the awareness went both ways.

Fighting it would do her no good.

Jude played to win, always had. If May knew anything at all about his history, she knew that much. And for right now, he intended to win her.

Connect with Us

Visit us online at
KensingtonBooks.com
to read more from your favorite authors, see books
by series, view reading group guides, and more.

Join us on social media

for sneak peeks, chances to win books and prize packs,
and to share your thoughts with other readers.

facebook.com/kensingtonpublishing
twitter.com/kensingtonbooks

Tell us what you think!

To share your thoughts, submit a review,
or sign up for our eNewsletters, please visit:
KensingtonBooks.com/TellUs.

More by Bestselling Author

Lori Foster

Available Wherever Books Are Sold!

Check out our website at **www.kensingtonbooks.com**

More by Bestselling Author
Hannah Howell

__Highland Angel	978-1-4201-0864-4	$6.99US/$8.99CAN
__If He's Sinful	978-1-4201-0461-5	$6.99US/$8.99CAN
__Wild Conquest	978-1-4201-0464-6	$6.99US/$8.99CAN
__If He's Wicked	978-1-4201-0460-8	$6.99US/$8.49CAN
__My Lady Captor	978-0-8217-7430-4	$6.99US/$8.49CAN
__Highland Sinner	978-0-8217-8001-5	$6.99US/$8.49CAN
__Highland Captive	978-0-8217-8003-9	$6.99US/$8.49CAN
__Nature of the Beast	978-1-4201-0435-6	$6.99US/$8.49CAN
__Highland Fire	978-0-8217-7429-8	$6.99US/$8.49CAN
__Silver Flame	978-1-4201-0107-2	$6.99US/$8.49CAN
__Highland Wolf	978-0-8217-8000-8	$6.99US/$9.99CAN
__Highland Wedding	978-0-8217-8002-2	$4.99US/$6.99CAN
__Highland Destiny	978-1-4201-0259-8	$4.99US/$6.99CAN
__Only for You	978-0-8217-8151-7	$6.99US/$8.99CAN
__Highland Promise	978-1-4201-0261-1	$4.99US/$6.99CAN
__Highland Vow	978-1-4201-0260-4	$4.99US/$6.99CAN
__Highland Savage	978-0-8217-7999-6	$6.99US/$9.99CAN
__Beauty and the Beast	978-0-8217-8004-6	$4.99US/$6.99CAN
__Unconquered	978-0-8217-8088-6	$4.99US/$6.99CAN
__Highland Barbarian	978-0-8217-7998-9	$6.99US/$9.99CAN
__Highland Conqueror	978-0-8217-8148-7	$6.99US/$9.99CAN
__Conqueror's Kiss	978-0-8217-8005-3	$4.99US/$6.99CAN
__A Stockingful of Joy	978-1-4201-0018-1	$4.99US/$6.99CAN
__Highland Bride	978-0-8217-7995-8	$4.99US/$6.99CAN
__Highland Lover	978-0-8217-7759-6	$6.99US/$9.99CAN

Available Wherever Books Are Sold!

Check out our website at
http://www.kensingtonbooks.com